Cliffs of Ochre

Donovan Hoult

Publishers:
Inspiring Publishers
P.O. Box 159 Calwell ACT 2905, Australia.
Email: inspiringpublishers@gmail.com

National Library of Australia Cataloguing-in-Publication entry

Author: Hoult, Donovan

Title: **Cliffs of Ochre**/*Donovan Hoult.*

ISBN: 9781925346749 (pbk)

Subjects: Inheritance and succession—Western Australia—Fiction.
       Models (Persons)—Fiction.
       Murder—Fiction.
       Suspense fiction, Australian.

Dewey Number: A823.4

1

The young lawyer studied the document with feigned intensity. He had already read it a number of times and was well aware of and fully understood its contents. He shook his head and whistled softly under his breath as he calculated the inherited wealth of the beneficiary. Although his eyes appeared intent on the wording, his mind was lost in thought as to how he might gain from a continued involvement with this client. Wills were a highly lucrative source of income for any established law practice as they were written up, witnessed and then filed away until the inevitable demise of the client – a veritable bank that paid no interest nor derived any income until the fateful day when the terms of the Will were revealed and the lucky beneficiaries began to express their undying love and concern for the departed. Estranged family and issue, disinherited relatives and discarded partners commenced action to lay claim to a share of the deceased's legacy.

The lucrative work commenced at that point, the fees guaranteed under the terms of the Will and the trickle, streams, or rivers of income commenced. First gain the confidence of the largest beneficiary and take their instructions to pursue or defend any claim knowing the tap would not be turned off until commonsense prevailed, or it was settled by the courts. It was truly a wonderful bank of future income Andrew Hanna was intent on nurturing. It was one of the reasons he had bought into the practice and finally purchased his deceased partner's share from his widow. It had been under extreme duress, but he had no alternative when he discovered the truth. The widow professed ignorance of her husband's malfeasance, but was resolute Hanna should pay the agreed purchase price, otherwise she would reveal all. It made no difference to her at her age she reasoned, and she had nothing to lose – she cared nothing for her husband's name or reputation.

The bank of Wills Hanna inherited was not large but it contained some high quality clients, and the woman he was about to meet was surely at the top of the list of beneficiaries of any estate he would handle in the foreseeable future. He knew who she was, her lineage and reputation. This one would have to be handled with the utmost care and attention. His potential client had been waiting about five minutes. Normally he would have adopted his standard practice of extending it out to fifteen to give the impression he was a busy attorney with a multitude of matters to attend.

He paused a second before opening his door to the waiting room. Normally his part-time secretary would show a client in, but in this case he dispensed with protocol and with an air of adopted professionalism greeted his new client with an extended hand.

"I'm pleased to meet you Ms Quartpot, won't you please come in?"

Her hand was elegant, the fleeting grip with a touch of firmness, the poise a studied acquired skill, but so natural. He could see she had evolved a long way from the roots of her heritage and upbringing. The unblemished olive complexion and features stunned him, but above all it was the soft brown eyes that betrayed a look of determination. The photos he had seen in magazines did not do his client justice. No wonder she had won international acclaim. He was instantly besotted as he tried to maintain his composure of professional indifference. He had fully expected her to be dressed in the style to which he had seen her in the media; a flowing evening or elegant day-wear number common to the venues in which she had modelled. Here she was dressed in an open neck blue shirt, and jeans that seamlessly moulded her perfect form.

"Please take a seat. Would you like a tea or coffee or a cold drink before we start?"

"No thank you Mr Hanna." Chloe tossed her broad-brimmed hat into a chair and pushed the sunglasses up into her hair.

"Please call me Andrew."

Chloe ignored the invitation. "What happened to Mr Fordyce? I thought he was handling my father's affairs?"

"Mr Fordye is deceased and I've taken over. I bought into the practice some months before his death, so I'm already familiar with most of his client's affairs. I'm confident I can deliver the same service as that delivered to your father. Can I ask you by what name you prefer. Do I call you Ms Quartpot or Boyce?"

"My natural father was Henry Boyce, so I will assume that name, although my birth certificate and passport register me as Chloe Quartpot."

Andrew broke into a broad smile. "I will need a name for my files so I will open it as Chloe Boyce. May I call you Chloe?"

She had taken an instant liking to him. It was his easy charm and manner with no pretensions that attracted her, but she had no intention of showing it at this stage.

"Let's keep it formal for the time being."

"As you wish Ms Boyce," Hanna replied as he inwardly cringed at his presumption and failed attempt at familiarity.

Andrew looked up from his legal pad. "I have your father's Will here. Are you aware of its contents?"

"I've read a copy I found in his safe at Venus Downs, before I went back to London to settle my affairs, but I don't know if it was his final version."

"Well, except for a cash bequest to his sister Elizabeth Murdoch, you are the sole beneficiary of his entire estate comprising the homestead property of Venus Downs along with another adjoining property and two very large cattle stations in the Pilbara region. Incidentally, I wrote to Mrs Murdoch and she has rejected the bequest in your favour. She said she had more than ample money to see out her days."

Chloe smiled at the thought of Aunt Liz. It was just like her. She had not said a word about the bequest when she visited her in Perth on her way back from London.

She had returned to sell her house in Eton Square, wind up her affairs, say goodbye to her closest friends, and shut the door on that side of her life forever. She was terrified of confronting the man she had come to detest, her husband Marcel Faroud. Her house was deserted when she returned, no antique furniture or expensive art, no servants and no Marcel. He had obviously sold what he could for cash and deserted the place. She made enquiries and finally hired a detective agency to trace him, but it was as though he had simply disappeared off the face of the earth.

Chloe had approached the police about their enquiries regarding the theft of a red diamond, only to be told the investigation had been terminated when Marcel had simply vanished.

"We interviewed Mr Faroud after he reported the theft and asked him to produce some evidence he had given you a red diamond, where he had purchased it and insurance details, as he would have surely taken such a precaution for such a priceless gem?" the detective told her. "If your husband could not produce such evidence, and we did have our suspicions about him at the time, there was not much we could do about pursuing our enquiries. He had agreed to supply the details including an invoice from DeGraff's, the Bond Street gem merchants he claimed to have purchased it from. He was due to meet me again the following week, but he never turned up. I of course contacted DeGraff's, and was told they had never handled a red diamond as described, and had no record of a Mr Faroud ever having purchased any item of jewellery from the firm. I decided at that point to make some further enquiries about your husband and became aware he had an associate by the name of Massoud Farhangi who was found with his neck broken in a council garbage transfer station. Turns out Farhangi was using a false passport and was wanted by Interpol for murder, drug running and extortion in Lebanon. We fingerprinted your house when we got the evidence confirming your husband was not who he claimed to be. He's not wanted by Interpol, but we've established he had a string of aliases, so you can take your pick which one he is using now. Did you know who you were marrying Mrs Faroud? Did you have any idea of his background?"

Chloe looked at him in shock. "Do you know if he's still in the country? I'm terrified of what he will do to me if he finds out I'm here."

The detective shook his head with a sympathetic look. "No, we don't know where he is. False passports are a fact of life and most borders are very porous. He could be anywhere in the world at this moment. We do know he caught a flight to

Australia soon after you left the country, but he got off the plane in Bangkok and simply disappeared. However, we did inform Australian Customs and Immigration and provided them with the details should he try to enter the country, but that's no guarantee he won't change his appearance on another false passport and slip through the net."

Chloe shuddered as the thoughts ran through her mind. Marcel would not simply disappear without trace. He was out there somewhere and she knew that someday he would walk back into her life.

She looked up and realised the lawyer was staring at her with a look of concern.

"Are you okay Ms Boyce. Can I get you something?"

"I'm sorry Mr Hanna, my mind was somewhere else entirely. What does this all mean to me?"

"In short, it means you have inherited title to some vast cattle stations, all of which have been experiencing record prices for cattle. You are indeed a very wealthy person. Do you think you'll be able to manage such a huge holding on your own? It's a pity one of your brothers isn't alive to assist you. I can see from the Will, Henry Boyce did intend the three of you would inherit the properties, but with Carl and Walter both dead, you are the sole beneficiary. If you ask my advice I would sell up."

Chloe slowly shook her head. "I haven't asked for your advice Mr Hanna, but I'll give it some thought. I can't see any need to make hasty decisions."

The picture of Walter's death was still vivid in her mind. It still resulted in nightmares, as did Carl's murder at the hands of his brother, which she had inadvertently witnessed. She had attended Carl's funeral, but could never divulge what had happened to Walter, or where she had buried his remains under a mound of stones. To do so would reveal a sacred site she had promised her grandfather would remain unknown and undefiled. She would never return to the sacred dreaming site of the rainbow serpent.

"I apologise for being presumptuous Ms Boyce," Hanna stammered. "But with your international background, I don't picture you rounding up and branding cattle." He saw immediately he had made a mistake as Chloe fixed him with a cold look. "Yes. yes, I'm sure you can."

"I was brought up on Venus Downs and I don't require your comments in regard to my perceived shortcoming or abilities. I've no doubt I will be able to find competent managers for Venus Downs and the other holdings."

She nodded. "There's something else I would like you to take care of. I was married in London. I want you to file divorce proceedings and handle the matter for me."

"I can certainly attend to that. Let me have a few details and I'll get straight onto it. I don't know the English procedure for divorce and will have to brief a London attorney. I will naturally need to put him in funds."

"You can contact this person in this London legal firm." Chloe handed over a business card. "I want this matter handled as soon as possible. Whatever it costs, just proceed. There will be complications which my London attorney has explained to me in regard to the divorce, so I want you to liaise with him."

Andrew caught the sharp edge in Chloe's reply. She was the consummate professional demanding service.

Chloe had been studying the lawyer as he wrote notes. He was certainly good looking, and someone she could relate to but it was far too premature to reciprocate, despite his charm. She had too much on her mind. She reached across for her hat and stood up to leave.

Hanna quickly rose to show her to the door. He was unnerved. He had blundered and was worried he was going to pay the price. "Will you allow me to continue as your lawyer?"

"I see no reason to change at this point Mr Hanna. Just make sure you can justify every account in the meantime, and I'll keep the matter under review." She did not take Hanna's extended hand and left him staring at her departing back.

He slowly closed the door and slumped into his chair contemplating his mistakes. He was not dealing with some unsophisticated country hayseed grieving over the death of her father. This was one beautiful and very smart lady with all the answers.

Ike Shulman had already filled him in on her background, or as much as he knew of her background and forebears. She was part-aboriginal adopted by her grandfather after her mother died of alcoholism, or at least that is what he had been told.

"How did she wind being adopted by her grandfather if her father was Henry Boyce? Why didn't he acknowledge her?"

"It would appear Henry had a fling with her mother who was probably part-abo herself. That would account for Chloe's stunning looks. A couple of generations of mixed blood lines and the abo features have been almost totally wiped out except for the olive skin and brown eyes. I don't know how Henry and her mother got entangled, but they did. The problem was Henry was already married and when Chloe arrived on the scene he had to make his mind up. He went back to the wife, and Chloe's mother took to the bottle. Somewhat to his credit Henry didn't abandon the child, but neither could he just bring her back to Venus Downs. His wife Margaret would have immediately realised the connection, so Henry did a deal with old Johnny Quartpot to adopt the girl. Henry loved the girl but would never acknowledge his paternity even when Margaret took off on him and went back to Sydney."

"What happened to Quartpot, there's no mention of him being provided for in the Will?"

"He's long dead. He went walkabout with Chloe one day way out east when she was about seventeen. Apparently, Johnny told her he was going to look at a sacred site which no woman could look at under his ancient lore and told her not to follow him. He just disappeared and no trace was ever found."

"And what happened to the two brothers, Carl and Walter?"

"They were supposed nephews of Henry and he adopted them when their father walked out and the mother couldn't control them. They were both always in trouble with the law until Henry took them under his wing, brought them up here and set them to work. He had no hesitation in kicking their arses if they got out of line. Anyway, Carl was gored by a bull under somewhat suspicious circumstances Henry confided to me sometime later, and Walter just disappeared. He had been to England to see Chloe for some reason which was rather odd, because he never acknowledged her while she lived on Venus Downs. She was treated as a servant rather than Henry's daughter. It was a very strange situation indeed. You would have thought once his wife took off he would have let it be known he was in fact, her father. It was a revelation to me she was his daughter and has inherited everything."

"So what happened to Walter?"

"His remains are on Venus Downs somewhere. He and Chloe arrived back from London, but not on the same flight. They met up in Perth and were due to fly up here together, but she chartered a plane and gave him the slip. She took off on foot for some obscure reason she didn't explain to anyone and he followed her when he arrived a day later. Chloe arrived back at the station a week later saying she had found a body at an outstation, but had not seen Walter. It took a couple of days for the cops to retrieve what remained of the body she reported. Mind you there wasn't much left of it after the wild pigs and dogs had dined on it for a week."

Hanna screwed up his nose at the thought. "Pigs do that do they?"

"Pigs will eat anything, animal or vegetable. They're the natural disposal units in the outback; Australia's answer to the hyena of Africa."

"Did they identify the remains as belonging to Walter?"

"No, they belonged to some poor Irish sod." Shulman sniggered at the thought. "And that was a real enigma. He was a geologist who had previously been the parish priest in Wyndham."

"Why the change from priest to geologist? Was he caught giving altar boys something other than religious instruction?"

"Not him. Dion Murphy as we knew him, was one tough character from the slums of Belfast. He nearly killed Carl Boyce after they had an argument over a game of pool, in which Murphy hustled him and cleaned him out. Carl was aware Murphy had been shagging one of the barmaids at Marge Tilley's pub, and tried to blackmail him to get his money back. Marge was aware what was going on as there was no confusing the orgasmic murmurings, and shaking of the bed in the room directly above her head, to that of the muted tones of a confessional. Anyway, Murphy pulled the pin as he knew the bishop would consign him to the boondocks when Carl opened his mouth, so he did a bunk. A few years later he's back here holding himself out to be a geologist with a particular interest in something he was looking for on Venus Downs."

"Sounds like a real character. Did he find what he was after?"

Shulman laughed. "If he did the pigs and dogs would have eaten that part of his knowledge by the time the cops retrieved his remains. Oh, and that's another mystery. There was enough of him left for forensics to find a bullet lodged in his spine. The bullet was identified as coming from a particular rifle, a Martini Henry dating back to the South African Boer war. The gun was registered to Walter, so he became the prime suspect."

"And you say Walter hasn't been sighted since? What about Chloe? Didn't any suspicion fall on her? Walter could have murdered Murphy for some reason and taken off. He may be lurking somewhere out there?"

"No, I'm sure Walter wanted to inherit Venus Downs. No need for him to commit murder for no reason, and he wasn't close enough to Carl to want to avenge his brother's humiliation at the hands of the priest. As for Chloe, the cops did give her a grilling about the murder, but gave it away when it became obvious she knew nothing. The coroner produced an open finding on the disappearance of Walter so that's how Chloe has inherited the whole kit and caboodle. By the way, I want a copy of that Will so I can read it first hand."

"That would be a gross breach of client confidentiality Ike. I've already told you more than I should."

Shulman smiled thinly as he ignored the remark. He was biding his time to enforce his control.

"Anyway, I think you know the guts of it Ike. You don't need a copy. You're well aware she's one wealthy lass."

"I can see you're thinking about how you're going to get into her knickers. But she might not be as wealthy as you think."

Hanna had been lost in thought, but snapped back to the present at Shulman's remark. "What do you mean by that?"

"Nothing, nothing."

"Is there anything else you can tell me about her? I would certainly like to get to know her better. She's a very smart and attractive woman, in fact she's beautiful."

Shulman nodded in agreement. "She walked the fashion runways of the world as an international model making millions as you know, but she tossed it all in to return to Venus Downs. I believe she was married in London, but I don't know anything about that as he hasn't turned up on the scene to date."

Hanna nodded. "Yes, she is married, but she's filing for divorce. There's some mystery surrounding the bona fides of the husband."

"So she might have to share her new found fortune when she gives husband the push. I wonder if she's thought of that? By the way Andrew, I would like to be kept informed of what she's up to. I had a business association with Henry and I want to ensure it continues."

"I can't do that Ike. That's again a breach of trust. I've already told you too much. I could lose my practising licence if she became aware any confidential information was suddenly in the public domain. This is a very small town and she would guess the source of the leak very quickly."

Shulman grabbed the lawyer's arm and fixed him with a cold penetrating look. The warm smile disappeared as the facial features hardened momentarily and then relaxed into a benign expression of understanding and friendship.

"If you want my business Andrew and want to survive, you will pay careful heed to what I've just demanded of you. Be rest assured, it is a demand and not a request for your compliance. If you intend to let your professional ethics get in the way of business you may as well close the door and leave town. You forget I pulled you out of the shit. You rushed into buying half of this practice not realising Fordyce had been dipping into his client's trust accounts to fund his gambling habits. And you soon realised you were jointly and severally liable for his debts and crimes. You would have been wiped out before you even started unless I covered those debts. I paid Bill Fordyce a fat retainer to act in my best interests by keeping me informed of everyone's personal business in this town. And now you've taken over the practice, I've no doubt you will want to retain that valuable source of income."

Shulman patted Hanna on the shoulder as the lawyer stiffened and was about to protest. "Don't be a fool boy. I can ruin you overnight by letting it be known Fordyce was not always acting in his client's best interests. The smell and distrust would permeate and as a newcomer to town your practice would crash. You've outlaid your life savings to buy this practice so don't fuck it up by getting all moralistic on me. As for myself, I don't have a reputation to safeguard. I have the money to ignore what anyone says or thinks, so what's it to be my boy?"

Disgust and repudiation raced through Hanna's mind, but he knew he was trapped. One of the first persons through his doorway when he bought the practice was Ike Shulman with his effusive welcome and promise of continuing business. The offer of the retainer to act exclusively for him, should there be a conflict of interest, was unsolicited, although quite normal for any law practice. Hanna was shocked by the size of the retainer and tried to suggest without conviction, it was excessive. Shulman dismissed the weak protest with a wave of his hand as he pulled out his cheque book and poised with his Mont Blanc pen those months before.

And now Hanna felt his blood run cold. Here was the piper confronting him for payment and he had the feeling the tune would be never ending.

"I"ve paid Fordyce's debts, saved your arse and now I'm about to write out a cheque for your next six month's retainer. Do I put ink to paper or not?"

Hanna nodded in resignation. He needed the money as he worked to retain the trust and patronage of Bill Fordyce's clients and here was the client who would guarantee his future and solvency.

However, in the last few minutes he'd become aware of the commitment he'd made with a man who could destroy him in moments. He should have been on his guard when Shulman burst into his office unannounced, for he was now aware Ike never went to anyone's office. They were summoned to his.

He was unaware Fordyce had committed to a similar arrangement, but it was now obvious he had also been on the take for the supply of confidential client information. Fordyce was in fact a hired pimp and now he had unwittingly followed.

"Wake up Andrew. You're washed up without me. Be in my office at ten tomorrow with a copy of that Will. There's no money in being a country lawyer hustling for nickels and dimes, at everyone's beck and call listening to all their petty squabbles, writing up penniless Wills, conveyancing property, rushing to court to defend some busted-arse cocky on a drink driving charge, while trying to get everyone to pay their outstanding accounts. Where's the money or future in that? Forget your principles. Money has no smell and no morals, so stick with me and you'll end up a very rich man. You never know your luck. You might get into Chloe Boyce's pants after all and you couldn't do better than that. We would become real partners then."

Hanna made no reply as he watched Shulman leave. What did he mean by that last remark? He slumped into his chair with his head in his hands. God, what had he got himself into? How could he have been so stupid?

"Oh Christ, I may as well join the conspiracy." He sighed as he straightened up and poured himself a strong black coffee.

2

Chloe was sitting on the veranda as she watched the vehicle approach followed by a cloud of billowing dust. She immediately recognised the driver as he alighted, and was somewhat surprised by his uninvited appearance. Still, that was the way of the outback and was to be expected and welcomed.

Now that she could study him as he walked towards her, she was impressed by his lithe physique, olive complexion and mass of black hair swept back with a careless gesture. What were his origins she contemplated?

"Good afternoon Ms Boyce. I hope I'm not being presumptuous by just calling in?"

Chloe laughed. She had caught the emphasis on the word presumptuous. It was obvious her lawyer could give as good as he got.

"No, you're not being presumptuous and I can see you're not concerned about just calling in unannounced. Come and sit down. Meet Jim Collins the new manager of Venus Downs. Jim, this is Andrew Hanna my lawyer."

The smile was perfunctory and without enthusiasm. The handshake was like having his hand crushed in a vice by a gnarled weather-beaten fist. It was obvious Andrew's presence was not appreciated and was being given the message not to expect friendship.

Collins was Andrew's height, but there the similarity ended. His hair was a natural flaxen and not bleached by the sun, the oversize Akubra lying at his feet attesting to the fact his head was always covered, as evidenced by the deep encircling furrow in his hairline. The long-sleeved open-neck shirt was tight across his chest and strained against the bulge of his biceps. The jeans were likewise taught against his thighs and gave the appearance of a carefully orchestrated ensemble along with the dusty boots in excellent repair. Andrew decided he was a man to remain wary of, the look of danger palpable. Here was a person who gave orders and did not get involved with the dust and filth-laden business of drafting, branding and handling cattle within the yards.

"So you've only recently taken over here as manager?"

Collins nodded, but made no reply. Sensing the tension Chloe broke in. "I appointed Jim before I went back to London. He's been doing an excellent job, but it will be some time before he's totally up to speed with our overall situation. He has his hands full running Venus Downs and Remus Park, the adjoining property."

"Sounds quite an undertaking. How many cattle overall would the two properties run?"

Chloe looked at her manager. "Jim, correct me if I'm wrong, but it's in excess of thirty thousand head, isn't it?"

Once again Collins just nodded, his unblinking eyes boring into Andrew's.

Andrew whistled in surprise. "That's a lot of steak on the hoof, one hell of an enterprise to manage."

"Jim's quite familiar with properties of this size and comes with the right qualifications and recommendations. He's talking me into buying a small bush plane or Robinson helicopter so I can fly around the properties. I would like to learn to fly."

Andrew could see Chloe was more than impressed with the attributes of her employee. Gone was the authority and remoteness Andrew had witnessed when she first came into his office. He was witnessing someone apparently enamoured with the man opposite.

"Hey, I'm jealous Ms Boyce. Flying is something I've always wanted to do."

Chloe laughed.

"Well, when I get my licence I'll take you around. It will be so much easier to fly into Wyndham rather than spending hours on dirt roads. I don't know why Henry didn't invest in a plane years ago."

"I'd like that, but I don't know about getting into a helicopter. From what I've read those Robinson's are always having accidents."

"Always pilot error, or due to poor maintenance." Collins suddenly grunted an interjection. "They take discipline and training to fly. Take risks and that's when the accidents happen."

"Jim was in the army flying helicopters. I think I'll be safe with him."

Andrew caught the faint look of a smile cross Collins' face. It was a look of total satisfaction and control. There was no need to explain or offer proof of his competency or expertise. It was already being done for him.

"Why don't you two chat while I get us some cold drinks?"

They both watched her as she walked inside, but Andrew dwelled too long on the sculptured butt in the tight jeans and turned to see Collins' deadpan eyes looking directly at him.

"No wonder she was an international model." Andrew was trying to break through the glacial ice of the subliminal message. "She's one classy lady, a real professional."

Collins stood and leaned forward gripping each side of Andrew's chair. He pushed his face within centimetres. "You stick to the law buster, and I'll stick to cattle. Make sure you don't trespass into my domain."

The words were spoken with venom, the intent of the message very clear. Collins spun around, picked up his hat and stalked off towards one of the outbuildings.

Chloe looked around in surprise when she emerged with drinks and biscuits on a tray a minute later. "Where did Jim go?"

Andrew was still recovering from the verbal attack and shock. "I.I think he said he had something urgent to attend to."

Chloe laughed. "That's Jim, always on the go. I count myself lucky I got him as manager. Good ones are hard to come by, but he's certainly lived up to his reputation so far."

Andrew watched as Chloe poured the iced drink. "You say he was in the army, but he must have been on the land before that?"

"Apparently he grew up on properties down near Esperance, but I haven't made too many enquiries. Mr Shulman said he was the man for the job and I should look no further. I must say, I'm more than happy with his performance to date. I really was at my wits end when Henry died and left me with a giant headache.

"Are you saying Ike Shulman recommended him?"

"You know Ike do you?"

"Yes, he's one of my clients."

"I saw the look on your face when I mentioned him. Is there something I should know about?"

"No, no Chloe, I mean Ms Boyce. it's just that..."

"It's Chloe, and I'll dispense with the formalities and call you Andrew. Now, as to my question, is there something about Ike I should know? Ike handled the sale of

Henry's cattle, but I don't think he's ever set foot on Venus Downs. I believe it was strictly business, because they never socialised. However, I did hear part of a conversation when I was sitting in the waiting room outside Ike's office waiting for Dad one day. Ike wasn't aware I was there and I heard him say in a quiet tone Henry would be broke if he didn't continue to comply with what Ike wanted."

"What did he want?"

"It wasn't clear, but it had something to do with Venus Downs and Ascot Downs to the north. Something about an arrangement Henry had better not renege on otherwise he would pay the price. What do you know about Ike?"

"Not a lot other than he's a client. I understand he's by far the wealthiest individual in these parts."

"Wealthy, he's super wealthy and into everything would be more to the point. Ike Shulman knows everyone's business and is known as the financier of last resort. Mind you, he exacts his price in return."

"He's offered to buy you out, has he?"

"What makes you think that? Has he been talking to you about my business affairs?"

Andrew held up his hands in defence. He was thinking fast trying to defend the lie. "Certainly not. It's purely a professional relationship, but it would seem obvious to me he would offer to buy your property in view of the fact he owns a number of cattle properties throughout the Kimberleys."

"And the fact I'm a woman and it's beyond my capability to run such a large undertaking?"

"It had crossed my mind."

Chloe nodded as though lost in thought. "He came on very hard when I first took over. He was almost brow-beating me that I could not possibly control an enterprise of this size and complexity. And then he did a complete about face. He apologised and from then on has been absolutely charming."

"Was that after you appointed Collins?"

"It was about that time, but I can only thank him for his assistance. What are you inferring. Is there a connection between Ike and Jim I should be aware of?"

"I'm not suggesting anything Chloe. I simply asked a question."

"Don't hand me that Andrew. You're a lawyer, and a smart one if my observations are correct, and isn't it correct an interrogating lawyer doesn't ask a question unless he knows the answer?"

Andrew laughed. "That's correct in the case of a courtroom barrister, but I'm not a barrister, I'm just a small-time country attorney."

Chloe fixed him with an amused smile. "I know you're not telling me something Andrew, but I'll let it ride for the moment. Now let's get down to business. You came out here today to see whether you still had my confidence to maintain you as my lawyer didn't you?"

Andrew shrugged and grinned. There was no point in trying to avoid the obvious. "Yes, it is. To be honest, when I bought Bill Fordyce's practice it was run down through neglect and in worse financial shape than I anticipated. He certainly gave the appearance of being well off with a steady fee income so I paid sight unseen as he led me to believe there was a competing offer. I was suckered if you want to know the truth, but there's nothing I could do about it. I need to build the firm up again and want every new client I can attract and that means making every effort to ensure you remain one of them."

"You can count yourself as being on the payroll Andrew." Chloe reached across to shake his hand. "There's no point in you heading back to Wyndham today. Stay the night and head back in the morning. There's plenty of room and you're most welcome."

"Thank you Chloe, I'll accept your hospitality." He watched as a rheumatic old native woman emerge from the house behind Chloe's chair.

"I be cookin for one or two?"

"Two Dotti," Chloe replied without looking around. "Andrew will be staying the night so would you get Hazel to make up a room. Come and say hello to Andrew. He's my new lawyer."

The old woman nodded and smiled at Andrew before disappearing.

"Dotti runs the house. Proper old tyrant, but she gets things done although there's not much she can do these days except give orders." Chloe lowered her voice. "She used to order me around as a child. I was the servant in those days and always at her immediate command. Any answering back and she would clip me over the ear, but she's really a darling at heart. She always looked out for me along with Gramps."

"Gramps?"

"My grandfather although he wasn't my natural grandfather, but he taught me everything and I loved him dearly."

Andrew noticed the change of tone in her voice and the fleeting look of lost memories. He decided not to pursue it as he believed he knew enough about her attachment to her adoptive grandfather.

They sat and talked and watched the incandescent orb which dominated the horizon slowly disappear to reveal the heavens and millions of points of variegated light.

"You two goin to sit there jawin all night, or are you comin in for dinner? I got a lot to do before goin to bed. Can't stan aroun waitin on you two." Andrew could see the old woman silhouetted briefly in the doorway.

Chloe laughed. "We're coming now Dotti."

"No teeth, but can still bark."

Chloe burst into stifled laughter. "You've got it in one Andrew, but don't you let her hear that sort of remark. You'll never be allowed to set foot on Venus Downs again."

The table was set for two, complete with a white table-cloth, properly laid out cutlery and a bottle of wine. Chloe glanced around to ensure Dotti was not within earshot.

"Boy, have you made an impression," she murmured. "I've never seen her give this treatment to anyone before, not even the visiting clergy when they occasionally turn up. You really have impressed her."

"Jim not dining with us?"

"Jim's my employee, not my lover Andrew. Do I detect a tinge of jealousy?"

"My apologies Chloe. I did not mean it like that."

"Don't make excuses Andrew. That's exactly what you meant. I've been propositioned by the finest gentlemen of France, Italy and Spain along with chinless aristocratic English with their witless and thinly disguised innuendo."

"You're quite right Chloe. I apologise for my clumsy approach. It's just that Jim said something to me out there...."

"What did he say?" Chloe flared as she asked the question.

"It was nothing Chloe. It's just my clumsy self stumbling again and drawing conclusions I shouldn't."

Chloe was about to say something when a girl appeared with two plates, each with an overlapping fish covered in a creamy sauce.

"Thank you Hazel, this looks lovely."

Andrew looked up at the girl as she smiled, a soft smile through perfect teeth and a round dark-skinned face. "It does indeed look wonderful Hazel. I can see you are a very good cook, or more to the point an excellent chef."

The girl nodded and poured them each a glass of wine before disappearing. He could hear Dotti's raised voice, but did not understand what was transpiring. By the look on Chloe's face he could see she understood every word.

"Wait for it. You're about to be set straight on who did the cooking."

Andrew was perplexed by Chloe's remark until Dotti suddenly appeared in the doorway.

"You like my cookin Mr Andrew? Caught that fish meself."

"The best chef in the land couldn't have improved on that Dotti, it's magnificent." The old woman beamed and disappeared into the darkness.

"What a bullshit artist you are Andrew. I caught you out on one barefaced lie and I've just witnessed another."

Andrew shook his head as he cut into the fish. "What was I supposed to say? You forewarned me about the old tyrant, and after all I'm only a guest in her castle, so I told her what she wanted to hear."

"Wise decision. Now tell me a bit about yourself. Are you married or have you been married?"

"Never married. Couldn't afford it and it's not on the horizon because I don't have the income to support myself, let alone a wife."

"Have you ever heard of marrying for love?"

"Is that what you did?" Andrew sensed immediately he had hit a nerve as she put down her knife and picked up the wine glass.

"To your health Andrew. I thought I'd married for love, but it was a terrible mistake."

"Tell me about him."

"Marcel was Lebanese. He caught me on the rebound. I thought he was one of the sweetest men I'd ever met and fell hopelessly in love with him."

"And what happened to change your mind about sweet Marcel?"

"Not long after we married he just switched to being totally possessive. I realised I was the central figure in a two act play, only to find out when the curtain went up for the second act I was no longer playing the lead role. I could not go out of the house without him, or one of his goons in tow. He was present at every fashion parade or photo shoot I was involved in. He was completely overbearing and I felt completely stifled."

"And you paid all the bills?"

"Yes, along with his gambling debts and women. And then one day I just snapped. I could see he was high on something with dilated pupils the size of frisbees. I'd witnessed enough drug addiction on the fashion scene to know what I was seeing. Marcel had tried to get me involved in it once before we were married, but that's another story. I didn't have to ask him what he'd been up to or with whom, as he smelt like he'd fallen into a tub of cheap perfume. Of course there was a scene when I accused him of cheating and that's when the violence started. He just went berserk. I thought he was going to kill me as he was completely out of control as he started to punch and kick me. Laurence, the butler intervened, otherwise I'm sure I would have wound up in hospital."

"I'll bet that cost him his job?"

Chloe nodded as she stifled a sob and wiped away tears. "Laurence was a former marine who had fought in the Falklands. He flung Marcel across the room in anger. Marcel cowered in fright as Laurence stood over him threatening to inflict real pain if he dared touch me again. When Marcel fronted the following morning he announced he was going to terminate Laurence's employ. Another blazing row ensued because I'd hired Laurence and saw him as my protector. Then he just disappeared and I really did fear the worst for the poor man. In his reference he had noted as the next-of-kin a sister living in Reading. I phoned her and she confirmed Laurence was staying with her, but he couldn't speak to me as he was unwell. It was the way she emphasised the word unwell that I feared the worst. Marcel had arrived home in the early hours and was in bed so I walked out and flagged a cab. I was sick to the stomach when I was shown into Laurence's bedroom. His face was pulp, most of his teeth were missing and he had broken ribs. He had been set upon when he was walking back from his favourite pub the previous evening. Three men dragged him into one of the gardens where he was found in the morning by a woman walking her dog. We both knew who was responsible. However, there was no point in reporting it to the police as nothing could point back to Marcel. I made sure he was adequately compensated for his injuries. The dental work alone cost a fortune and the cosmetic surgery to his torn face cost even more. I apologised to him as best I could, but I'll forever feel responsible for what happened."

"Did you confront Marcel with it?"

"No, I wasn't going to give him the satisfaction of asking him whether he knew anything about it. However, he couldn't help himself and commented a day or two later that Laurence appeared to have left without giving notice and I should be more careful in hiring responsible staff."

"But the violence towards you continued I take it?"

"No, he was all sweet and concerned again, but I could see there was a marked change happening in his general demeanour. He was continually uptight and stressed and whenever I caught him on the phone he would lower his voice or just hang up. The staff were instructed he was not home to anyone who phoned, which happened constantly throughout the day and night. I often had to take the phone off the hook to get sleep. Then he started demanding money saying he was expecting a bank draft from Lebanon to hit his account within the week. Of course the next week never happened and the excuses became more familiar, the demands more urgent and always for larger sums of money. Finally, I'd had enough of carousing and gambling and refused to give him any more. He pleaded with me and when I held firm the violence started again. I couldn't resist and gave in despite the fact I had given him more than half a million at that point."

Andrew whistled softly and shook his head. "You knew he was cheating, but how did you know he was gambling?"

"When you move in the circles I did at the time, some jealous cat with a grudge will always sink her claws into you by passing on some rumour or truth she has been told by her best friend or lover. There's no such thing as a woman possessing a juicy bit of gossip keeping it to herself. The social hotline, is a twenty-four hour operation in London. It never goes off the air. Then one morning there were a couple of unsavoury looking types at the door demanding to speak to Marcel. They didn't wait for the maid to check with Marcel, but simply walked right past into the drawing room. They said they would wait until Marcel was available. The message was very clear. Marcel was shaking when he came down, gathered himself and strode into the drawing room, slamming the door behind him. I couldn't help myself and stood outside to listen. At first it was just muffled conversation which I could not understand and then Marcel began to raise his voice. He was suddenly cut off in mid sentence and then there was a scream of fear. I forgot about danger and opened the door to see one of the intruders holding him up on his tip toes by the throat. In the other hand he had a knife pushed into the flesh of his neck. When he saw me he simply dropped Marcel, pocketed the knife and the pair strode past me without saying a word. I was petrified. It wasn't funny at the time, but on reflection I often chuckle about it. I don't know if Marcel was embarrassed about his scream or the fact I noticed he'd wet his pants when he picked himself up off the floor. He couldn't support himself for a few minutes. He was just a heap of jelly."

"So that was the end of him sponging off you?"

"It got worse from that point, so I started to lay the groundwork to get out of what I'd got myself into."

"Was Marcel roughed up again?"

"Yes, but not by the original assailants or any other London thug. It was in fact someone more local to here who finally humiliated him the next time."

"Who was that?"

Chloe ignored the question. "Marcel hired a thug by the name of Massoud whom he said was Lebanese. He often threatened he would have Massoud cut me up if I didn't comply with his frequent demands. Believe me, if you'd been confronted by Massoud you would have seen real trouble staring you in the face. He was death. Marcel moved him into the house. I had no say. However, Massoud wasn't the only one. There was another one, only bigger and uglier who filled in when Massoud wasn't around."

"Marcel must have really been in debt to the mob? I suppose he started to stay home at night?"

"He did for about a week and then he suddenly went back to his old routine, but always with Massoud in tow. It became obvious why he had recommenced his routine when about three weeks later I picked up the *Mirror* paper and inside were photos of two known criminals who had been found dismembered in bags tossed into the Thames. They were the two I confronted in my house. I shudder when I think about it."

"Did you tell the cops what happened?"

"You've got to be joking. I was scared I would also wind up as sushimi in the Thames if I'd done that. Then one day the police arrived at the door wanting to speak to Marcel and Massoud as to their whereabouts on certain dates. Apparently someone had put the finger on Massoud as being involved in the murders. Marcel convinced the police they were in no way involved and gave alibis that obviously checked out. The police never came back. However, I could have blown his alibi out of the water if they'd asked me and I was sorely tempted to contact them, but thought better of it."

"You were once again listening at the door?"

"No, I wasn't. By that time I'd learned it was not healthy to listen at doors so I purchased a small voice-activated recorder which I left on a concealed shelf under the coffee table in the drawing room. I never used the drawing room except when a visitor called, as Marcel claimed it as his own. If I was out being accompanied by Massoud, I would simply check it in the evening when Marcel was not around. It was from those recordings I learned the extent of his gambling, involvement in drugs, and womanising. I knew if I didn't make the break and get away I would end up in psychiatric care."

"And that's where the person from around here became involved and helped you?" Andrew already sensed he knew the answer, but decided to remain ignorant.

"Not exactly. He had a different motive for wanting to talk to me, something I wish I had never become aware of."

"Who was that? What did he want?"

Chloe did not answer for a few moments while she thought through the implications of what she should divulge. "I'd rather not say. I would like to think about it."

"But he helped you get away from Marcel?"

"Yes, he did."

"Where is he now?"

"He's dead."

"And you know that for sure?"

Chloe looked down at her hands and then raised her eyes to meet Andrew's enquiring look. "Oh, yes he's most certainly dead. I witnessed ...." She broke off and covered her mouth with her hand to stifle a cry of pain evident in her eyes. "Please don't ask me anymore about him."

"Okay, okay. Now tell me about Marcel. You've asked me to file for a divorce, but I've already found out from your London lawyers he may be dead. They can find no trace of him."

"Marcel is not dead, I'm sure of that. I recorded him boasting to someone one day about how he could get any records he liked altered. Forged birth, death, marriage certificates or passports were not a problem. He could have anybody's identity altered overnight. When I decided to make the break he followed me to Bangkok on another flight and then simply disappeared. He's out there somewhere."

"Could it be he had to disappear? Gambling and drugs are not forgiving occupations. Do you know if he owed money, or had fallen out with anyone more powerful than him?"

"I'm sure he owed money. He cleaned out my safe of all my jewellery. All my antique furniture and paintings had gone from my home when I returned. I learned from my lawyer he had even tried to sell my house, but my lawyer had been smart enough to suggest I put a caveat on it when I consulted him about Marcel's debt problems."

"And that's why you think he's still alive?"

"Yes, I do. You see, the caveat was put in place some months prior to me deciding to quit modelling and return to Australia. Marcel tried to sell the house after he disappeared in Bangkok so I know he's not dead."

"That's pretty convincing I must say. It's going to be an involved process to get him to show his hand again though."

"How long will that take?"

"Some years I'm afraid. London has set the wheels in motion by making application that Marcel is presumed dead and you are seeking a divorce. I believe there is a statutory period of some years before it becomes absolute."

"Is he entitled to any of my property?"

"Yes, I would image he would be. The law here in Australia is that he can most certainly make a claim. Mind you, there's no set quantum and it's up to the court to determine the extent of his contribution."

Chloe rested her head on her clenched hands and slowly nodded. "I know he's not dead, so I guess I'll have to wait and see what happens. In the meantime, I'll just get on with life."

ndrew was sitting on the veranda with a cup of coffee. He had risen early, but Hazel was already in the kitchen.

"You like a coffee Mr Andrew?"

"Thank you Hazel."

"You go sit on veranda and I bring out. Breakfast ready when Ms Chloe gets back from the yards."

Andrew lay back in the squatter's chair and let the warmth of the morning sun soak into him.

"Did you sleep well?"

He had not heard Chloe walk up and snapped back from his somnolent state. She slumped into the chair beside him. Hazel immediately appeared from the kitchen with coffee.

"Yes, I did Chloe and it's certainly pleasant just sitting here listening to the birds bringing the place alive. You must have got up early?"

Chloe chuckled. "Yes, it's a far cry from my modelling days working no set hours. Up before daylight to prepare for a photo shoot in some mist shrouded location advertising Vodka, or some new car, or a new fragrance from one of the leading perfumeries, or at some fashion function until the early hours of the morning humouring sycophantic advertising directors who wanted every last minute of my time to justify their fees to their client."

"Putting Marcel aside, you must have enjoyed your work. It took you all over the world didn't it?"

"It's like anything Andrew. It was all excitement to begin with, but then the excitement starts to wear off. I admit, the money was fantastic, but I certainly worked for it. And there's the sleaze side of the business where every male is on the make, from the faggot fashion designers who think they can stick their business into you just to prove they're really bisexual, to millionaires, feaux royalty, judges, doctors, company directors, film stars and politicians of every nationality who think you're fair game. Models are the same as film stars. Some will assume the missionary position immediately to gain an assumed advantage, only to see their career come crashing down when they're dumped for fresh meat. Some think they're being swept off their feet by an adoring admirer with marriage in mind, only to wake up in the morning to discover they've been drugged and raped. The admirer is safe in the knowledge the publicity and damage to your reputation will preclude you from complaining to the police. It's a sleazy world out there Andrew. I think that's why I fell for Marcel. He offered tenderness and protection. He never tried the direct heavy approach, but took me under a protective wing. He was always by my side to make sure no one got out of line. I think back now and realise some of the rumours were true that I was not a person to be messed around with. I thought about it at the time, but I do remember how a politician who made a very frontal approach had fallen from the first floor balcony of a reception onto the roof of a car below. He was drunk and tried to paw me. Poor fellow survived with broken ribs and arm, but it made the papers the next morning showing him sitting up in a hospital bed. He claimed he'd lost his footing and simply fell. I'm sure Marcel had something to do with it. Another was an

American impresario who relied on his reputation for immediate submission and conquest. Bimbos fell at his feet, or rather into his bed in the hope of some advancement up the career ladder. I was horrified when he grabbed my breast while helping me on with my coat as I was about to leave a Monte Carlo function on a particularly cold night. He made a comment into my ear which I won't repeat. I was hoping Marcel hadn't witnessed the incident, but when I looked up I saw him glaring at the assailant. I noticed him mutter something to Massoud. He didn't mention what he'd witnessed and was jovial as we went back to our hotel. However, the morning news carried the story the impresario in question had been badly beaten up and all the fingers on his right hand broken."

"He'll be more careful where he puts that hand in future," Marcel had muttered when I expressed concern. "Before I married Marcel, I was hopelessly in love with an Italian and we planned to marry. A gorgeous man in every sense."

"And?"

"We had been away together when he suddenly said he had to go to Naples because his private yacht had been burnt to the waterline. He dropped me in Milan and drove on to Naples saying he would be back in a day or so. He was shot dead in Naples."

"Was Marcel implicated in any way?"

"It would appear so. The police had me go through hundreds of computerised mug-shots until I was finally able to identify the man I had seen at a restaurant Pietro and I had lunched at, and then later arguing with him at his vineyard in Valpolicella. Ricardo, Pietro's cousin who managed the vineyard told me at Pietro's funeral the Cammora, the Naples mafia, had caught up with his assassins. The one who pulled the trigger described Marcel as being the person who paid for the murder, although he did not know his name. He was an Albanian who got paid in cash for the job."

"So Pietro was involved with the mob?"

"It's hard to believe, but there must have been some connection. They say that nothing moves or happens in Naples without the blessing of the Cammora, so I suppose he was paying for something."

"So the Albanian and his accomplice are in jail I suppose?"

Chloe gave a hollow laugh. "I asked Ricardo that question, but he didn't answer. He simply wiped a finger across his throat."

"And that's where the person from around here, as you described him, entered the picture. What was his involvement?"

"No, not then, but it was very soon after that Walter Boyce came to see me. However, by that time I had decided to leave Marcel and London. I just wanted to get away."

Andrew could see by her hesitation she was hiding something. "What did he want?"

"He wanted me to show him something I denied any knowledge of. By that I mean it does exist, but there was no way I could possibly show him the location of what he was looking for."

"Walter is the brother who simply disappeared somewhere on Venus Downs from what I've heard. Is that correct?"

Chloe nodded in agreement. "That's true. He followed me back from London and then simply vanished."

"Why do I think you know more than you're telling me?"

Chloe sighed as she looked up at Andrew's penetrating accusatory expression. "Yes, there is more. He followed me to London because he thought I knew the exact location and source of a red diamond I'd been given years ago by my grandfather. It was from a sacred site I'd sworn to Gramps I would never divulge."

"How did he find out about it? Did you give it to him?"

"No, I didn't give it to him, he stole it from me."

"Did you report the theft. A red diamond would have to be very rare wouldn't it?"

"The monetary value of the diamond was immaterial to me. The cultural significance and the vow I made to Gramps was all that mattered."

"And so you recovered the diamond? Therefore you must know what happened to Walter?"

"You sound like one of those detectives who subjected me to hours of questions when no trace of him could be found. They concluded he had murdered a geologist who had also seen the diamond, but that's where the trail ended." Chloe could see that Andrew did not fully accept her story.

"Who else knew the diamond existed? Who had actually seen it?"

"Gramps, myself, Walter and Dion Murphy the geologist and a London journalist. The police maintained a diamond merchant in Perth had left notes of seeing the stone, but he was found murdered."

"So, you're the sole survivor? Did Marcel see the diamond?"

"No, he didn't, but he knew of its existence. He at one stage laid a complaint with London police I'd stolen it. The journalist who came out to Australia with Walter was interviewed by the police, but she couldn't help them other than saying she'd seen the gem. She said her sole purpose was to write an article about me, the international model who came from a cattle station in the remotes of Western Australia."

"And Marcel has also vanished, so that diamond is really cursed in leaving a trail of death."

"It is the eye of the rainbow serpent." Chloe murmured to herself as her mind wandered into the past.

"Rainbow serpent? That sounds like superstitious bunkum to me."

Chloe flared. "Think what you like Andrew, but the rainbow serpent is real and I can assure you I've experienced its power."

"I'm sorry Chloe. I didn't mean to be offensive. It's just my legal instinct to dismantle and reassemble circumstances. I've heard many stories about aboriginal lore, but never witnessed it."

"You don't need to witness what I've told you. It's true because I've experienced it. The eye of the rainbow serpent is real, but you'll never see it and neither will anyone else. It is a sacred place."

Andrew smiled inwardly. It was clear to him the diamond came from somewhere on the property, but she wanted it and its source to remain forever hidden. He held up his hands in submission. "I won't ask you anything further Chloe. I will never raise the subject again."

"I accept that assurance, and please respect that assurance by not discussing it with anyone. If anyone starts getting too inquisitive, just remember I'm your client and a blank sheet. You know nothing."

"You have my pledge on that. Changing the subject, do you have any business dealings with Ike Shulman other than him being an agent for your cattle?"

"I know Henry and he had dealings. As I've already said, he did try to buy the place, but I haven't heard from him since. Why do you ask?"

"No real reason. I'm just curious about the man. He appears to have a lot of influence."

"Your question is quite transparent Andrew. You wouldn't have asked that if you didn't have something on your mind."

"Ike has retained me to look after his legal affairs, and to ensure there's no conflict of interest I wanted to make sure there was no conflict, legal or otherwise between you and him. I don't want to be put in the position of choosing sides. I can act for you as long as there are no impending disputes or litigation. If there is any conflict I'm duty bound to tell you to get someone else to represent you."

"I hear what you're saying Andrew, but there's no business or other relationship between us. I've no contact with Shulman other than him buying my cattle, but if a conflict does arise I will certainly let you know."

Andrew nodded. He was mystified why Shulman had retained him and demanded to be kept informed of Chloe's business affairs. He was uneasy, as he was already in breach of his professional ethics, but he needed the income so he pushed the concerns to the back of his mind. However, nagging doubts continued to surface. What was Shulman really up to? He was positive it wasn't just idle curiosity. People like Shulman always had a motive when they started paying for information. He knew he would have to watch his step, but he was determined to find out the real reason and he had a premonition he was going to become involved. He just hoped Shulman's motives remained obscure so that he could build up his practice and dispense with the man's retainer.

"You two goin to keep talkin out here, or you comin in for breakfast?"

It was Dotti standing in the doorway who broke his line of thought. Something had occurred to him momentarily, but he lost it as they got up and went inside. They made idle chatter over breakfast, but Chloe could sense Andrew's thoughts were not concentrated on the plate of bacon and eggs as he slowly ate. He finally pushed his plate aside and turned to Dotti to thank her. He knew she had not cooked the breakfast, but was claiming credit in any case.

"First class Dotti. If you get sacked from here, you can come and cook for me."

The old woman chuckled. "Too much to do aroun here keepin this mob in line Mr Andrew. An I'm too old to be learnin where someone else's pots and pans are stowed."

Andrew noticed Collins walking towards the homestead from the yards full of milling and bellowing cattle.

"Good morning Jim."

"Morning Chloe," the manager muttered as he sat down and threw his hat onto a vacant chair. He acknowledged Andrew with a nod, but said nothing. "Early start Chloe. I've got six trucks with trailers arriving in the morning to take a mob to Wyndham."

Hazel put a plate heaped with bacon, eggs, hash and toast in front of Collins without saying a word. He reached for the bottle of Worcestershire sauce and poured it over the eggs without further comment. Andrew could see from her look Dotti did not like the man as she stood in doorway just staring at the back of his head. Her eyes were hard and cold. What was it about Collins he could not put his finger on, Andrew wondered? It was apparent Chloe was the only person who could not read the negative atmosphere the man generated. The table fell silent as they all tried to ignore his noisy eating habits. Chloe and Andrew pretended to be interested in the cacophony of bird life springing up around the nearby billabong.

"How many cattle is six trucks?" It was an idle question from Andrew in an attempt to draw the man into conversation.

"Enough to fill six trucks," was the curt reply. Collins shovelled the last of the food into his mouth and drained the mug of tea, before standing up and with a nod to Chloe, walked off.

"Quite a conversationalist," Andrew commented wryly.

"Without him this place wouldn't operate. When Henry died I was way out of my depth."

"But you were brought up on this station."

"There's a gulf between being aware of what happens on a cattle station and actually managing one. I'd been in London for a number of years and was way out of touch with reality."

"He's a very strange fellow. I wonder what he's hiding?"

Chloe laughed. "Why would he be hiding anything, but whatever it is, its not interfering with his job here. He's paid well and works hard, so what more can I ask of the man?"

"And Ike Shulman got him the job?"

"What's this all about Andrew? That's the second time you've commented on that fact. Is there something I should know about, or is it just because he's not very vocal or communicative? You don't like him do you?"

"Can't say I'm particularly enamoured with his attitude, but that doesn't mean he just doesn't show his true personality in front of me. I know for a fact he doesn't like me. He made that very clear when we first met."

"Why, what did he say to you?"

Andrew waved the question aside. "It's of no consequence really, but I did get the message he felt I was stepping on his toes. Encroaching on his territory so to speak."

Chloe picked up the inference and laughed out loud. "Really Andrew, grow up. There's absolutely nothing between

Jim and myself except an employer employee relationship, and you fall into the same category. The last thing I want or need is romance. I need a fresh coffee." She stood up ignoring Dotti's outstretched hand for the cup and walked inside.

"Dat man no good," Dotti murmured loud enough for Andrew to hear. "Chloe can't see it, but he bad news in my book. I heard you ask how many cattle those trucks hold an I tell you Mr Andrew. Prime mover with three deck take sixy head, with same number in each of the two attach trailers."

"Thanks Dotti." Andrew was about to ask another question when Chloe reappeared.

"What have you two been talking about?"

"I was asking the question Jim would not give me an answer to, and that was how many head of cattle can six trucks take."

"What makes you so interested in that?"

"Aren't you? I would imagine you should be interested in every detail of such a large undertaking as running cattle stations."

Chloe looked thoughtful as she stirred her coffee. He could see she was mulling over the strength of her imminent rebuttal. "Andrew, I hire you for your legal input, and not your gratuitous management opinions."

"Point made and taken. You're quite correct and I will refrain from commenting on anything outside my brief. Now, thank you for your hospitality, but I think I should be heading back to town."

Chloe got up and followed as Andrew strode off towards his ute. He was about to step into the vehicle when she restrained him.

"Andrew, please accept my apology. I didn't mean to be so rude. It just came out the wrong way."

"Forget it Chloe. I was out of order making a comment like that. It's just that I'm concerned for your welfare and future. You've taken on an incredible task and workload."

"And you think as a woman I can't handle it?"

"I've already told you I'm not going there again," Andrew replied with a smile. "I'll stick to my knitting from here on in."

He caught her completely off guard as he stooped, kissed her on the cheek and then swung into the cab. She was still smiling at his audacity as he swung the vehicle around and drove off. What she had not noticed and the reason for Andrew's sudden affection, was the sight of Collins leaning up against the doorway of an outbuilding nearby. Chloe was walking back to the homestead veranda with her back to the departing vehicle when Andrew gave him a wave as he drove past. The acknowledgement was not reciprocated.

He decided he would make it his business to find out more about Collins. There was something about him that did not add up. Following his graduation from law school, he'd spent his first few years defending and representing petty criminals as he trawled for work of any kind to bring in a meagre income. He had become quite used to the multi-facets of humankind, their weaknesses and strengths, the liars and truthful, the shifty and shiftless, the thieves and honest, the degraded, the pitiful and pitiless. Collins fitted into one of those categories and if his judgement was not astray, he had already put him into the correct pigeonhole. It was just a matter of time to confirm that assumption as it would be a comparatively easy task to pull up court records, search credit agency files and make a few discrete enquiries. And if all else failed, pull in a couple of favours he was owed in return for services already rendered. But then again, what was his real interest in Collins? Why was he so interested in checking on the man's background. It was none of his business.

Chloe thought he was an excellent manager and certainly wasn't in any danger of being threatened by him. He had the hots for her, that was quite obvious, but then again so did he. Was that the real reason he didn't like the man? He tried to put it out of his mind, but somewhere in the background a tiny bell continued to ring and it was somehow connected with Shulman.

"Well, how did your weekend go? Did you make any progress?"

Andrew did not notice Ike Shulman had come out of his office and was walking close behind him down the street. He stopped, confused by Ike's queries. How did he know where he'd been for the weekend, and then it occurred to him the source had to be Collins or Chloe. "You've been talking to Chloe then?"

Shulman slapped him on the shoulder with a laugh. "No, Jim Collins told me of your social visit. It apparently went very well. You got to stay over I'm told."

"Yes, I did. It was a very pleasant weekend."

"She's one classy lady that one. Brains as well as beauty, a rare combination. Play your cards right and you may wind up catching her."

"I don't think that's any business of yours Ike."

"Calm down lad. I'm looking out for your future. No money in small town law. You've got to expand your horizons."

"Ike, where does Jim Collins come from? What's his background if I may ask?"

"Oh, he hails from somewhere in the south of the State. I don't know a lot about him, but someone recommended him, and I put him in touch with Chloe as I knew she would be looking for a competent manager. What's your interest in him?"

"Nothing Ike. Just a casual enquiry."

"When I first met him I was not very impressed with his manner, but Chloe totally relies on him and that's all that matters." Ike sensed further probing questions and with a wave broke off and strode across the street.

Andrew could not get Collins out of his mind as he walked back to his office. He had spent several years in the law courts as both a defense and prosecuting attorney. He had represented clients who he knew were guilty as charged, but was duty bound to defend. What a sham it was representing the liars, cheats, scam merchants, thieves, standover men, thugs, pimps, drug peddlers, drunk drivers and the remainder of everyday society who claimed to be innocent misunderstood victims who looked to the leniency of the court. The magistrates were never fooled, all the while trying to present a passionless expression of impartiality, although more often than not it was a visage of total boredom. The client had already been sentenced before Andrew opened his mouth. They had seen it countless times before and knew every excuse invented by man. Andrew had often caught the look of disbelief on the magistrate's face as he listened to Andrew's submission on behalf of his client. At first Andrew was inclined to give his clients the benefit of the doubt, but after awhile he adopted the same impersonal attitude. He smiled when he greeted them, listened to their defense and ensured they put him in funds before agreeing to represent them. They were just a number, they paid him in advance and he mouthed their protestations of innocence to the court. He had already made up his mind as to their guilt or innocence after only a few minutes of their initial meeting, but it was his job to try and persuade the magistrate to show leniency, or at the very least accept the plea they were really sorry and would never offend again. He sat down at his desk and picked up the phone.

"John, it's Andrew Hanna. How's things?"

"Hi there Andrew. Things are great. Now what do you want? As you know I'm a very busy man."

"Listen John, and cut the crap. I can see you now with your feet up on the desk reading the comment on Saturday's games. When are you going to learn there's no money in giving your hard earned dough to the bookies?"

"Yeah, yeah. You know, life's been quiet since you left town. A guy has got to do something to occupy his mind. I used to enjoy putting those people you represented behind bars. When are you coming back? Surely, you're not going to lock yourself away in some shit town for the rest of your life?"

"By my account, I think I got more people off than you ever sent down when you were opposing me." Andrew made the remark in jest, but he knew by the silence his jibe had struck home. John Lusty was a police prosecutor and a good one, but he hated to lose. However, they had been on good terms and occasionally compared notes over a beer after a particularly gruelling case.

"So what can I do for you?"

"Does the name Jim Collins strike a note with you?"

Lusty repeated the name a couple of times while searching his memory. "Can't recall I have. At least not in Perth. Why, what's he done?"

"Nothing that I know of, but let's just say I'm suspicious. Could you do me a favour and run a search on him?"

"Hang on and I'll see what's on file."

Andrew had not been expecting such an easy compliance. Lusty could have easily claimed police confidentiality and denied the request, but it looked as though the police prosecutor did not hold any grudges.

"There are half a dozen listed by that name, but some of them go back years. Can you be more specific. Have you got an address or middle name, a nickname, an aka, or something I can go on. Is he a murderer, bank robber, rapist. Does he even come from Western Australia? I'm not hooked into the other State data bases so I probably can't help you."

"I heard he came from down south of Perth, possibly Esperance."

"How old is he?"

"Looks to be around thirtyfive-forty, somewhere in that range."

"I've got a couple of young abo kids, a wife basher in his sixties, two shoplifters and a vagrant, but I guess they don't fit the picture. I need something more definite, and then I may be able to help you. I know you well enough to realise you have a strong suspicion this guy has form. Am I correct?"

"Just a hunch John."

"Say, you're not caught up in some love triangle are you? The jealous lover being challenged for the virgin's affections?"

Andrew laughed. "It's nothing like that. From our experience in the courts we both know we can spot a perp from a hundred metres, even before they open their mouths. It was a long-shot John. I thought it might just ring a bell. In the meantime I'll see if I can't get a better profile on this guy."

"You do that Andrew. In the meantime, why don't you give up that crummy lifestyle in the backwoods and come back to the city? I miss sparring with you."

"Thanks for your help. If you do get anything on Collins or a likely suspect with that alias, would you put me in the picture?"

"An alias you say. You really do have a fixation on this guy don't you? Leave it with me."

Andrew sat back in is chair lost in thought. Why was he so interested in Collins? Was he that paranoid about him becoming romantically attracted to Chloe, or was there some other reason. Chloe seemed overawed by her manager's capabilities and appeared to be infatuated with him, but was this a superficial assumption, or a romance? Something occurred to him and he picked up the phone again.

"John, it's me again. I just thought of something. Would you be able to check with the military regarding Collins? He was apparently an army helicopter pilot before he got into managing cattle, or it could be the other way around."

"Jeez Hanna, I need more detail than that. Don't waste my bloody time until you've got this guy's full name or some other means of identification. I've got a good contact in military legal, but I'm not going to call in a favour until I've got something solid to go on. You're obviously not representing this person, and you're not prosecuting him otherwise you would have his complete background by now. I don't like getting involved in fishing expeditions I'm not involved in. It could get embarrassing if someone higher up gets wind of it and I'm asked to explain. Every incursion into the data base is recorded, and I could get a kick in the arse if I haven't got a good excuse. Now is there anything more detective Hanna while you've got me? I've got a load of work on my plate at the moment."

"No John. Have good day. I apologise for bothering you." Andrew could hear Lusty drawing a deep breath.

"I didn't mean to be rude Andrew, but I really am up to my neck in shit at the moment. I'll do what can, but I can't take it on as a priority."

e was leaning back with his hands behind his head staring vacantly at the ceiling when his office door opened. He got a shock as he knew he had no appointments and he'd told his secretary not to bother coming in today.

"Mr Hanna, my name is Bill Hargraves. I haven't got an appointment, but could I talk to you please?"

"Yes, come in Mr Hargraves." He hurriedly put his feet down and shook the man's gnarled sun-cancer blotched hand as he indicated a chair. He was a big man, but he appeared to have shrunk within his clothes, as they hung loosely on his frame. The flesh of his face hung loosely, the two cadaverous jowls reminded him of a bloodhound, but it was the sight of the man's eyes when he took off his hat. They were the deep yellow of death. He had seen the same eyes when he witnessed the death of his father. He tried to avert his gaze as he picked up his pen and shuffled his legal pad.

"You've seen the look before haven't you Mr Hanna? No point in being polite by denying it. I can see you've looked death in the face, so let's get on with it."

"Yes, Mr Hargraves I have. How can I be of assistance to you?"

"I want you to make out my Will. I've only got a short time to live. A matter of days or weeks according to the doc. It's got me in the guts and has spread to my brain. There's nothing they can do for me. The doc said I should already be booked into the palliative care wing of the hospital, but I don't want to go into that death house. I told him I'll die at home and they can bury me under a tree somewhere nearby." Hargraves winced in pain as he pulled a bottle out of his pocket and swallowed a handful of pills.

"These knock the pain down for a while, but it soon comes back with a vengeance. It's getting real bad."

"I'm certainly able to assist you Mr Hargraves."

"Call me Bill."

"Okay Bill. So let's get started. What's your full name, occupation and present address?"

"William Augustus Hargraves. I'm the manager of Ascot Downs Station and that's my present address."

"Do we already have a Will on file here? Did Bill Fordyce make one for you?"

Hargraves shook his head. "No, never thought much about dying, but now I'm looking at it head on."

"Do you have any family?"

"Nope. The wife died about five years ago and the son copped it in Vietnam."

"Any other beneficiaries like relatives, friends or bequests to charities you would like to make?"

"I took a job as a ringer on Ascot Downs more than fifty years ago and have lived there ever since. Let me tell you a story and then you can decide whether you wish to help me."

Andrew leaned back as Hargraves began to relate his very beginnings at Ascot Downs, his life and experiences and meanderings down the various tracks of recollections. Andrew could have cut him off, but decided to let the dying man carry on without interruption as the chronological happenings over the years emerged. His mind began to wander and several times snapped back to the present at the silence only to see his client staring blankly at his hands clasped in his lap with his head bowed like a penitent sinner. He heard the name Henry Boyce mentioned, but did not make an immediate connect. What followed caused him to straighten and then switch to full alert as he listened to what was being relayed. The implications of what he was hearing were profound as his client poured out the full confession without breaking his monotone dialogue.

"And there you have it Mr Hanna. What should I do?"

Andrew looked at Hargraves in shock and disbelief as he finally dropped his pen onto his notepad and slumped back in his chair.

"Bill, what you have just told me is an admission of a criminal offence. This is not a petty matter, but theft on a grand scale and what's more, it's continuing even as we speak. Not only have you confessed to a crime, but you've put me in an invidious position in that I have a total conflict of interest. I act for Chloe Boyce so I cannot possibly act for you and I must report this offence immediately to the police."

"You can't do that Mr Hanna. Please let me die in peace. I wouldn't see the night out if Wally Smith arrests me. As I've just told you, I believe Smith is involved. He would make sure I died before I could sign a statement implicating him."

Andrew looked at the ceiling as the enormity of the crime flashed through his mind. Ike Shulman had introduced him to the fat cop when he first arrived in town. He formed the opinion the man was to be respected as representing the law, but was to be given as wider berth as possible. Smith gave off an aura of conceit and power which he made no pretence of hiding as he crushed the young lawyer's hand in his powerful paw.

"Just out of law school are you, and you've bought into that old drunk's practice Ike tells me? Keep your nose out of what doesn't concern you and we'll get along fine."

Andrew had been mystified by the remark at the time. He now understood what Smith meant. He realised he was in danger as was Chloe, whether or not she was party to what was going on. He had the feeling Smith would stoop to anything to cover his tracks if word leaked of the real reason Hargraves was in his office. Finally, he overrode the guilt of his glaring obligations. Perverting the course of justice by withholding what Hargraves had just disclosed and compounding his quilt by being party to the knowledge and preparation of the document would cost him his career and a likely criminal sentence if it ever came to light. His better judgement was to forget everything he'd just heard. The defence would be valid because the man would be dead. By committing it to paper the record was complete, but a nagging thought compelled him to do exactly that; an insurance policy that could protect as well as destroy the client uppermost in his mind.

"What I'm going to do is prepare your Will which will deal with beneficiaries and distribution of assets and any bequests, a standard document. Then I'm going to prepare an affidavit which will give full particulars of what you have disclosed to me in the way of criminal activities and those involved with you. Whatever you tell me is in the strictest confidence, but this is against my better judgement as I believe you know very well what you should do."

Hargraves looked up and slowly nodded. "I know what I should do, but I haven't the guts to do it now. I'll be dead in a matter of weeks and nothing will matter any more."

"Okay Bill, your admissions are secure with me. Why don't we get down to what assets you have? Can you list them for me please?"

As Andrew began to list the man's assets in property and cash he was astounded as to the extent of the crime which had provided the wealth. Only Hargraves would escape the fall out. Although Henry Boyce was dead, his estate was not beyond reach.

"Now for the affidavit. Are you sure you wan't to do this Bill? Why do you want to involve your co-conspirators? Is it an act of revenge for something they may have done to you in the past?"

"Mr Hanna. I want you to record everything concerning the crime and those involved. It's on my conscience and if it affects the people I name, I offer no apologies. They knew what they were getting into. The details of my sole beneficiary may raise a few eyebrows when it's probated, but the rumour mongers will just put it down to Bill Hargraves having lost his mind."

"Are you sure about this?" Andrew was trying hard to extricate the one person he wanted to protect. He knew why, but couldn't admit it to himself.

"Yes, I've had a good life, but since the good Lord punched my time card I've decided I have to make some amends for what I've done. Not that I believe for a moment there's a God, but I will go with a clear mind."

"So you're not going to tell your sole beneficiary the reason for this bequest?"

"I don't think there'll be any need for that. It won't take much for them to work out why, but I would like a clause in the Will alluding to a vague criminal activity and recommending an immediate audit of cattle numbers. You can make it vague, but I'm sure the Ascot landlords in England will be able to read between the lines. That should be enough to scare Shulman."

Andrew raised his eyelids with a frown of concern as he thought of his involvement. He was in an invidious position. He was aware of a crime and people involved, but could he claim professional privilege in not reporting it? He was standing on very thin ice.

"The affidavit is for your eyes only Mr Hanna," Hargraves replied as though reading Andrew's mind. "If you don't reveal its existence, no one will know about it or be any the wiser."

"That's correct Bill, but just because you're gone doesn't mean these people won't continue. I think they should be stopped."

Hargraves gave a shallow laugh. "It probably will if you let it be known, but be bloody careful to watch your back if you do. I think the wording in the Will be sufficient to scare the hell out of them"

"But it's still going on today. It's criminal," Andrew protested as a sudden thought sprung to mind. "Is my client Chloe Boyce aware of this? Is she mixed up in it?"

"I don't really know Mr Hanna. I've only met her as a child. I don't know how much Henry Boyce told her, if anything, which I believe would be the accurate assumption."

"You've put me in a terrible situation Bill. I should really report this to the police immediately."

Hargraves sat emotionless as he studied the lawyer with a look of despair. "I thought you might do that Mr Hanna and I suppose I cannot blame you if you so decide. However, if Shulman gets the message in my Will the crime will cease soon after my death, and you now hold the key to ensure it does. The victim is totally unaware a crime has been committed, so why bother to say anything at this stage. I realise I'm making only partial restitution, but that's all I have to offer.

I believe the wheel always goes the full circle Mr Hanna and one day it may run over the others involved before they also face the inevitable. I just want to be able to walk out of here in the knowledge I've confessed to what I've been involved in, but the beneficiary knows only about the level of the inheritance and from whom, but not its real source. And oh, I want to add a codicil, I think its called, but only to be revealed if a certain event happens. I want it in a separate document."

Andrew listened, but showed no emotion. Someone could be in for a nasty surprise if his assumptions turned out to be correct.

"Your Will and codicil are straight forward, but what if your beneficiaries reject your bequest. It's a great deal of money and they may reject it on the grounds it will reflect badly on their management. They certainly have a high ethical standard to protect in the U.K. business world and if it appeared they'd been shown to be less than diligent in Australia, they might just ignore what you're trying to hand back. Stranger things have happened. Have you thought of that?"

"I will then leave it to you to disperse it as you see fit."

"I will need an Enduring Power of Attorney for that. It's a simple document saying I can handle your ongoing affairs and make all decisions on your behalf."

Two hours later Andrew finished the documentation. "I can sign as a witness to your signatures, but it will require another witness. We'll go next door to the chemist."

Hargraves gave him a shocked look. "That's Bill Murton. I don't want him knowing anything."

"He'll only be signing on the witness pages Bill. He'll most probably guess its your Will as he obviously dispensed that pain-killing medication you've been swallowing. All he'll be doing is witnessing our signatures."

Murton eyed them as they walked in. What did Hargraves want? He had only just filled his morphine prescription and what was he doing with Hanna?

"Mr Murton," Andrew beamed. "Can you witness a couple of signatures?"

Murton nodded and pulled out a pen from his white smock coat.

Andrew folded two copies of the Will and indicated Hargraves where to sign. Andrew then scrawled his signature and then pushed the documents in front of Murton to witness. It was quite obvious to Murton what he was witnessing, but made no comment as he signed.

"And now these two Mr Murton and that's us done." Andrew produced the documents which Hargraves and he signed. He pushed them over to Murton, but was caught off guard as Murton flipped it over to reveal the cover page. Andrew quickly turned them back.

"Just there if you would Mr Murton," he said indicating with his pen. He watched as the chemist signed. "Thank you very much for that sir."

Murton nodded, but said nothing as he watched Andrew and Hargraves walk out. Why was Hargraves signing an affidavit and codicil, at least that's what he thought he saw, as Hanna had been too quick in folding the documents back. It had to be an affidavit. He recognised a Will when he saw one, and the Power of Attorney, but why the other two. He was sure Ike would be interested in that piece of information.

Andrew handed Hargraves a copy of the Will as they stood on the pavement. "Put that in a safe place Bill. I'll keep a copy on file along with the other documents you just signed. Are you off home now?"

"Probably in the morning. I want to call on a few people first. Thank you for your help. How much do I owe you?"

"I'll send you an invoice. Four hundred will cover it."

"It might be too late for that." Hargraves took a wad of notes out of his pocket, peeled off a number and handed them to Andrew.

"That's too much Bill."

"Give it to some charity then."

They shook hands and Andrew watched as Hargraves climbed into his vehicle and drove off. He knew it would be the last time he would see the dying man in person. Hargraves probably felt he had expunged his crimes, while unwittingly making Andrew a party to it. He knew he had a real problem on his hands, the enormity of what he now knew would destroy people he had become involved with. In one way it was the perfect crime, in that the target had no knowledge any loss had been suffered. And it would remain that way until the death of his client potentially brought the house of cards down. He had to shield one whom he felt was not knowingly involved, but was she ignorant of what was going on? He turned into his office lost in deep thought as he considered his own predicament.

He felt it more than co-incidence when Ike Shulman phoned a couple of hours later, summoning him to his office. He had to stall to collect his thoughts as he knew for certain either Ike would have seen Hargraves leaving his office, or Murton would have contacted him.

"I can't Ike. I'm very busy today." He knew he did not sound very convincing, but he simply did not want to talk to the man.

"I realise you've got more work than you can handle Hanna," Ike replied with a clear tone of sarcasm in his voice. "But you will always have time for me. That's one of the terms of my exclusive retainer for your time and advice. I want you over here in the next ten minutes."

Andrew was not in the position to tell his practically one and only client to go to hell. However, what he now knew about the man would surely see him in a cell for a few years. He pondered how Ike would endure prison. He put down the phone without further comment and mentally prepared himself for what was coming.

Ike was beaming as his secretary showed Andrew into his office. "Tea, coffee, cold drink Andrew?"

Andrew turned to the secretary and shook his head as he sat down in one of the armchairs opposite Ike. The chairs demonstrated the man's wealth, power and position in the town. They were sumptuous, but meant to demean in that the person was seated a good head height below that of person sitting on the other side of the desk. They were forced to look up at the slightly built man with the penetrating accusatory eyes.

"Now what can I do for you Ike?"

"You know very well what I want. Don't fence with me, but just to make sure you're on my wave length, I want to know what Bill Hargraves was doing in your office, and don't tell me it was a social call?"

"You know very well I can't tell you that Ike. Anything discussed between Hargraves and me is covered by professional privilege."

"The man is as good as dead, and you know it, and I know it because Doc Barrett told me last week. Hargraves has only days to live."

Andrew was not surprised Ike's tentacles stretched to control of the local medico. "Make's no difference Ike. I can't tell you anything."

Ike's tone of voice hardened as the two tiny black eyes focussed on him with unblinking intensity. "You've suddenly become very defensive Hanna. You've learned something that involves me, haven't you?"

"Ike, why are you so concerned about what transpired? Have you something to hide? Is something about to catch up with you?" The questions were rhetorical as he already had the answers, but he took a delight in baiting his inquisitor. While walking across the road he had been tormented as to how he was going to fill the income gap when Ike fired him, which he felt was coming. But now he was relaxed. Inwardly he was dreading the moment, but remained expressionless.

"You're not much help to me Hanna. You've broken our contract so your retainer is in the balance."

"I wrote up Bill Hargraves' Will, but that's as much as I will tell you."

"He also signed an affidavit. What was in it?"

"Murton couldn't get on the phone fast enough to you, could he?"

"I pay for good advice," Shulman snapped. "I want you to tell me what it contained."

"And I've no intention of doing so. However, he did make some interesting comments which I think should preclude you from terminating my contract. Bill did tell me things that don't exactly reflect on your probity or that of other people involved."

"Are you trying to blackmail me Hanna?"

"I don't see how I could be blackmailing you Ike. What have I blackmailed you with? I merely made the observation you can't fire me because I'm the only lawyer in town and you need my expert services. You need me on call. You simply can't engage another firm hundreds of kilometres away and expect to get the kind of service I can provide."

Ike leaned forward on his desk and rested his chin on the pyramid formed by his hands. "You're very astute Hanna. You come into town with the arse out of your pants and now you appear to be holding a stacked deck. There's always a weak link in the chain I suppose and now I've got to find a way to deal with it."

"Are you referring to me or Hargraves? I don't like where this is travelling Ike."

"Calm down Hanna. I'm just thinking out loud."

"Well, I'm just a lawyer with no intrinsic interests in my client's affairs. So I can't help you with your musings or your problems if it should compromise my ethical position."

"It's obvious Hargraves really spilled his guts to you. It's a very dangerous situation and that's why I want to know what was in the affidavit. How long has Hargraves got?"

"I thought Doc Barrett told you it was only a matter of days? Look Ike, I've already breached client confidentiality, so let's just leave it at that."

"You've put yourself in a dangerous position Hanna. Have you thought of that?"

"You're fishing Ike. What you're forgetting is Hargraves didn't need to consult me. He could have consulted any law firm and you wouldn't be any the wiser. He could have easily made an earlier Will that will come to light on his death. And then the bomb, if in fact there is one, would have gone off before you became aware of it. Have you thought of that?"

"Could be, but Hargraves never moved far from the property and I doubt whether he's been anywhere else in the past forty years. Okay, you've made your point so I'll let you get back to your office. Chloe Boyce is one beautiful girl, don't you agree? I know you've got more than a passing interest in her, or you should have if you've got any red blood in you. Pity if something should happen to her."

"And now you're trying to blackmail me?"

"No Hanna. I'm just sending you a message."

Andrew stood up and started to walk out, but turned when something occurred to him. "Jim Collins. You know more than you're letting on don't you?"

"I know nothing about him. He came recommended, so I just passed him over to Chloe Boyce. I had no work for him."

"Is he implicated in something sinister? Is he hiding from something or someone?"

"Implicated in what? I know nothing of the guy's background."

"Forget it Ike. Just an idle question. However, there's something about that guy I can't put my finger on."

"Everyone has secrets Hanna, and more than one person in this neck of the woods would be a little irritated if someone started to delve into their past or particular predilections. What are you really doing up here? What are you trying to hide? Doesn't make a lot of sense that a Perth attorney with a good income would suddenly decide to buy into a near defunct practice run by the town drunk. I would advise you to be careful about opening doors into people's private lives. Take a look in the mirror lad, but I would advise you to be careful otherwise you could have a nasty accident. I've been in this town for thirty years and know where all the skeletons are hidden, so take my advice and just stick to your knitting."

Andrew nodded. "I'll keep that in mind Ike."

Ike was deep in thought as he watched the lawyer leave. He picked up the phone. "Smith please."

The young cop recognised the voice, but did not acknowledge him. "One moment, I'll see if he's in." He got up from his desk and walked down the short corridor before standing in an open office doorway. "Ike Shulman is on the phone for you sarg."

"Put him through, and close that door," was the brusque order as the young cop retreated.

"Hi Ike, what's it this time?"

"We need to have a quiet chat Wally, and I don't mean in your office."

"You've got a problem?"

"We've both got a problem. A small inconvenience has arisen, but with your input and advice I believe it can be overcome."

Smith could sense the urgency in Shulman's tone and made no attempt to query him further.

"Where?"

"Ten this evening. Same as usual. Come around the back. The door will be open."

The policeman drove slowly along the laneway with his lights out. He pulled into a darkened courtyard and waited for a few minutes studying his surrounds for any signs of movement. Satisfied, he stepped out, locked the vehicle and quickly entered the building, making sure to lock the door behind him. They never associated with one another, and just nodded when they passed each other in the street, or at a social function. That was the way they both wanted it; no rumours and no idle chatter as to why the town cop and the town's wealthiest individual, but most loathed citizen, were seen too often in each other's company.

Ike swung around in his chair and stood up as he signalled for the cop to sit down. He pulled a bottle out of a cabinet and poured two glasses of Lagavulin, handing one to the sergeant.

"The finest from Islay." The cop raised his eyes as he savoured the spirit. "The finest scotch there is, but one unfortunately I cannot afford."

"That's what I like about you Smith. Anyone would think you're the only cop in Western Australia not on the make."

"I've only got a couple of years to go before retirement. I don't want anything screwing that up. Show a bit too much wealth and it will quickly leak up the chain that something doesn't smell right with Sergeant Wally Smith. Now, let's cut shooting the breeze Ike. What's this all about? I don't like crawling up back alleys in the dark."

"It's Bill Hargraves."

"What about him? Don't tell me he's not satisfied with what he's getting?"

"No, it's more serious than that. He's dying."

Smith shrugged his shoulders as he took another sip of the liquor. "What's out of the ordinary about that? I can't recall how many stiffs I've looked at over the years. What will make Hargraves' death any different?" The cop trailed off as his brain began to click into gear. "You mean our little game is finished. So what? We've had a great run and made a shitload of money. Maybe we can strike a deal with his replacement."

"If only it were so simple Wally. What do dying people generally leave behind them?"

"The usual. Debts, assets, cash, goods and chattels etc."

"And what is the document the majority of people leave when they don't want the bloody government getting their hands on everything?"

The cop looked bewildered for a few seconds. "You mean a Will?"

"You've got it in one Wally. Hargraves is dying and has written a Will."

"I suppose he has, but then most people do."

"He called on Andrew Hanna today. Hanna confirmed he'd prepared a Will and Bill Murton witnessed their signatures. Murton phoned and told me about it. But the real dynamite is most probably in an affidavit he also signed in front of Murton. Any guesses what might be in that document, or who might be mentioned in it?"

"You suspect it might refer to your little caper? Surely not."

"It's not my little caper as you intimate. It's our little caper. It's plural and you're in it."

Smith grasped the significance of what Shulman had just emphasised. He put his glass down and screwed up his face in thought. "Holy shit, if my name's in it, I could be in a lot of trouble."

Ike nodded at the shocked realisation. "I suspect there will be many names getting a dishonourable mention, not just yours."

"Why would he tip a bucket on us? What's his motive? You don't think you're panicking a little too quickly do you? Why would he suddenly turn against us? It just doesn't make sense."

"There could be many reasons. He could have got religion. He could have suddenly acquired a conscience. Who the hell knows what his motives may be, but are you prepared to take the risk he's about to shop us?"

Smith took another long swig of the scotch. Ike could see his hand was twitching as he tried to conceal the nervous movement. His mind was racing as he looked up at Ike. "You don't appear to be too concerned."

"You're bloody right I'm concerned. Why do you think I called you here? It wasn't to drink my expensive scotch and chew the fat, I can tell you that much."

"But if he's left a Will and affidavit, we're cactus if he's revealed everything."

"Not if he's dead and no incriminating documents can be found."

Smith looked into the two little black beads of sight fixated on him. "You're not suggesting we murder the man are you?

You're way out of line Ike. I won't be party to that." Smith drained his glass and stood to leave.

"Sit down, sit down. I'm not suggesting that, but I've certainly contemplated it. Hargraves will have a copy of the documents with him as he's still in town. Hanna will have kept copies. You, Sergeant Smith have got to locate and destroy any incriminating evidence."

"And simultaneously Hargraves is to be found dead on an outback track to ensure he doesn't go and sign another fucking affidavit is what you mean, isn't it?"

Ike smiled and poured another measure into Smith's glass. "We don't have any choice Wally. I'm a pretty astute reader of people and their reactions, and the mood written over Hanna's face when I fronted him about what possessed Hargraves to consult him, really said it all. Hanna knows everything and the bucket will be tipped over us when Hargraves dies."

"But he can do that in any event, can't he? He doesn't need the affidavit or the Will."

"He could, but he would have absolutely no evidence if the documents don't exist. As an experienced prosecutor he knows full well you can't just point the finger of suspicion at someone. You need facts and proof. Mind you, it would be convenient if Hanna suddenly disappeared."

"Oh Christ." Smith leaned forward and cupped his forehead in his hands. "I couldn't do it Ike. I'm too close to handing in my badge and doing a bit of fishing. It's too risky."

"Wally, if we don't get those documents, and I include the Will because there maybe something in that implicates us, the only travelling you'll be doing is looking through the window of a paddy wagon as they haul you off to jail for a long stretch. And you know how they treat coppers in jail. Every crim you've sent there will be itching to beat you to a pulp. You won't need plastic surgery on release as you'll have a whole new face, that's if you get out in one piece. Maybe they'll scramble your brain with the leg of a chair, or jam a broom handle up your arse, but be assured you're going to suffer, and you certainly know that."

Smith's brain was racing. He'd taken every precaution possible to make sure there was no track leading directly back to him.

"I know what you're thinking Wally, so put it out of your mind. You're in this up to your neck. You don't think I was just going to let you take the money, but not accept any responsibility, do you? It doesn't work that way. I always buy insurance and to that end I've recorded every transaction and the distribution to each member over the years. Your name is clearly visible. If you like I'll quote the number of your bank account in Singapore. I always take precautions to ensure that if things go pear-shaped, I don't take the complete fall."

"You're a hungry bastard Ike. I could shoot you dead now and I don't think there would be too many people attend your funeral or mourn your passing."

"You're quite wrong Wally. A lot of people in this town would gladly turn up at my funeral to make sure I was dead and buried. But, let's not dwell on the melancholy. We've got a potential major problem which must be dealt with immediately. Hargraves is going to cash in his chips any day now according to Barrett, so we've got to make a move before he dies."

"What do you suggest?"

"It's obvious isn't it? You've got to get hold of whatever Hanna prepared for him. There might be something in his Will that implicates us, but I believe it's the affidavit that contains the bombshell. How you get hold hold of those documents I'll leave up to your imagination."

"Why aren't you getting your hands dirty, or do you assume you can direct everything from the sidelines?"

"Wally, Wally. Haven't I directed everything to date and ensured you've got more money than you'll ever need to retire on? How many properties do you own in Perth now? That was a nice pub you installed your son in last year. Don't look surprised, as I've already said, I always take out insurance in case anything goes wrong."

The cop had wanted to get out of the arrangement a year ago. He had enough money and wanted to distance himself, but Shulman had made veiled threats as to the consequences. More than once he had contemplated just murdering Ike during one of their quiet meetings. Although he would conduct the following investigation and the killer would not be found, he suspected Ike would have already covered that eventuality, a fact he'd just revealed.

"How the hell do I do it? I just can't walk up to the man and shoot him."

"I don't care how you do it Wally, but this is the only chance you'll have. Hargraves will most certainly have those documents on him when he leaves town. His ute is parked outside Marge Tilley's pub now and knowing him it will take a lot of scotch to kill the pain. I'm sure he'll flop at Marge's for the night and head home in the morning. And you can't wait until he's back at Ascot Downs before you make a move as there are simply too many witnesses around the homestead. You have to take him out somewhere in between, so if you head out early in the morning you'll catch him on a quiet stretch of road."

"Okay, but how do I get Hanna's copies? I can't just walk in and demand them?

"That one's quiet simple really. In fact you could do it this evening, but I would suggest you do that tomorrow night after you've dealt with Hargraves."

Smith's hand shook as he tried to contain the spill of expensive liquor. "You're not suggesting I do Hanna in as well are you?"

Ike held up his hands. "Nothing of the sort Wally. I would suggest a little stocktaking will suffice."

"Stocktaking? What the hell are you referring to?"

"Hanna's office catches fire in the dead of night and burns to the ground. The insurance company starts an investigation that will occupy Hanna for some time. He's not travelling very well so the suspicion will be he started the fire to claim the insurance. He may be able to put two and two together and assume Hargraves' death and the fire are connected, but he'll have nothing concrete to go on. All his records will be gone and Hargraves is dead. No copy of his Will or the affidavit can be found. You'll conduct an investigation and come up with nothing so we can both live happily ever after. I will of course spread rumours Hanna was responsible for the fire and put the skids under him to leave town."

"Aren't you forgetting something Ike?"

"And what's that?"

"Hanna is sure to have a safe or one of those fireproof filing cabinets."

Shulman shook his head as he topped-up Smith's glass again. "I've already checked that out. He has neither. He's still using Bill Fordyce's old wooden filing cabinets. Those, along with the building constructed of wood early last century will just disappear in a ball of flame within minutes. That will be game, set and match as regards to the Hargraves material."

"It's okay for you Ike. You just sit there conducting the whole bloody orchestra while I do the dirty work."

"You're not thinking clear Wally. If you louse this up we'll all be going down the gurgler. It's just that I think more rationally than you, but I'm just in as much danger if things go wrong."

Smith stood up and drained his glass. "Okay, I'll head out for Ascot Downs first thing and wait for him." Inwardly he was shaking with anger at Shulman's cunning. He was trapped and standing on a rug that could be pulled from under him at any moment. He knew at some time he was going to have to deal with the problem. First he had to deal with Hargraves and then set fire to half the town and yet remain above suspicion. He could feel the net closing around him.

Ike did not reply as the he watched the policeman leave.

5

Smith pulled over on the side of the gravel road and swung around to face the direction in which he had come. He had driven out to within a couple of kilometres of the track that turned off towards Ascot Downs. He smoked as he tried to control the turmoil in his stomach and brain. How was he going to do it? He idly watched as he noticed a rising cloud of dust some distance off. It could be a willy-willy whipped up by a current of hot air or Hargraves, but it was still too far away to see if it was Hargraves or a natural occurrence. Finally, his mind was made up as he got out of his Toyota, stubbed his cigarette out with the heel of his boot and urinated on the same wheel his dog had done moments before. A sharp command and the wandering dog was back in the passenger seat. He was about to pull out when he heard the warning bellow of an air-horn as the roadtrain and trailers loaded with cattle drew level and then enveloped him in a cloud of choking dust and flying gravel which peppered his vehicle as it roared past. He was so lost in thought he had not heard it coming although normally the unmistakeable roar of a turbo-charged diesel would have signified danger minutes before. The truck would not have been able to stop if he had suddenly pulled into its path, nor would it have attempted to do so as to run off the road in this rugged terrain would inevitably result in the death of a large number of cattle along with the driver. Smith shook his head at the ignorance of the drivers of these vehicles. He was known as the menace of these cowboys as they tore up the outback roads with no consideration for other drivers or the condition of the road. He had written out hundreds of heavy fines, but it made no difference. He caught a glimpse of the driver as he turned sideways and looked at him while at the same time reaching up and pulling the air-horn cord in a further blast of defiant challenge. Smith had no intention of trying to pass and pull over thirty tons of truck and bellowing cattle. He recognised the driver and would just follow him into the town cattle yards and book him there. First he had to deal with Hargraves. He waited for a few minutes to let the dust settle and then pulled out and followed. He was just cresting a small rise further on when in the distance he saw the truck jack-knifed across the road, with one of its trailers on its side spewing injured and escaping cattle. The driver was out of truck and just peering over the edge of a small ravine when Smith pulled up.

"I warned you this would happen one day Tippet, didn't I?" The man took no notice of the challenge. Smith could see he was not listening as he stood transfixed at what he was looking down at. He was oblivious to the overriding sound of injured and dying cattle.

"He just came at me. I just couldn't stop in time. He took no notice of my horn or flashing headlights. Christ, I think I've killed him."

Smith looked down into the gully and the pile of twisted metal he recognised as Bill Hargraves' vehicle. His mind snapped to attention.

"You start shooting those injured cattle and start cleaning up this mess. But first get on your satellite phone and call through to town for an ambulance. I'll deal with what charges to lay against you in good time, but you can count on something akin to manslaughter if Hargraves is dead. You were driving like a maniac when you passed me."

"Jesus sarg, the mad bugger just ignored my warnings. He had plenty of time to pull over." Tippet shouted in anquish as he turned back towards the cattle.

Smith slowly picked his way down into the gully. He heaved a sigh of relief as he noticed Hargraves' lifeless body some distance further down from the wreck. The twisted position of the torso and smashed skull told him he was dealing with a corpse. He knelt down and went through the man's jacket pockets, but could not find what he was looking for. He scrambled back to the wreck and looked inside the cab strewn with rubbish and broken bottles from an overturned case of scotch. He pulled a battered brief case from under the liquid mess. He sprung it open and rummaged through the papers. A manila folder at the very bottom produced two copies of the Will, but the possible vital incriminating document was not there. Could Murton have been wrong in what he thought he saw? He folded the contents of the file, shoving them down his shirt front. All the while he quietly thanked Tippet for his luck while cursing Hargraves. What had the old bastard done with the affidavit? It had to be somewhere and it was now obvious Hanna had it. He clawed his way back up to the roadway.

"Honestly sarg, I just didn't see him until the last moment when I came over the rise. He was travelling at a hell of a clip. He must have been asleep at the wheel because I'm sure he didn't see me coming."

Smith walked around to study the front of the truck. "You didn't hit him then?"

"No, I jammed on the brakes which caused me to jack-knife. He just shot past me and disappeared over the side. He's dead isn't he?"

"He sure is. But the fact you didn't hit him doesn't let you off the hook just yet. You've been in constant trouble with me Tippet. How many times have I booked you for speeding, fighting, being drunk and assaulting people and generally making a pest of yourself? How many times have I listened to your bullshit excuses when you've come up before the magistrate. You went past me like an express train back there, and even had the bloody nerve to give me a blast. Not so bloody cocksure of yourself now, are you? I think this time I've got you nailed for dangerous driving causing death. You'll pull at least a couple of years for that."

He watched as Tippet sank to the earth, leaned back against the tire of his truck, and held his head in his hands. "It was an accident sarg. I didn't see him until the last minute."

"You know who you've just killed, don't you?"

The kid nodded. "Yeah, it's Bill Hargraves. But I didn't kill him. The old bastard just drove off the road. You can see I didn't hit him."

Smith was savouring the agony he was putting Tippet through. "You're directly responsible for his death, not to mention the damage to both vehicles, the death of the cattle you've just shot and the economic loss. You're a no-good arsehole who's finally going to get his comeuppance."

Tippet was a tearaway from a family of mixed breed who lived in shacks on the outskirts of town where drunkenness and brawling were an everyday occurrence. However, he had noted from Tippet's last court appearance where he was threatened with jail if he re-offended, he appeared to be drifting off the police radar screen.

Tippet stood up and looked Smith in the eye. "It was an accident sarg. You've got to believe me. I'm the only member of my family with a job. My father has diabetes bad and

Mum is not so flash herself. I'm gonna lose my job over this anyway. Metcalf will fire me the moment he gets here and sees the state of his new rig and the damage. You send me to jail and my folks will just die without my income to support them. I'm fucked."

"You've been fucked since the day you took your first breath Tippet. Your whole mob is the same. A complete waste of time and space. Your old man hasn't worked a day in his life just bludging off welfare, and those brothers of yours are no better."

Tippet stiffened and clenched his fists. "Go screw yourself copper. You're a first class cunt." He was quick, but not quick enough as Smith had been anticipating the move and stepped forward, his massive hand closing around the young man's throat, thrusting him back into the body of the truck. The pressure was relentless as Tippet flailed helplessly under the iron grip which was slowly choking him. His face reddened and ballooned to a brilliant crimson, before Smith buried his fingers in flesh and pulled him forward so that their noses were almost touching.

"You get personal with me again Tippet and I'll pound you to a pulp. Now listen you little motherfucker and listen carefully. Maybe there's a way I can overlook what's happened here in return for you doing a little job for me." He released his grip and stepped back as Tippet sunk to his knees gasping for breath.

"What do you want?"

"That's the tone I like to hear Tippet. Now let me explain how you're going to get out of this mess with a clean sheet. I'll speak to Metcalf and can assure you here and now you'll not get the boot. If Metcalf doesn't want his trucks pulled over for speeding or load checking every day, he'll know what's good for him. There will not be any charges against you. It was all Hargraves' fault for being on the wrong side of the road."

Tippet's eyes widened as he slowly took in what Smith was telling him. He could not believe what he was hearing as Smith related the intended crime to him.

"And don't think you can get away with not doing it tonight, because if you don't I'll throw the book at you in the morning. It must be tonight. Do we have a deal?"

"If I'm caught I'll go to prison," Tippet protested weakly.

"You sure as hell will if you're caught, but you've got to weigh up whether you take the risk, or I arrest and charge you now for what's happened here. You've served time already so don't expect the magistrate to believe any bullshit about me inciting you to commit a crime. So what's it to be?"

"I want time to think about it. I don't like what you're asking me to do."

"You've got all the time in the world." Smith nodded towards the approaching sound. "The moment that ambulance arrives I'm going to arrest you, so that leaves you about two minutes to make up your mind."

Smith remained poker faced, his stance tense as he awaited the reply. He was playing a dangerous game as he realised if Tippet refused, he and Ike and others had some serious accusations to defend if Hargraves had in fact spilled his guts to Hanna. The continued silence from Tippet finally convinced him he had failed. As the ambulance pulled up he reached over to take his arm and arrest him.

"Okay, okay, I'll do it. But do I have to do it tonight?"

"If you don't I'll lay the charges in the morning and if you do I'll make sure Metcalf takes my advice and has a change of heart. You're a valued employee after all."

A ute with Metcalf Transport blazoned on the door pulled up in a cloud of dust beside the ambulance and the enraged driver flung himself out to take in the scene.

"What in Christ's name have you done Tippet? How many cattle have you killed you fuckwit, not to mention the damage to the rig and trailers. You're fired."

The driver was charging at Tippet when Smith stepped in between them.

"Metcalf just calm down. It was not Mark's fault. Bill Hargraves is in the gully there dead. Mark came over the brink of the hill there and Bill was in the centre of the road. Mark tried to pull up as you can see from the brake marks in the gravel. In my opinion it was unfortunate accident: inattention on the part of Hargraves. Your driver is in the clear in my book and I don't think there are any grounds for you to sack him. Your truck and rig are insured so there's no huge loss on your part. It's unfortunate about the dead cattle, but insurance should cover that. The only person who has lost out of this disaster is Bill Hargraves, and he's in no position to complain, so why don't we leave it at that?"

Metcalf nodded as he calmed down. "Yeah, I hear what you're saying. It's a pity about Bill. I daresay Ascot Downs will be looking for a new manager. Not a nice way to go, but he did tell me himself he had only a short time to live. Okay, Tippet you're off the hook. You stay here and organise things. I'll send out a loader to right the rig and I'll see you in the office in the morning." Metcalf threw the remark over his shoulder as he turned away.

It was after midnight when the policeman got the call he had been anticipating. It looked as though Tippet delivered his end of the arrangement. As soon as he opened the flyscreen door and stood on the veranda he could see the flames erupting from the office building midway down the street. A couple of vehicles raced past in the opposite direction towards the fire station. Five minutes later the appliance, with siren blaring, trundled towards the fire. Smith hitched up his belt and casually strolled in the direction of the blaze. No need to hurry. He could do nothing except stand and look concerned from the opposite side of the street. Shulman was standing outside his office watching Hanna's office and two adjoining businesses being consumed by the flames as Smith drew level.

"Not much the brigade can do about that sergeant. Probably an electrical fire. Those buildings must be at least a hundred years old."

"Yes, Mr Shulman. I hope nobody was inside."

Shulman looked around to see if there was anyone with earshot. "I'd say it's been a very successful day sergeant. Let's hope everything has gone up in flames. Very convenient that Bill Hargraves killed himself and now this. How did you arrange it?"

"Hargraves' death was an accident. I had nothing to do with it. How this fire started was an arrangement between me and that feral Tippet."

They watched as Andrew Hanna came hurrying down the street. "That's my office sergeant. Oh my God, I will have lost all my records. How did it start?"

"Too early to determine Hanna. It could have been an electrical fault of some kind. Someone could have left a fan on, a computer could have blown up; who knows? Not much I can do until they put the fire out, so it will be sometime tomorrow before I can have a proper look. If I suspect arson I'll call in the specialist squad from Perth. I'm just glad no one was inside. I've already had to witness one tragic death today, or rather yesterday," Smith said looking at his watch. "And I can certainly do without another."

"Anyone I know?" It was a casual question from Hanna as he was distracted by the fire and not really listening.

"Bill Hargraves, the manager of Ascot Downs. Did you know him?"

Hanna turned around slowly with a look of shock on his face. He had a sick feeling in his stomach. It was during the night he had suddenly awoken and realised he may have given Hargraves both copies of his Will, one folded inside the other. "He was a client of mine. How did he die?"

"Nothing sinister about his death Hanna. I saw it happen, or rather I got there a few moments after it happened. He didn't see an oncoming road-train loaded with cattle and swerved off the road to avoid it. I'm sure he was drunk as his vehicle was awash with booze. I know he spent the night at Tilley's so you can draw your own conclusions. He was thrown clear, but was certainly dead when I saw him a few minutes later."

"What were you doing out there?"

Smith gave the lawyer a withering look. "I don't have to tell you what I'm doing at any one time Hanna, but I will tell you what I witnessed. I was on a routine patrol which I do a couple of times a week. Yesterday I was out near Ascot Downs when a cattle-laden road-train passed me. I was parked at the time, but decided to follow a couple of kilometres or so behind to avoid the dust. I also suspected the driver may have been speeding so I decided to follow him back to town. I came over a rise and there was the road-train jack-knifed across the road. It wasn't until I drove up that I saw Bill Hargraves' ute over the side. There was nothing suspicious about his death."

"And now my office goes up in flames."

"Are you inferring something Mr Hanna? Are you suggesting there's a connection between Hargraves' death and what is happening across the street now?"

"No, it could be pure co-incidence I suppose? I take it the road-train driver survived the accident?"

"He did, but he's severely shaken up by the smash and the death."

"Can I ask you his name?"

The question was ignored as Smith hitched up his belt and began to walk closer to the fire in the pretence of interviewing the gawking townspeople who were gathered. No one had seen anything suspicious which the policeman already knew. At that time of night the street would have been deserted.

"Do you know who was driving the cattle truck?" Hanna had turned to Shulman.

"I don't have a clue, but I daresay it will be common knowledge later this morning. What's your interest in the driver?"

"Just curiosity. I'd like to talk to him."

"Andrew, I would suggest you drop the role of policeman and let Smith handle it. Hargraves' death was an accident and it would appear this fire will result in a similar finding. Just leave it alone."

"That's alright for you Ike, but I've just lost my total records. I may as well pack up and leave town."

"Cool down Andrew. You're still on a healthy retainer from me and I'll make sure you get more business pushed your way."

"Did Smith retrieve any of Hargraves' effects from the smash?"

"I haven't enquired. It's not my business, but you were his solicitor so I suppose you've every right to ask him. Is there something in particular you were after?"

"Don't fence with me Ike. You know full well Hargraves had me prepare his Will. I gave him a copy and it should have been with him. I saw him stuff it into his battered briefcase. If it's missing, then I have a problem, as the original was in my office." Andrew trailed off and looked into Shulman's eyes to notice the fire momentarily dancing off the cold smirk of obsidian reflection contained in the expression.

"If nothing was found in his ute, I can guess exactly what's happened. You don't think you're going to get away with this, do you Ike?"

"Get away with what? I don't know what you're talking about."

"You know very well what I'm talking about. I suppose Smith found the Will and it's now in his possession."

"The way I see it Andrew, Hargraves is dead, his Will is missing and your copy has gone up in flames, so the case is closed. You have absolutely no proof Smith found any papers, including his Will. No crime has been committed, so don't waste your time or mine. And if you go around making enquiries or mouthing off, you may find you wind up like Hargraves."

"I take that as a threat?"

"It's not a threat Andrew, but be aware Smith is one hardened copper and if you call him a thief, he's liable to get very angry. Well, what's it to be Andrew?. Do you want to keep your retainer and practice, or do you want to be like Quixote, and tilt at windmills?"

Andrew nodded and walked away without a reply. He called into Smith's office later in the morning but it only confirmed what he already knew.

"I was first on the scene and there was nothing other than a few Ascot Downs documents in the case." Smith indicated the opened briefcase on a side desk.

Andrew pulled a wry smile of disbelief and shook his head. "I gave him a copy of his Will. He must have had it with him. You must have seen it?"

"I don't like what you're inferring Hanna. I repeat, there were no documents other than what I've already told you. Now if you've got no more questions, I've got work to do. Hargraves' death and the fire will fill my day." Smith eyed Andrew dismissively and started to open a drawer. He stopped and leaned back in his chair as the lawyer left, closing the door behind him. This man was a problem, and a problem he felt sure would have to be addressed at some point. He could smell danger; the danger of a cell door being slammed behind him. He picked up the phone.

"Ike, I've just had Hanna in here. What do you make of it?"

"Don't worry about him Wally. As you saw, there was nothing in the Will that incriminates anyone but Hargraves. He has a lot of unexplained wealth, but nothing to suggest a crime. It's wealth accumulated over forty years of saving. After all, he's never had to put his hand in his pocket for anything like accommodation or living expenses. It's all been included in his job as manager. A few eyebrows will be raised when it becomes known who he's left it all to, but nothing will come of it. People make strange bequests like leaving it to their cats or dogs. He left it to his employer because he enjoyed working for them. He had no one else to leave it to, so they got the lot. Who's to query that? On the other hand the affidavit could be dynamite. We'll all be in jail if a copy of that surfaces. One weak link is that Tippet kid. Are you sure he can keep his mouth closed?"

"He fell right into our laps Ike. I wasn't going to miss an opportunity like that. It was like winning the lottery."

"Yes I know, but that kid comes from the wrong side of the tracks. He's a drinker, and a troublemaker just like the rest of his mob. He could really give us some grief."

"I fully realise that. It was a spur of the moment thing on my part and it sounded just right at the time. Leave it with me."

But Shulman could tell from the hesitation in the policeman's voice he wasn't confident he had committed the perfect crime.

"Are you Mark Tippet?"

The lanky kid slowly straightened from under the bonnet of the prime-mover and turned to face his inquisitor. He picked up a piece of rag and started to wipe his hands of the accumulated grease and oil which penetrated into the creases of his skin and embedded under his nails. His jeans and shirt matched the filth of his hands.

"Yep, that's me. What can I do for you?"

"My name's Andrew Hanna. I'm a lawyer and Mr Hargraves was a client of mine. I believe you were involved in the accident that caused his death?"

The smile quickly disappeared off the kid's face. It was replaced by a look of suspicion and defence.

"I'm in the clear mate. I didn't cause his death. It was an accident. The cops have already said he was driving on the wrong side of the road. I couldn't avoid him. You can't pull thirty tons of truck and beef up in a few metres. The silly old coot just drove straight at me, so what are you on about?"

Andrew held up his open hand. "Hold on there Mark. I'm not suggesting anything other than what the police have established. I just want to ask you about what happened."

"I've just told you what happened. Hargraves nearly ran into me. I almost lost a new rig and trailer, not to mention the twenty head of wounded cattle I had to shoot, and

I almost lost my bloody job. As it is I'm grounded doing all the shit-kicking jobs around the yard here until the boss let's me drive again. I make good money driving, compared to the lousy wages I get for hanging around here changing oil and tires and being up to my balls in oil, diesel and dirt all day long. The diesel burns shit out of your skin in this heat."

"Okay, okay Mark. Just tell me what happened. That's all I want to know."

"It's simple. I came over a rise and there was Hargraves in the centre of the road right in front of me. I couldn't pull up, but like a fool I slammed on the brakes and jack-knifed the rig."

Andrew gave a wry smile. "Why do you think you were a fool?"

"Because I almost lost the rig. I should have just carried on and run right over the top of the old bastard."

"So you consider the rig was worth more than a man's life?"

"Yeah, that rig was worth more than that old turd's life. I've heard he was near to popping his clogs anyway."

"So you hit Hargraves' ute. What happened then?"

"I didn't hit him. He just went over the side into a gully. He got flung out of the ute and busted his neck I suppose. I'm not very interested in the actual cause of death."

"Where was Sergeant Smith?"

"I'd seen him some way back sitting on a sidetrack. Those fucking cops are always lurking somewhere waiting to pick on us truckies for overloading or speeding. I saw him pull out and follow me, but he was way behind keeping out of the dust. Dunno whether he saw what happened, but he was only a minute or so behind when the accident happened."

"What did he do when he got there?"

"He went down to see if Hargraves was okay. I could see from where I was standing he was dead."

"What did the sergeant do then?"

"What do you mean, what did he do then? Hargraves was dead. End of story."

"Did he look in the wrecked vehicle?"

Tippet thought for a moment as he continued to rub at his hands with the cloth. He was cunning enough to realise this line of questioning was leading somewhere, but he could not as yet catch the thread.

"Yeah, he did."

"Did you see him take a briefcase out of the cab?"

Tippet nodded. He had clearly witnessed Smith retrieving and opening Hargraves' briefcase. He had also seen him rifle through the contents and take out a folder, briefly study the contents before folding some papers and stuffing them into his shirtfront. The empty folder was hastily shoved back into the case. It was at that moment Smith noticed his actions had been witnessed.

"Did you see him open it? Did he take anything out of it?"

Tippet stared at him blankly. He could sense danger. Smith was not a copper to be messed with, but what was this lawyer trying to hang on him. He would gladly shop Smith if he thought the finger would not be pointed back at him. Smith had often used him and his family as punching bags when one of them got out of line. No use complaining about police brutality in this town. Smith was the law.

"What's it worth if I did see something, not that I did?" A look of alarm appeared in Tippet's eyes as they suddenly heard approaching heavy tread. Andrew slowly turned.

"What the fuck are you doing Tippet? I don't pay you to stand around goofing off all day. And who the Christ are you? Who gave you permission to just walk into my yard? Didn't you read the sign that all visitors must report to the office. This is a busy yard and a dangerous place with all these trucks moving around. You get run over and I lose my insurance, and I'll have government health and safety wankers making my life misery."

"I'm Andrew Hanna, Bill Hargraves lawyer, or I was. I just wanted to ask Mark a few questions about what he saw yesterday."

The finger felt like a piece of steel reinforcing rod as it was thrust into his chest. Andrew staggered back in surprise.

"And my name's Walter Metcalf, and this is my yard. So get your fucking arse out of here now before I kick it all the way out the gate. If you want to talk to one of my staff, you come and talk to me first."

Andrew could see there was no point in arguing with this barrel-chested hulk with massive arms hanging from an over-stretched Jackie Howe singlet. The shorts were equally strained around the thighs in contrast with the trunk-like legs. The worn runners were without laces. The ruddy face surrounded and surmounted by ginger stubble added to the menace.

"My apologies Mr Metcalf. I didn't see the sign," Andrew lied as he turned and walked away.

Metcalf waited until he was out of earshot before turning to his employee. "What did he want?"

"He was just asking me about the accident and what I'd seen."

"And what did you tell him?"

"What could I tell him? I told him the cops had cleared me and that was about it."

"I was watching you both from the office. You were telling him a lot more than that. Watch yourself Tippet. You're skidding on greasy ground around here, so don't push your luck. Smith saved your arse yesterday and I'm still trying to fathom out why he did that."

The red stubble was pushed within an inch of his employee's face. "Has he got something on you I don't know about?" Metcalf drew back with a look of sudden understanding. "Why would he do you a favour unless you've got something on him? Is that what it is? You two are up to no good, aren't you?"

"You're dreaming boss. I can't stand the prick, you know that."

"I don't buy that Tippet, but as long as it doesn't affect your work or my business I couldn't give a shit. Let me give you a warning though. Watch your arse as well as your back when it comes to Smith. There are some stories I could tell you about that character, and none of them pleasant."

Tippet laughed. "I can look after myself boss. I've taken a hiding from Smith more than once, so he doesn't scare me. I learned since I was a kid just to roll with the punches."

"I'm not talking about a slapping. I'm talking about a very nasty accident when your corpse is found by the side of the road. And take it from me, no one in this town is going to give a stuff, or ask any questions as to who was responsible when it comes to your family."

"Me and Smith will get along just fine from now on boss. I'm not worried."

"Tippet, I've got the distinct feeling something occurred between you and Smith out there yesterday. He saved your job. I was going to fire you on the spot when I saw the mess, but he went into bat for you. You agreed to do something for him, but for the life of me, what for or why, is beyond me."

"As I've already said boss, nothing happened, but if it had I wouldn't tell you anyway." Tippet turned and stooped to bury his head in the engine bay again.

Metcalf did not reply as he walked off lost in thought. There had to be a connection between Tippet and Smith.

He was already paying Smith to lay off stopping and booking his trucks for real and imagined infringements, but for how long? How long was Smith going to protect Tippet for his part in whatever they were mixed up in? There had to be a compelling reason why he was protecting the kid. Tippet was in grave danger, but Metcalf knew there was nothing he could do about it. It could not have anything to do with Bill Hargraves' death, so what was the connection? Once Tippet had served his purpose Smith would dispense with him, and probably permanently. Smith found out his wife was having an affair with one of his senior constables several years previously. The constable was transferred to Geralton and Smith's wife followed him. The pair were discovered dead in their car a few months later. It was a murder suicide. He had shot her then himself. However, Metcalf had a cousin in the homicide division who shook his head in disbelief while relating the story to him.

"The man's foot was jammed between the door and the door ledge. There's no way he would have been able to shut the door, let alone stand the excruciating pain, yet the door was firmly closed on his foot. Why would you do that and then blow your brains out? Why not just leave the door open while you completed the job? I've got no doubt someone took them for a ride, murdered them both and then for some strange reason slammed the door on his foot. It was no suicide, I'm certain of that."

By the time he got back to his office Metcalf had shrugged it off. Why should he be concerned about Tippet? His real concern was Smith would keep his word and layoff targeting his trucks. It was hard enough making a living in this business without some bent cop delivering the message every year that brown-envelope payments were not keeping abreast of the consumer price index. At first he would dismiss it as some careless driver exceeding the speed limit or overloading, but when the number of fines started to climb to three or more incidents a week, he got the message it was time to call on Smith and satisfy his greed. He would phone Smith for an appointment, a social call to see if he had any complaints or concerns. The greeting would be loud and cordial as he was shown into the policeman's office. For the listening ears Metcalf was not here to register a complaint; it was merely an exercise in public relations. Smith always left the door of his office open when Metcalf visited for the benefit of eavesdropping staff. There could be no suggestion of criminal collusion if anyone should come sniffing from Internal Affairs. They talked about the weather, sport, the problems of the region and politics, sure categories of conversation that would dull the senses of anyone listening in. While they could be heard, no one could see into Smith's office, so they could not see the stuffed envelope being slid across the desk by the trucker.

"I believe there's been a three percent increase in the cost of living this year, don't you? Costs are never ending."

Metcalf had already estimated the increase required and nodded towards the envelope as he lowered his voice to an inaudible murmur. "Yeah, I would say it would be about that figure, but you'll see I've already allowed for that."

"I wish a cop's pay was adjusted every year. God, we're underpaid for the working conditions and hardships we have to put up with."

"Well sergeant, I've got to be going." Metcalf wanted to get away from the thieving bastard and smell of corruption surrounding him. The rumours abounded, but then rumours were rife about any cop running a thriving country town. Someday Smith would get his comeuppance. He hesitated as though lost in thought.

The sergeant looked up from the envelope on which his eyes had been glued once Metcalf turned to leave. "Something else?"

The trucker placed his hands on the desk, leaned over towards Smith and lowered his voice. "I don't know what happened out there on the road between you and Tippet, but I can sense something did go on. I just can't figure out why you would go into bat for the likes of him when he hates your guts. I'll bet you've lost count of how many times you've arrested him. And what was that bloody lawyer Hanna doing sneaking into my yard to question Tippet?"

Smith raised an eyebrow. "When did this happen? What did he want to talk to Tippet about?"

"I haven't clue, and Tippet has clammed up. You haven't answered my question why you're protecting him?"

Smith smiled thinly. "Tippet needed a break. I could see he'd kept his nose clean while working for you. He wasn't getting drunk or getting in my hair so I thought I'd give him a hand up. Pity those other useless family layabouts of his didn't get the same message. Do you have any problem with that?"

"I don't believe you sergeant, but I'll have to accept it. I've known Tippet all his life and I'd be careful that whatever arrangement you have with him, doesn't blow up in your face."

"I'll remember that advice, but I can assure you Mark Tippet knows his place in this town, just as you know yours. I would strongly advise you to stick to trucking cattle and keep your nose out of what is none of your business." The smile had turned to an ice-cold look on the sergeant's face.

The remark bit. Metcalf was about to say something, but straightened and walked out. The listening ears had noted the sudden drop in tone and all eyes turned towards

Metcalf as he walked past them with a nod of acknowledgement. They knew there had been a payoff, but it was Smith's turf and there the interest died. Smith thumbed the contents of the envelope before shoving it to the back of his desk drawer. Although he had brushed Metcalf's warning aside, he knew it was real, the Tippet kid was dangerous. However, he would deal with that when and if the need arose. Right now Tippet had performed and the immediate danger had passed. It was quite obvious what Hanna was after. He wanted to know if he had seen him removing any documents from Hargraves' briefcase. He realised Tippet had seen him and would keep his mouth shut, but for how long? The only copies of any documents had gone up in flames. Although Hanna was very aware of the contents, there was nothing he could do about it. He did not have a copy of the Will, therefore it would be deemed Hargraves died intestate and the government would get the lot. But where was the affidavit Murton claimed he had witnessed? If it wasn't in Hargraves' possession and Hanna's files had gone up in smoke, there was nothing to worry about, as there was nothing in the Will implicating anyone other than some vague reference as to a possible illegal activity. Smith gave a loud snort and belly laugh when he read the identity of the main beneficiary of the estate. Hargraves making restitution for his crimes? The poor sod was probably waving the Will in front of St Peter pleading to be let in. But the thought of the existence of a damning document and its contents gnawed away at his conscience. The threat would come from Hanna and it would have to be handled quickly and finally if it did. He sat back staring at the ceiling for a few minutes before picking up his khaki bush hat that matched the colour of his immaculate uniform pulled out of shape by his protruding belly.

"I'll be out for half an hour," he muttered as he jammed the wide-brimmed hat on his head and walked past a couple of constables. They waited for him to step outside before one turned to the other with a broad grin.

"Must be going to collect another envelope?"

"Shut up you bozo. Wait until he's out of earshot, or you'll be sent out to patrol some abo camp. Keep your mouth shut and enjoy the air-conditioned comfort of shuffling papers."

The sergeant stood on the veranda and surveyed the street. He had heard some of the conversation. Here was another young upstart who would be consigned to some alcohol-drenched outpost which would invariably break his spirit and determination to remain a cop. Nothing would be said, but the young constable would realise very quickly the error of stepping out of line. The booze induced fights, the threats to his safety, the endless hammerings on his door by some abused drunk female trying to escape another violent bashing and rape. Rape was an atrocious crime when reported in the big city media, but in the native lands it just did not rank investigating. Both sexes could expect to be sexually assaulted, raped and gang-raped long before puberty. The sight of drunken figures lying in the filth of their surroundings, clothes filthy or non-existent, was endemic while children with snot-streaming noses and gummy diseased eyes, defenceless against moisture-seeking flies and scabies-ridden dogs which foraged and slept amongst the filth of the habitation, were ignored. Children staggering around in a stupor sniffing from tins and jars of petrol, or noses thrust into a petrol soaked rag, anything to give them a high and escape the boredom of their existence. The entire contents of houses built by well intentioned, but misguided uncaring successive governments laying in ruins with holes punched into their hollow concrete-block walls. The construction was meant to counteract vandalism, but they merely represented a challenge. There were no doors, door frames or windows. Every scrap of combustible material torn out to provide heating in the cold desert nights. Other artefacts of orderly human habitation, toilets, sinks, kitchens, ripped out and strewn in the street along with mattress's and metal bed frames. They lived in filth and debris of their desperate existence. Yes, the constable was about to pay the price. Nothing stirred except the heat and flies. Smith walked off the veranda and heaved his bulk into his Toyota cruiser.

"What do you make of it Harry?"

"Straight out arson Wally." The fire-chief did not turn and acknowledge the policeman, but kept his gaze fixed on the smouldering remains. "The place stinks of petrol. Can't think of why anyone would do it. Why would anyone torch Bill Fordyce's old office? I know it's not an insurance job as the council owned it. Doesn't make a lot of sense. I've spoken to the young lawyer who took it over. He's really upset at all his records going up in flames. He was depending on them to maintain a steady income while building up a new clientele. He lost some law books, but said they were of no real significance anyway. Why would anyone do this beats me."

"Maybe someone wanted to give Hanna a warning?"

"Nah Wally, he hasn't been in town long enough to have any enemies. Seems a thoroughly nice young fellow to me."

"Has he said anything to you about who he thinks may have been behind this?"

The fireman scratched the stubble of his unshaven face dislodging flakes of white ash. "He did make a remark I thought rather strange."

"What was that?"

"He said the game was getting too rough, and he was considering getting out of town. He could see no future in staying."

The fireman did not see the faint smile of satisfaction cross Smith's indifferent stare.

"What's strange about that? When a person's distraught they will often make odd statements while stressed."

"I thought it strange he would say the game was getting too rough. I tried to draw him out on it, but he just clammed up."

"Oh, I wouldn't put too much store on that comment." Smith turned and started to walk away.

"Do you want me to secure the site so the forensic boys can give you a full report?"

"No Harry, there's no point in that. It's clear what happened. Someone was smoking near a can of gas."

"Aren't you concerned we could have a firebug in town? This could happen again."

"I'll file a report, but I don't buy the firebug theory. It's a one-off. I'm not worried about it re-occurring anytime soon."

The fireman shook his head as he watched Smith get into his vehicle and drive off. He had an uncanny feeling the cop knew more than he was letting on. He was too casual. Smith had a reputation of knowing the life history of everyone in the town and surrounds. He controlled the riff-raff living in broken down caravans and car bodies on the outskirts. He knew the reputation, lifestyle, gossip and income of every town resident. He knew the life history of the young tearaways who got drunk or got into fights disrupting his peaceful existence and that of the residents. He could pick drifters the moment they got off the bus. A couple of days in town just mooching about with no purpose was enough for him to encourage them to get back on the next bus and leave. Any resisting found themselves driven out of town and dumped beside the road. The message was clear and the bush telegraph worked; unless you've got a job, don't go near Wyndham. The fireman did recall him dropping his guard after having more than a couple of beers at the bush picnic races. Normally he retained the attitude of a tough cop who was there to maintain law and order and brooked no back-chat from anyone. He was known as a tough bastard, but there were rumours about him.

On one occasion he was off duty at the races and began to tell about an incident the previous day. "There were these two young hoons in an old Holden weaving all over the road. I just tagged along behind watching as they tossed empty beer cans out the window. They were unaware I was there, or too drunk to care. They got really aggressive when I finally cut them off. The one in the offside seat jumped out and came at me. He was a tattooed long-haired gorilla who hadn't seen a bath in a month. He was shirtless, filthy jeans and bare feet. However, he soon realised the error of his ways and they turned the car around and took off back the way they'd come."

The group watched as Smith took a long pull on his stubby of beer, but one of them could not be contained. "How did you manage that Wally?"

Smith let out a loud guffaw. "I put two bullets right between his legs. I told him if he took another step I'd blow his balls off and shoot him and his mate. I wouldn't be making too many enquiries when someone reported they'd found two stiffs in a burnt out car. The piss literally began to run down his legs in fright. All the beer he'd put in was flowing like a waterfall. I reckon he crapped himself at the same time, as it sure smelled like it. He jumped back into the car and I walked around to the other side and put my gun right against the driver's ear. I then told him to turn the car around and go create trouble somewhere else. He wasn't as smart as his mate, or too drunk to care, and he tried to answer back. I tapped him on the nose with my Glock real hard and he started to bleed like a stuck pig. He still had some fight in him and was about to open the door, so I put two shots through the windscreen. He was already bleeding, but now he had the problem of not being able to hear as a Glock fired an inch from your ear can be rather deafening. I've never seen a car do a one-eighty so fast leaving a trail of rubber in its wake. I don't know how the hell they could see they were so pissed. I'll bet they're holed up somewhere still scraping shit out of their daks."

The group went silent as Smith belched and stood up. "That's enough for me lads. Stay out of trouble." They did not see the smirk of satisfaction as he walked away, leaving dead-silence behind him.

7

ndrew pulled up in front of the homestead and sat for a few moments lost in thought. The place appeared deserted, but then he saw a horse and rider cantering towards him from the distant cattle yards. He got out and watched her draw near. She was certainly one strikingly vivacious woman. He could not believe she was mixed up in this crime, but maybe there was a side of her he hadn't seen yet?"

"Hello Andrew. What are you doing here?"

"I came to see you."

"Business, or is this a social call? You know, you're welcome at anytime."

"That's kind of you Chloe. No, this is strictly business."

"Well let's get out of this dust," she said as she swung down and tethered her horse. She took the Akubra off and shook her black curls loose. "Dotti will have a cold lime juice ready. Just go and sit under the veranda while I wash my hands and freshen up."

Andrew could not keep his eyes off her figure and jeans-clad rump as she walked away.

"Hello Mr Andrew." Dotti placed the tray containing two glasses and pitcher of lime juice on the table. "So good to see you. You come outa see Chloe, ain't you. Bout time someone show that girl some love."

Before he could reply she hurried off, brushing past Chloe and disappearing into the homestead with a faint giggle.

"What's she been saying to you?"

"Nothing really. She just commented it was nice to see me."

"Well, what's on your mind?"

"You probably haven't heard my office was burned to the ground yesterday. I've lost everything and I don't think there's much of a future for me in Wyndham. I've just come out as a matter or courtesy to tell you I cannot handle your affairs any longer."

"What happened? How did the fire start?"

"According to the fire-chief someone emptied a can of petrol against the back wall of the building. Being wood and very old it went up in a matter of minutes. They couldn't save a thing."

"Who would do a thing like that? You haven't been in town long enough to have made any enemies. Have you any ideas?"

Andrew took a draft of the cool drink before answering. "I have some ideas, but they're only ideas without too much substance."

"Have you spoken to the police?"

Andrew gave a wry grin and shook his head. "No, I don't believe that would help the situation."

"But, if you have some idea who's behind this, surely you should report your suspicions?"

"Not a very wise move Chloe. Police departments leak like a sieve, nothing is confidential. It would quickly emerge who was spreading malicious rumours and who was the suspect. Rumours and scuttlebutt are like a grassfire that cannot be put out and must burn their course. I've no wish to point the finger at anyone without absolute proof. Besides I don't want to find myself as the defendant in a libel case."

"Is there anything I can do to help? I don't want to see you leave. Is it a money problem? I can certainly assist in that direction."

Andrew could see the concern on Chloe's face. "I really appreciate that, but it's not only money. It wouldn't take me much to start up again, although I've lost all the files I rely on for continuing work. They were my lifeblood. That's what I paid for."

"I can arrange an office for you." There was concern and desperation in her voice. "Mr Shulman has a whole building just down the road from his present office. I'll go into town tomorrow and talk to him."

"No Chloe, I really don't want to owe Ike Shulman any favours. There are other things happening in this town I would like to distance myself from."

"And what are they?"

"I can't go into that."

Chloe leaned back in her chair with a look of concern. "I'm so sorry you've decided to pack up and leave. Surely, you're not going to toss it all in because of a minor setback. I've obviously read you wrong."

The comment stung and Andrew glanced up to intercept her penetrating look. "How did you read me?"

"As someone setting out on a new adventure. Someone who had rejected the partnership of a large city practice to move to the country and become involved in the local culture and scene. But maybe I have you wrong? Maybe you're hiding something and that's why you've landed up here?"

Andrew finished his drink and placed the glass back on table. He had been goaded and it hurt. Of course she was correct. He was about to run from something he had no control over, nor wanted to know about. He knew too much and felt that he was already a target.

"Is Jim Collins still with you?"

"Of course, but why do you ask?"

"Just a lame attempt to change the subject Chloe."

"You don't make a very convincing liar Andrew. There was something behind that question, so why don't you out with it?" Chloe held up her hand as Andrew was about to answer. "No, don't tell me. I don't want to know anything about Jim that may degrade my opinion of him. He's a first-class manager and that's all I care about."

"I don't know anything more than you know Chloe." Andrew caught the flare of annoyance and defence in her answer. "I'm not here to tell you anything disparaging about the man. I won't mention him again."

"Jim is in Wyndham today. We are continually moving stock into the markets now the overseas live cattle trade demand has accelerated."

"Ike Shulman still handling everything for you?"

"Yes, he is. He makes sure we get good consistent prices. Not always the top, but Jim says they average out very well. We're going to have another excellent year. The Asian trade has really picked up of late. Henry could see it coming apparently, but sadly he didn't live to see it. You know Andrew, I still get the distinct impression you know something I should know? Or do you think I'm hiding something from you?"

"I don't know what to think Chloe. You will have to forgive me, but I'm very confused since the fire. Oh, by the way I've got some news for you, but I don't know whether it's good or bad. I got a letter regarding your husband. It appears you are correct and he's very much alive. Following his disappearance in Thailand he attempted to enter Australia a few months ago on a false passport and was immediately deported, not to the U.K., but to Lebanon. He had assumed the identity of a Lebanese doctor who has been dead for ten years. So your husband is still alive, but whereabouts and circumstances unknown.

"Does that mean I'm still married to him?"

"Yes, you are, but that doesn't stop you from divorcing him. You've got to go through a process that may take some time. You've got to file the appropriate papers in England and take out newspaper ads and make some attempt to locate him. It will not be an easy process. It will take time and money."

"Will you continue to handle that for me?"

"I'm leaving Chloe. I don't know where I'll be and I don't see how I could give you the service required to carry it through."

"Andrew, I really do need your help. I'm not concerned about the money, I just want to rid myself of Marcel. He's evil and I want him right out of my life. If he has been barred entry into Australia is there a possibility of him getting a false passport and trying again?"

"From what you say about him I believe he would have all the contacts in the world to run him off another false passport. If he does turn up on the scene, just contact Immigration and they'll deport him."

"If I'm still married to him, does he have a claim on me and my assets?"

"He could have, although it's really going to boil down as to what he contributed to the marriage in the way of income and assets."

"He always said he would kill me if I ever left him and I believed him."

"No point in killing you Chloe. He would have nothing then."

"But what if I'm still legally married and I should meet with a nasty accident. He would have a full claim to everything.

Marcel is capable of arranging anything. I know first-hand people who crossed him met with violent ends and that's why I get some comfort from Jim being around. I don't think anyone would mess with him, do you?"

Andrew was about to reply when he saw the vehicle approaching. It pulled up in the yard and Collins stepped out and walked towards them. Chloe broke into a smile as he approached.

"How did it go Jim?"

"We got good prices and Ike wants another five hundred head next week." The stockman slumped into the squatter's chair, swinging his boots up and out onto the protruding wings while dropping his hat onto the floor. Chloe poured a drink and handed it to him. He did not acknowledge Andrew as he downed the liquid in a couple of deep gulps and poured himself another. Finally, he sat back and eyed the lawyer coldly.

"I hear you got burnt out counsellor. You must have rubbed someone up the wrong way or stuck your nose into someone's private affairs?"

Andrew returned the look with a shrug and wry smile. "You're correct on the first count, and as for becoming involved in people's affairs, that's what I earn a living at, looking after people's affairs."

"Looks like you were looking too closely for your own good."

"What do you mean by that?"

"Obvious isn't it? Someone wants to run you out of town."

"You appear to be making assumptions Jim. I take it you've had experience of being run out of town?"

Collins straightened in anger as he dropped his feet onto the floor. He picked up his hat, ignoring Andrew as he turned to Chloe. "I've got too much to do to be sitting around here chewing the fat, so I'll be off."

Chloe nodded with a pained expression, but said nothing.

Collins strode off towards his vehicle. The engine roared into life and the wheels churned up a cloud of dust as he took off.

"He's a very angry man, isn't he?" Andrew murmured as he watched the departing vehicle. "I'm sorry, I didn't mean to be rude, but I find him particularly obnoxious." He continued to watch Collin's vehicle as he thought about his predicament.

"And you don't trust him?"

"No, I don't. Chloe, what do you really know about Venus Downs and your father's business affairs?"

"This is my home. I know everything about it and I certainly know certain things about this property my father never knew." Chloe was indignant. "Henry Boyce was an open and honest man. He had nothing to hide. He was a hard working pastoralist who toiled to the end of his life to build this holding into what it is today. Just what are you implying?"

Andrew ignored the demanding question. "I accept you know everything about the physical aspects of the property; the billabongs, the landscape, the dream time of your grandfather's ancient lore, but I put it, you know very little about the business of your entire holdings, including Venus Downs. And by that I mean how many head of cattle the property can sustain, what are current prices for beef and the market, and what are your projections for the next two to three years. The list goes on, but what I'm getting at is do you really understand what makes a property of this size tick? And what of the other properties you've inherited including those in the Pilbara. Do you really understand?"

Chloe leaned back in her chair searching her mind for the answers. "I left here at seventeen. I spent two years in Perth before going to London for seven years and have been back here for almost a year. I don't know much about the business side of things. That's why I rely completely on Jim to manage. Without him I would be completely lost."

Andrew nodded without expression, but inwardly he was relieved he had finally been given the answer he was seeking. Either that, or Chloe was not only a model, but an excellent actress who knew how to portray innocence without the slightest trace of deceit or guile.

"Maybe so, and I can see you rely on him completely, but I think you should take a more hands-on approach to running your properties as a real business. By that I mean you should have an accurate count of how many head of cattle you're running and how many you're selling, how many staff you're employing and what are your overheads. Do you have any idea?"

"I leave that side of it to Fred Carter my accountant. He gives me a report every month."

"Carter is the accountant with offices in one of Shulman's buildings isn't he? Ike did introduce me to him when I first arrived. May I ask what his latest report looks like financially?"

"I don't think that's any of your business Andrew. You're my lawyer, not my accountant."

"Chloe, I can see you've taken offence at my treatment of Collins, but I make no apology for it. If you want me to continue representing you I want to ensure I'm doing so with your complete interests at heart, and of course your approval. From my casual observations, Venus Downs must have an enormous cash-flow from the number of cattle being run-off and marketed through Shulman. I estimate those numbers far exceed what a station of this size should be carrying. Can you explain that?" He let accusation sink in. It was a long-shot, but he was looking for confirmation she was not mixed up in what was going on.

"How do you know this? Have you been talking to Carter? He has no right to discuss anything with you, despite the fact you are my lawyer."

Andrew shook his head. "I can assure you I've not spoken to Carter, nor would I."

"Then how do you know?"

"My background as both a defender and prosecutor has armed me with an antenna of suspicion, as I call it. There's an old Russian proverb: *doveri non proveri* – trust but verify. I observe people, their mannerisms and reactions to questions and their answers. It is very easy to establish whether someone is lying or trying to obfuscate an answer. Some people do it in all innocence because they've blindly accepted something that someone has told them in order to mislead. In that instance their innocence crucifies them as no one will accept they were not aware of being misled at the time. That's why the judges of our courts are so erudite and full of ethereal wisdom. They act with the support of total hindsight. Their adjudication is unchallengeable because they can determine what a person should have done at the time the offence was committed. I've witnessed it time and time again."

Chloe smiled. "So you can read my mind?"

"No, I can't read your mind, but I've observed enough to know you are concerned about something. I don't know whether it's because of Marcel, or it's Venus Downs, but I suspect it's a combination of both. You're trying to conceal it, but I can see it."

Chloe bent forward, put her elbows on her knees, held her face in both hands and slowly rocked back and forth lost in thought. Andrew turned to idly watch a flock of cockatoos screeching in a eucalypt. Their protests were overpowering and blocked out the haunting call of the magpies perched nearby. He made no attempt to press home his case. The accused would either admit or deny.

"Yes, you're correct. I don't know enough about my true financial position other than what Carter tells me. He says everything is traveling well, but I feel uncomfortable about the man. He appears to be evasive at times."

Tell me, is Ike Shulman mixed up in this somewhere?"

"I don't know, but what makes you think that?"

"Ike has his fingers in every pie and I'm getting the impression he has somehow got involved in what is concerning you."

"Dad did comment once Ike had helped and supported him when he was almost wiped out by a drought which lasted for a number of years. Can we leave the subject and talk about something else? I'm getting very stressed. Venus Downs is my life. I could never go back to modelling."

"What's this rumour about a source of red diamonds somewhere on the property?"

The question caught Chloe by surprise. "How did you hear about that?"

"Is it true?"

"No, it's not. I can assure you there are no diamonds of any colour on Venus Downs."

Andrew smiled and nodded. "I can see you've dodged the question because I didn't put it correctly, but let me ask you this. You may not be aware of any diamond occurrences on Venus Downs, but are you aware of diamonds anywhere close?"

"I am, but I will never disclose exactly where."

"By disclosing the location of something not on your property could really mean great wealth, particularly if it turns out to be a discovery of major importance. You could easily obtain mining title to it with my assistance."

"I will never disclose what I know and what I've been shown, or its locality. It is my grandfather's sacred dreaming ground and I gave him my oath I would never disclose it to anyone."

"But he was not your grandfather, so why not cash-in on what you know?"

Chloe flared. "You don't know a damned thing about me Andrew. You may know of my lineage, but you don't know of my feelings, convictions and beliefs. I made a commitment which I will never dishonour. How dare you suggest I should just cash-in as you put it, and spit in the face of my grandfather's beliefs. I made a commitment. Can't you get that through your head? It would appear to me you would be quite prepared for me to forget any obligation or promise if I thought there was a pot of gold in return for my deceit."

Andrew realised he had overstepped the mark. His line of questioning could have been handled with much more sensitivity. "Chloe, I apologise. That came out the wrong way and I totally accept your condemnation."

She made no comment and they sat in silence looking out at the ochre cliffs rising up as a backdrop to the surrounding landscape. Finally Chloe broke the silence.

"I've been questioned by police, the press, geologists, mining companies, government officials and entrepreneurs about a fabulous red diamond I was supposed to have found on Venus Downs. It was a diamond and it was a beautiful red, but at the time my grandfather gave it to me, I just thought it was a red stone he said was sacred. He called it the eye of the rainbow serpent. It was part of his dreaming. To him it had absolutely no material value other than as part of a sacred site. It's no secret I had it in my possession. When I left London, Marcel complained to the police I'd stolen it."

"So how did Walter get hold of it?"

"He saw it in a jar of unusual stones I'd collected over the years and kept in my bedroom. I don't know how he found out it was a diamond, but someone must have told him. He brought it to London to show me in the hope I would disclose where I got it from. I was at a function in the Savoy at the time, but I denied all knowledge of it and my link with him as he had a journalist in tow and Marcel was within earshot. However, I got a message to him through the journalist to meet me at my house the following day when I knew Marcel would be out for a few hours. Unfortunately, Marcel must have suspected something as he turned up unexpectedly. He ordered Walter out of the house and then proceeded to shove me around and threaten me until I disclosed the purpose of Walter's visit. From that moment I knew Walter was in grave danger as I overheard Marcel make some phone calls and then tell Massoud, his hired thug, to get the diamond at all costs. However, it didn't work out as planned, as Walter killed Massoud in self-defence and Marcel was mugged by Walter while he was sitting in his car. He robbed Marcel of a couple of wallets stuffed with money, his solid gold necklace and bangle, his Pierre Cardin watch, diamond pinky ring and for some strange reason his bespoke shoes, obviously to make it look like an opportunistic theft by some vagrant. At first Marcel thought Massoud must have been responsible because he had disappeared, but when his body was found in a garbage bin, Marcel somehow connected the dots and realised Walter was the perpetrator of the mugging and robbery and Massoud's death. He hired a couple of Serbian or Croatian killers to go after him and a journalist by the name of Annie Brittan who had been helping

Walter. They managed to get out of England and on a plane to Perth where a couple of crooked police were waiting for him. Fortunately he spotted them and passed the diamond to Annie. He then made the mistake of mailing the diamond to my aunt in Perth to hold until he could retrieve it from her. He was afraid the police would stop and search him at anytime as they knew he had it, so he wanted her to hold it until he found a way of getting out of Perth with the diamond. My aunt Liz had no idea what the package contained. I had already made the decision to get away from London and Marcel so I caught a flight home only to be met at the airport by Walter and Annie. My arrangement with Walter was that I would show him the source of the diamond if he returned it to me."

"Which you had no intention of doing?"

"No, but at that point I had no idea how I would get hold of it again. I was winging it. However, providence prevailed in that I phoned Liz when I got into Perth and went to see her. It was only when I was leaving she casually mentioned she had received a small parcel Walter was due to pick up. I guessed immediately what it was, but ventured nothing other than to say I was meeting Walter for dinner and would give it to him. Liz detested Walter and was only too happy not to have him call on her. As soon as I was outside her building I opened the package and sure enough there was the diamond. I was due to fly back to Wyndham with Walter the following day on a commercial flight, but I chartered a jet and flew directly home. I wanted to return the diamond to its sacred site before Walter caught up with me. You can do a lot of thinking on a long flight. I realised Walter had in fact murdered his brother Carl so he could inherit Venus Downs. I sensed somehow I would be his next victim, but could not work out why I could be a threat, as I was not related. However, just before he died Walter revealed Henry was in fact my father and the estate was to be divided among the three of us. With Carl dead I remained the sole impediment to him inheriting everything. You can imagine my despair when I saw Dad helpless in a wheelchair with a full-time carer after being away all those years overseas. He'd had a stroke which totally debilitated him. I wanted to stay, but I knew Walter would only be a day or so behind me, so I immediately left to return the diamond to the rainbow serpent."

Chloe looked up to see Andrew smiling at her. "I can see you don't believe in the rainbow serpent or sacred sites, but they do exist."

"Chloe, I'm not doubting you or being derisory in any way. I was merely reflecting on how resourceful you are. The drive and determination to leave Venus Downs and make an international success of yourself is truly admirable. It's obvious you managed to return the diamond to its rightful home, but how did Walter die? You must have had some hand in it?"

Chloe's face turned ashen as she shook and tried to hide her emotions. "I was not responsible for his death. I did not kill him."

"You might not have directly, but I'm convinced you were present at his death and know how he died. When I first became aware of the diamond saga I pulled up the archives of *Prix* magazine and read the article by Annie Brittan about you and the diamond. She confirmed she had seen it. I made a few discrete enquiries from police records and read your account of returning home and immediately departing for your grandfather's dreamtime grounds. It was established that Walter followed you the next day and disappeared. You returned to the homestead a few days later and reported you had found the body of an Irish geologist who'd been looking for diamond pipes east of Venus Downs. The bullet that killed him had been fired from a Martini Henri rifle. The station staff knew Walter owned such a weapon, but it had disappeared some years previously. You denied seeing Walter while you were out there, but Dotti confirmed he had followed you immediately after he arrived at the station homestead. I've no doubt that Walter was an expert tracker and could easily follow you. The police established he had murdered the geologist and then wandered off with the rifle and committed suicide. It amazes me they didn't put you in the frame. They really didn't try very hard, did they? I believe you know exactly what happened to Walter."

Chloe began to sob quietly. "I didn't do it. You must believe me."

"He caught up with you though, didn't he?"

"Yes, yes he did. He saw me return the diamond and was going to rape me before he murdered me. He was gloating that Venus Downs was his and he now knew the source of the diamonds I was of no further use."

"Diamonds? So there was more than one?"

"The rainbow serpent was guarding many more that Gramps had hidden in a crevice. They were sacred and belonged to the rainbow serpent."

"So you're telling me it was the serpent that killed him?"

"That's correct. The snake struck when he attempted to retrieve the bowl. He died within a few minutes. It was a horrible and painful death."

"So, Walter's remains are still out there along with the diamonds and you could not tell the police because that would have immediately brought a horde of exploration companies looking for the source. Your grandfather's secret would likely be discovered if you said anything."

Chloe nodded. "Precisely, but that didn't stop the exploration companies descending on the station. I was offered the world if I would assist them. After all red diamonds are a complete rarity. Argyle nearby has its fabulous pink diamonds, Ellendale has its priceless yellows, but blood red was nothing anyone had seen."

"And you've never been back?"

"I go out there occasionally to sit with Gramps and talk to him. Walter shot him very close to his sacred site, and it is a place I know he would want to be in, the dreaming spiritland of his ancestors. Hopefully, he will never be disturbed by exploration as the area has now been excised into part of a national park and that means no exploration or mining allowed."

"Chloe I want you to know I would never disclose what you have just told me. I just couldn't see any purpose in doing so."

Chloe wiped her eyes with the back of her hand. "Thank you Andrew. I don't know why, but that's a burden of guilt lifted. I've been wanting to tell someone, and I really can't understand why I told you."

"I don't see why you should feel guilt. You didn't kill Walter, nor did you have a hand in his death, so put it out of your mind. Has Collins ever queried you about the diamonds?"

"Yes, he did attempt to do so, but I soon put him straight in that regard. I told him he was the station manager and I expected him to confine himself to that job."

"But he didn't, did he?"

"You're very perceptive Andrew, but no he didn't. On a number of occasions he just rode off by himself saying he wanted to spend a few days in the bush on his days off. I had one of the native station hands follow him on occasion and he tracked him to the outstation where Walter murdered the geologist. He wandered around, but found nothing as I knew he wouldn't. I didn't let on I knew what he was doing and he hasn't mentioned it since. I think he may have spotted the tracker and realised I was aware of his intentions, because he hasn't been out there since."

"But he does frighten you doesn't he?"

"What are you, a psychiatrist now?" Chloe gave a nervous unconvincing laugh. "No, he doesn't frighten me, but I do feel uncomfortable at times. I'm aware of him looking at me with those piercing blue eyes of his."

"He gave me a warning not to get too fond of you the first time I came out here. He's a very dark character is Jim Collins, if in fact that's his real name."

Chloe looked startled and was about to ask something when Andrew made to stand. "I suppose I'd better be getting back to town. I've a lot to sort out if I'm to stay and re-establish my practice. I'll get an office and then start with talking to Fred Carter about your finances."

"You won't get back until dark. Why don't you stay the night and leave in the morning?"

Andrew nodded and sat back. "I think I'll take you up on that offer. I've been living in my office. It was very comfortable really, but that's all gone now so I'll have to look for new digs."

"You can use Dad's old room. Call it your own whenever you're out here. By the way, there's an envelope on his desk addressed to you. I didn't want it getting mixed up with the station mail and getting opened accidentally."

"Thanks Chloe. It's mine. I addressed it here because I didn't want it in the office. It must have been a premonition something would happen."

"It must be important then?"

"It is. Very."

Chloe could see he was not going to venture any more information as to its contents. She dismissed it as none of her business.

"Jim won't like me staying."

Chloe laughed. "Now look who's frightened of him. It will do him good to see he may have a bit of competition?"

"When you divorce Marcel, are you going to marry again?"

Chloe nodded. "I would love to have children. I know marriage is not a precondition for children in this day and age, but I would like to get rid of Marcel first."

They talked long into the afternoon and the light was fading when Dotti poked her head through the doorway. "You two want to eat out here or inside?"

"We'll sit out here Dotti. It's a lovely night and there don't appear to be many bugs to annoy us. Andrew, why don't you clean up in Dad's room? I'm sure you'll find everything you need in there. And don't be concerned about sleeping in his bed. He died out here on the veranda in his favourite chair."

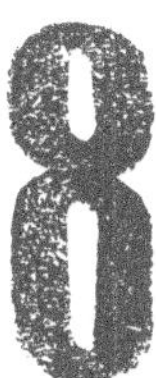

ndrew pushed open the door to the dead man's room. It was large with a made-up double bed on a copious wooden frame. He picked up his self-addressed envelope and slowly opened it. He could tell by it's weight he had made a terrible mistake in his haste. The Power of Attorney, affidavit and codicil were there, but there was no copy of Hargraves' Will. He had given both copies to his dead client. Without that the papers he was holding were worthless, and amounted to nothing. He put it out of his mind as he looked around. Two large wooden chests of drawers and a wall-length wardrobe opposed each other on either side of the room. One panel of the wardrobe had a full length mirror. He studied some old framed photos on the walls of what he could only imagine as being of Boyce in his younger days along with groups of non-descript people. It was the same in any old homestead where the present descendent occupants could point out relationships and events, but other than that the photos were of vague memories, meaningless to the next generation. He walked through into an office with a large desk, filing cabinets and an ancient safe in one corner. The top of the filing cabinets were covered with books, old farming and grazing publications and diaries. Andrew picked one up and began to idly flick the pages with his thumb, the years of a man's everyday life chronicled with observations and remarks, meaningful only to the person who wrote them.

A particular entry momentarily flashed into his mind, but he was already closing the journal and the significance faded. A heavy wooden swivelling captain's chair was pushed back from the desk, with its leather-covered cushion and horsehair stuffing bursting through its exploded stitching. He imagined Henry Boyce had only just got up from it and left the room. He walked through to an adjoining bathroom, attached as an afterthought, blocking off part of the veranda that had once circled the whole homestead. He grinned at the sight of the ancient bath with rusting plug-hole, chipped enamel and green-mould encrusted taps. There was no plug. It was evident Henry Boyce did not soothe his aching limbs in a hot tub, but rather bathed under a rudimentary shower with exposed plumbing and a drainage tray obviously retrieved from a junk yard. No creature comforts here. Hot water was sourced by lighting a fire under a forty-four gallon drum, the hot water rising to be adjusted with cold water from an overhead tank as well as replenishing the water drawn for the shower. There was a washstand with an overhead locker and attached mirror. He noted the cake of fresh soap along with a shaving brush, razor and toothbrush. The towel was fresh, but stiff from being aired in the open. It was not going to be as primitive as he imagined as he washed, felt his chin for stubble, but decided against shaving. It would be too obvious he was trying to make an impression.

"Did you find everything?"

He had been sitting on the veranda again for about ten minutes when Chloe finally appeared. "It's a bit primitive, but that's the way Dad liked things, rough and ready with no frills or gadgets. I got rid of all his personal things, clothing and the like. It's aboriginal custom to completely erase all evidence of a dead person and never to mention their name again. I won't go that far. Henry Boyce will always be my father."

"And you still go out and talk to your grandfather."

"Gramps has a special place in my heart. I will never forget him." Chloe was lost in her memories as she looked out into the dark.

Dotti pushed the screen door to the kitchen open. "You two ready to eat. Hazel will bring it out here."

"Thank you Dotti. I'm not sure whether Jim is going to join us."

"Mr Collins hummf." Dotti snorted as she let the door swing shut.

"I see he's got another admirer."

Chloe ignored the remark as she heard the approaching footsteps. Collins pushed open the outer screen door and entered the fully screened bug-proof veranda.

"Good evening Jim."

Collins nodded at Chloe but once again ignored Andrew. "Sorry I'm late, but I had a few things to do and give the boys some instructions for the morning."

Dotti held the door open as Hazel appeared with two plates of food which she sat down in front of Chloe and Andrew. She was back in a minute with a plate for Collins who began to eat, as though ignorant of their presence. Chloe and Andrew watched him for a few moments before following him.

"Andrew has been giving me some advice and help Jim."

"As long as he doesn't get under my feet I can't see a problem with that Chloe." Collins flicked the top off a stubby of beer with a quick twist and drank straight from the bottle.

"Andrew thinks I should be more acquainted with the day to day running of the property. Become more involved."

"You own the place Chloe. You call the shots as far as I'm concerned. Where do you want to start?"

"I would like a full rundown on how many cattle are being run on Venus Downs for a start; breeding cows, steers, heifers and weaners and how many we turn-off a year. Can you give me those figures?"

"Not off the top of my head, but Fred Carter would have those numbers at his fingertips. He's the bean-counter so why don't you ask him? Why the sudden interest if I may ask?"

"Andrew has agreed to look into my affairs and has suggested I start to take a more serious look at what's involved."

"I've got Venus running how I want it Chloe. I don't need any outside input, interference or advice."

Chloe glanced at Andrew with raised eyelids.

"What do you know about cattle Hanna?" Collins demanded as he continued to eat.

"Nothing, but from what Chloe tells me I get the impression the ledgers don't balance in terms of what is being run-off and sold and income."

Chloe looked up in surprise, but said nothing. She had not implied any such thing to Andrew. What was he up to?

"You're out of your depth Hanna. Why don't you stick to law and leave the running of the station to me?"

Andrew could see he was getting nowhere. He would have to start with Carter and try to figure out what was going on. "I'll do that and thanks for your advice."

Collins finished his beer, pushed his plate aside and stood up. "I'll be going to town early tomorrow Chloe. I've got some spare parts to pick up."

They watched him leave. "He really doesn't like you, does he?"

"He made that very clear on the first day, but now he perceives me as a direct threat and I intend to find out why."

"But he's such a good manager."

Andrew didn't answer. He was lost in thought. He was dredging his memory for any traces of a connection somewhere with the man. He had encountered hundreds of miscreants in his time as a prosecutor. He could not possibly remember them all, but somewhere at the back of his mind something was nagging him. Had Collins recognised him? Was that the reason for his open hostility? There had to be something, but it was eluding him.

"I'm pleased you agreed to stay Andrew. Although I love this place, I get very lonely at times and probably that's why you think there's something between Jim and I, but he's someone to talk to, nothing more."

"You don't miss the international stage and all the glamour life you must have led?"

Chloe laughed. "It's like anything Andrew. It's all excitement to start with and then the pressure and novelty starts to take its toll. I was not cut out for it and knew one day I would have to make the break. The glamour life is so false, with endless functions, fashion shows and parties and the parasites and effete posers that infest the business. I don't miss it for a moment and I certainly don't miss Marcel. I lay awake at night thinking of how I made the mistake of marrying him. I just pray you can track him down. Although I detest his memory I have Walter to thank for being the catalyst that got me out of that scene." She suddenly got up and went inside, appearing again with a bottle of wine and two glasses. "Will you join me?"

Andrew twisted the top off the bottle and poured. They touched their glasses and silently toasted one another.

He was gazing aimlessly as he followed the endless ribbon of dirt road stretching out into the distance. He finally became aware of a vehicle pulled up in the middle of the road some distance ahead. As he slowed and drew closer he could make out the form of Collins leaning over the bonnet aiming a rifle at something in the surrounding open space. He heard the distinct crack of the rifle and watched as Collins chambered another round and leaned forward again to re-sight. Andrew slowed to drive around the vehicle and realised he would have to pass in front of the shooter as his path was obstructed on the near side by a large washout. Collins did not move his position, or acknowledge the vehicle about to overtake him. Andrew was shaken by the blatant intimidation, or was it something worse about to happen? Just as the front of his vehicle drew level another shot was unleashed. His reaction was to jam on the brakes in fright and look out at the leering antagonist who was casually ejecting the spent shell and chambering another. The grin broke into a laugh of pure contempt.

"Just getting rid of a dingo Hanna. We don't tolerate vermin of any sort on Venus Downs."

"Well you're obviously not much of a shot Collins. You missed the dingo with the first and no dog's going to hang around while you reload. You're shooting skills match your attitude, very poor."

Andrew realised instantly the taunt had hit home with electrifying effect as Collins raised the rifle and pointed it directly at him. The shot was deafening as he felt the pressure wave of the bullet pass a fraction in front of his face. Both windows were down, otherwise he would have been covered in shattered glass. He remained stock still, too shocked to move. The man was bloody mad. Collins lowered the rifle and walked around to face him.

"I'll bet that scared the crap out of you. You start sticking your nose into where it shouldn't be and the next shot won't miss. Anything can happen on a lonely road like this Hanna.

People disappear in the outback and no one asks too many questions."

Andrew slowly put the Toyota into gear and started to move. He was anticipating another shot as he gathered speed. He looked back in the mirror. Collins was standing in the middle of the road, the rifle dangling from one hand. The encounter had the desired effect. What the hell was he doing thinking of staying on in Wyndham? What was he thinking of? Let Chloe sort out her own bloody problems. He owned nothing, nor had any commitments to tie him to the town. He had been threatened and it was obvious his life was in danger. Collins was not making an idle threat and he knew it was no use reporting it to the police. Something told him Collins knew he was immune. The whole core of the town was corrupt, but he could not prove it and had no intention of sticking his neck out. He started to calm down and think rationally as the distance rolled by. He realised he was in love with the woman, but how long would it take her to realise it? Andrew pulled up outside Ike's office block and waited for a minute or two to collect his thoughts. He was surprised to look up and see Ike standing in the doorway looking out at him.

"Hi Ike, I'm looking for some office space." Andrew got out and swung the door closed.

"I can help you there. You've been out to see Chloe Boyce have you?"

"Yes, I went out to tell her I was leaving town and she'd have to find someone else to represent her."

"So what changed your mind, or have you fallen in love with her? She's one hell of a looker. Any number of young bucks would love to get into her pants. That light coating of chocolate colour would bring anyone on. I could die just licking her all over. She even gets me horny at my age every time I lay eyes on her."

Andrew ignored the remarks without expression. "Strictly business Ike. She wants me to look after her legal matters."

Shulman showed Andrew into his office. "Take a seat lad and let's talk about what you can do for me and how I can assist you."

"I want office space Ike if I'm to stay in town."

"You already have my retainer so you have an income and I can easily set you up with an office. You'll have to answer your own phone though. My largesse doesn't extend to paying for staff."

"Thanks Ike. Now let's get down to business. What do you really want. You didn't rush out of your office to say hello. That's no the way you operate, so what are you after?"

Ike settled back in his chair and studied the lawyer. Hanna was smart and dangerous, but did he realise how dangerous he was? "You know very well what I'm aiming at. You know what's going on so don't look dumb with me."

"I haven't a clue what you're referring to Ike."

"You wrote and witnessed Bill Hargraves' Will, a Power of Attorney and an affidavit, that's what I'm referring to."

"True, I did write a Will and Power of Attorney, but I don't recall preparing an affidavit and Ike, I've got no doubt you've already acquainted yourself with the contents of the Will. However, I can assure you there was no codicil naming you as a beneficiary."

Ike ignored the flippancy. "Bill Murton swears it was a affidavit he saw."

"If I had prepared one I would have given Hargraves a copy and it obviously hasn't turned up otherwise you wouldn't be asking me about it. And if I had a copy it would have gone up in smoke with my entire files. Anyhow what's the importance of an affidavit? What's it to do with you?"

Ike dismissed the question with a wave of his hands. Maybe Hanna was telling him the truth. "Tell me about Chloe Boyce. I would be interested in buying her out if the price was right."

"She hasn't mentioned selling to me, but she has asked me to look into her books and I'm going to go see Fred Carter later today."

"I thought you said you were handling her legal problems? What's this about getting involved in her finances?"

"She wants me to look at everything. I need the work Ike, if I'm to stay in this town."

Shulman nodded slowly. "Yes, I suppose you do. I've heard she maybe about to experience some problems. She inherited a great deal of property, but she's got no experience of how to run Venus Downs, let alone her other holdings."

"She has high praise for Jim Collins and is really thankful for you recommending him. He's apparently doing a first-class job. If Collins is that good I would imagine the property would be making real money what with current beef prices being high."

"I'm pleased to hear that Jim is working out well," Ike replied with obvious satisfaction. "I recommended him. However, I know she's into the bank for a heap and you know those guys are not sympathetic to interest payments not being met or the fact a woman is attempting to run such a large operation. She's part abo to boot and the abo's are hopeless at management, or with money. As soon as they get an income the whole bloody mob lands on them and starts to bleed them dry. You only have to look at the stations where the blacks have been given ownership and control. They've all gone bust and rely on the government tit to keep them alive simply because no government wants to admit its patronising policies are a failure. Give them a hand-up, not a hand-out is the only way to deal with the problem. Make the buggers work for a living and cut the booze supply off instead of handing sit-down money to them every week."

"You're not being too judgemental are you Ike? Chloe Boyce is not in that league and never has been. But touching on morality, you own the Argent hotel down the road, or that's what I've been told. Cut the snake-pit's grog supply off and your interests would suffer, wouldn't they?"

"Touché Andrew," Ike replied with a smile. "I can see you're not entirely ignorant of my business interests."

"Ike, people in small towns know or guess they know everyone else's business. You have a certain notoriety in this town so people are naturally interested in what pies you have your fingers in. It's only natural just as you want to know their business which may be to your advantage."

Shulman ignored the riposte. "Tell me, do you have a feeling Chloe might be interested in selling her holdings and cashing in? I'm particularly interested in Venus Downs."

"The only comment she's made to me is that she loves the place. It's her home and she's glad to be back. Why don't you ask her yourself?"

"I did when she found out what she'd inherited, but she said she wasn't interested. It had too many memories for her and she went on about something to do with her grandfather and how attached she was to him. I couldn't fathom what she was on about really. Johnny Quartpot was just an old black fellow who claimed he was born on the property and it rightfully belonged to him and his tribe. They're full of it, those old bludgers. They just sit under a tree all day yabbering away to themselves. Need a good kick up the arse really. As it turns out he wasn't her grandfather anyway and she knows that, so I can't see what the attachment was."

"We all think differently Ike and everyone has different values, beliefs and attachments. Venus Downs and her grandfather are her particular obsessions so it would seem."

Andrew watched as Shulman stroked his chin lost in thought. "I need that property and I'm going to have it. I want your help to get it."

"I don't see how I can help if she doesn't want to sell Ike. I realise you have retained me, but I've also agreed to act for Chloe. As long as everything's above board and transparent and Chloe is aware and happy with the arrangement I'm quite happy to approach her on your behalf. Why don't you get someone to prepare an independent valuation and then I can approach her."

"I'm not going to pay what some bloody valuer says it's worth. It would be multiples of what I'm prepared to pay. Those guys work on a commission and the higher the valuation the more they earn. Bunch of fucking blood-suckers," Shulman exploded. "I want it at my valuation and I'm going to get it."

"You may have to wait a long time Ike. You're no spring chicken. She's very young and unless she meets with a nasty accident or illness, I can see her outlasting you." Andrew trailed off and bit his tongue at his naivety. The man was rich, powerful and vain and he had just impugned his vanity.

Shulman swung on him with a look that penetrated deep into his mind. The man was ruthless, but he was witnessing to just what depths that trait extended as Shulman leaned forward and crashed a fist onto his desk.

"Listen Hanna. I pay you for your advice, not for your smart-arsed observations. And as for Boyce and her properties, I will get them at my price. Boyce is not going to have any say or control over the transaction." He trailed off as he realised he had gone too far. Andrew had touched a nerve and he had replied in a moment of anger and frustration he now regretted. He was a person who always went out on a concealed hand. No black-jack for him, flipping cards until he won or went bust, he always laid down a straight flush. Winner take all.

"I can see you have a move up your sleeve she's not aware of?"

"Henry Boyce overextended himself which is not a smart move when it comes to grazing properties subject to the vagaries of weather, cattle prices, staff and a dozen other problems. Chloe Boyce hasn't a clue how to manage such an undertaking. She'll go broke."

"Then why don't you wait until she goes broke and pick it up at the auction? On the other hand if Collins is such a brilliant manager there's no chance of it going pear- shaped, or is there a game plan I can only guess at?"

Andrew had already established why Shulman wanted Venus Downs, but was not going to give the man any inkling he knew.

Shulman did not answer the question, but eyed the lawyer with suspicion. "I think it's an excellent property and I want to own it, in fact I want them all. I made the mistake of not buying Henry Boyce out when I had the opportunity, but it didn't suit me at the time."

"But it does now? Would you like me to approach Chloe on your behalf? I don't think for a moment she'll sell, but at least I can get a reaction. It would probably be better coming from me seeing she's asked me to advise her on legal matters and a sale of the property would come within that ambit. I would be happy to do so if you like?"

Shulman contemplated the offer for a few seconds before slowly shaking his head. "No, I've already said I want to buy the property at my price, not at the price some outsider will value it at. Beef prices are heading north and the seasons are good. I'll just have to wait, but I'm not going to wait too much longer."

Andrew was about to say something, but checked himself. Was Ike testing his loyalty in expectation of a protest at his intended treatment of Chloe, or was it a heat of the moment outburst? "I'd better have a look at the office you've offered me and get on with some work."

Ike rummaged in a drawer and tossed a couple of keys on the desk. "Take any one that appeals and move the furniture to suit yourself. There should be enough in both offices to make up one suitable for your needs."

Andrew walked down the street and climbed the ancient wooden staircase. He tried the handle of the first door he came to. It was not locked. The large office was well set up with a desk, a couple of chairs and filing cabinets. He would have to be his own secretary as there was no reception room. He looked into a small room to one side that had no entrance from the corridor. It contained a sink and an ancient fridge. All he needed was a sofa bed and it would be adequate. The main office looked out over the street and directly at the bank opposite. He flopped into one of the chairs and put his feet up on the window sill to contemplate his position. He had a glaring conflict of interest. He could either represent Shulman or he could deny his professional integrity and work for them both. Maybe Shulman had just put him through a little test and the real position was that Ike and Chloe were in fact accomplices. He tried to put the thought out of his mind, but it kept reoccurring. He felt trapped at his predicament. He needed the money and Shulman had locked him in. The overriding temptation was to simply walk out, get in his vehicle and drive out of town. He had no clothes other than what he was standing in as everything else had been lost in the fire. He was deep in thought when he noticed Ike cross the road and walk into the bank. Probably had enough money to buy the bank he chuckled to himself as he swung his feet down and stood up. His next stop would have to be for new clothes, but he doubted the local emporium would have anything to match a professional look. He would just have to settle for jeans and double-pocketed shirts. He walked out and was closing the door when he noticed someone approaching from the wash-rooms at the end of the corridor.

"Hi there, you must be Andrew Hanna, I'm Fred Carter. Looks like we're going to be neighbours. Too bad about the fire."

Andrew shook the extended hand of the genial-faced balding accountant. "Yes that's correct. I've got to get a few things to get going again. I don't even have a pad or a pencil to my name at the moment, but I would like to come and see you about Chloe Boyce's affairs. She has asked me to look into them for her."

Carter's demeanour changed. "She hasn't spoken to me about this. I wonder if she's told Ike?"

"What's it got to do with Ike?"

The sharp retort caught the accountant off guard as he stumbled for an answer. "Oh, nothing really. It's just that Henry Boyce and Ike were very close business associates, so naturally I thought Chloe would have informed Ike of any plans she had regarding yourself. What is it you want to go over with me?"

"I just want to satisfy myself. I've no doubt everything your end is fine, but she wants some reassurance as to her legal liabilities so to speak."

"I don't understand. I did the books for Henry for a number of years before his death and Chloe has continued the arrangement. She has never raised any concerns with me. I find this rather irregular with no notification from Chloe and at such short notice."

Andrew could see the geniality was only a front. The man had adopted a worried look. Someone was stepping onto his turf and he did not appreciate it. Was it that, or was he hiding something? He smiled and patted Carter on the arm. "By all means check with Chloe. In the meantime I've got to get some clothes to make myself look presentable, so why don't we make it in the morning?"

"I, I'm rather busy in the morning," the accountant stammered. "But if you just want a general outline I can give you that. However, I'll need more time if you want to discuss the accounts in detail."

"It's only a first pass meeting Fred. I don't want to go into forensic detail at this stage as I'm going to be very busy over the next few days. All I really want now is the financial position of the various properties she owns, the liabilities such as any bank overdrafts or mortgages, the number of cattle she's turning off and selling and the income and outgoings. Back of the envelope profit and loss data is all I need. I'm not an accountant, I'm a lawyer. I'll leave the counting of the beans up to you. I only want to be able to report to my client that I'm happy with what I've seen."

The look of relief was almost audible. Carter would be hopeless at pokcr. The facial expression immediately gave him away. "I'll look forward to seeing you in the morning then. Anytime will be convenient." Carter beamed with sickly conviction as he scuttled past towards his office.

Andrew nodded and made to descend the stairway, but halted when he judged Carter was out of sight. He quietly followed him down the long corridor and around into another short corridor. He could see a door ajar and could hear

Carter talking on the phone. He stepped closer and looked through the open doorway, quickly pulling back as he was in plain view of the accountant leaning down at his desk. He would have immediately seen Andrew if he had been looking at the doorway.

"Did you know about this Ike?" It was not a demand, but the pleadings of a very worried man. "What the hell am I to do? I can give him some notes and blind him with bullshit, but what if he wants to delve deeper? He doesn't look like any dumb-bunny wanting to run up some fees to push out an invoice. He gives me the impression he wants to look deeper. How much does he know?" Carter went silent as he listened to the reply, but his right hand clutching the side of his head as he leaned into the phone was all the observation needed as Andrew turned silently to retrace his steps.

"I'm coming down now Ike. We need to be singing from the same hymn sheet if this guy gets around to comparing notes. This has really got me worried."

Andrew was at the top of the landing when he heard Carter's door slam and the fast approaching footsteps. He went down the steps two at a time and out onto the street. Who in this bloody town didn't Ike Shulman control he pondered to himself? He determined if Chloe was party to what was going on he would just leave town. They could all swim in their rotten little cesspit.

"Hey there Mr Hanna. How are they hanging?"

Andrew looked up to see Mark Tippet walking towards him. "Fine thanks Mark." He made to walk past, but Tippet stepped in front of him.

"I want to have a word with you Mr Hanna. I might have something of interest for you."

"And what might that be Mark?"

"When you came out the other day you asked me if I'd seen Smith remove anything from Bill Hargraves' truck. I said I hadn't but that wasn't the truth. What's it worth if I tell you what I saw?"

"That's very interesting Mark, but I think I can guess. You saw Smith remove a folder from Bill Hargraves' bag didn't you?"

Tippet looked surprised. "Yep, that's correct. He thought I couldn't see him, but I saw everything. He shoved the contents of the folder down his shirt front and tossed the bag back into the wagon."

"But he did see you looking?"

"He must have. He called me in to make a statement. I tried to give the true version of what happened which would've put me in the clear, but he'd already prepared his version which he forced me to sign."

"And what did that say?"

"It said I admitted to causing the accident and was responsible for Bill's death."

"And you refused to sign it?"

"I did, but he took me out to the cells and hammered shit out of me." Tippet took off his sunglasses to reveal two swollen eyes. "My ribs are worse. I've been spitting blood for a couple of days."

"So you signed?"

"No choice. I know when I'm fucked. I thought we had a deal, but the bastard reneged."

"So it was you who lit the fire. And if you opened your mouth the negligent driving charge causing death with five years jail attached, would suddenly appear?"

Tippet looked at him in shock. "You've got it in one Mr Hanna, but I'll never admit I told you that. Either way I'd be facing jail. Smith can't lose."

"Wasn't anybody else at the station when he beat you up?"

Tippet chuckled while holding his hand to his chest to stifle the pain. "Smith is king. None of those lilly-livered cunts would ever be game to say a word. Now what's it worth to get what you're looking for. I know it's Hargraves' Will and I know you lost your copy in the fire."

"How do you know Smith has Hargraves' copy?"

"Jerry Briggs, the probationary constable in the office is my cousin. He heard Smith yelling at me while I was making the statement and saw me come back from the cell after Smith did me over. He doesn't like the bastard either, but he needs the job."

"Does Smith know you're related?"

Tippet pulled a face. "Do you think Jerry would have a job if Smith knew? Anyway Jerry realised that whatever was worrying Smith must be contained in the docs he'd seen him shove into his desk drawer. Unbeknown to Smith, Jerry has had a key to the drawer for ages. Smith made the mistake of taping it under the lamp on his desk. Brilliant. No wonder the shit has never risen above sergeant. Anyway, while Smith was out of the office for a couple of hours on patrol Jerry read the file. It was Hargraves' bloody Will. That's why you're interested in what I'm telling you, isn't it?"

Andrew ignored the question by pulling an indifferent expression. "Did your cousin copy it?"

"No, he didn't want to be seen using the copier and Smith could have come back at anytime. He reckons he was shitting himself with fright by the time he finished."

"So your cousin told you and by now it's all around the town."

"Not on your Nelly. Dumb as he is, we both know it would only take Smith a couple of seconds to work out what had happened and who was the source of the leak. Jerry would be shipped off to a godforsaken one-man station in the boondocks. We'd both be dead meat if Jerry ever said anything."

"So why are you telling me this. I wrote Bill Hargraves' Will. I'm perfectly aware of what it contains."

Tippet leered at Andrew. "I may look like a cabbage Mr Hanna, but I'm not green. Why would you give a damn about what Smith took from Hargraves when you would have kept a copy yourself? I figured that's why Smith got me to burn down your office so your records would be destroyed."

"And now you want to shake me down?"

"It's only business Mr Hanna. I've got something you want, but my real motive it to stick it to Smith. Let me lay it out for you. Metcalf was going to fire me for pranging his truck although it clearly wasn't my fault. Smith got him to back-off, so I kept my job, but for how long I don't know. In return Smith wouldn't book his trucks for overloading or speeding. We knew Smith had to be on the take from Metcalf, and if he got a little behind in his payments Smith would touch him up with a reminder by pulling up his trucks. I'm only a dumb-arse truck driver and it took me a while to work out what the connection was between Smith letting me off the hook and then getting me to light the fire. Smith knew if he had one copy of the Will you must have another in your files, but those files don't exist any longer. You, Mr Hanna don't have a copy, so Hargraves dies intestate and you miss out on fat fees for administering his estate, because the government gets the lot. At least that's how Jerry explained it to me. Now, let's get down to business. How much is it worth to get you a copy of what Smith has?"

Andrew protested. "I can't possibly get mixed up in something like that. I cannot condone what you're proposing."

"Come off it Hanna," Tippet snapped, any signs of politeness gone. "It's common knowledge you've got the hots for a certain station owner mixed up in this. When this comes out she'll be looking out from behind bars with Smith and a few others."

Andrew eyed his antagonist with some admiration. He was certainly brighter than he first appeared. "Mixed up in what? I've no idea what you're talking about."

"It doesn't make sense that Hargraves would leave all his money and assets to the pommie owners of Ascot Downs. I've moved a heap of cattle off Henry Boyce's property over the years, and the common knowledge is a large number of those cleanskin cattle came from Ascot, were branded by Boyce and sold through Shulman as the agent. Smith must have known about it and was in for his cut at some stage. Jerry is positive he's up to his neck in it along with Shulman and now Chloe Boyce, no doubt. Jerry said there's a clause making some reference to restitution. He believes Hargraves wanted to give a hint of what was going on so it could be shut down on his death. That's the case isn't it?"

"That's not proof of a crime, that's just supposition."

"You're wrong Mr Hanna. There's enough smoke to suggest a fire somewhere and I believe I can start that fire. Jerry says he can write an anonymous letter which would make Smith's superiors in Perth sit up and take notice."

"There's absolutely no proof Chloe Boyce is mixed up in anything and without strong proof to the contrary, it really won't stand up."

"I wouldn't put money on that. If she's employed that thug Collins, she's in it up to her pretty neck."

"What about Collins? What do you know about him?"

Tippet laughed. "There's plenty to tell about him. His name's not Collins, it's Dave Bonham. I served time with him. I was in for kicking the shit out of a young copper trying to arrest me and he was doing time for rape amongst other things. He's an Afghan veteran. He served in the army as a chopper pilot. No one messed with him and you certainly had to look after your arsehole in the showers when he was around. Is he shagging Boyce, because if he isn't she'd better watch out? She's liable to end up on the receiving end of something throbbing if he gets horny. I know the cops are looking for him in regard to another rape. Smith must know who and where he is and is protecting him for some reason. Truth be known, Bonham has done some of his dirty work for him, or is about to do something."

Andrew tried to hide his shock. "That's all very interesting, but rather irrelevant. Anyway, what precisely do you want? If it's money, you can forget about it because I don't have any."

"No, you wouldn't be able to pay what I'm after. I've always wanted to start my own trucking company and I think Shulman will finance me into a new rig and Smith will never bother me again. I'm sure Metcalf can be persuaded to give me a couple of his good accounts with what I know. Bribing a cop is a criminal offence according to Jerry."

Andrew whistled softly. "You're playing with fire Mark. Do you really think Shulman or Smith are going to let you live the moment you make the demand?"

"That's where your end of it comes into play Mr Hanna. Jerry said I should get you to prepare a statement regarding what I saw Smith doing at the Hargraves scene, and what Smith told me to do under threat regarding your fire. Then there's Bonham which Smith is going to find hard to explain. His career would be finished. I can also tie Shulman into the cattle theft from Ascot. It should cause quite a stir when

I flash it in front of Shulman and Smith and tell them you have a copy. They'll know who holds the whip-hand then. That protects both of us doesn't it? I've got to hand it to Jerry, he's a smart thinker. I can't wait to stick it right up Smith's keester."

Andrew trawled through the implications for a few moments stroking his chin and looking down at the pavement. "Okay, I'll give it some thought, but I will need the original and not a photocopy."

"Jeez, I can't ask Jerry to do that. It would only take Smith two seconds to point the finger at him. It will have to be a copy."

"Okay, but when can you get it for me?"

"Give me a couple of days." Tippet's face suddenly turned from delight to shock as he looked past Andrew. "Oh shit. Someone's seen us talking and been on the phone." He suddenly turned and slowly walked off. No use hurrying as he knew he had been spotted.

Andrew turned pretending to be about to cross the road when the Toyota pulled up beside him. Smith was looking straight ahead at the departing form and did not avert his gaze. "You're keeping bad company there Hanna. That boy is bad news. I don't suppose you'll tell me what you two were discussing?"

"Nothing that would interest you sergeant. Just passing the time of day."

"Is that so? It looked to me as though he'd been caught playing with himself behind the garden shed, the way he took off. He sure looked guilty when he saw me coming. He seemed to be doing all the talking."

"That's my profession sergeant, listening, counselling and advising people."

"That's okay, but don't get caught jerking off with him otherwise it may become my business." The policeman slowly moved off without looking at Andrew.

ndrew tapped on the door and began to open it. It was obvious Carter had been anticipating the visit because he was halfway across his office when Andrew entered.

"Hi Andrew, take a seat. Can I get you a coffee or tea?" Carter swept his hand towards a small table on which an urn was situated along with cups and a plate of biscuits.

"I'm fine thanks Fred. I'd like to get down to business if we could."

Carter sat himself down behind his desk which was clear of everything except a writing pad, phone and computer screen. Andrew got the distinct impression the meeting was being staged. He was not going to be shown anything in hard copy, but rather explained with a pen being used as a pointer on the screen.

"Where would you like to start?"

"Give me a general rundown on the financial position of Chloe's total holdings."

Carter made a pyramid of his fingers and looked into the air. "She owns Venus Downs and the adjoining Remus Park, as well as a couple of larger properties to the south in the Pilbara. They are Baracool and Ironstone Park. In my opinion they're not worth a cracker and I've yet to fathom why Henry Boyce bought them."

"Are they viable?"

"Yes, but they aren't being managed well in my opinion. They could be doing a lot better. I've advised her to get rid of them, but she won't hear of it."

"What about Remus?"

"It does very well for its size, but it's simply not big enough. You can't make real money running cattle on a few hundred square miles in this country. It should be sold or amalgamated with an adjoining property."

"Where is it situated?"

"It practically adjoins Venus Downs. There is a similar sized holding that separates them."

"What's the name of that property, and who owns it? Surely, it must have occurred to Henry Boyce to acquire it?"

"It's Romulus Park, and the person who owns is not interested in selling although it's in the same financial situation as Remus, too small to be really viable. Combining the three properties would make an enormous cattle run and the economies of scale could be realised. Romulus and Remus were originally one before being split and sold off separately. Henry bought Remus."

"So who owns Romulus?"

"It's owned by Issac Investments."

"And I can safely assume that company is controlled by Ike Shulman?"

"That's correct."

"Have you suggested to Chloe she should sell Remus to Shulman?"

"I have, but she won't sell at the price Ike is offering. It is substantially below what Henry paid for it."

"And Ike won't sell Romulus. Doesn't sound as though either of them is thinking straight."

"Ike's not in any hurry or under any pressure, unlike Chloe who may be forced to make a decision soon. Let's face it

Andrew, running a cattle property is not her business. She's dreaming. I've advised her to sell up and enjoy a less stressful existence."

"She doesn't accept your advice, does she?"

Carter sighed and shook his head. "I've tried to tell her she should re-arrange her finances by selling off some of her holdings. But she's very stubborn and won't hear of it."

"Is Venus Downs a profitable operation?"

"Yes, but nothing like it was when Henry was in control."

"How many head of cattle is it running off every year?"

"The current season will see around five thousand go through the saleyards."

"And in Henry's day?"

Carter fidgeted and looked awkward. "I really can't tell you that. I would have to go back through the records."

"You've got a computer in front of you Fred. You've obviously got the accounts for the last year before Henry died, so stop beating about the bush and pull them up please. I want to know."

Carter looked offended at the sudden demand and change of tone. He adjusted his glasses and tapped the keypad to bring up and scroll through the accounts. Andrew had no doubt Carter could quote the numbers without referring to his computer records. He was an old-school accountant who memorised a client's exact position because he manually recorded everything on paper, prepared the profit and loss account and balance sheet and filed the tax returns. Now he was giving the impression he relied on a computer. There was silence as he scrolled through the records.

"Oh yes here it is. It's just over ten thousand head."

"That's a hell of a difference. Why the sudden drop? Give me the three years previous years."

"I can see you have no understanding of the cattle industry. Droughts, poor cattle prices, low export prices, are all factors that directly affect the industry. You just can't pick a high figure in one year and maintain that as the average. I would stick to being a lawyer if I were you."

"Well, you're not me and don't insult me with your patronising advice." Andrew got up and walked around to stand behind Carter as he nervously tapped the keys. The man was rattled as he pointed at the figures. "The previous year was fifteen thousand." There was silence as he pulled up the previous two years to that. "Fifteen thousand in each of those as well."

"Would you print off the accounts for those four years please?"

"I can't do that today. My printer has been out of action for a week. I'm waiting for a replacement."

Andrew nodded. He had been expecting such an excuse. He walked around to his chair and sat down again. "What is the stocking rate of Venus Downs?"

"I, I don't have that at hand. It would be better if you asked Chloe or her manager. I believe the number can vary according to......"

"Seasons, cattle prices and exports, yeah, yeah I know that Fred, but you prepare the accounts and I've no doubt you can give me an average. Just don't hand me any bunkum. Even to me it's obvious Venus Downs could not be running off that many head, even in the best of seasons. So where have these cattle come from?"

Carter went red in the face. "You've got a bloody neck Hanna, coming in here and throwing your weight around."

"I'm acting for my client and that's exactly what you should be doing. You had ample warning of what I wanted and yet you've treated me as ignorant. You could have just slapped financial returns for the last five years down in front of me. I could have taken them away and studied them, but no, you've hidden behind that computer screen. However, don't bother yourself any more today, but I want copies of the full accounts for the past five years and don't give me any bullshit about printer problems."

Carter sprang up and leaned forward with his clenched fists resting on the desktop. "I reject your accusations Hanna." The spittle sprayed from his mouth. He was too furious to express himself coherently.

Andrew made no reply as he nodded and walked out. Carter had to be aware of what had been going on. He wondered what Carter's cut was although it could not be much going by the appearance of both the office and the man. Maybe he just hid it in offshore accounts or under his mattress.

Carter slumped into his chair lost in thought. He finally picked up the phone. "Ike, I've just had Hanna in here demanding Boyce's accounts for the past five years. I'm sure he knows what's going on."

"Calm down Fred. You didn't give him the accounts did you?"

"No, but he wants them just as soon as I get a new printer."

"Anything can happen in that time. Just cool it and let me handle everything. His client will have more on her mind than accounts by then."

"What do you mean by that?" Carter could not keep the worried tone under control. He could feel the uncoordinated beat of his heart. He was feeling faint.

"You're not going to resort to violence are you? I've a heart condition as you know. I just can't handle pressure of any kind."

"Oh shut up princess. Everything will be okay, I guarantee it. Look, I'm too busy to talk to you at the moment."

Carter replaced the receiver and slumped back into his chair. He could feel the walls closing in around him. He reached in the drawer for a pill container and shook two valium into his hand and swallowed them without thinking. He tried to create the saliva to wash them down, but they stuck in his throat as he rushed coughing to the sink to pour himself a glass of water.

Ike Shulman studied the rangy youth sitting opposite him. He was as tough as ironbark, the biceps bulging from under the cutaway sleeves of his filthy shirt. The tattered cap was pushed back on his head to expose a lock of dark hair which almost matched the colour of his soft brown eyes which were full of dancing life. The infectious smile was gone, to be replaced by a determined satisfied look. He knew he had the advantage of the person sitting opposite.

"So what can I do you for you Mark Tippet? I don't like people just barging into my office without an appointment."

"I think you can do a lot for me Ike, in fact I know you can."

Ike did not flinch although he was uneasy. Tippet's confidence signalled trouble. He knew who he was by reputation and would never normally have given him the time of day. He could sense there was a problem about to loom large.

"Well, let's hear it."

"I know what you and Smith and Boyce are up to."

Ike nodded and smiled. "And what might that be?"

"Don't play dumb with me Ike. It's going to cost you a packet for me to shut up."

"Is it something criminal you're referring to?"

Tippet let out a large guffaw. "Anything to do with you is criminal, the whole town knows that."

Shulman studied him for a few seconds and then smiled thinly. "Get the hell out of here Tippet. If you think I'm mixed up in some sort of crime you should report it to the police." He picked up the phone and thrust it towards him. "Here, I'll dial the number and you can speak to Sergeant Smith directly. He looks after the crime and criminals in this town. In fact you know the sergeant very well, almost on first name terms with him you've been in his cells so many times."

He waited for the bluff to work. Tippet was going to call it or retreat. He could see fractional hesitation in his manner, but the determination returned as he took the offered hand-piece and tossed it back across Ike's desk.

"Don't try that on me Ike. It ain't going to work. I've got you and your friend cold and it's going to cost you. Smith got me to toss the can of gas into the lawyer's office and I now know the reason why."

Ike slowly leaned back. Here was a menace that had to be handled like one would pick up tiger snake; with extreme care.

"And why was that?"

"Bill Hargraves had made a Will. Smith found a copy at the crash site and Hanna had the other in his office, hence the need to burn it down. Smith gave me the bullshit story that by doing so he would put the pressure on Wally Metcalf for me to keep my job. Well fuck my job driving for him for shit wages. I'm going to get my own truck and you're going to help me."

Ike remained motionless. How did this dead-beat know about the contents of the Will? It had to be a bluff because there would be no way he would have seen a copy. He doubted Tippet could even read as he knew his whole family and extended family were illiterate. If that was the case, who had put him up to this? It was time to listen to the demands and terms.

"Tell me what you want then."

Tippet grinned in satisfaction. "That's more like it Ike," he said as he put one Blundstone boot up on his knee and began to roll a cigarette. The toe of the boot had disappeared to reveal the steel cap. The elastic siding of the boot had long since perished and the sole was worn to one side. The leather that remained was soaked with oil and grime.

Ike did not show any emotion as Tippet blew a cloud of smoke as he began to relate his terms. Finally, he held out his hands in a wide gesture. "That's about it Ike. I reckon that's fair deal to keep you lot out of the slammer. Smith wouldn't survive in there ten minutes, you may last a little longer and Chloe Boyce's pussy would be sucked dry by every dyke in the place."

"Have you spoken to anyone else about this?"

"No, but someone else knows what I know and if anything should happen to me, you'll find yourselves up shit creek."

Ike was fascinated as to who the informant was. He had been given a clue, but who did Tippet know who had any brains, or could read or comprehend a lengthy document. Was Hanna behind this? How else would Tippet know about the contents of the Will?

"This will need a little thought Mark. I just can't give you an answer on the spot as I will have to look at how I'm going to finance this. You're talking about a great deal of money. I'll need some guarantees you'll keep your word, so naturally I'll hold the mortgages over your truck and plant. One word of this gets out and the deal's off."

Tippet got up and thrust out his paw-like hand, the broken finger nails encrusted and underlain with grease and filth. Ike hesitated for a second, but then offered his spotless manicured hand which was crushed, not with malice, but with excitement. Tippet had no idea of the absolute power, but limited strength of the hand he was shaking.

"Give me two days Mark. I should be able to set it all up for you by then."

"I'm glad we were able to reach agreement Ike. One final thing, you make sure Smith keeps off my back in future. That bastard is always giving me a rough time for no reason."

Ike nodded as Tippet turned and strode out of the office. Did Tippet have an accomplice, or was it a bluff? He determined it was a bluff as he felt certain Tippet did not know anyone with the mental capacity to have read or understand a Will, or had such a contact. It had to be Hanna. Smith had already told him he'd seen Tippet talking to him in the street. He picked up his phone and sat back in anticipation of the explosion of incandescent rage when he explained the meeting and the terms demanded and agreed to, but Smith had remained silent.

"You don't appear too upset sergeant. How are you going to deal with it?"

"Just a minute Ike while I close the bloody door." By the time he had sat down and picked up the receiver he had thought it through. "This is not only my problem Ike. I can assure you if the balloon goes up, you won't escape." The menace is his voice was palpable. "I'll deal with it, but here's what I want you to do."

Tippet entered the bar and looked around. He caught the eye of Mouse and his mate Retread. Mouse was okay, but so-named because he had a face like Mickey Mouse with big ears and a black plum for a nose, and Retread, a name that had stuck from when he started fitting tires at the local servo. Tippet had never liked Retread, he didn't trust him and the feeling was mutual. Retread could not overcome the look of smouldering hate towards the person who had given him a hiding on a number of occasions. Mouse was simple, always good for a laugh and knew where to lay his hands on good weed. Tippet nodded to Retread who immediately excused himself and moved down the bar.

"Retread doesn't like you mate. Here, let me buy you a beer."

Tippet ignored the disparaging remark. He was amused Mouse had offered to buy him a drink. It was usually the other way around. He was immediately on his guard.

Mouse pulled out a packet and rolled himself a toke. He pushed the packet across before lighting up and blowing out a cloud of smoke. "Real good shit. I've got more in my wagon if you want it."

"Hey, this is better than the crap you generally try and sell me." Tippet felt the narcotic creep into his brain. The barmaid looked up and raised her eyebrows, but said nothing. No one else in the crowded bar took any notice. "I'll take a hundred bucks worth."

Mouse eyed him. "You come into money or something. Where'd you get a hundred bucks from?"

"I got paid today and in future I'll be able to afford your very finest."

"In that case let me buy you another beer. I'm always on the lookout for good cash-paying customers. You onto something good are you?"

Tippet nodded as he downed the beer and picked up another glass the barmaid had slid in front of him. "This time in a week or two all my troubles will be over. I'm going into the trucking business. Fuck Metcalf, I'm going into competition with him." Tippet began to lay out his plans.

Mouse gave a low whistle. "What'd you win lotto?" He was eager to know where Tippet's sudden wealth was coming from. Normally, he did not have the price of a tank of gas, let alone a powerful semi and trailers. Maybe it had something to do with the call from Ike: Fill him with beer, sell him your best shit and I'll square it with you, was the instruction.

Mouse continually pressed the package towards Tippet and bought him beer after beer. Tippet was at first suspicious, but the effects of the beer and marijuana quickly dulled his senses. He agreed to give Mouse a job in his new trucking company. Mouse was following Ike's instructions to the letter. After all, they were partners. Ike had financed the irrigation equipment for his hidden plantations and ensured Smith never had him in his sights. He was doing very well, but was at pains never to show his wealth other than a new Toyota cruiser he'd just bought. Ike always handled the finances with bank accounts in various names. Another year or two he could give it all away, get out of this mosquito invested hole and retire to the Gold Coast.

"C'mon mate. I've had enough. Let's go out and do the deal."

Tippet nodded and unsteadily got down from the bar stool. He could feel the effects of both the beer and narcotic as he followed Mouse out and into the parking lot behind the hotel. Mouse opened the door of his vehicle and reached in behind the seat. He passed over a stuffed brown paper bag as Tippet reached into his back pocket for his money.

Mouse counted the money and climbed into his vehicle. "Be seeing you Mark. I hope everything works out for you." He was glad to get away. He did not know what was going on, but whatever it was he didn't want to be around to see it happen. He had fulfilled Shulman's instructions.

Tippet staggered towards his battered ute parked at the back of the yard. He swung open the door and was about to get in when he sensed someone was standing behind him. He turned, recognised the person and attempted to swerve away from the danger, but he was off balance and too late. The flat of the shovel caught him on the side of the head and the curtain of oblivion overtook him. Half an hour later he started to come out of the haze. He was lying on the ground, but curled up in scrubby surrounds he did not recognise. He started to get up when he realised he was stark naked and Smith was standing a couple of metres away with a shotgun dangling from one hand.

"Whaat, what the hell are you on about? We had a deal you bastard." His anquished scream was lost in the empty landscape.

"That's where you're wrong you shithead. The agreement was you would keep your mouth shut, but I saw you with Hanna and you were doing all the talking. Did he offer to help you in some way?"

"No, he didn't and I didn't tell him anything."

"Bullshit. I think you spilled your guts. And now you've resorted to blackmail. That's a serious crime you could do a long stretch for normally, but I'm going to overlook charging you."

A flash of sickly relief crossed Tippet's face. "Christ sergeant, you didn't have to bring me out here to scare me. Where are my clothes? Are you some kind of pervert?"

Smith laughed. "You won't be needing your clothes. I thought I would do the wild pigs a favour. They'll be able to chew up your remains without getting fibres in their teeth."

Tippet began to vent himself when it dawned on him what was about to happen. He sank to his knees. "For fucks sake sergeant, please don't do it."

"How did you find out about Hargraves' Will and its contents? Who told you?"

Tippet gave a guttural moan as he considered whether to wait for the inevitable or make a run for it. He started to get to his feet. His befuddled mind was racing. "Hanna told me."

"You're lying and don't even think about making a bolt for it. You can't run far with a load of twelve-gauge shot up your arse. I'll ask you once again. Who's your informant?"

"Hanna, Hanna told me." Tippet cried as he stood rooted to the spot in fear with excrement running down his legs.

"Don't hand me that bullshit. Now try again one last time."

Tippet jumped back as the blast tore a hole in the barren earth separating them. It galvanised him as he gained his full height and clenched his fists in defiance. "Fuck you Smith. You're going to kill me so why should I tell you anything?"

"Your brain's screwed up Tippet. Too much booze and dope tonight." Smith raised the gun and pointed it directly at Tippet's head as his legs began to fold under him in realisation of the inevitable. His face blasted into a thousand pieces of bone, brain, blood and gore. There would be no identifying jaw and teeth to identify the remains. Smith stood over the twitching body, casually reloaded and emptied the charges into the torso. No need to bury it as the feral pigs would wait a few days for it to putrefy before devouring every last scrap, including the marrow-rich skeletal remains.

Smith broke the gun, pulling out the empty shell casings and putting them in his pocket. He slid the gun in behind the driver's seat and retrieved a can of petrol which he poured over Tippet's clothes and boots. He leaned up against the cab, lit a cigarette and watched the flames, and beyond it the corpse. The flames died away. He laughed as he saw the evidence of the last remains of Tippet's worldly possessions; the steel toe caps from his boots. He drove slowly back into town and pulled in at his darkened office. He sat in the dark for a while smoking. He felt absolutely no remorse at what he had just done. He had too much to lose. He reached across and picked up his phone. It was immediately answered. "It's done Ike. We won't have any more to worry about from that direction."

"But how the hell did he know?"

"He was smart enough. I think he put two and two together when he was talking to Hanna, first in Metcalf's yard and then yesterday when I saw them talking in the street. I've got no doubt Hanna was asking him whether he'd seen me take the documents from Hargraves' truck. However, I think it was a bluff he'd seen anything."

"I'm not so sure about that Wally. He was very sure of himself when he came to see me."

"Be as it may, we won't have to worry about him any more and it's immaterial if he did say something to Hanna. Tippet's dead and Hanna is intelligent enough to know his testimony is worthless, no matter how much Tippet told him. Anyway, I'm going to put my feet up and have a drink. Goodnight."

Smith sat in the darkness smoking. The scotch bottle was half empty. Suddenly he sat upright and retrieved the key from under the lamp and opened the drawer. He sighed with relief as he saw the folder was exactly where it should be with a piece of rock paperweight made to look as though it had been casually dropped onto one corner. He opened the folder and read the contents again under the light of the desk lamp. Fucking Hargraves, he cursed under his breath. Why did he have to go and find God and spill his guts and incriminate them all. Why could he not just die without visiting his sins on everyone else. Weak bastard. He replaced the folder, locked the drawer and went and lay down on his office couch for a few minutes. He felt tired and exhausted.

He was awake in a second when he heard the backdoor of the station being unlocked. Light was streaming in through a window. He sat up and looked at his watch. He had been asleep for hours. It was far too early for any of the staff to arrive as he sat motionless waiting for the intruder to enter. He heard the soft foot-treads and then watched fascinated as the door handle to his office began to slowly turn. A head appeared. It was looking directly at his desk and had not noticed Smith sitting in the shadows.

"What do you want Jerry? A bit early for work isn't it?"

Briggs spun around. He was startled but quickly regained his composure. "I've got some reports to complete so I thought I would come in early."

"What did you want in my office?" The question was blunt and accusatory.

"I saw your wagon outside chief so I knew you were here, but I didn't see any lights on when I came in. I was concerned and just wanted to make sure you were okay."

Smith looked at his deputy and sighed. "Okay Jerry. I'm okay. I had a late night and just fell asleep." He dismissed Briggs with a wave of his hand. The explanation was reasonable. He doubted Briggs would have the brains to be up to no good. He was honest and hardworking, but was never going to make it above the rank of constable. He was probationary at the moment and spent most of his day assisting the prosecutor in court. Drunks and traffic offences were about the sum total of his responsibilities. He pushed his hands through his hair and felt the growth on his chin.

"I'm going home for an hour or two to shave and shower and cook myself breakfast," he said as he walked past Briggs sitting at his desk. As he pushed open the flyscreen door to the veranda he turned as though lost in thought. He noticed Briggs glance up at him.

"You know Mark Tippet don't you?"

"Sure do sergeant. I don't know how many times I've read out the charge sheets in court. What's he done now?"

Smith ignored the question. "Did you know him in any other capacity? Was he a friend of yours?"

Smith did not catch the flash of shock. Briggs had caught the unintentional past tense in Smith's question. He shook his head. "No chief, our association was strictly prosecution."

Smith nodded and let the door go. Briggs waited for him to start his vehicle and drive off before getting up and retrieving keys to a locked room. He selected another key to open the gun cabinet. The rack that contained the shotgun was empty. He picked up the record book and noted Smith had signed it out early the previous evening. Strange that he signed it out so late. What did he need a gun for at night and particularly a shotgun which was only good for threatening an angry mob, and there had been no civil disturbances in town for as long as he could remember. There was no record of him signing it back in again so it must still be in his wagon, which was strictly against regulations. Briggs quickly went back to his desk and took out a camera with which he photographed Smith's entry showing the date and time on the bottom of the photo. It was for his own personal satisfaction as he knew he could never use it as evidence. The code of silence was strict and his fellow officers would quickly close ranks around Smith if he was ever accused of the minor misdemeanour of not checking the weapon back in the same day or at the very latest, the following morning. However, Briggs had no doubt if he checked the register later the gun would have been signed as being returned the same day it was checked out. He locked the cabinet and returned the keys. It did not require premonition to realise he would not be seeing Mark Tippet again. He regretted ever telling Mark about the contents of Hargraves' Will, and the inference of a crime. He had sworn him to secrecy, but the headstrong Mark had gone and said something to someone and the word had rebounded right back to Smith. He began to sweat with fear. Had Mark mentioned his name? If he had, he had no doubt he would be next in line for the shotgun. However, the more he thought about it, he realised Smith could not know he was the source of the leak, otherwise he would have already accosted him and his attitude towards him that morning had been his usual abrupt self. Smith had no friends and could never hide his emotions. If the person was a suspect, Smith made it very clear through his actions or tone of voice he was under suspicion, but nothing Smith said to him since coming in today suggested otherwise. He wondered how long before someone reported Mark as missing.

It was nearly a week later when he heard a commotion at the front desk to see Mark's mother shouting at the desk clerk. He pretended not to notice as he returned to his paperwork.

"Where's Smith. I want to talk to him now. That rotten bastard can't hide. I know he's in there." The agitated woman tried to push past the clerk. The tussle and the shrieking woman brought Smith out of his office. He slowly walked through to the front.

"What do you want? If you don't shut up I'll charge you and throw you in a cell."

"My son Mark has disappeared and you've murdered him you bastard," she screamed across at him. "I haven't seen him in a week, and he ain't been at work."

"Probably still lying under some bush sleeping it off. Either that or he's busy throwing a leg over some slag down on the river bank."

"No, he ain't doing neither. I've been checkin around and he was last seen at the pub."

"You mean Marge Tilley's, the Majestic?"

"Don't give me that shit. You know bloody well Marge wouldn't let him in the place. He was down at the snake-pit, the Argent."

"Well, I wouldn't know anything about that. I don't go near the place unless someone kills someone," Smith replied with a laugh. "Get them to check the shithouse, he's probably still in there."

The woman lowered her voice, but her intent was menacing. "You, Smith were at the Argent the night my son disappeared. Mark was in there with that weasely little bastard Mouse. You know, your partner in that marijuana plantation you think is a great big secret."

Smith's face went red as he tried to control his anger. "Your son may have been there, but I wasn't, so don't come in here with any accusations unless you have proof."

"I've got a witness alright. It turns out that someone who will remain anonymous was having a piss in the bushes behind the car park when he saw Mark and Mouse come out. Mouse sold him a bag of shit and then drove off. The witness then saw you come up from behind and lay Mark out flat with a spade. You then bundled him into a white Holden ute and took off. You own an old Holden ute don't you sergeant?"

"Listen Ma, if you've got a witness I suggest you tell me who it is because I'm not the person he saw."

"He's too scared to point the finger at you Smith. His life wouldn't be worth a dime and he knows it. You may not have been in uniform, but he recognised you by your gut and your waddling walk. You're the only one in town with a gut that large. It's because you sit on your arse all day instead of working. It's a wonder you can find your dick under all that overhang. You probably have a bit of string tied to it."

The insult stung. Smith leaned forward, but not too close that the woman could spit in his face as he knew would happen if he tempted her. "Well, in that case your accusations are worthless. If your witness won't come forward there's nothing more I can do. We will record your son's disappearance and hopefully he will turn up some time, as I've no doubt he will. I only hope he's taken off to another town as he really is a piece of garbage I'm tired of arresting."

He turned on his heel and walked away with the woman's screams of abuse in his ears. The worry was written on his face as he passed Briggs' desk. Who the hell was the witness? He was safe if it was Mouse as he had too much to lose. One peep and he would close it for him. Was it Retread? It could be any one of a dozen low- life's that frequented the snake-pit. Despite his precautions someone had obviously seen him. The ute was locked away in his garage, but that would have to disappear and quickly. A burnt out wreck on some lonely road following a stolen vehicle report would fix the problem. Forensics was just too good these days. He could not afford to have a single hair of Tippet's head to be found in the vehicle. He slammed his door to the shouting resonating from the front desk and flopped into his chair.

10

"Andrew, can you come out and see me urgently? I've got a real problem on my hands and I don't know what to do."

"What's wrong Chloe? Can't you tell me over the phone?"

"I've got two problems Andrew. One's business and the other is personal. I need your advice. Please, please come."

"Okay calm down. I'll head out first thing in the morning. You're safe aren't you, you're not being threatened?"

"It's nothing like that Andrew, but I am in danger. It will wait until morning though."

"I don't understand. At least give me some idea of what's this about?"

"I'll expect you tomorrow Andrew, and I want you to stay over for a day or so. I've got to go now. I can see Jim walking across the yard."

The phone went dead and Andrew considered phoning her back, but surely she would have given a hint if she thought Collins was one of the problems she was referring to.

He was on the road before dawn. There was not a single person or vehicle on the street at that time as he drove out of town. He gathered speed as the road stretched out before him. Several times, as his thoughts drifted he was shaken back into the present by a roo appearing suddenly from the surrounding scrub and threatening to smash through the

windscreen or radiator. The dead weight of a roo or wandering wombat could easily tear the wheel off a vehicle. It was
mid-morning when he pulled up in front of the homestead.
Chloe came out to meet him.

"I'm so pleased you came Andrew. Come in and I'll get
Dotti to fix you something to eat. You haven't had breakfast
have you?" The relief on her face clearly evident, but it was
accompanied by a drawn look so obvious he could see she
had not slept.

"Just a cup of tea will do Chloe. I can see you're worried,
so why don't you tell me what this is all about."

Chloe took his arm and ushered him down to a table at
the far end of the veranda well out of range of Dotti's acute
hearing. It was no spontaneous decision as there was a
folder topped by a newspaper already in place. She flipped
the newspaper to one side and pushed the folder towards
him.

"Could you read that first please? That's the most urgent."

Andrew opened the folder and picked up the single sheet
of paper containing a bank's letterhead. He read it slowly
while absorbing the implications, aware Chloe was watching his expression. He sat back without comment and slowly
read the letter again.

"What do you think Andrew? Can they do this without any
warning whatsoever? I'm at my whit's end."

"Banks are not answerable to anyone Chloe. They are a
law unto themselves and you can't fight them unless you've
got very deep pockets. As you know this letter states they
are cancelling your overdraft and working capital loans, but
they don't give any figure as to what they amount to. Have
you any idea?"

"I thought you were doing that for me Andrew. Did you
contact Fred Carter?"

"I did, but he wasn't a lot of help and in fact I thought he was quite evasive. I wasn't very impressed with the man and was going to recommend you change accountants. I've asked for the last five years of financials and have a meeting with him next week."

"This is my home Andrew. I don't want to lose it. What I can't understand is why I've not heard a word from the bank until this. Carter did make some vague noises, but told me not to concern myself as he had it in hand."

"Surely, Carter must be aware. This letter states several letters have been written to you care of Carter and none have been answered. I can see why the bank is not happy."

"Can I stop them from foreclosing? I see they've given me a month to comply and that letter is dated a week ago which means I've only got a few weeks before they move against me."

"It certainly looks that way, but don't panic at this stage. I'll go and see the bank after I get the accounts from Carter. In fact, I'll get you to phone him in a minute and tell him I'll pick up the accounts tomorrow morning. He said his printer wasn't working, but I can copy the data onto a USB stick and get it printed somewhere else. Now what's your other problem? I take it that was the business side, so tell me what's the personal matter?"

Chloe picked up the newspaper and unfolded it. She pointed to a photograph above an article. Andrew glanced at the heading and then at the photo. "What am I supposed to be looking at?"

Chloe put her finger on the figure of a man with arms outstretched being patted down by a person wearing overalls with Customs clearly imprinted on the back.

"That's Marcel my husband."

"Are you sure? He's almost side on. How can you be so certain?"

"I know my own husband Andrew and that's him."

He read the article about another load of illegal immigrants landing on Christmas Island. He looked at the date of the paper. "This article is a couple of weeks old. Did someone send it to you? You don't get *The Australian* newspaper, so how did you get this copy?"

"It came wrapped around the eggs I ordered with the groceries last week. It was only by chance I saw it. You can imagine my shock. Would it be possible to find out where he is?"

"I would imagine he's still on Christmas Island. I've read it takes at least a year before Customs & Immigration clears them and issues them with a temporary visa or sends them back to where they came from. And if he is there, he may not be using his proper name. All those boat people toss their passports overboard the moment they're picked up by navy patrol boats. That way they can claim to be genuine refugees, rather than economic refugees just looking for a better lifestyle. A passport immediately gives their identity away which along with their circumstances can be checked. Without that document it's a long process which causes an unsustainable backlog in the camps so the government is forced to give them temporary residence in Australia. They then simply disappear into the general population. The government is too understaffed to care and forgets about them."

Chloe leaned her chin on her clenched hands and slowly shook her head from side to side. "I know Marcel and I know he'll be trying to get off that island with every means possible. He knows where to find me. Is there any way of informing Immigration of his true identity?. He's been refused entry already, so maybe they'll deny him again."

"I'll write to them and include a copy of this photo. It may help, but I wouldn't count on it. Anyway he's the least of your problems at the moment. Why don't you get on the phone to Carter now and also set up a meeting for me at the bank later in the week. I want to walk in there fully armed with the facts if I'm going to be of any help." Chloe got up and went inside to the phone.

"Hello Mr Andrew." Dotti beamed as she set a beaker of iced tea and sandwiches in front of him. Despite her claimed chronic arthritis she moved silently and he was not aware until she was at his side.

"Thank you Dotti. I appreciate that."

"Chloe not a happy girl. You help her won't you Mr Andrew?"

"I'll do my best Dotti, you can count on that."

She smiled and patted him on the shoulder before disappearing back down the veranda and inside to her domain. He could hear Chloe's raised voice on the phone. She was clearly arguing with someone, but he could not make out what she was saying. Finally, she came back and sat down stoney faced.

"Well, that's taken care of. Carter wanted more time and argued with me about your involvement. I guess he thinks you're standing on his toes and sticking your nose into where it's not wanted."

"Either that or he's hiding something he doesn't want you to know about. I don't think it's anything to do with professional pride."

"He said he'll also arrange the bank visit as he wants to accompany you. I agreed to that. Do you have any objections?"

Andrew screwed his face up. "Not really. I don't suppose there's any harm in that. I would have liked to have talked to the manager by myself, but I can live with Carter being present."

Chloe gave him a cold look. "Andrew, a bell keeps ringing in my head you're not telling me something?"

"What makes you think that?" He attempted a genuine smile, but it was not convincing.

"I was involved in a world of deceit, intrigue, back-stabbing, gossip, lies and sleaze; a life I'm glad that's behind me. I became adept at reading people and their transparency, so don't try your innocent look on me. What is it I should know about?"

Andrew was on the verge of telling her, but now was not the time. She had enough on her plate without collapsing into total panic. He was now sure she was not mixed up in what had been going on.

"I'm concerned about your position. I just wish I'd become involved earlier and hope it's not too late."

"This place is everything to me. I don't really care about the other properties. I'd sell them in a flash if it meant keeping Venus Downs."

"Don't be too hasty in that decision Chloe. You really don't know what they're worth , but what I understand from Carter is that they pay their way. They've got to be worth something."

"I cannot understand why Henry bought them. Why down there in the Pilbara when he could have bought better stations in the Kimberlys?" It was a frustrated and angry outburst.

"I've got a feeling Remus Plains maybe worth something to someone. It may have a strategic value you're not aware of."

"There you go again. You're not just plucking suggestions out of the air Andrew. What are you not telling me?"

He gave her a disarming smile. "You know Chloe, you're quite beautiful when you get angry. The colour rises in your cheeks. They absolutely glow."

She looked at him with an expression of realisation at what he had just said. She was about to say something when he cut her off.

"I mean it Chloe. I'm in love with you." It was a simple direct statement that took her off guard.

"I, I'm already married Andrew and I'm not in love with you," she replied abruptly. "Oh God, I didn't mean it to come out like that. I'm sorry, that was rude and ungrateful. You do understand don't you?"

"I understand Chloe, but it makes no difference. I'm still in love with you."

"Is that why you didn't leave after the fire and agreed to stay and help me?"

Andrew thought for a few seconds. "Yes, I suppose it was, now I come to think about it."

Chloe reached out and put her hand on his. "You're a very sweet person Andrew. I'm sorry I don't feel the same way about you. In fact I don't have any feelings about anyone at the moment, I'm just so confused. First Marcel and now the bank. I don't know which is worse."

Andrew covered her hand and squeezed it. "Forget about Marcel for now. The bank is your real worry, so let me see what I can do about it."

As if on cue Dotti's head appeared at the end of the veranda. "Dat lazy Hazel has prepared lunch. It's all set out in here. You musta finished talkin by now"

"She's a mind reader, nosey and a real pain in the back-side at times, but I love her," Chloe murmured quietly as she stood up. "Come on, let's see what Hazel has prepared."

Chloe chatted cheerfully over lunch. It was as though a valve had been suddenly opened and the pressure within released. Andrew finally looked at his watch.

"That was great Dotti." He indicated to the smiling figure hovering in the doorway to the kitchen. He did not miss the fact Hazel had been directed to stay in the background so the compliments would not be misdirected.

Chloe looked at him with disappointment in her expression as he stood. "You could say the night and leave first thing in the morning."

"I've got too much to do Chloe. I want to see Carter first thing and then spend the day looking over what he gives me."

She followed him out to his vehicle and put her hand on his arm as he closed the door and started the engine. "Thank you, I really appreciate what you're doing for me."

"I don't know if I can do anything, but I'll certainly give it my best shot."

She stood and watched the departing vehicle until it was out of site, then walked back to the homestead deep in troubled thought.

Andrew meant to ask where Collins was, fully expecting to be accosted once again around some turn of the road ahead. It was near midnight when he parked in front of his office and trudged up the old wooden stairs. No need for a burglar alarm in this place. Any intruder could be heard coming. It reminded him of a tour of the ancient palace in Kyoto where the floorboards were purposely loose-sprung so it was impossible for an assassin to enter or move around at night without being detected. When the reason was explained to him by the tour guide, he could literally feel the razor sharp blade of the samurai sword about to take his head off.

He opened the door and walked into his office. He didn't bother turning on the lights as the weak moonlight was providing enough visibility through the unshaded windows. He threw his jacket onto a chair beside the hand basin and was about to lean down and wash his face when he sensed he was not the only person in the room. He spun around to make out the outline of a figure sprawled in a lounge chair against the far wall. He was asleep.

"Who the hell are you? What do you want?" He moved across the room to turn on the lights.

The startled figure sprang up out of the chair. "Mr Hanna please don't turn on the lights. It's not worth my life to be seen in your office. I must have dropped off and didn't hear you come in. I don't mean you any harm. I'm Jerry Briggs and I've got something for you."

The man came closer until Andrew could see his face. He did not sense danger, but was wary as he could not at first place the name or the face. He was exhausted and his brain was just not functioning as normal.

"Ah yes, you're a policeman aren't you? I remember now seeing you when I went to see Smith about Bill Hargraves' death. You're related to Mark Tippet, aren't you?"

"Correct on the first point Mr Hanna, but you've got the wrong tense on the second. Mark is dead. He's been murdered."

"Murdered. I was only talking to him a couple of days ago. What happened?"

"I'm sure Smith shot him."

Andrew indicated a chair. "Please sit down and tell me what you know."

"Mark had been drinking down at the snake-pit."

"Snake-pit?"

"Yeah, the Argent hotel. It's known as the snake-pit. Anyway he bought some dope off one of the locals. He went outside to complete the deal and Smith was seen to flatten him and bundle him into his old ute. He hasn't been seen since. It's my fault because I told him what I'd read in Bill Hargraves' will. I always go through Smith's files when he's not there. Mark was a real tear-away. Would never take advice and that's why he was always in trouble. I think he shot his mouth off to someone about what I'd told him because he was raving on how he was going to buy a truck and go into competition with Metcalf." Briggs pulled a folder from the inside of his jacket. "This is for you."

Andrew took it and flipped it open. It was exactly what he was missing; Hargraves' Will. "You've taken a hell of a risk Jerry."

"I made you two copies. I don't think Smith will ever be any the wiser. I know it was Mark's fault in opening his mouth, but that doesn't condone murder. It's about time that mother-fucker Smith and a few other people in this town got their comeuppance. I give you fair warning now, don't ever try to implicate me in what I've just done Mr Hanna. I will deny any knowledge and I promise you I'll blow you away with a shotgun just like Smith did to Mark, if you ever try to subpoena me as a witness."

Andrew nodded. He could see the man meant business. It was not an idle threat. "I've got the message Jerry, and thank you for the file."

Briggs nodded, got up and walked out the door without saying another word. Andrew heard the retreating footsteps as they slowly descended the ancient stairway. He got up and pushed the file under his mattress before flopping down and drifting off into a troubled sleep.

Carter was expecting him. There were a series of folders on his desk. He gave a weak smile which barely concealed his nervousness as Andrew walked in.

"You got your printer working I see. If you don't mind I'll take these back to my office to go through. I daresay I will have questions, so I may call on you during the day."

Carter looked at his watch. "I've arranged a meeting with the bank in an hour."

"That doesn't give me enough time to go through these. Did you arrange the meeting?"

"No Chloe Boyce did apparently. Roy Briscoe, the bank manager phoned me to confirm the time. He said he couldn't make it any other time this week as he's extremely busy. I did look into your office earlier, but saw you were asleep. I didn't want to disturb you as I knew you would be tired. It's a long drive out to Venus Downs and back again on the same day."

"Tell me Fred, you are aware the bank wants to call in Chloe's overdraft and loans? You must have had correspondence to that effect. Why didn't you notify her of the problem?"

Carter fidgeted with a pen. "It's my fault entirely. I thought I would be able to negotiate with the bank and take the burden off her. She has no experience in dealing with finance and she just wouldn't understand how to manoeuvre."

"You didn't even give her the chance and now you've got her petrified she's going to lose everything. This is nothing short of professional bloody incompetence on your part. It's criminal and you know it. Tell me, what's your end in all this? Who paid you to put her into this predicament?"

Carter could not contain his anger as he face went crimson. "You two-bit fucking ambulance chaser. If you think you can waltz in here and make those accusations, you've got another think coming."

Andrew could see the situation was going to get ugly as Carter came around the side of his desk with his fists clenched. Andrew stood just as Carter looked down as his phone started to ring. The blow caught him on the side of the jaw sending him sprawling backwards. Andrew picked up the files, not bothering to check on the condition of his motionless opponent and walked out. That was close he mused. Saved by the phone. He doubted whether Carter would lay charges.

Briscoe kept him waiting for ten minutes before the door to his office opened and he summoned Andrew with a broad smile. "Good morning Mr Hanna, my name is Roy Briscoe. I'm pleased I've gained someone's attention at last." He motioned for Andrew to take a seat. "Where is Mr Carter? I thought he would be joining us?"

"Fred is indisposed at the moment Roy. He won't be attending."

Briscoe gave him a quick look of surpise. "Oh, no problem so let's get on with it."

"As I understand Mr Briscoe, Fred Carter has been discussing Ms Boyce's affairs and the present predicament with you?"

"I've had one meeting with Mr Carter and that would have been more than a month ago. I've sent him letters since, but have never been favoured with a reply. I decided last week I would write directly to Ms Boyce as the matter was getting out of hand."

"I can assure you Mr Briscoe she was completely unaware of any problems. Carter has never brought it to her attention. I'm here to see if the situation can be rectified."

"I'm sorry Mr Hanna, but head office has given me firm instructions to call the loans supporting the mortgages and sell her up if she can't satisfy the bank's demands."

"But surely there is room for negotiation here Mr Briscoe. Chloe only became aware of the problem a couple of days ago and asked me to help her as her lawyer. Is she badly in debt?"

Briscoe opened a thick file on his desk as though trying to refresh his memory.

Andrew had no doubt the man could quote the figure down to the last cent without resorting to the charade.

"It's not so much the overdraft but the mortgage liability. The overdraft is managable, but the mortgages are another matter."

Andrew looked querulous, but Briscoe had not seen the gesture as he was pretending to be buried in the document before him.

"That doesn't make sense to me Mr Briscoe. If the overdraft obligations are being met, then surely that would include any interest payments due on the mortgages. You've just stated in effect the business is profitable, so why is the bank intent on pulling the pin and selling her up?"

"I can't answer that Mr Hanna. It's out of my hands and I must follow instructions."

"I believe that is totally unreasonable Mr Briscoe. Surely, the bank will let her sell one or two of the holdings to reduce the overall liability?"

Briscoe closed the folder. "No, that is unsatisfactory Mr Hanna. Head office has taken a dim view of its correspondence not being answered. Obviously, they took the attitude Ms Boyce was not taking things seriously. Banks don't like to be ignored Mr Hanna. If Ms Boyce had got in touch when I sent out the first letter, or Mr Carter had conveyed the problem too her, there would have been a very good chance the bank would have listened to any proposal she may have suggested. I'm not suggesting for a minute it would have taken a different attitude, but the bank would have been bound to listen. I'm afraid it's far too late for that now."

"How much time has she got?"

"She's got less than a month to settle. We'll move immediately after that and put the four properties up for sale in one lot."

"What if she sells one or two properties in the meantime? There would have to be a surplus to cover the outstandings?"

"The bank will not allow the properties to be sold individually. They will be offered in a single lot by auction."

Andrew snorted. "From my calculations that would run into a substantial figure. There wouldn't be too many people around who could afford four grazing properties in a single package. I believe the bank is being entirely unreasonable in its demands. The sum of the parts is worth more than the whole. Why not give her time to discard the properties in the Pilbara or Remus Plains adjacent to Venus Downs?"

"That's probably a reasonable proposition Mr Hanna, but I've my instructions and they're final. There is nothing more I can do to assist."

A sudden thought occurred. "Mr Briscoe can I ask you whether Henry Boyce was in serious financial trouble prior to his death?"

"Not just prior to his death, but some years previously the bank was going to foreclose according to these records. I should not say this, but I do have some sympathy for Ms Boyce's predicament."

Briscoe read some of the diary notes out to him, dry and clinical to the manager, but forming a pattern of understanding in Andrew's alert mind. He could almost pinpoint the day the crime commenced.

"Could I have a copy of those notes for my client?"

"Most certainly not Mr Hanna and I trust what I've read to you remains confidential?"

"You have my word on that Mr Briscoe."

It was clear the meeting was over as Briscoe got to his feet. Andrew did not move as his brain looked for a bargaining position. "Can I ask you where your instructions came from in regard to this current matter?"

"Certainly. Head office is in Perth."

"Would you be so kind as to contact the appropriate person so I may go down and discuss this with them? Would you make an appointment for me?"

It was clear Briscoe resented people attempting to go over his head and showed his displeasure. "I'll do that for you Mr Hanna, but I can assure you you're wasting your time."

"Well, it's my time Mr Briscoe and I will be the judge of whether I'm wasting it."

"You forget Mr Hanna you will also be wasting the valuable time of one of our senior managers. I can't say he will agree to meet with you as I've been given clear instructions. After all Ms Boyce is the client."

"Mr Briscoe, this matter is extremely serious and Ms Boyce has asked me to help. I believe I'm competent to handle any negotiations on her behalf. I agree Carter has been grossly negligent on behalf of his client, but I would like to see if I can rectify that. Would you at least convey Ms Boyce's concerns to Perth and ask for a meeting. It may only take five minutes. Surely a senior manager can afford that?"

"I'll see what I can do," the banker replied as he rose and ushered Andrew out. "I will phone you if it can be arranged. If you don't hear from me by close today you'll know your request has been denied."

Briscoe sat down behind his desk and stared blankly at the folder. He could not understand what the bank was doing. Why was it calling up the mortgages when the cash flow alone from Venus Downs was satisfying the terms covering all properties. The sale of one of the properties would clear up any debt. Hanna was correct, the bank was being totally unreasonable. It was not as though the bank was out on a limb as there was a substantial guarantor supporting the overdraft and working capital loans. Why was the bank getting mixed up in this? The effect of the guarantor pulling the plug left the bank with no option, but to call the mortgages to protect its position. Henry Boyce must not have realised the implications of what he was doing when he signed the documents. The guarantor had him over a barrel and he didn't realise it. Obviously, a competent accountant had not advised him, otherwise he would have immediately picked up the potential trap. And now the trap had been sprung and there was no escape for the prey. Briscoe was well aware of the motive and the identity of the person behind it. He opened the file again and turned to the last page. He had looked at it many times before and shook his head in frustration. How much did this client want? He tossed the file into a tray and picked up the phone. No use pondering it further. He wanted it over and done with.

"Mr Geddes please. Roy Briscoe from the Wyndham branch calling." He was transferred and after confirming with Geddes' secretary and kept waiting, his superior came on line.

"Hello Roy. How's it going up there? Has the heat affected you yet? Tell me, what can I do for you?"

"Arthur it's about the Boyce matter. I've explained the bank's position, but Ms Boyce's solicitor, Andrew Hanna, who she has only recently engaged, would like to come down and discuss it with you. He believes the bank is being unreasonable and there are grounds for negotiation."

The pleasantries suddenly dissolved as Geddes took on an overbearing tone. "Briscoe, you have very clear instructions regarding Boyce so carry them out and no, I will not be available to Hanna or anyone else. Just get on with it and don't call me again."

Briscoe's phone rang almost immediately he put it down. "I saw Hanna leaving your bank. What did he want?" The tone was demanding, the identity unmistakable.

"I think you know very well what he wanted. He's acting for Boyce and wanted to know if there was room for negotiation. I told him the bank's position and he asked me to contact Perth to see if he could meet with my superior."

"You phoned Geddes, and what did he say?"

"As I told Hanna it would be pointless, but I did as he asked. Geddes refused to see him."

"Good. Hopefully that should put paid to it."

Andrew sat in his office pondering Chloe's predicament. Why would the bank call the loans when there was positive cash flow and plenty of collateral which they could fall back on? Why the urgency? Her position did look hopeless. He had the nagging suspicion Shulman was mixed up in this somewhere. Maybe he should play the ace card and see what he could shake out of the tree. He picked up the phone and paused before putting it down again. Why phone him when he could just walk in?

"Hello my boy. How's it all going for you?" Ike's welcome was open and effusive as he indicated for Andrew to sit down on the huge boardroom sofa rather than a lounge chair in front of his desk.

"It's not easy Ike. I don't have much of a cash flow at the moment. That fire has really stuffed me up."

"I can increase your retainer to keep you going for another few months. By then you should be okay. Listen, I'm glad you called in as I've heard on the village drums Chloe Boyce is going to be sold up by the bank. I want you to handle the legals for me as I intend to buy the lot."

"News travels fast Ike. There must be a hotline between you and Briscoe?"

Shulman's face immediately drained of its conviviality. "What do you mean by that crack?"

"Pure deduction Ike. Unless Briscoe told you, how would you know, unless of course Carter is the source? I will opt for Carter because I believe in my brief observations of Briscoe, he seemed to possess some banker integrity."

Ike waved his hands. "What does it matter who told me? The fact is Boyce is going to the wall and I intend to takeover."

"How do you know someone won't overbid you?"

Ike gave a derisory laugh. "No one's going to write a cheque out for four properties at the one time. I can assure you I will own the lot very soon."

Andrew decided to play his trump card. He had the distinct feeling his days of receiving a retainer from Shulman were about to end. It was not a spur of the moment decision.

"You've been getting your cut from Venus Downs for years. Why the sudden urge to get greedy?"

Shulman bridled at the comment. "I agree I've done very well handling cattle sales. It was been a very lucrative arrangement for Henry Boyce and myself, but now I intend to take full control. Let's face it Andrew, there's no way Chloe Boyce can manage such an enterprise with her operating funds cut-off; she's finished."

"But I thought Jim Collins was doing an excellent job? Chloe appointed him on your recommendation. She speaks very highly of him, so does Chloe really have to be a hands-on manager?"

"Maybe it's time for her to go and run a fashion house in Perth, or wherever."

"She's not part of your criminal activities then? She doesn't know about it does she, and you want to get rid of her before she finds out and blows the whistle?"

He watched as the coal-black unblinking eyes burrowed into him.

"You're standing on dangerous ground making accusations like that Hanna. Libellous and defamatory. I don't pay you to call me a criminal. I pay you to represent my interests. As of this minute you're fired."

"I expected as much Ike, but you see I do have the evidence you along with Hargraves, Smith and a number of others, including Henry Boyce have been implicit in stealing thousands of head of cattle over the years from Ascot Downs and running them through Venus Downs. It was a foolproof arrangement until Bill Hargraves decided to put it on paper."

Shulman gave an unconvincing laugh as he tried to disguise his shock. "I merely acted as agent. Boyce verified the cattle came off his property. I know nothing other than that and nothing can be proved to the contrary."

"You don't sound very convincing Ike. Bill Hargraves signed an affidavit which spelled out the complete details of his involvement, and your name certainly features. I made four copies of the Will, two of which I gave to Hargraves and are now in Smith's possession; one I filed in my office and the fourth along with a very incriminating affidavit are now in a safe place. You see, Mark Tippet told me Smith had set him up to light the fire. He didn't know the real purpose, but he soon worked it out and I've no doubt he tried to blackmail you."

"That's only supposition on your part. In any event Tippet has disappeared so his testimony can't be verified. What other evidence do you have implicating me in this so-called crime?"

"Hargraves' declaration says it all. He found God when he knew he was terminal and wanted to make sure those pearly gates would not be closed when he got there."

Shulman smiled derisively and shook his head. "You're bluffing, you don't have anything otherwise you'd be waving that affidavit in front of me now. Too bad everything went up in smoke. Mind you, you've obviously got designs on Chloe

Boyce, but you wanted to find out whether she was involved. Of course she is and I doubt whether any jury will accept otherwise. Why didn't you come clean with me? I would be quite happy to let you have a corner of the action. Now you're a broke lawyer with no income, no office and no prospects. I want you out of that office today and I would advise you to get out of town for your health."

"I'm not concerned about my health Ike, I'm concerned about my client."

"Bullshit Hanna," Shulman exploded. "You accepted my retainer and I was your exclusive client. You were bound to me and behind my back you start working for Boyce. I would call that a giant conflict of interest, wouldn't you? A breach of trust?"

"Not where criminality is involved Ike and you're correct, I did want to confirm whether Chloe was involved, but it's now clear she is totally innocent. You introduced Collins to pull the wool over her eyes to ensure the theft continued, which it does to this day."

"Okay Andrew, you say you've got the evidence and the game is over. Any investigation is certainly going to take time and it may even get lost in the filing system along the way. My name is trashed by implication and your client tries to establish her innocence in the face of Collins testifying to the contrary and I daresay Carter will be likewise inclined. You're on a hiding to nothing Hanna, so I would give it away if I were you."

"I'll move out of the office today." Andrew stood up to leave. "I was hoping you'd see things differently."

"Differently, differently? What do you mean by that? I can see you're attempting to blackmail me. That's a crime in itself."

"Wrong choice of words Ike. I apologise."

"Well, what the hell do you want? I'm quite happy to double your retainer and let you have the office rent free if you work for me exclusively. What is it you're really after?"

"Somehow I suspect your involvement with Venus Downs and Henry Boyce goes much deeper than is apparent. You don't need the property. With your wealth and influence I'm quite sure you could put some pressure on the bank to reassess their position. The properties are viable and the mortgages fully serviced. This is a real bastard act on the part of the bank. I can only assume it's due to some outside pressure."

"And?"

"Why don't you let Chloe have Venus Downs? You don't need it. Hargraves is dead and any new manager might not go along with the present arrangement."

"And in return?"

"I'll forget I've got a certain document and get on with my life."

"You don't have a bloody thing Hanna. You're bluffing. That affidavit went up in flames, if in fact there was one. I want Venus Downs and I'm going to get it. Nothing personal. It's just pure business."

Andrew made to protest, but Shulman held up his hand. "Get lost Hanna. Go get into Chloe Boyce's nickers and live happily ever after, but you're finished in this town. Go and do your worst."

Andrew felt a wave of depression engulf him as he walked out. However, he was determined to set the ball rolling and bring Shulman down, but how would he do it without incriminating Chloe? He was lost in thought as he strode into the doorway of his building, and barged into a fat figure blocking the entrance. He looked up in shock.

"What the hell do you want?"

Smith held a paper up in front of Andrew, but withdrew it when Andrew reached for it. "This is a search warrant Hanna. I've just searched your office for drugs, but you're in the clear. I didn't find anything, so you're lucky."

"Can I have a look at that warrant? Who authorised it?"

"I only have to show it to you counsellor.'" Smith hissed between gritted teeth. "I don't have to give it to you. Go check with the magistrate, he'll confirm he signed it. Oh, and by the way, next time you ask one of my staff to copy something for you, tell him to be more careful, although there won't be a next time."

Andrew was pushed aside by Smith's bulk as he stepped out onto the pavement and walked away. Andrew walked slowly up the stairs. There was no point in hurrying as Smith would have been thorough in his search, which would not have taken more than a few minutes as there was no place to hide anything. He pushed open the door of his office and studied the sum total of the disarray of his life. He picked up the mattress off the floor and tossed it back onto the bed. Smith had found what he was looking for. Intuition had prompted Andrew to toss the second copy into the post on his way to meet Briscoe. He lay down in complete defeat, contemplating his predicament. Smith must have suspected Briggs had something to do with Tippet. Had someone seen Briggs leaving his office last night? Maybe Smith had just suspected something and shaken it out of him? His impression of the man was it would not take a lot of shaking to get a confession, not when being stood over and threatened by the likes of Smith. In any event it was too late now, but he felt responsible for Briggs, because he had most certainly lost his job. He threw his feet over the side of the bed. No use staying around here. He realised he was in danger as he gathered his few papers and stuffed them into his bag. He closed the door without looking back at the mess. So much for the smart young lawyer who wasn't thinking clearly. He should have taken more care. He tossed the bag into the backseat and slowly drove out of town.

He did not see Smith watching him from his parked Toyota down the street. The gaze followed him until he was out of sight. Smith climbed out of his vehicle and walked slowly into Ike's premises and into his office without acknowledging his secretary. She looked up momentarily to challenge, but resumed her gossip on the phone, as she smiled in recognition.

Shulman looked up as Smith sprawled himself into the lounge. "I could do with one of these in my office. You sure look after yourself Ike."

"You're welcome to it Wally. I'll have it delivered today if you like. I've been thinking about throwing it out and getting something new."

Smith guffawed. "Can you imagine what the commander would say if he visited and saw that in my office. The bastard would immediately think I had my hand in the petty cash tin or was involved in graft and corruption."

"I'll have it delivered today then Wally."

The smile faded as Smith dissected the riposte. "There's no call for that crap remark Ike. If I go down, you go down with me. Just remember that."

"My apologies Wally, I didn't mean it like that and there's no need to threaten me. I understand the situation very well." Talk about thick in the brain department and thin-skinned. It's a wonder he ever made sergeant, he silently mused.

"Did you get it?"

Smith pulled the document out of his jacket, leaned forward and tossed it onto Ike's desk. "He'd hidden it under his mattress of all places. Mind you there wasn't much to search. I was hoping I would be in and out of the place before he got back, but he ran into me just as I was walking out. You should have seen the look on his face."

"How did you get a search warrant? On what grounds?"

"I can put anything in front of old pissmark Hoben and he'll sign it. Fine upstanding magistrate he may be, but the moment I caught a kid giving him a blow-job in the park toilet block, I owned him."

"How did you know Hanna had it?"

"I've been a bit suspicious about Briggs for awhile. Someone tipped me off there maybe a connection between him and Tippet. I've got a locked drawer in my desk where I keep anything sensitive. It's well understood anyone going into that room without approval will be registering for unemployment benefits if I find out. I always leave a mark such as a paper clip or pen on top of any files. Briggs was good, but he wasn't that clever. He was particularly agitated the morning after I took Tippet for a ride. The desk clerk confirmed later she'd seen him looking at the gun register. I'd forgotten to check the gun back on that day. Not a hanging offence, but he had me on ice if he wanted to create trouble. Anyway, I stuck a bit of blue-tack underneath the drawer and sure enough when I looked next, it was still stuck to the bottom, but was no longer attached to runner. As a precaution I also took all the paper out of the copier that night. I was first in in the morning and sure enough it was loaded with paper. Someone had used it during the night. It didn't take me long to work out who the culprit was. He confessed to having run off a copy of Hargraves' Will and given it to Hanna, but I've covered that base so Hanna is back to square one. On a pretext I said I wanted to go and have another look at the site where Hargraves crashed and invited Briggs to come with me. He was excited because he never got past doing the desk work. He didn't suspect a thing."

Shulman's eyes widened. "Did he meet with an accident out there?"

"Yes, and it could have been life threatening. The poor sod slipped with a little help, went arse over down about ten metres and landed in a pile of very nasty ironstone. Broke three ribs, really made a mess of his face and also broke an arm. He's on sick leave for a month. Silly boy should have been looking where he was stepping."

"Can you trust him?"

"Of course I can't trust the bastard, but I'm willing to take the chance. He's not like Tippet who couldn't keep his yap shut. Anyhow, Briggs is a probationary constable which would have required a full scale investigation if he'd simply disappeared. The last thing I want is Internal Affairs sniffing around this neck of the woods. Briggs will not utter a word. I went through his desk and found his camera and photos he'd taken of the gun register. I just filled the register in with the required date to prove I'd returned it the same day. Simple. I then went to see him in hospital and gave him the camera as I was leaving. I'd put a bullet through the lens. He got the message."

"What about Hanna? He's a loose cannon liable to ignite at any moment. You've got to take care of him. By the way I just fired him."

"Yeah, I just saw him driving out. And tell me, why is it me who has to take care of him? You forget Ike, we're in this together. If you think you can walk away and leave me holding the baby if the balloon goes up, you'd better think again. However, I doubt whether Hanna will open his mouth. I know he's got the hots for Boyce and I doubt whether he would want to see her in the slammer should he decide to go public with what he knows. She would have extreme difficulty proving she hasn't been complicit in carrying on where Henry Boyce left off. Collins has already run ten thousand Ascot cattle through the place since she took over and we both know, ignorance is no defence."

Ike smiled and chortled to himself. "Yeah, I'm certain Hanna is out to catch the wealthy lady grazier? He must realise she's about to suffer a severe setback, but somehow believes he can ride to her rescue. Once I've got control of her properties, I've cut out the middleman so to speak. Hanna has no solid proof of what's been going on. He told me he had Hargraves' Will and signed affidavit, but I don't believe him, otherwise he would have shown it to me and if he does say anything the beautiful Chloe is likely to serve time."

"What about Collins? He should really be back in jail where he belongs. I'm going to have police Internal Affairs demanding answers if it's discovered I've been harboring him. I don't think I'd survive the investigation."

"I intend to leave him on as manager. He's very effective and knows what will happen if he steps out of line."

"I don't like the prick. Knowing his type he'll want more and attempt blackmail. Believe me, it will happen."

"Then I pay him a bit more Wally: a bonus. When this all blows over and Boyce and Hanna are out of the scene, surely you could arrange for his permanent disappearance. After all there's a lot of open country around here a man could vanish into, and I doubt you're going to look too hard for a criminal with his background. You said Hanna has left town?"

"Yep, I'm sure he's headed out to shack up with Boyce which worries me a bit. He's a very smart lad and yet you say there's no way Boyce or he can delay the sale?"

"He's already tried with the bank, but Briscoe was under instructions to knock him back. I had to put that jumped up bank-Johnny in his place. He started to argue with me he could see no reason to pull working capital and overdraft facilities as they were adequately covered by the income. It was an arrangement I had with Henry Boyce to give the bank some comfort when he was getting himself out of financial problems at the time. But now Chloe has taken over and I'm certainly not going to allow her to take advantage. I got Arthur Geddes to sort Briscoe out, but he wasn't happy about it. Now that he's sitting in his ivory tower in Perth he's taken the position he's not involved, but still wants his payoff."

Smith pricked up his ears. "I didn't realise Geddes was involved? What's his end?"

Shulman realised he had stumbled. "Oh, nothing really. Just a few dollars now and again. He was able to give me an update on anyone's financial position. Find out what any-one's assets and liabilities are and you've got an advantage if you're dealing with them."

"And mine?"

"I know what you earn, but it doesn't come anywhere near what I've paid you over the years.You've been well looked after."

"So you're going to keep the game rolling when you take over? With Hargraves gone, how to you know the new man-ager will be bought?"

"I've already taken care of that."

11

Chloe saw the concerned look on his face as he got out and walked towards her. He motioned for her to follow him to the far end of the veranda out of earshot. Dotti was immediately at the doorway instructing Hazel to hurry up with the cold drinks. They remained silent as she poured two glasses and hastily beat a retreat when she did not receive Andrew's normal greeting and light banter.

"It didn't go that well did it?'

"No, it was far from satisfactory." He picked up the glass and took a long draught before fixing her worried look. "Chloe, I want you to level with me. Are you party to what's going on around here? If you are I will say nothing and simply drive away. I don't want any part of it."

She looked shocked. "What do you mean? I have no idea what you're implying?"

"So you have no idea your father was a criminal? An integral part of a conspiracy involving Ike Shulman, Bill Hargraves, Wally Smith and I've no doubt it doesn't end there?"

"Oh my god, what are you saying?"

"Your father was a key figure in a cattle duffing program that's been going on for years and is still operating at this precise moment. You haven't been aware Collins is involved and that explains why he's so hostile to me."

"Are you sure? When did you find this out?"

"I'm quite sure. I found out when Bill Hargraves, the manager of Ascot Downs asked me to write up his Will. He had only a short time to live and wanted to get the guilt off his chest. He disclosed exactly what was going on and who was involved."

"I don't believe it. My father would not be involved in anything like that." She trailed off with an incredulous look on her face. "How much money are you talking about?"

"I don't have a precise figure, but the monetary loss to Ascot runs into the millions. We're talking about a major criminal activity."

"But the Ascot accountants must have picked up on it. You're talking about tens of thousands of cattle."

"Ascot is the largest pastoral holding in this area. The company is owned by absentee English landlords who apparently wouldn't have the foggiest idea of how many head the property is running. As long as it is paying some sort of dividend they're not interested and haven't visited the place in years. Tens of thousands of unbranded cleanskins were run off to Venus Downs, branded here and shipped into the saleyards as belonging to Henry. The proceeds were split between Henry, Ike Shulman, Bill Hargraves, and Smith was also on the take for his silence. Oh, and I've no doubt your trusted accountant Fred Carter along with someone else is also involved."

"I can't let this go on Andrew. I will have to report it immediately."

"And who are you going to report it to? No point in running to Smith. I think it best if you let me think this through."

"I can't do that Andrew. You're suggesting I just ignore it. You're talking about a major crime." She suddenly went quiet with a look of sudden realisation crossing her face. "You knew about this when you were last here, but said nothing about it. You thought I was involved didn't you?"

"I admit I had my suspicions, but now I've no doubt you were totally ignorant."

"I find that very strange. You said you loved me, but obviously you were hiding all this. What would you have done if it proved to be correct? Was that love conditional?"

"No, it's not conditional. I love you. I've been fighting with the demons of doubt, praying you were not involved."

"What changed your mind?"

"My meetings with Carter, Briscoe at the bank and finally Ike Shulman. The crime and extent fell into place when I talked to Ike."

"But I don't owe Ike anything. Where does he come into this?"

"I'm positive Ike is behind the bank's move to sell you up. He was quite open with me that he intends to take over all your properties at bargain basement prices when the bank puts them up for sale."

"But why would he do that?"

"Chloe, it was okay when Henry was in control, but he cannot trust you to maintain the same arrangement as he knows very well you wouldn't have a bar of it. You are now superfluous to him and he wants you gone. But he's not going to give you a fair price. That's not in Ike's nature."

"How did my father ever get involved in this?"

"It was near the end of years of drought from what I can ascertain. From what I gather, the bank was foreclosing on properties all over the Kimberleys. Henry was over extended and the bank moved to sell him up. I can only assume Shulman put up a guarantee and got the bank off Henry's back. And from then on his financial position never looked back. And that fits in with what Hargraves told me about the timing of Shulman's approach to him."

"But why didn't Shulman just let Henry go broke and buy the property? Why share the proceeds of the crime?"

"That puzzled me my dear Chloe, but the answer is rather simple in my opinion. Ike wanted to keep his hands clean. He was selling cattle branded and supplied by Henry and was merely acting as agent. It was Hargraves and Henry who were the real criminals and not him. I don't know what the percentages were, but Henry's must have been significant to buy the other grazing properties you've inherited. There is no doubt in my mind Henry was involved in a major criminal activity. The partnership worked a treat until Henry died and you assumed total control. And that's why Shulman's got to remove you."

"So I may as well pack up and go?" Chloe cupped her head in her hands and stared vacantly at the floor. "Will it ever come out that Henry was involved?"

"No, I don't think so. Ike has too much to lose and will want to keep it quiet. He wants to carry on. He knows I won't say anything because he's guessed I want to protect you, and you're not going to say anything because of the damage to your father's name. I think you're better off by making a clean break. In that way if anything happens you are in a much better position to deny any involvement."

"How long have I got?"

"The moment a sale goes through you'd better be packed to go. Shulman will want to move in immediately."

"What are you going to do now?"

Andrew chuckled to himself. "Well, my brief career as a lawyer in Wyndham has come to an end. Also I know too much for my own good and would always be looking over my shoulder if I stayed."

"You think Shulman is that much of a threat?"

"It's not Shulman, it's Smith who concerns me. I have reason to believe he personally murdered someone who found out about his involvement in the duffing and tried to blackmail him."

"In that case why don't you stay here and help me? I feel threatened now you've told me that. I don't want to be on my own if Smith or Shulman should drive up. They know you've come here and must realise you would tell me everything. They may not believe I would keep my mouth shut to protect Henry's memory. I'm just as much a threat as you, isn't that correct?"

He was aware of the danger, but had said nothing. He considered she would be removed from the threat when the properties were sold and she moved away. He now realised his mistake mentioning the murder. She was quite right. She was in real danger. Why let her just leave when at some time in the future she could level an accusatory finger at Shulman and Smith?

"I'm quite prepared to pay you until the sale goes through. If you don't want to, I'm sure I can rely on Jim to protect me."

Andrew shook his head slowly. "No you can't. There's something you should know about Jim Collins. I've always been suspicious of him, despite your confidence in his management abilities."

"He doesn't like you either Andrew, but he's never threatened other than a harmless pass at me, but I can see you're about to tell me something to the contrary."

"His real name is David Bonham. He's wanted for rape and a string of other offences." He watched her face as she absorbed the revelation. It turned from the look of a challenge to that of horror.

"Where is he now?"

"He, he left yesterday for a break. He's been working very hard so he's entitled to a week off."

"Did he say where he was going?"

Chloe shook her head and started to tremble. "No, he just said he'd be away for a week. I assumed he would just go into Wyndham. Andrew, I'm terrified of him now. A rapist working for me under an assumed name. I can't possibly stay here when he comes back. I thought I'd escaped fear when I got out of London, but fear is stalking me again."

"Calm down Chloe. Of course I'll stay and you can forget about payment and don't worry about Collins as he's not coming back."

"How can you be so sure of that? You don't really believe you can stand up to him do you?"

Andrew pulled a wry expression. "I admit I'm no match for the man physically, but I'll make a phone call to a police contact in Perth who will be most interested in locating David Bonham. My guess is he will not be coming back if Perth acts quickly on my tip-off. I think Sergeant Smith will be asked some embarrassing questions of how he allowed Bonham to go undetected in his jurisdiction."

"That takes a load of my mind. And to think I had total trust in the man. Please, can you make the call now?"

Andrew pulled out a small notebook and thumbed it for a number. "Let's go into Henry's office." Chloe followed him and closed the door behind them.

"John Lusty in prosecutions please. Tell him it's Andrew Hanna who would like to speak to him." He looked at Chloe. "John's not in investigations, but he'll convey it to the right division."

Chloe could hear the burst of laughter and a greeting as Lusty answered. They exchanged insults and pleasantries for a minute before Andrew stopped the banter.

"Look John, this is not a social call. Your people are looking for a certain David Bonham, a real bad arse. He's in Wyndham at the moment. He goes under the assumed name of Jim Collins. He's well known to Sergeant Wally Smith who's in charge up here. Smith's aware of his real identity, but is protecting him. I won't go into the reasons why because it's not relevant to this call. You'd better tell the demons not to telegraph their arrival to Smith, otherwise Bonham is likely to do a runner. And do me a favour, this is strictly an anonymous tip-off. You can take all the credit and buy me a beer when I'm next in town."

Andrew put the phone down and smiled across at Chloe. "That should do the trick."

"Demons? What are they?"

"Detectives. I wouldn't be surprised if a couple of them aren't on the plane in the morning and the threat of Bonham removed permanently in the next few days."

"Will you stay until that's confirmed?"

"I'll stay until the sale contract is signed and then we can talk about what we're going to do after that."

Chloe reached over and put her hand on his. "Thank you Andrew. I don't know that I love you, but I do have feelings for you. I appreciate everything you're doing for me."

"I'll keep working on it. I'm in love with you."

"Yes I know. I just can't get the thought of Marcel out of my mind. I don't suppose you've made any progress?"

"No, I just haven't had the time, but once we're out of here I'll attempt to pick up on his trail. It may be very difficult if he's here under an alias. There are so many illegals flooding in on boats and even planes. Immigration just hasn't the time to check their backgrounds because of the numbers involved. There will always be undesirables among the genuine refugees."

Chloe nodded. "I suppose I shouldn't worry so much about trying to find him. Knowing Marcel as I do, it will be him who finds me. He knows about this place. I'd love to see the look on his face when he turns up and finds a sold sign on the gate."

"Can you run the place without Collins for a few weeks?"

"Yes, Joey Moonlight the head stockman and his mob are very capable. I imagine Shulman will have to find a replacement for Collins. I shudder when I think about him."

"I would say Collins was warned off by Smith not to threaten you in any way. He was secure while he was here under the protection of Smith and he wasn't going to jeopardise that."

"Even so, I had one psycho maul me on demand and I don't want to experience another. Marcel was an animal. If Collins had done so I would have gone around the bend. To think I put my full trust in the man."

Andrew got up and put his hand on her shoulder. "Put it out of your mind Chloe. I'm here and you've got nothing to worry about."

"Yes I know." She reached up and squeezed his hand. "Why don't you get your gear. I'll see what Dotti has prepared for dinner, or should I say Hazel. Dotti always takes the credit, but I let her get away with it. She'd give Hazel a hard time otherwise."

"That's the way of the world Chloe. Someone is always trying to take advantage of someone else. You're witnessing it right now with Ike Shulman."

Andrew retrieved his bag and was about to pass the kitchen when Dotti suddenly appeared. "You not goin to walk past without saying hello to Dotti, are you Mr Andrew?"

"Yes, Dotti I was. I wanted to sneak past and freshen up and then blind you with my good looks and pay compliment to your fine cooking."

She burst out with a giggle. "You full of goanna shit Mr Andrew. You wouldn't have stood a chance when I was younger, but you safe now. I'm too old for that sort of thing. However, I know you can't resist my cooking."

She didn't notice Andrew glance over her shoulder at Hazel who was standing in the background slowly shaking her head at the audacity she had just witnessed. She quickly broke off her look of disdain and smiled when he gave her a knowing wink.

"This is really good." Andrew looked up from his plate, but could see Chloe's mind was elsewhere. She was staring directly at him, but was not seeing him. "What's bugging you now may I ask?"

It took her several seconds before Chloe realised he was talking to her and gave him a startled look. "I've been thinking about the number of times Jim has sat exactly where you are now and what was running through his mind. Me chatting away making conversation and trying to initiate a rapport, while he just remained absolutely clinical with his answers which were confined to cattle, and cattle prices. Although I tried to ask him about himself and his background he would just clam up."

Andrew snorted and shook his head. "He was very smart in that regard. He wasn't going to drop his guard with idle conversation. He'd obviously learned that in prison. Keep your mouth shut and you could never be caught out on a lie. Have you noticed when people get excited they're liable to let drop a snippet of their background they would otherwise keep hidden. Everyone has a secret."

"What's yours?"

"I'm not at the stage of divulging secrets," he grinned. "That's for another day."

"But you will tell me?" Chloe laughed as she pointed her knife at him.

"That may take some time. I like to know people really well before I take them into my confidence. Are you willing to wait?"

"You were thinking about Collins, weren't you? He's due back tomorrow. That's why you've been depressed all week, isn't it?"

Andrew did not need to look across to see Chloe's drawn look.

"I'm just praying your friend passed the message on and Jim's been arrested. I can't stop thinking about it. What do I do if he turns up? I'll have to fire him as I can't have him back."

Andrew patted her hand. "You won't be seeing Collins again around here if Lusty has acted on my tipoff. I can assure you of that."

"Thank you. I just can't bear to face him."

Lusty walked down the corridor, knocked on a door and opened it without waiting.

Pratt cut off the conversation and closed his mobile with an annoyed look at the intruder. "I'll call if I want to see you Lusty. Don't just barge in here without warning. What do you want?"

"Detective, are you by any chance looking for a character by the name of Dave Bonham, also known as Jim Collins?"

Pratt shook his head. "Doesn't ring any bells. What's he supposed to have done?"

"A real nasty bit of garbage according to our computer records. He's wanted for rape amongst other things, but he's been on the run for a couple of years now."

Reg Pratt raised an eyebrow. "So you've tracked him down have you? I assume he's in custody, and you've been lined up to prosecute?"

"No, he's not in custody, but I've been tipped off as to where he is."

"Well, where the hell is he? And who gave you the tip-off? I don't have all bloody day sergeant, so get on with it."

"He's in Wyndham. You were stationed there once weren't you?" Lusty already knew the answer to his question. Pratt was a tough cop with a dubious reputation amongst the force. *'And that's in cash'* were the words he overheard when he pushed open his door moments before. It was the reason for Pratt's rebuke. The detective was obviously organising another payday.

"None of your bloody business where I've been. So who tipped you off?"

"Andrew Hanna, a friend who bought into a legal practice in the town."

Pratt screwed up his face. "Andrew Hanna. Hanna, where do I know that name from?"

"You know him alright. He was a bright young barrister here in Perth who successfully knocked over some of your prosecutions."

"Yeah, yeah, I remember him now. Cocky young bastard. And you say he is a friend of yours? If I recall correctly, you were the police prosecutor who lost a few of my watertight cases to him; crims who I had banged up for sure, but he got them off. Was he that good, or was it just because you are hopeless at your job?"

Lusty's expression changed to ice at the insult and the sneer on his superior's face. "That's the way the law works detective. You aren't guilty until proven. I lost because the case for the prosecutions you launched weren't strong enough on the occasions I opposed him."

Pratt tried to ignore the stinging riposte. "What did he do wrong to move to a place like Wyndham. Who or what is he running from I wonder? You haven't thought of asking for a posting there yourself, have you? You should give it some thought sergeant. You could continue your cosy arrangement."

"I'm only passing on a message regarding the whereabouts of a wanted felon. It's over to you now."

A thought occurred to Pratt. "Has Hanna ever defended Bonham? How does he know it's him?"

"That had occurred to me detective, but according to the records they've never been in the same courtroom together. And I didn't bother to ask Hanna how he knew Bonham was in town. It just didn't occur to me as being relevant."

Pratt waved his hand in dismissal. "Okay sergeant, I'll handle it from here."

Lusty nodded and turned to open the door when he was interrupted. "Sergeant, this place has too many ears. I don't want Bonham getting a tip-off he's about to be arrested, and doing a disappearing act, so keep this confidential."

Lusty grinned as he closed the door behind him. Pratt was lying when he denied knowing about Bonham and his form. Any senior detective with more than twenty years in the force would be aware of someone with the reputation of Dave Bonham. Like hell was he going to keep it to himself. He was going to have a quiet word with the head of his division, and cover his arse by making a record of the time and date and content of his meeting with Pratt. It was well known Pratt was as trustworthy as a fox in a chook-house.

He would turn on anyone if it suited his purpose, as many a young constable had found out. He realised he should have gone directly to the station chief, but risked being reminded in very strong terms there was a chain of command that had to be adhered to. Pratt was the appropriate starting point.

Pratt cursed silently to himself. He knew full well Lusty would make a note of their meeting. He had to act before Lusty took it higher up. He got up and walked out of the station to his car and drove off to find a quiet spot from which to make a call. He pulled out a private unregistered mobile phone.

"Sergeant Smith please."

"May I ask who's calling and the purpose?"

"Just tell Wally it's his old classmate. He'll know who wants to talk to him." He tapped his fingers on the steering wheel impatiently as he waited.

"Is that who I think it is?"

"Yes Wally, but just get into your wagon and I'll call you back in ten minutes. What's your mobile number?" He could envisage Smith heaving his bulk out of his chair and trying to look casual as he walked past his staff and out of the station.

Pratt glanced at his watch. Fifteen minutes was adequate time for the fat-one to have cleared the station and the listening ears.

"Wally, what the bloody hell is Dave Bonham doing in Wyndham?"

"I didn't know he was still here. I warned him to get out of town."

"Don't give me that horse-shit brother. Nothing moves in that rat-hole without you knowing about it. Why are you shielding him and what's he up to?"

Smith knew there was no point in lying further. "He's managing a cattle station out of town and doing a good job according to reports I hear."

"Well, someone recognised him, and now I'm in the picture. Did you give him the job."

"No, Ike Shulman got it for him, but I arranged it. I thought he was well out of sight."

There was silence for a second as Pratt's mind raced. "I told you to get him a job on that prawn trawler. He would have wound up as prawn food by now if you'd followed instructions. The skipper of that boat is an ex copper who owed me a big one for not pinning complicity in a murder on him."

"Bonham took one look at your mate when he came up from below deck and refused to step aboard. It was obvious he recognised him and was well aware of what was going to happen."

"So you referred him to Ike. What's the name of the person he's working for and the property."

"He's on Venus Downs."

Pratt caught the hesitation. "And the name of the owner?"

"Boyce."

"And the Christian name?"

"Chloe. It's Chloe Boyce."

Smith held the phone away as the explosion of abuse filled the cab. "You're talking about Chloe Boyce, the ex model, aren't you? You fucking numbskull Smith. She doesn't stand a chance if Bonham gets horny. I can't believe you introduced a rapist the likes of Bonham to a single woman, or is she married by now?"

"No, she lives on her own with the station staff, but she does have a boyfriend by the name of Andrew Hanna. He's the local lawyer."

"Bonham will rape and murder her when he gets the inclination. You've taken leave of your senses Wally. The shit will hit the fan when that happens and heads will roll, and one of them will be yours."

"Don't come the heavy with me Reg. You sent him up here, so you must be covering for him. You point the finger at me and both our heads will roll. What did you two have going?"

Pratt did not answer the question. He was the initial contact to engage Bonham as the hit-man to take care of the drug dealer who wasn't keeping up with his payments. In fact, he was becoming a total liability with veiled threats. The prawn boat skipper was the bent copper out to make an easy ten grand by acting as middle man to set up the hit. Only it all went wrong. Bonham shot, but didn't kill the dealer who lived long enough to identify the cop. The charge didn't stick when Pratt stepped in and gave evidence the cop had been with him all evening. The cop never got his ten grand, but was eternally in Pratt's debt. He didn't realise Pratt was not acting as agent, but rather the master-mind of a drug syndicate.

"Listen carefully Wally, I don't know what Shulman's motive is, but it's got to be something sinister. When will you be seeing Bonham next?"

"He comes into town every week for supplies. He should be here again in a couple of days."

"Okay, I'm heading up there tomorrow. We'll arrest him on sight and take him for a little ride in the wilderness after dark."

"You're not pulling me into this Reg. It's your problem. I can only be fingered for incompetence for not recognising Bonham, but you're suggesting something far more serious, and I'm too close to retirement to go through a departmental investigation about the sudden disappearance of someone I'd just arrested."

"Wally you forget I can nail both you and Shulman at any-time of my choosing. You'll both serve time if I should open my mouth about the cattle duffing. I appreciate the payments

I get every month from Ike, but I would like something more in return."

"How the hell did you find out about that?"

"You forget I was the relieving cop who stayed at your house while you were down here having that hernia operation a year or two ago. You really should get yourself a better safe, than a fire-proof filing cabinet. It took me about ten minutes to open it and find your list of assets, and most revealing of all, your bank statements. I can see Ike never let on to you I'd worked out he was your source of all that extra wealth. He buckled very quickly when I showed him some of your paperwork with his name prominently mentioned. Make sure you pick me up off the flight tomorrow."

Smith was left staring at the dead phone. Fuck Pratt, but what was his alternative. The risk was they would be both charged and thrown out of the force if Pratt opened his mouth about the duffing or Bonham. However, the risk now was, that unlike with Tippet, he had an accomplice; a dangerous accomplice to a crime to which he was going to be a party. And what if Pratt then turned the gun on him and then shot Bonham claiming self-defence. He wasn't prepared to take the risk. He made two phone calls. He told Pratt to go to hell and forget about Bonham; he would take care of him and accept the risk.

"Ike, get hold of Bonham and tell him to disappear for a couple of weeks until the dust settles. Hanna tipped off our mutual friend detective Pratt, that Bonham is still around and he's petrified something will happen to Boyce, now he's aware who he's working for. I told him not to worry as I'd take care of it, but you never know, he may just fly in any day and arrest him. In any event, Bonham will have to leave permanently. We'll just have to give him an incentive to go, and soon."

12

hey were both sitting on the veranda as the golden
early morning light with its attendant cacophony of
bird life signified the new day. He had been unable
to sleep. He quietly dressed and made his way out
to the veranda. Chloe was reclining in a squatter's chair with
her head to one side in deep sleep. He sat down quietly, but
she was instantly awake in fright.

"Oh Andrew, you startled me."

"You've been there all night haven't you?"

She nodded. "I just couldn't sleep. I want this day over."

Andrew looked sideways and strained his ears. "I don't
think you'll have long to wait. I can hear a vehicle coming."

It emerged with the trailing cloud of dust, but it was not
Collin's ute, but Smith's Toyota cruiser. They could see Ike
Shulman seated beside him.

Chloe got up to move and go out to meet them. "Don't do that
Chloe. Just stay where you are and let them do the talking."

They watched as Smith rolled out of the cab, hitched his
trousers up over his bulging gut before waddling towards
them with his inward-bent knees straining to support his
weight. Shulman was slightly to one side and behind, content on letting Smith assume authority and command.

Andrew nodded to Smith as he pushed open the screen
door and entered, closely followed by Shulman. They both
sat down without invitation.

"You're out of bed early aren't you sergeant? You must have something urgent on your mind?"

"You're quite the pimp aren't you Hanna?" The look on the policeman's face was menacing.

Andrew looked at him blankly. "And what are you referring to sergeant?"

"Don't give me that bullshit Hanna. It was you who tipped Perth off, but for your information they didn't get him."

"I don't know what or who you're talking about."

"You think you're so bloody smart you could tip Perth off and me not find out about it. Five minutes after you called Lusty, I got a call. By the time detectives arrived he'd already shot through."

Andrew shrugged. "So they went home empty handed, but they will get him one day. Not all coppers are bent sergeant."

Smith ignored the remark as he turned to Chloe. "Where's the country hospitality Ms Boyce? I would like a cup of tea and something to eat. It's been a long trip and we left without having breakfast."

"Well, you'll just have to wait until you get back to town because there's nothing here for you."

Andrew smiled inwardly at Chloe's defiance. She was not about to be intimidated. He had seen Dotti appear at the doorway and quickly disappear when she caught Chloe's comment. "What do you want Mr Shulman. Is the sergeant your bodyguard?"

Ike shrugged. "I'm doing you the courtesy Ms Boyce of informing you I will be buying Venus Downs, Remus Plains, along with Baracool and Ironstone Park in the Pilbara. I want you off the property the moment the contract is signed."

"I'm already well aware of your intentions. There was no need to come out here in the heat and dust to tell me that. You were my father's partner in crime along with the sergeant here. You made a fortune, but it's not enough for you, you want everything."

"You are wrong Ms Boyce. I was not involved with Henry Boyce's activities. I merely acted as agent to sell cattle on his behalf. You haven't a shred of evidence I was involved. The bank is about to foreclose on the properties and I'm a ready buyer. It's as simple as that. The bank wants to sell the whole lot in a single transaction and I'm willing to pay on the fall of the hammer."

"If that's the case why not offer Chloe a good price now and give the bank what it's owed."

"Because that doesn't suit me Mr Hanna. I'm a business man, not a charity. I know the properties are heavily mortgaged and the bank wants to wipe its hands of the liability. As you know, they want to sell in a single line and are not prepared to sell individually."

"And that leaves you as the only person with the deep enough pockets to buy them. You know Ike, there's something that doesn't smell right about all this. I don't know how you've swung it, but somehow I believe you're behind the bank's move."

Shulman laughed. "Banks don't operate with compassion or get into sinister transactions as you are implying. They only deal in money, not conspiracies." He turned to Chloe. "Ms Boyce you have my sympathies, but I cannot let an opportunity like this pass by without acting. I realise you're still suffering the loss of your father. It was common knowledge he was your father, but he never acknowledged you while he was alive. Not only was he guilty of stealing cattle, but he obviously felt guilty about liaising with your mother, a native. He was not a very honourable man, was he?"

Andrew tried to restrain her as she furiously sprang to her feet, but she shook off his arm. "Get off this property

Shulman. You might own it soon, but you don't at the moment, so get off. You were just as guilty as my father and so is this fat swine."

Shulman was unmoved. "Take care Ms Boyce. I've been handling cattle on your behalf since you took over. Therefore, you've been party to the crime you refer to. I've sold at least ten thousand head in that time and Sergeant Smith should be laying charges right now. There's no way Venus Downs could legitimately have run-off that many cattle, so I would shut my mouth if I were you young lady, otherwise you might find yourself in the watch-house. You would have a hard time and it would be a very costly exercise to defend the charges."

Chloe slumped back into her chair defeated as Shulman and Smith stood to leave. "Two weeks is all you've got Ms Boyce so I suggest you start packing. I take it you will be helping her Hanna? You should have played ball lad. You could have wound up being the wealthiest lawyer in these parts."

"And become as crooked as you and your friend here Ike? No thanks."

They silently watched as they drove away. "Why did he do that Andrew? What a cruel and vindictive person he really is."

"He wanted to crush and humiliate you. He doesn't want you opening your mouth."

"He's not going to get away with it. I'm going to get advice if you won't help me."

"Chloe, I said I would help you, but you are wasting your time. You're only going to drag your father and your name into the mud, you would also most certainly get me de-registered as a lawyer. I'm in an indefencible position in that I'm in possession of a document which proves a crime has taken place and is at this moment ongoing, and yet I've not acted upon it. I'd be torn to shreds when they put me on the stand and I was forced to reveal I'd been withholding such a document. I'd be made to look an accomplice by protecting you.

Forget pursuing it further and walk away is my advice. The cost of legal advice is prohibitive. I don't know what you're worth, but reserve what you have to re-establish somewhere else. You could still go back to modelling."

"I'm over that Andrew. I've told you that already, so please don't mention it again."

"Okay, okay I promise I won't, but have you any idea where you're going or what you want to do, because I will be close behind."

Chloe sighed in resignation. "There is something I've got to do before I leave. I want to do it because I'm never coming back once I walk off."

"I hope you're not thinking of getting a gun and shooting those two vermin?"

Chloe laughed at his vain attempt to lighten the situation. "No, I've got to go and talk to Gramps one last time."

Andrew raised an eyebrow, but quickly understood. "Sounds fine. I'll come with you then."

"No, Andrew I must go alone. I just want to be with him."

"I want to make sure you're okay out there. Anything could happen." He cut her off as she was about to protest. "Look Chloe, I won't let you go by yourself. I don't want to know where Gramps is. We can camp somewhere in the vicinity and you can go alone from there. I promise I will not follow you, or ask you anything about it ever again."

She pondered his argument and then nodded. "You're right, I would like the company, but I will hold you to your promise. We'll leave in the morning early. It's a two day ride both there and back. I'll get Dotti to prepare some food and the boys to have a couple of riding and packhorses ready."

It was still dark as they made their way to the stables. The horses were standing outside fully saddled. The jackaroo handed Andrew the reins and gave him a leg-up into the saddle. He then walked around the flank of the other horse and started to talk to Chloe in a hushed tone before she sprang into the saddle without assistance.

"You look worried. What did he tell you?"

Chloe did not answer as she dug in her heels and pulled on the rope tethered to bridle of the packhorse. He followed in silence out through the yards into the first filtering light of dawn. Once in open ground he drew level. "Chloe what did he say to you?"

"He said on his way back from town yesterday he passed the police Toyota heading back. That would have been Smith and Shulman. However, he said the same vehicle had pulled up on its way to the station. He said a person got out and never got back in."

"How the hell would he know that? The road is nothing but bulldust and gravel. You can't even see a tyre track."

"That's what you think. Tommy was born on this station. He's an expert tracker and absolutely reliable. He followed the tracks for a few hundred metres to confirm whose they were. They were heading in the direction of the homestead."

"So who was it?"

"Jim Collins."

"I'm completely confused Chloe. We've got some obscure footprints in the dust, but your man Tommy can positively identify the owner? I find that incredible."

"Believe it Andrew. I've seen them do it many times. They can look at a footprint and tell you who left it and it doesn't matter if the foot has a boot on it or not. In this case it was easy because Tommy was well aware of Jim's bootprint."

"But he didn't turn up. So where is he now if your Tommy is so sure it was Collins?"

"I don't know, but Tommy also said there were two horses missing and the storeroom was unlocked when he went to prepare our horses for us this morning. There was also food missing from the storeroom, and the only persons with keys are Jim and Joey Moonlight and Joey told Tommy it wasn't him."

"So he's got horses and food? But what's he up to?"

"There are a couple of outstations once used for mustering. They're no longer used because it's much quicker and easier with helicopters these days. I think he's heading for one of those and he'll hide out until Shulman takes control. He'll wait until Smith gives the signal the dust has settled and then resume management of Venus Downs. Even if police suspected he was out here, they'd never find him."

"But Tommy knows."

"Yes, but I told him to keep it to himself for now. I said I'd explain everything when I got back in a week or so."

"But we know he's out here. I'll put in another call to my so-called friend John Lusty when we get back."

"Andrew, they didn't catch him this time and they won't catch him next time. You heard Smith say he got tipped off."

"I suppose you're right." He constantly changed position trying to relieve the cramp he was already feeling in his thighs. "Horses are not my style. I'll be walking bow-legged when this is over."

Chloe laughed. "You've got two days of it there and two on the way back. You'll get used to it. We're in no hurry, so if it gets too uncomfortable we can walk."

"Walking's not my style either. I'm used to sitting in one place all day listening to people tell me their problems."

"Well, you can turn around and go back. I'll be fine by myself, but I will miss you."

"That's nice to hear. In that case I'll just have to put up with the pain." They rode along in silence, Andrew fascinated by the timeless land, and the constantly changing hues of the landscape. The chattering parrots and communicating sounds emitted by swirling waves of budgies and flocks of tiny multi-coloured finches held his attention. Then suddenly as if on cue all sounds ceased to be replaced by the raucous call of black crows as they claimed their tenure of the day. The morning had melded into the harsh light of the approaching afternoon.

Chloe walked her horse through a group of gnarled euca-lypt and dismounted by a clear billabong. She stood watching the placid water lost in thought.

"I'm glad we've stopped. I was about to fall off." Andrew held the horse's neck and slid clumsily to one side. "Gawd, my backside's sore. I hope this is as far as we go for the day?"

Chloe did not answer as she kicked off her boots, peeled off her jeans, walked into the water and turned towards him. "Come on in. It's beautiful."

"I will, but I want to see if a croc takes you first." Andrew was laughing as he sat down struggling to take his boots off.

"I thought you said you loved me and now you're worried about a crocodile. You're not my Sir Galahad after all. However, you're safe. There are no crocodiles around here."

He stumbled on a rock as he walked in and was completely off balance when she shoved him backwards. He thrust out his hand and caught the front of her shirt, dragging her down with him as they collapsed in a laughing heap. She was on top of him and held his head under the water as his hands thrashed to gain buoyancy. He came up spluttering and coughing.

"Okay Chloe Boyce, so you want to play dirty." He rose and lunged towards her, but she spun around and effort-lessly stroked away from him.

"Not much of a rider and a hopeless swimmer, aren't you?" She taunted as she rolled on her back and floated with her arms outstretched.

"I can't swim with jeans on."

"Well, take them off you wimp."

Andrew tossed his sodden clothes on the bank and struck out after her. Several times he was within reach, but she would turn and sprint away again further out into the billabong.

"You'll have to do better than that Hanna."

"I can't while I'm distracted by your lovely backside bobbing up and down." He tried to gain momentum while laughing and gasping for breath.

Finally, she let him catch her. "Hold me tight Chloe. I think I'm drowning. I need mouth-to-mouth resuscitation."

"Don't try that on me Andrew Han…." He pulled her head forward and his lips muffled the protest. They milled around lost in the embrace, with neither wanting to break it.

"I do love you Chloe, you know that don't you?"

"Of course I do. You keep telling me. I can also feel that you love me." Her head motioned below the surface as she burst into another peal of taunting laughter.

"Be careful, there are large baramundi in this billabong always looking for a tasty dangling morsel."

His face flushed red as he tried to regain composure. "Stop the bloody laughter. I'm serious. Do you love me? I've got to know."

Chloe stroked the side of his face and put her head on his chest. "Of course I do. I'm starting to feel cold so let's get out before I lose my love for you." She spun around and stroked for the bank.

"Unless I lose my love you I won't be able to make it," he shouted. "I'm dragging the bottom now."

He was still laughing as he staggered up onto the bank and stood over her naked body bathed in the afternoon light. He kneeled down and with one knee thrust her legs apart. She did not resist as he lowered himself to enter her slowly and then withdraw again and again to stimulate and tease. She raised her knees and reached back clutching his buttocks, urging him to increase the rhythm as the orgasms flowed in ceaseless waves. Finally he threw himself sideways, propped himself on an elbow and gazed at her spreadeagled form with arms outstretched. She slowly opened her eyes and looked across at him with a broad smile.

"I do love you Andrew."

"That's what I want to hear. You're beautiful, seductive and very, very promiscuous."

"Why am I seductive and promiscuous?"

"You just seduced me. I had honourable intentions until you enticed me into the water and showed your promiscuous intent."

"You're full of it Andrew." She laughed as she leaned over and threw her arms around him, rolling him onto his back. She lay on him and clutched his head in her hands and kissed him gently. "I couldn't resist the moment Andrew. I didn't have any intention either, but intentions can change in a flash when you realise you love someone, and that's what happened." She leaned back and straddled him as she began a slow grinding movement of her hips. She could feel him responding as she rubbed her excited vulvas back and forth along his engorgement. She cried out as the teasing climaxed and they exploded into one another.

They lay in the grass talking and caressing quietly as the sun faded behind a high bluff on the western edge of the lagoon. Chloe got up, retrieved their wet clothing and spread them over rocks to dry. He watched her, as apparently devoid of inhibitions, she walked around naked oblivious to his devouring gaze and arousal in his loins.

"Why don't we just stay here for a couple of days?"

She walked over and smiled down at him. "No chance. We've lost half a day already so we'll camp here the night. Now you gather some wood and start a fire while I look to the horses and see what Dotti has packed for us. I'm really hungry."

After the meal they sat staring into the dying embers. The night was empty of sound, but faintly lit by a canopy of millions of tiny bright lights.

"Magnificent, isn't it?"

"They're all Gramps mob. Every one of them is part of the dreaming. They will shine in the heavens forever."

Andrew nodded. "Yes, I believe they will. It's absolutely timeless and beautiful out here. Possessions mean nothing. The real world is so far away."

"This is the real world Andrew. Gramps people have lived in this land for millenniums without wealth, possessions and completely unclad to roam free at will."

"Don't you count yourself as one of Gramps mob?"

"I can't claim that. My father was white, my mother a mixed-blood aboriginal. I respect Gramps beliefs and what he taught me, but I'm too removed to immerse myself in the lore of his secret traditions and ceremonies."

"Henry never acknowledged you while he was alive. Why do you think he did that?"

"I've constantly thought about it and can only conclude he was ashamed of me. That's probably not correct. He was not ashamed of me, as he always protected me. I think he was ashamed of himself. I was the result of an affair while he was still married. I find it very strange, but there's nothing much I can do about it, or blame my father for. Everyone has their weak points and when you look at it in the hard light of day he was weak in not recognising me as his daughter until his death, and he was weak in that he got involved in cattle theft."

"Perhaps you're being too hard on him Chloe. He may have loved your mother, but there may have been a barrier that could not be overcome. We simply don't know the circumstances and never will."

"Dotti has told me since my mother had been promised to an older man who she rejected. She was apparently a very beautiful young woman who wanted to break away from her family group where one person's possessions belong to everyone. Henry was threatened by a group related to the older man so he broke it off. I was born soon after and my mother took to the drink and died an alcoholic. Henry managed to rescue me from a certain life of degradation, by having Gramps claim me as his granddaughter and adopting me. But that doesn't explain resorting to crime."

"Chloe, once again you don't know the circumstances. Life's tough when droughts hit and beef prices are low. Desperate men do desperate things. Maybe Henry was right up against it and it was either steal cattle or go bankrupt and walk off. I would imagine once in bed with the likes of Shulman there would be no way out. No use threatening Ike's money tree by announcing the drought had broken, prices were good and he no longer wanted to be party to the crime. Ike wanted the tree to keep blooming and produce and endless harvest of money, the source for which couldn't be laid at his feet."

"You really think that's how it happened?"

"I've got my suspicions. Hargraves said there was another person involved besides Henry and Ike, but didn't know his identity. He had asked Ike and Henry on many occasions, but they wouldn't tell him and that person hasn't surfaced since."

"What about Henry's share? Surely, I'm not still receiving that? I've got to stop it immediately if it's going into my account."

Andrew shook his head. "I was wondering when you would come to that. I saw from Carter's accounts you're still receiving more money from sales of cattle Venus Downs cannot possibly be supporting. It puzzled me at first. Why Ike didn't grab your share when Henry died? You would never have been any the wiser to the arrangement, but I'll give it to Ike, he's smart. He had to maintain you as an unknowing party to the crime. To cut you off would signify you knew nothing about it and that would be your defence if it was ever discovered. He's about to gain control and is relying on the fact you won't go to the police. It would involve you in time and money defending any actions the police would surely investigate and bring against you. Your hands are tied, and I advise you to forget about Ike Shulman. You'll just have to forget you've lost Venus Downs and the rest of your inheritance and just get on with life. I'll start another practice in some other town. We'll do okay."

"He makes my blood boil thinking about it. You said there was a fourth person involved. Is there any way of finding out who it is? I take it you're not referring to Smith?"

"No, I think Smith is a minor player. Hargraves and Henry are both dead, so that only leaves Ike and he's not going to confirm anything. All the cattle are sold through Ike as agent. Hargraves alluded to a fourth person being involved, but never found out who it was, nor was he interested. Ike is the only person who would know, but I'll bet he's got some incriminating hold over him. And yes, I can see it from your expression, but I can confirm Carter is a crook. He's been siphoning off excessive fees from Henry's accounts for a number of years. I didn't have time to really go over them, but I guarantee Henry was not getting his full share of the proceeds. Henry was just too trusting and too busy to ever pay too much attention while everything appeared to be going well."

They sat silently staring vacantly at the dying embers, each lost in their own thoughts. Chloe suddenly broke out of her trance, stood up and brushed down her jeans.

"Time for sleep. Are you joining me?" She rolled out the double swag and they both climbed in fully clothed. Within minutes they were asleep.

As if on cue they awoke to the faint light of dawn. Within minutes he had the fire going and the billy perched on a rock beside it. Soon Chloe had bacon and eggs frying in a large iron pan. Next a loaf of Dotti's damper appeared and a couple of pieces were sliced off and coated with butter. She took the pan off the stove, sat it down between them on a large rock, and handed Andrew a knife and fork.

"What no plates?"

"Why carry gear you don't need? Less to wash up this way."

"I thought we'd be travelling rough, but this is luxury." He filled his mouth and hunger. They wiped the pan clean with damper and sat back, each with a mug of tea.

"You do the dishes and I'll pack up and saddle the horses."

Andrew tipped the remainder of the tea over the coals and went down to the lagoon with the pan and utensils. He watched fascinated as tiny fish darted to the surface to dine on the scraps.

"Come on Andrew. We've got to get going." He handed her the pan which she shoved into a packsaddle, secured it with two leather buckled straps and patted the animal on the withers before turning and effortlessly mounting her mare. She was already moving as Andrew put his foot into the stirrup and clumsily swung up into the saddle. He winced as his legs spread astride and he felt the pain in his thighs, back and buttocks.

"You'll get used to it in a day or so. You're a real softy." She gave him a mocking laugh as she turned in the saddle noticing his discomfort. "We'll stop for a short rest at midday, but other than that I want to keep moving."

"You mean we won't be having a swim and a leisurely lunch? I think we should do it every day."

She ignored his remark and remained silent as the horses plodded along until after what seemed an eternity to Andrew, they pulled up at a small spring-fed water hole overhung with a large bloodwood. He dismounted and lay down in the long grass to ease the pain.

"What! Aren't you coming for a swim?" Chloe taunted him as she stripped off and dived in. Andrew did not move as he closed his eyes and prayed for relief. It was as though moments later she was standing over him fully dressed. "Up you get cowboy. You can't stay here all day."

He moaned and rolled on his side. "We did yesterday. My backside will never recover from this. I'm never going to get on a horse again." He stood up and slowly remounted.

It was late in the afternoon when Chloe finally pulled up at a stream slowly running from within a sandstone formation with stunted mulga bush on either side.

"Don't think much of this place, but the water's deep enough I suppose to sit in and get some relief for my backside and back."

"We're lucky it's running. I was worried, because it's not a permanent stream." She swung down and walked forward to tether the reins to a branch, when she stopped and glanced down with a curious look which he noticed.

"What have you seen?"

"Someone else has been here recently. See that hoof mark. It's not from a wild brumby as I can see it's been shod and there's a boot mark where someone has hopped a couple of times as he tried to mount while the horse was moving."

"I can't see what you're looking at." He searched for an outline within the disturbed sand, until he recognised what she was pointing out.

Chloe slowly walked towards the creek bank before stopping and kicking a pile of sand to expose blackened coals. "And here's his campfire."

"How long ago?"

She leaned down and put a hand on the remains. They were cold. "A day or so at the most."

"Are you thinking what I'm thinking?"

Chloe nodded. "Yes, I think it could be Collins. It certainly isn't anyone else from the station. We'll have to be careful. There are two outstations about thirty kilometres apart. One has been there for more than fifty years and the other is a couple of abandoned shipping containers put there more recently by an exploration company."

"So which one are we heading for?"

"The oldest one. You unpack and start a fire while I go for a walk around and try to find out which one he's heading for. There's sure to be a track somewhere."

Andrew was sitting under a mulga with his back propped up by the bulk of the swag watching her as she moved around in expanding circles until she stopped about two hundred metres away across a barren gibber-strewn plain. She walked straight ahead for about a hundred metres before turning and heading back.

"You found something?"

"Yes, I came across a soft patch of sand. It would appear he's headed for the containers, but he could easily change direction. Unless we follow him I can't be sure where he's heading, but I've no intention of doing that. We don't want to run into Jim Collins under any circumstances. However, we'll be safe here for the night as he'll be a long way in front."

He could see she was worried as she silently prepared a meal of cold corned beef, sliced tomato, onion and a slice of Dotti's damper. "You're on a Jenny Craig menu." She indicated with a feigned laugh.

"Have you considered turning back Chloe? We may be riding into a whole lot of trouble by continuing."

"It's been on my mind, but once I'm off Venus Downs I won't be able to return. Shulman wouldn't let me near the place and I wouldn't dare with Collins in the homestead. No, I've already told Gramps I'm coming and I don't want to let him down. I'll never come out to this place again, so Collins or no Collins I'm not turning back. You can if you want to."

"You know I can't do that," Andrew protested. "I'm glued to you no matter what happens."

Chloe could see there was no point in arguing further. "Okay, it's off at first light again. We should get to the old outstation by late afternoon."

It was a slow trek picking their way along dry watercourses, across barren plains covered with patches of spinifex and native grasses and around timeless weather-worn formations exposed to the ceaseless elements of attrition.

"That clump of trees is where we're headed. They surround a permanent spring." Chloe pointed at the vegetation a couple of kilometres ahead.

"Good, I was feeling like the kid in the backseat of the car, asking are we there yet?"

"How's your bum?"

"Don't ask. It'll never be the same again."

Chloe laughed as she guided them through the trees, past a small clear billabong and up onto a slight rise. "We've arrived." They pulled up in front of a small rough-hewn timber shack with an enclosed post and rail yard beside it.

"This is a nice setting." Andrew slid down from his horse, holding onto the saddle for support as he looked around.

"It maybe a nice setting, but it's not a nice place. It gives me the shudders just being here. This is where Walter murdered Dion Murphy."

"And then he tried to murder you, but you got in first?"

"No, I've already told you, the rainbow serpent did that."

"And you couldn't come clean with the cops because that would have led them to the sacred site you swore to Gramps you would never reveal?"

"That's correct."

"But it's somewhere close to here, isn't it?"

"I'm not going to answer that Andrew. I'm not going there tomorrow, so it's of no relevance."

"I still want to come with you. In fact I'm not going to let you go without me. I'll stay a safe distance away so as not to disturb you, but I want you within earshot."

Chloe smiled and nodded. "I can see you're worried about me, and yes, I'm petrified of running into Collins."

"Are we going to stay here tonight?"

"No, we'll camp down by the water. We'll take the horses down and unload them, then I'll bring them back up here and put them in the yard for the night."

Andrew handed her the reins. "I'll walk down thank you. I've had enough riding for one day." He followed her down holding a painful thigh while trying to straighten his tortured back and wondering whether his legs would ever come together again.

Chloe had already unloaded the contents of a pack when he arrived. "You start a fire. There are baked beans, corned beef, tinned potatoes and corn cakes Dotti prepared. You take your pick and surprise me with your culinary skills, but I expect it to be fine dining on par with top London restaurant standards to which I became accustomed."

"Yes madam, you can expect the full silver service laid out on a fine linen cloth complete with candelabra and crystal glasses. Of course it will be served in a communal frying pan as usual. Would you like toast on the side with that?"

He could hear her laughing as she kicked her horse into a fast canter while dragging the others behind her. He busied himself with the fire and preparation of the meal, while pondering what had brought about the complete change of disposition. She had been quiet and withdrawn all day, hardly exchanging a word, but now it was the usual Chloe striding back down the hill with a beaming smile.

"Why are you so cheerful? You look like the cat that swallowed the canary."

"I'm happy because you're here with me. That's a good enough explanation, isn't it?" She leaned down and kissed him and then put her arms around his neck. "I do love you so much."

"Will you marry me then?"

"You know the answer to that, but isn't there a slight impediment to that at the moment?"

He reached up and held her arms. "Well, I'll just have to locate a certain Marcel Faroud and serve him with divorce papers. In the meantime we'll live together."

"I want children Andrew."

"That shouldn't present too much of a problem, but you realise of course we'll have to get in a bit more practice?"

She laughed, squeezing him tighter and kissing him on the neck. "Come on, what have you prepared? I need food to make love."

After they finished they leaned back supported by the rolled up swag and gazed into the fire. Andrew put his arm around her shoulders and pulled her towards him.

"I know what you're thinking Andrew."

"You do?"

"You're thinking I should retrieve a couple of red diamonds and pay the bank out, aren't you? You're wondering why I'm being so stupid?"

"It had occurred to me."

"You know the answer to that, so put it out of your mind."

"I won't mention it again then."

She nestled up to him and gently stroked the side of his face. "I know you're only trying to help me, but money doesn't concern me. I've got enough and I've got my London house on the market. Although I'm going to really miss this place and it will be forever in my thoughts, I'm not interested in selling my soul to retain it."

"Shall we make love then?"

13

*C*hloe awoke and listened to Andrew's heavy breathing. He was sleeping with the god's as she gently eased herself out all the while listening for any break in his rhythmic pattern. She picked up her clothes and boots and walked slowly away trying to step over any twigs or stones that would signify her intent to the sleeping form. She grinned at the thought of Gramps along with whole of the dreaming watching the naked nymph bathed in bright moonlight as she silently dressed. Ten minutes later she was quietly stroking the nose of her horse as she slipped the bridle over its head, saddled it and led it out of the yard. She mounted and gently dug the animal in the flanks to set it on a steady walk. A kilometre away and well out of earshot she set it into a steady canter. It was cool and the horse appeared to enjoy the increased exercise after the slow walking pace of the past few days. As they approached a broad barren plain it started pulling on the reins so she let it have its head as it broke into a gallop, before tiring minutes later and dropping back to a steady canter. The morning was cool and as she rode steadily east she saw the streaks of light which signified the bursting ball of fire she was riding into.

It was an hour later when she finally approached the base of the jagged bluff. She tethered her horse under the sparse cover of a tortured mulga bush and began to slowly climb, picking her way through the rocks, holding on and pulling herself up step by step. It was steeper than she remembered, but the memories were still painful. They would never be erased. Finally, she looked up to see the particular boulder and stepped around it. The cairn of stones was undisturbed and exactly as she had left it. She picked up a large stone and gently placed it on top, adding it to the pyramid structure. A sudden anabatic wind crested the edge of the slope, throwing up a swirling willy willy of dust which subsided as quickly as it had formed. She smiled and sitting down on a rock, looked to the south-east in the direction of the rainbow serpent. She felt depressed and yet elated; depressed she was losing what was hers and elated the location of the sacred site remained hidden forever. Finally, she got up and stood in front of the cairn.

"Goodbye Gramps. I will not be coming out here again." She turned and slowly picked her way down the slope. Her horse instinctively turned and began to retrace its steps as she swung into the saddle. It was late afternoon when her mare suddenly pricked its ears and looked to the north-west. She scoured the horizon, but at first could see nothing, until looking further to the west she could make out a moving object within the haze. She stopped, wiped the sweat out of her eyes and reduced them to mere slits to concentrate the aperture and field of vision. The figure rode up onto a ridge and then slowly began to descend the other side, before disappearing. The shock hit her. It was someone on a horse leading another horse. She realised instantly who it could be. Collins had probably decided the northern most out-station was uninhabitable or unsuitable and had decided to look at the old camp, which was directly where he was headed. Chloe could see he was too far ahead for her to swing around to the south to flank him and warn Andrew they had an unwelcome visitor. The horse would die under her if she tried in this heat. She felt sick in the stomach at the trick she had played on him. What was the point in not taking him with her? She was never going there again and he would have no motive to do so or reveal its location, so why did she do it? What would Collins do when he rode up to find Andrew? She shuddered at the thought as she prodded her mount into a steady canter.

It was an hour later when she she stopped, tethered her horse and picked her way through the scrub until she could see the shack. She stood there for some minutes watching for any movement before slowly walking towards it, expecting at any moment to be challenged by Collins. The horses were still in the yard, so Andrew was still there, but there was no sign of Collins. The horses whinnied as she approached and slowly walked around the side of the shack and glanced inside. It was empty.

She turned, looked down the slope and gasped in shock. Collins was standing over the prone form of Andrew, who was no match for the hard physical stature of his aggressor. She watched horrified as Collins shouted something at him and he began to groggily rise to his feet. He was almost upright when Collins stepped forward and with one powerful blow sank his fist into Andrew's stomach. He casually raised the rifle hanging loosely in his left hand and fired a shot into the ground near the sprawled retching figure, before breaking into a peel of laughter. Chloe stifled a cry as she watched Andrew once again begin to rise to his feet only to be flattened with a blow to the side of the head.

Chloe edged around the side of the shack and into the debris-strewn interior. She stood up onto the frame of the windowless opening on the opposite side of the room and reaching up, felt around until her hand locked onto what was concealed. She pulled it down and checked it. Satisfied, she slowly walked out and began to descend the slope, hiding behind rocky outcrops and stunted trees. She was shaking with fear as she approached. Collins had propped his rifle against a rock and was sitting under the shade of a tree with his back to her. Andrew was a few metres in front of him moaning quietly and posing no threat.

The fear disappeared in a second. A sheet of cold hatred descended as she stepped into the open. Collins caught the sound of movement and looked around, breaking into a sneer of recognition while getting to his feet. Her eyes gave her away. He could see the fear although her hands were rock steady.

"What do you think you're doing Chloe? Come to rescue lover boy have you? He wouldn't tell me where you were, but I figured you'd turn up before dark." He made a deliberate unhurried move towards his rifle and picking it up began to turn. "Now I can take care of both of you."

The bullet caught him in the kneecap, blasting it into a shower of shattered bone and blood. He screamed in pain as he rolled backwards clutching his leg while trying to staunch the arterial flow. Chloe ejected the spent casing from the ancient Martini Henry while trying to stop her hands from shaking at the realisation of what she had done. She inserted another bullet and snapped the lever-action breach shut. She was not taking any chances although she could see Collins was no longer a threat. She picked up his rifle and cast it further out of his reach.

"For Christ's sake, help me. I'm bleeding to death you black bitch." The obscenities flowed from the man's tormented mouth as he rolled around cursing between bursts of ever increasing pain as the shock set in.

Chloe stood her ground. It was too dangerous to go closer or to offer any help. She realised the man could die, but there was nothing she could do about it. She knelt down beside Andrew who had raised himself on one elbow.

"Talk about arrival of the cavalry. You were just in time." He groaned between laboured gasps.

"Has he broken anything?"

"No, I don't think so, but he's sure put in a few dents where I don't need them. Where did you get that rifle?"

Chloe ignored the question as she put it down and helped him to a sitting position with his back to a water-smoothed boulder.

"Did you mean to do that? You've made a real mess of him by the look of it."

"Yes I did, but I didn't know where I was aiming. I just pulled the trigger. You didn't really think he was going to let us get out of here alive did you?"

They watched as Collins tore off his shirt and ripped it into strips as the blood continued to flow with each pump of his heart. He wrapped them tightly around his thigh before falling backwards in a dead faint.

"He may die if we don't help him."

"I'm not going near him," Chloe replied.

Andrew pushed himself to his feet and walked over to the unconscious figure. He looked at the shattered knee and rebound the tourniquet's until he was satisfied the flow had been stemmed.

"He's in a bad way. We've got to pack up and get out of here now. You go get the horses."

Half an hour later they were ready to move. Collins had come around, but all colour and agression had drained from his face as they helped him onto his horse.

"Just hang on and I'll lead you."

Collins snarled and jerked the reins out of Andrew's hand. He made to dig his heels into the horse's flank. A tortured cry was strangled in his throat as he attempted to flex the wounded leg. They rode all night lit by the half-tone of a full moon. Three figures riding in complete silence except for the steady tread of horses sure of their direction.

Andrew riding alongside, had been watching Collins' drift in and out of consciousness as the bouts of nausea and pain swept over him. He was waiting for him to fall, but every time he was on the brink of it, he would stiffen and ignore Andrew's outstretched steadying hand.

"I think we'd better stop and take a break Chloe. You boil the billy and I'll have a look at his leg."

Collins did not resist as he rolled sideways into Andrew's outstretched arms. Collins was bordering on the unconscious as he sat him down and propped him into a sitting position with the aid of a rolled swag. He looked at the leg and pulled a wry face which did not escape Chloe.

"Is he that bad?" She was stirring beans and bacon in the large pan having already ripped the last of Dotti's loaf into portions.

"Here, put some of that into this." Andrew held out a pannikin. "He's worse than bad. He's lost too much blood and what's left of that knee is going to turn real ugly unless we get him medical help."

Andrew turned to Collins and spooned the food into his mouth as he chewed ravenously with closed eyes. He felt Andrew nudge his arm with the mug and taking it, swallowed the mixture of tea and sweetened condensed milk before dropping his arm and letting the mug fall from his grasp.

"He won't give us any more grief." Andrew sat down beside Chloe and picked at the food.

"I should have killed him," she murmured. "He was going to kill us. You're a very compassionate man Andrew."

"Tell me. Where did you get that rifle?"

"It was Walter's. He was going to murder me with it. After he died, I took it because I thought I would be in real danger if I ran into Murphy, but he was dead when I got back to the shack. I was going to throw it away, but decided to hide it in the rafters. Thank God I did, otherwise things would have turned out differently."

Andrew threw the remainder of his tea into the fire. "I think it would be wise to bury it now, and for good. I don't want you answering difficult questions as to how a bullet taken out of the spine of a dead geologist matches the bore of a rifle now in your possession. I know you are innocent of the murder, but you would have a lot of explaining to do."

"But what if the police do question me?"

"They don't have the bullet that shattered Collins' knee, so they can't match it to your gun and will have to accept your version of what you shot him with. Of course they'll ask, but you can easily say you managed to get hold of Collins' weapon. It will be your word against that of a criminal so I wouldn't be at all worried. I'll confirm what took place."

They sat watching Collins as he moaned in pain and drifted in and out of reality. Andrew looked up at the moon and got to his feet. "Come on. There's no point in wasting time. He'll die on us if we don't get him help."

Collins was delirious as they came in sight of the homestead late in the afternoon. Andrew had been riding beside him holding him by the arm to make sure he did not fall from the saddle.

"Dotti." Chloe yelled as the old woman appeared out of the homestead. "Phone the hospital and ask them to send an ambulance. It's an emergency."

Andrew pulled Collins from his horse and lay him on the ground. He was comatose. A jackaroo came running up. "Joey, get a ute and fill the tray with hay. It won't be a comfortable, but I don't think he'll feel a thing. He's certainly in no condition to ride in the cab. I'll meet the ambulance on the road. It will save time."

Ten minutes later Joey Moonlight and a couple of jackaroos helped lift Collins onto the tray and lay him down on the thick layer of hay. "Don't like the look of that boss." Joey was looking at the blood encrusted mess. "How did it happen?"

Andrew, ignored the stockman's question as he climbed into the cab.

"I'm coming with you."

Andrew pulled her aside out of earshot. "Chloe, that wouldn't be wise. I think you should stay here and let me handle it. I'll save time by meeting the ambulance on its way out. Then I can follow it back to the hospital to get an idea of his condition. If he dies, and he may well do looking at him now, you're going to be subject of some hard questioning and you certainly don't want to run into Smith just yet."

"But I'm responsible. I shot him."

"Chloe don't bloody argue with me," he snapped. "I'm your lawyer and I'm strongly advising you to not make any admissions before I've had time to think about this mess. Smith will be itching to slap a charge on you. Just don't rush into his arms and let him dream up a charge of attempted murder or the like. At present you feel guilty and responsible and you're vulnerable. Do as I ask and stay here. And for God's sake don't talk to Dotti or any of the staff about what happened, because whatever you tell them may come out in court and be unwittingly used against you."

Chloe nodded and stepped away from the moving vehicle. She watched helplessly as it disappeared into the darkness.

He drove as fast as he dared, conscious of roos suddenly appearing in his lights. Three hours later he saw a faint light coming towards him. He let out a sigh of relief as the light slowly separated into twin beams with flashing lights either side and on the roof. He pulled over and waited for the ambulance to come alongside. One medic swung open the rear doors while the other followed Andrew into the tray of the ute. He tested for vital signs before turning to the leg and whistling softly.

"This is bad. His blood pressure is low and that leg looks necrotic. Give me a hand to lift him onto the gurney. Don't worry about being gentle, he's out to it."

Within minutes the ambulance had turned and sped off with Andrew following close behind. He felt exhausted from holding Collins on his horse for near twentyfour hours. His mind was confused and blank. He needed a long rest and time to think.

The ambulance pulled into the hospital. The emergency doors opened as the medics dragged out the gurney and rushed it inside. Andrew was close behind and watched as the doctor stood over Collins with a stethoscope applied to his chest. He pulled the instrument out of his ears and studied the leg before standing back and screwing up his face as the odour struck him. Andrew recognised him, but now was not the time or place.

"Twelve hours on duty and now this." It was a weary, but concerned comment. "Just my bloody luck. Why wasn't this man brought in earlier? Where's he been?"

"I've been riding with him for nearly two days." Andrew stepped forward, but the doctor did not recognise the exhausted, disheveled, unshaven individual with the blood-shot eyes of exhaustion.

"How did he get this injury?"

"It's a gunshot wound."

The doctor nodded as he shook his head with a pained expression. "The leg's got to come off, but first I've got to stabilise him. I'll see what I can do, but I don't like his chances. If he gets through the night, I'll have him flown out to Perth in the morning. I just don't have the facilities to handle this."

"I might stick around and wait."

"You're welcome to do so, but I would advise you to go and get some sleep. You look a lot worse than I feel."

Andrew slumped onto a hard bench, before accepting the futility of his vigil. He walked out and drove into town.

"Hi there Mr Hanna, I heard you left town." Marge Tilley was wiping down the top of the deserted bar. "What brings you back? You just couldn't stay away from the bright lights of a big city could you?" She let out a raucous laugh, the hilarity of which drew a blank look. "What would you like to drink?"

"Two double scotches and a bed for the night."

Marge poured the scotch into one long glass and watched him finish half of it without stopping. "My God, where have you been lad? You look real beat up and you don't smell too good either from where I'm standing. I'll get you a key."

She re-appeared from her office and handed him a key which he glanced at and walked out with a nod of thanks. He trudged up the stairs, opened the door of his room and began to kick off his boots as he sat on the edge of the bed. He rolled backwards into oblivion. He was awoken by someone shouting at him and shaking his shoulder. Smith was standing looking down at him. It was broad daylight.

"Who shot Collins?"

"It was an accident." Andrew sat up rubbing his eyes. "Look sergeant I'm in no mood to face your inquisition now. I stink of horses and myself, so I'm going for a shower, breakfast and then out to buy a change of clothes. After that I'm all yours."

"That's not good enough Hanna. I want answers now." Smith took a step back repelled by the odour.

"Listen sergeant, if you're going to arrest me then do so and I'll immediately reserve my rights to remain silent and ignore your demands. If on the other hand you want a full explanation to assist you with your enquiries, I suggest you toddle off and I'll be ready in a couple of hours."

Smith made no reply as he swung on his heel and stormed out leaving the door open.

"Gawd, you were a mess when you came in last night boy. You feeling any better now? What would you like for breakfast or rather an early lunch?"

"Bacon, eggs and anything else your cook can stack on the plate thanks Marge. I've showered, but I'll have to remain in these clothes as I didn't bring any money with me. Is my credit good for a couple of days?"

"Go look in the storeroom for clothes. Plenty in there that'll fit you. Travellers, salesmen, geologists are always leaving stuff behind. You're welcome to take what you want."

"Thanks Marge. I'll do that."

The waitress emerged from the kitchen and gave a startled look as Marge took the plate of food off her and crossed the room to set it down in front of him.

"Apparently Collins is at death's door. Who shot him?"

"News travels fast in this town Marge." Andrew stuffed in a mouthful of food, not caring the bacon was overcooked and the eggs hard. It was food.

"Rumour is that you shot him and waited a couple of days before you brought him in. Is that true?"

"Who's been spreading that rumour? It wasn't sergeant Smith by any chance?"

"Oh, I can't tell you that, but I do know a couple of staff at the hospital. All I know is you took him in last night with half his leg blown off. Last I heard he's still alive, but only just."

"Did they remove his leg?"

Marge shook her head. "Doc wouldn't do it. Said Collins would die on the operating table if he did, so he's handed the problem to Perth. They're trying to stabilise him first, but Wally reckons he won't make it. He's got you labeled as the shooter. Mind you, from what I've been told about Collins, he's no clean potato. Would you know about that?"

"Not a thing Marge." Andrew finished his meal, wiped his mouth with a napkin and stood up. "It's all news to me and anyway, I don't like spreading rumours. Thanks for the offer of the clothes, but I must be going."

Marge was affronted by the sudden departure. She was just settling in for a session of traded gossip. The waitress tried to stifle a knowing grin as she came across and picked up the empty plate. Radio Tilley would have no hot gossip to add to her broadcast that day. The nosey old bat did not like being rebuffed.

Andrew got into the vehicle and sat there listening to the steady rattle of the diesel. He'd told Smith he would see him when he was ready, but decided he was not ready as he swung across the street and headed out. He grinned maliciously as he thought of Smith sitting in his office with his concealed voice activated recorder and all his questions prepared, fuming as the non-appearance of his witness dragged on.

Smith answered his direct line. He knew who was calling. "What did Hanna have to say for himself?"

"He claimed it was an accident, but I don't believe it. I'm waiting for him to come in so I can take a full statement."

"No point in waiting any longer Wally. I just saw him drive out of town."

Smith slammed his fist on the desk. "If that smart bastard thinks he can play me for a fool, he'd better think again."

"Did Hanna actually say how the accident occurred."

"No, and I don't believe it was an accident. I can't imagine Collins being so careless as to shoot himself. Shit, I'm not looking forward to driving all that way out there tomorrow to question Hanna."

"Leave it until you see what happens to Collins. If Collins dies, the problems solved. Don't be in a hurry."

Smith drummed his fat fingers on his desk. "I can't believe Collins picked a fight. I told him to make himself scarce for a few weeks until you called him back to run Venus Downs. Why didn't he just stay clear?"

"Wally, I think you'll find Collins was very jealous of Hanna. She's one striking woman that Chloe Boyce. Maybe Collins thought he could eventually win her over. You ran the real risk of him raping her and have you ever thought about the consequences if that happened. You knew he's a wanted rapist and yet you got him the job. I would say that's perverting the course of justice, wouldn't you?"

"Don't hand me that shit Ike." Smith was trying to control the anger in his voice. "I thought we were partners, or are you suddenly changing the rules of the game?"

"There you go again Wally. Just calm down before you have a stroke."

"It's okay for you Ike, but it's me that'll carry the can and get booted out of the force. I'll lose my pension. You can deny all knowledge and leave me completely exposed."

"I've got a solution for you Wally."

"Yeah, what's that? It had better be good because it's compulsory to report all gun-shot wounds and I've got to do it before the hospital beats me to it. If I don't I'll have Homicide in Perth wanting to know why. And those boys can get very nasty"

"Wally, I sometimes wonder about you. I'll bet money Hanna didn't say who shot Collins. He just arrived at the hospital with a patient suffering a gunshot wound. The quack isn't interested in who shot him?"

"So?"

"So you file a report after interviewing the doctor today as to what was said when Collins was admitted. If he confirms my suspicions, you then file a report stating it was self-inflicted; a shooting accident. If Collins dies your report stands and it will end there."

Smith sneered. "You've missed the obvious Ike. If Collins survives and thinks he can hit back at Hanna by pointing the finger, I'm still in the shit. At any investigation Hanna would surely reveal my connection with Collins and tip a bucket on what's been going on around here for years. We'd all be dead meat."

"I've told you what to do. File your report as being a supposed accidental gunshot wound."

"What if Hanna decides to open his mouth?"

"I don't think for a moment he'll say a word. He doesn't have to unless you try to shake him down for a statement. Then it's all going to be on paper and on file. As much as you despise Hanna for what he knows and what he's apparently just done to Collins, I wouldn't mount a personal vendetta. It might blow up in your face, so I would leave well alone."

"They were going to move Collins to Perth this morning, that's if he's still breathing. I'll check whether they've done so. It's out of my hands and jurisdiction if Perth detectives

get interested and start asking him some awkward questions. They'll very quickly establish who he is and what he's
wanted for. And if he mentions me in connection with you
getting him the job with Boyce, my goose is cooked."

"No, Collins won't drop you in it even if they do arrest him.
He's due for his share of a big payout from the last three
months of cattle sales. He won't jeopardise that by opening
his yap."

"Yeah, I suppose you're right. I'll go out to the hospital now
and have a word with the doctor. Hanna, or even Collins in
his delirium might have told him how the wound occurred,
so I want to get my story straight before I file anything."

He put the phone down and sat back running his hand
through his greasy hair. He was sweating, but he felt cold
with dread. It was okay for Shulman to be so calm, but he
was not going to be in the direct firing line. He would take
the bastard down with him if anything happened. He had
enough evidence to connect the dots to all the participants.

"Be back in an hour or so," he muttered to Briggs as he
walked past. The constable grunted, but did not look up until
Smith had his back to him and was walking out the door.
News and gossip travelled by mental telepathy in this town.
The fat prick did not look comfortable and Briggs knew the
reason. He knew who Collins was and what he was wanted
for. Smith would be in for early retirement if he ever bothered
to post that evidence along with an explanation of Tippet's
disappearance in an anonymous letter to Internal Affairs. He
determined he was going to do it one day to avenge Tippet's
killing and the injuries he had suffered at Smith's hands,
but not just at the moment. The justification being Tippet
should have known better than open his mouth. Unbeknown
to the sergeant, Shulman was giving him a handy sling every
month to keep him informed of what Smith was up to and

who was under investigation. After all, the police station was the nerve centre of town, so why not cash in on selling information to someone who could well afford to pay? Smith was selling his soul, so why should he not also be in the queue for a handout?

Smith pulled up in front of the hospital. The smell of antiseptic and the squeak of polished linoleum under his boots was the only sound as he moved towards the desk.

"The doc who's looking after Collins. Is he in?"

The nurse was about to answer when a tired and harassed looking individual in shirtsleeves appeared from a doorway.

"I'm doctor Gibson. What can I do for your sergeant?"

Smith looked him up and down. "You operated on Collins? Where's Tim Barrett, I thought he was the senior surgeon?"

"Doctor Barrett is on leave for a week." Gibson fixed Smith with weary eyes. He was not going to be browbeaten by this demanding, overweight individual standing in front of him with the pretence of an air of authority. His initial diagnosis was he was a prime candidate for diabetes, if he was not so already, or he would next be treating him for cardiac infarction. He gave him two years at the most.

"I want to know how Collins is?"

"Collins died early this morning of a cerebral embolism. I was going to remove his leg, but it would have been pointless. It was already too late when he was admitted."

"Did he say how the injury occurred?"

"He was unconscious sergeant. It was clearly the result of a gun shot. The knee was non-existent with just skin and bone fragments holding everything together. Two days without treatment for such a massive injury is just too long for the system to endure. I've already prepared my report and forwarded it."

"Did Andrew Hanna, the person who brought him in say anything?"

"I had no time to talk to Mr Hanna, nor did he say anything to me."

"What did you say in your report doctor?"

Gibson gave him a puzzled look. "I said it was a gunshot wound. What more could I say? The patient wasn't in any condition to tell me how it happened and it was not relevant to my position as a doctor. I'm not a policeman."

"But it could have been an accident, self-inflicted. That's not uncommon is it?"

"No, its not sergeant."

"Good, well that's the way I'll record it." Smith felt a tide of relief. An accident. A self-inflicted gunshot wound would close the file. However, he still wanted to interview Hanna to ascertain what really happened. If Hanna admitted to pulling the trigger, he could resurrect a charge of attempted murder or manslaughter if he thought Hanna was going to be a threat. That should encourage him to keep quiet.

"Will that be all, as I'm extremely busy?" The look of annoyance was clearly visible.

"Nothing more thank you doctor. I'll take it from here."

Gibson watched for a few seconds at the departing policeman. He could have sworn the policeman had tried to stifle a smile when he told him the patient had deceased.

Smith climbed back into his Toyota and sat with the air-conditioner on full blast for several minutes. That was a close call. There was a God after all. The thought of claiming Collins' share of sales overtook any compassion he felt for his dead accomplice, although he could see an argument looming with Ike.

14

Chloe put down the phone and turned to Andrew in despair. "Collins has died." She collapsed into a chair with her head in her hands and burst into tears.

Andrew put his arm around her shoulders. "It was self-defence Chloe. He was going to murder us both, but you got in first. All gunshot wounds are potentially fatal and what killed him was the loss of blood and time it took us to get him to hospital. When I met the ambulance one of the medics just shook his head when he saw the extent of the wound. You didn't murder him. If that was your intention you would have put another shot into him and we would have buried him out there and no one would have been any the wiser. In hindsight it would have saved us a lot of grief, but neither of us would have done it, so we've just got to live with the consequences."

"But I will be charged, won't I?"

"You may plead manslaughter if that happens, but I will be representing you all the way. I will be right there with you."

"I don't know how I ever pulled that trigger. I hate guns and as for deliberately shooting someone, I just cannot believe I did it."

Andrew squeezed her shoulders and kissed her on top of the head. "It was the primordial sense of survival over which you had no control. Your brain recognised the threat and instantly reacted to the danger."

"What does manslaughter entail?"

"Look Chloe, let's wait and see what happens. You had absolutely no control over future events the moment you shot Collins, so you've got to try and control yourself. It's no use working yourself into a state, although I can understand."

"I should go and see Smith and tell him what happened, shouldn't I? Make a statement?"

"No, that's the last thing you should do at this stage. Let Smith make the first move, but remember, I won't leave you alone with him for a moment. Sergeant Smith has a few problems to think through first before he charges or calls you in to make a statement."

"What problems?"

"I'm thinking ahead Chloe. He's got to think of the ramifications if he lays a charge of manslaughter. I'll make sure his connection to Collins, Shulman and Hargraves gets a very solid airing. I've no doubt it will finish his career and put him behind bars. There will be a money trail from Shulman which he won't be able to explain or defend. I've got no doubt he and Shulman have already got their heads together thinking it through. Smith has to act. He just can't sweep a death under the carpet, but he will have the counselling advice of Shulman to guide him. Let's see what happens in the next day or so, but in the meantime he knows where you live, so let him make the first move."

"Where would I be without you Andrew?"

"I shudder to think if I'd let you go out there without me. You would have surely run into Collins and I would never have known what happened."

She reached up and gripped his arm. "I know, I realise that now. I should never have sneaked away in the morning by myself, but I wanted to be alone with Gramps."

"Well, your trick worked, because you exhausted me and I didn't hear a thing until the birds woke me up," he laughed. "On the other hand you saved us both. If he'd caught us together the outcome would have been inevitable. It would have been a chance too good to miss. I think he was about to finish me off when you walked up with the gun. I saw the look of absolute shock on his face when he saw you. Make no mistake, he was intent on murder."

Chloe wiped the tears off her cheeks with the heel of her hand. "I suppose you're right, but it doesn't get over the fact I killed him. I will never forget it."

"It's better you're alive with those regrets, rather than dead as he intended. He wouldn't have forgotten it if he had murdered you, but he certainly wouldn't have had any regrets either. Look at it that way. Now try to put it out of your mind and just wait to see what Smith does."

She smiled at him weakly and nodded. They sat on the veranda for the rest of the day trying to make conversation. She jumped when the phone went, but Andrew restrained her as he went inside to answer it. She could hear his voice, but not what was being said. The conversation was brief.

"Who was that?"

"It wasn't Smith if that's what you're thinking. It was Ike and I told him you were unavailable. I said he should get on his bike and pedal out here if he's got anything to discuss. I don't want you talking to anyone at this stage as you may say something in complete innocence that rebounds on you. I've told Dotti to tell anyone who calls, you're not in."

"Not anyone?"

"That's right. You wouldn't know if the person on the other end isn't just pretending to have your interests at heart, or isn't recording the conversation. You have to be really careful in this situation. Just think about it. What did Ike really want? He wants to know if you're going to tip the bucket on his whole operation. He wants to try and ascertain your state of mind. Just steer clear of that phone and don't be tempted to pick it up and call anyone."

Dotti did not disturb them as she would silently appear with a fresh jug of iced drink or a plate of sandwiches.

Andrew noticed the whole station had gone quiet. He could hear none of the usual laughing and carrying on by the jackaroos or the children in their housing scattered among the trees near the adjacent billabong.

"Where are they all?"

"Joey Moonlight will have ordered them to be quiet. He knows what happened, but he's perfectly capable of running the place and I hope Shulman will keep him on. Although they appeared to be getting on well, Dotti told me there were arguments starting to happen and she felt Collins was going to get rid of him if he could."

"But he was born here, wasn't he?"

"He was and there's no way he would leave voluntarily, but if you fire someone they lose all their dignity and in Joey's case that would have meant relying on welfare and then the decline into alcohol. I've seen it so often. Henry was tough, but he treated them well."

The phone went a number of times and they could hear Dotti answer it. He caught the irritation in her raised voice when it rang a couple of times in quick succession and grinned to himself.

The look did not escape Chloe. "You know who that is, don't you?"

"I would say it's the good and honest upholder of the law sergeant Walter Smith getting very irritated. You don't deny Smith when he makes a demand that you grace him with your presence in his office. We can expect him tomorrow if I'm correct in my assumptions, and he'll be fuming he's been made to drive out here. His fat gut will get a real work-out on those roads and the thought of not eating and satisfying his large intestine when he gets here will be uppermost on his mind."

Chloe protested. "Is that wise? I can't not offer him something. That's simply unacceptable hospitality, even to the likes of him. Doesn't he have every right to make me call on him?"

"A cold drink or a cup of tea will be enough and no, he doesn't have the right to demand your presence. You're not under arrest, so you can ignore his demands. Knowing him, I've got no doubt he's going to adopt a very threatening stand-over attitude when he arrives, but you must let me deal with it while I get an idea of where he's coming from when he starts asking questions. Remember, this guy is a cop and showing him hospitality is not going to cut any ice. You must let me handle it."

It was late morning the following day when Chloe suddenly turned and pointed to the cloud of oncoming dust.

"You were right. This looks like him now."

"Now just remember what I said. Don't volunteer anything. He's not here to see you. He's here to see me."

Chloe gave him a startled look. "What do you mean, he's here to see you? Those calls were for you then?"

"They were, but you'll soon discover why he wants to talk to me. However, don't say a word or attempt to correct me in any way. You must promise me that."

"But I shot Collins. I cannot possibly deny that." She looked at him horrified. "You're not going to say you did it, are you?"

"Of course not. Look Chloe, I may sound as though I'm talking in riddles, but I don't have time to explain. Just let me handle it."

They watched as Smith heaved his bulk out of the vehicle and stormed towards them with all the resemblance of physical strength and authority he could muster. He was already mopping his brow as he swung open the screen door and stood there surveying Andrew and Chloe with a look of malice.

"Why didn't you take my calls?"

Chloe was about to answer when Andrew cut her off. "Sit down sergeant, and tell us what you want."

"You know bloody well what I want Hanna." He lowered himself into the squatter's chair and heaved his fat legs onto the protruding arms.

Andrew ignored him as he poured a glass of iced lime juice and reached across placing it on the arm of his chair. Smith took it and drained it before letting out a subdued belch.

"You know Collins died, don't you?"

Andrew nodded. "Yes, I'm aware of that."

"I need to take a statement and I don't appreciate driving all the way out here to get it. You were supposed to come and see me, but you bolted. I phoned yesterday but I was told you were not available."

"Sergeant, there's no requirement for me to answer a phone or to make a statement. If you want to lay charges, you can go right ahead and do so. However, you might be a bit premature in that regard, don't you think?"

"You can wipe that stupid look off your face Hanna. This is serious and you admitted to me Collins had been accidentally shot."

"That's correct. We heard a shot and found him in that condition." Smith did not notice Chloe flinch at the lie.

"And you think his death was a trivial matter that can go unreported?"

"I know from experience that two things would already have occurred. The doctor who signed the death certificate would have already filed a report as required for all gunshot cases, and you would have done likewise, otherwise you would be failing in your duty. Tell me sergeant, what did you say in your report?"

"That's none of your business Hanna. I'm here to ask questions, not you. You appear to take the attitude the death of Jim Collins is not serious."

"Oh, don't get me wrong sergeant. I do take it very seriously, but I'm not sure whether you're referring to a person calling himself Jim Collins, or to a Dave Bonham, the criminal you've been shielding. You've got a real problem, haven't you?"

Smith's face reddened. "You're too smart for your own good counsellor. I've come out here to take a statement to complete my investigation and make a report to the coroner. It doesn't matter what name he was using, the fact is you said you heard a shot and found him with the wound from which he died. I don't buy your explanation. Either you make a statement as to the facts, or I arrest you now."

Andrew smiled and shook his head. "You're bluffing sergeant. If you thought you could pin manslaughter on me you would have already done so, and you're well aware I don't have to make a statement or say anything to you. You know what I think?"

"What do you think smartarse?"

Chloe gasped and raised her hand to her mouth with a look of shock. Had Andrew gone too far?

"I think you've already filed you're report stating the death was due to an accidental self-inflicted discharge of a rifle. In fact, I'll bet my last dollar that's what you've done. Your sole purpose in coming out here was to get me to make an incriminating statement with which you could blackmail me with by threatening to lay a charge if I dared open my mouth as to the facts of crime to which you're a party."

"You've pushed your luck too far Hanna, you're under arrest." Smith threw one fat leg after another onto the floor and stood up as he reached behind for his cuffs. "You're grasping at straws guessing what I might have reported as to the cause of death."

Chloe could not believe how Andrew calmly remained seated.

"I know exactly what you wrote Smith. You see, I've known Dr Carl Gibson for a number of years. We played together in the university cricket team. I phoned him after Chloe took the call Collins had died. I introduced myself and he apologised for not having recognised me. We chatted for a while about old times and I don't know what triggered it, but he brought up your discussion with him and the fact you were going to record the death as a self-inflicted accident. You're now going to have to change your report if you arrest me. That's not going to go down well with a jury when they hear Carl Gibson's testimony and combined with the fact you've perverted the course of justice by knowingly shielding Collins, you're in deep shit. You know Smith, you're a standover man and you're just as big a bloody criminal as Collins and your pal Shulman. And don't think for a moment Ike wouldn't dump on you if the balloon goes up. After all, he's the only one who would almost escape unscathed, by claiming he was only acting as agent and wasn't directly involved in the cattle duffing."

Smith was florid and shaking with rage, but then slowly deflated as he realised the implications. "You're going to tip a bucket on me are you?"

"I've no intention of doing so Smith. You can drown in your little cesspit for all I care. Chloe and I will be leaving very soon and that's the last you will be hearing from us. I gather you understand what I'm saying?"

Smith nodded and walked out, letting the screen door slam behind him.

"You're not staying for lunch sergeant?" It was Dotti standing in the kitchen doorway with a large grin on her face. "Good riddance you bag of fat."

Smith did not acknowledge her insult as he climbed into his Toyota, swung it around in a vicious circle of dust and drove off. It was not until the trailing dust began to diminish did Chloe turn to him.

"I want you on my side in future Andrew, but I wouldn't have let him take you. I would have told him the truth. I really thought he was going to call your bluff, and I couldn't let that happen."

"It wouldn't have made any difference if you had admitted you pulled the trigger. I was holding all the cards and I wanted to play them in my own good time."

"And you think that's the end of it?"

"I do. Smith realises full well he can't do a thing without also putting himself in the firing line. However, he'll always be sweating I'll go back on my word and reveal his crimes. He's got the problem, not me."

"I wouldn't have been able to handle it. I would have crumbled. The man is completely overbearing and frightens the life out of me."

"I know that Chloe. Shulman is going to steal your properties and for good measure Smith would have blackmailed you. There's no way you could have handled the pressure and he knew it. He would have threatened to charge you with murder or manslaughter if you revealed anything about the theft of cattle. I wasn't going to let that happen."

She got up and sat on his lap and wrapped her arms around his neck. "You're a wonderful person Andrew Hanna. How can I thank you?"

"We'll work on that tonight, but you must realise my fees are very high." He chuckled as she leaned down and smothered his mouth.

"You two comin up for air, or comin in for lunch." Dotti giggled as she poked her head out the doorway. "What'd he want? He don't look to happy when he left. Looked like he had a rat up his backside, he was clenching those fat cheeks so tight."

Andrew and Chloe burst into laughter as they followed her inside.

"Where do we go from here?" Chloe was idly picking at the remnants of the corned-beef salad.

"I thought I might go back to Perth and try and re-establish myself in a practice. There's nothing up here for me now."

"What about me? Am I included in your plans?"

Andrew reached across and squeezed her hand. "That goes without saying. Of course I want you to be with me."

"I wonder where Marcel is?"

"Don't worry about him for now. I'll start a more intensive enquiry once we're out of here. We've only got a week left according to my reckoning before Ike comes knocking with his eviction notice. I think you'd better start packing."

Chloe laughed. "What's to pack? There's nothing here I want to take with me. Just the memories will do."

"What about all Henry's papers and old records? There are piles of them in his office."

"I'll get some of the boys to take them all out and burn them. I wouldn't know what's there, but I'm sure they don't have any value. I'll get them onto that in the morning. Now I'm going to saddle my horse and go for one last ride. I want to listen to the birds and look at the trees and sit beside a waterhole for an hour."

"I'll come with you."

Chloe held up her hand. "No, you stay here. I want to be by myself." She saw his sudden look of concern. "Don't worry, I'm in no danger."

Her horse was already standing by the rails waiting to be saddled when they walked up hand in hand. He watched her stroke its blaze as she inserted the bit and pulled the bridle over its head. The blanket and saddle were quickly fastened and with a fluid motion she mounted and gently dug the animal in the flanks.

"See you in a couple of hours."

"If you're not back by then I'll come looking for you. In fact I should come with you now. We could find a nice shady spot to relax."

Chloe laughed as she spurred the horse into a canter. "I know what kind of relaxation you've got in mind. See you soon."

He watched her until she was out of sight before slowly walking back to the homestead. It was too hot on the veranda so he went through to Henry's office, turned on the large overhead fans and sat down at the battered roll-top desk. His mind wandered as he looked at the sum total of the man's accumulated diaries stacked neatly four-high the length of the top. He reached and picked one up, blew off the thick red dust and began to flick the pages quickly through thumb and fingers, stopping now and again to read the neat hand writing. It was all cattle and rain and the recordings of seasons past, dull and boring information only relevant to the author and devoid of any jottings of personal life. He snapped it shut and was about to replace it when he opened it again and began a more intense study. Something had caught his eye. He went slowly back through the diary, marking each page of interest with a dog-ear. The recordings were meticulous, detailed and deliberate, but what did they mean? It was as though Henry Boyce had laid out a trail of bread crumbs which to the casual observer were just meaningless statistics, but which pointed back to where the first crumb of the trail commenced. The numbers varied, but the initials and percentages remained constant. Beside each entry was a separate numerical figure in brackets. His hands started to shake as a flash of recognition went off in his brain and he grabbed another diary and began the search, flicking through month by month.

He did not notice her enter the room until she wrapped her arms around his neck and kissed him. He looked up. It was dusk with the last light fading quickly. He had not noticed she had been away far longer than expected.

"What are you doing?"

"I'm going through Henry's diaries." He was trying to hide his excitement. He knew what he was looking at, but where was the key? What he had discovered was circumstantial. It would cast a dark cloud of suspicion, but could not be proven.

She kissed him on the cheek. "Well, I smell like a horse, so I'm going for a shower before dinner. Do you want to join me?"

She heard him murmur something, but he did not turn or acknowledge the invitation, which was strange. She stood there for a second watching him lost in thought while turning the pages. She realised she may as well not been in the room as she turned with a sniff of rejection and walked out.

"Mr Andrew, Mr Andrew, dinner is on the table. Chloe already there with candle going and bottle of wine. You on a promise tonight Mr Andrew," Dotti giggled salaciously. "You better hurry as Chloe don't look happy. What you done to her?"

"I'll be there in a minute Dotti." Andrew waved her away without looking up.

"Boy, you be in big trouble if you don't come now." She whistled and shook her hand as though it was in pain. "You be in trouble with me also. Your dinner is on table."

"Okay, okay Dotti. I'll just finish reading these last few pages and be right there. It will only take a minute."

Twenty minutes later Chloe was still seated at the table staring at the flickering candle. The bottle of wine was untouched. Dotti witnessed the mood and had hidden in the kitchen waiting for the reaction, knowing that love was being tested.

The sudden shout of excitement from the office broke the silence and jolted them both as Andrew came running out holding a diary. He dropped it on the table and pulling Chloe to her feet, whirled her around in a circle while kissing and hugging her.

"I'm angry with you Andrew." She tried to maintain the mock look before finally succumbing to his excitement.

"No you're not Chloe Boyce. You're in love with me. You can't be angry with me because I'm in love with you."

She broke into laughter. "Stop it Andrew. Stop. You're making me dizzy. What are you so happy about?"

Dotti appeared, put their reheated meals on the table and attempted to slip away, but Andrew grabbed her and began to twirl her small frame off her feet. She beat his chest with her strong hands all the while laughing along with him. "You be in trouble Mr Andrew if you don't put me down an behave yourself. Chloe and I both very upset with you."

Andrew let her go, but held her hand to make sure she was steady on her feet.

"Let's eat." He picked up the wine bottle and poured two glasses. "Here's to us Chloe Boyce."

Chloe winced as they touched glasses so heavily she expected them to shatter. "What are you so happy about Andrew? Tell me, tell me now. I've got to know?"

He grinned at her as he finished half the glass. "Do you know your father kept meticulous records? And to think they were all going into the fire."

"But they're only diaries. What's so important about them?"

Andrew lowered his voice as he had no doubt there would be a pair of old, but sharp ears listening from the kitchen. "They're important because they're a complete record of the crime."

Chloe shook her head. "You're crazy. I already know about the crime. So what's so new that's got you so excited?"

"I'll explain it to you" He stood and picked up the bottle and diary. "Bring your glass and let's go out on the veranda."

She followed him out to the far end of the veranda. "Now tell me before I break that bottle over your head." Chloe fluffed up a cushion and leaned back in the squatter's chair.

"What I've discovered is a complete sequence of diary entries giving dates, the number of cattle stolen from Ascot Downs, the dates sold through Shulman and the split up of the proceeds and to whom. It's theft on a grand scale worth millions."

"What's new about that?"

"The revelation is the name of the fourth person involved. Hargraves told me he was involved along with Henry and Shulman, the three musketeers, but in fact there was a fourth musketeer."

"Andrew, come down to earth; would you please and explain it to me? You've said the trail is cold. Henry and Hargraves are dead, which only leaves Shulman and you can't pin anything on him because he was only acting as agent. Smith is obviously involved, but he's not worth the trouble. Shulman is taking over, I'm finished and we're both leaving, so why don't we forget about the whole thing. It's too late."

"No Chloe, you're wrong. I think I can pull the rug right from under Ike's feet, at least I think I can and I'm certainly going to try. The fourth person is the key."

"So who is the missing musketeer?"

"Arthur Geddes."

Chloe screwed up her face. "I've never heard of him, have I?"

"I'm sure he was Henry's bank manager. At first I could not recall where I'd heard his name mentioned and then it struck me, I hadn't. It was when I was in Roy Briscoe's office I noticed a name badge lying on a shelf. The name was Arthur Geddes. Henry, Hargraves and Ike each had a third interest in the stolen cattle. Geddes was the silent partner with the remaining ten percent. Smith wasn't mentioned, so Ike must have been paying him somehow. It took me awhile to get back to this diary which dates from ten years ago. It took me sometime to work out what the entries meant, but I was only surmising until I picked up this one, the year it all began. Henry has made very precise notes as to how he was in a desperate financial position because of the prolonged drought. Ike pressured him into the arrangement with Hargraves whereby they would run Ascot Downs cleanskins through Venus Downs and then Ike would market them. It would appear it was Ike who got Geddes to threaten to cut off Henry's overdraft and in return Geddes received a kickback. Henry agreed never to reveal Geddes' involvement, but that didn't stop him recording it in his diaries. You can see from these annotations the number of Ascot cattle moved through Henry and then onto Ike and the dates they occurred. The figures on the side represent the money received and who received it. Henry must have suspected the wheels would fall off one day, and Ike would try and escape involvement."

"But surely it's too late to do anything about it now?"

"Maybe and maybe not, but one thing I have established is that Ike is conclusively involved in what's been going on. I'm also convinced Ike's behind the bank's actions, but I can't figure out how he's managed it. What influence he would have with the bank, I just can't fathom. Okay, he could threaten to pull his business, but no bank would listen to that threat. There's something else motivating the bank. Someone is pulling the strings. It has got to be Shulman."

"Why not confront Ike and show him what you've discovered?"

Andrew mulled over Chloe's suggestion before dismissing it. "Maybe, maybe not. Let me think about it. He knows he's safe to a degree. You see, if I threaten to blow the whistle, he'll threaten to take you down with him. In that event the Ascot Downs owners would sue Henry's estate for damages. You will come out with a very blemished record after the court and press work you over. You may not do time, but you most certainly will lose everything, because I've no doubt the Ascot owners would be successful. You can't win and Ike would know it."

"But can he afford to call your bluff Andrew? After all, it wouldn't be me that asks him to withdraw from the bidding for Venus Downs. It would be you, my lawyer. Ike is a man with a big ego. He's money and power hungry and the threat of winding up in jail and losing a substantial part of his fortune would not appeal to him either. And if he's really behind the bank's move it maybe enough for him to stop it?"

"I'll tell Joey Moonlight in the morning he's not to accept any more cattle from Ascot Downs. The thieving's got to stop now."

"No Chloe, don't do that. You're almost finished with Venus Downs, so don't make waves."

"I just can't believe this has been going on for so long without the owners becoming aware."

"This is only one of their huge holdings. Because of the size of Ascot it would be near impossible to arrive at an accurate head count in any year. Cattle are moved from one property to another so it's easy for crooked managers to disappear thousands of head spread over thousands of square kilometres. Being an absentee landlord just leaves the door wide open for crime."

"Joey Moonlight is the head stockman, he should have told me what's being going on."

"Don't blame him Chloe. He was not going to confront Henry or Collins or yourself. It's not his business, but I agree he would have known all about it. As for Collins, we had a lucky escape. When he saw me out there he must have guessed you would be close by. He was going to make sure neither of us posed a threat to his income."

Chloe shuddered. "I still have nightmares about that. Not so much the man, but images of that shattered leg and the pain he must have endured will never leave me."

"Put it out of your mind. You would have been dead if you hadn't got in first."

"So what do you think we should do?"

"Your suggestion of the direct approach is the only thing I can come up with. I'll walk into the lion's den and call on Mr Shulman, confront him with what I've discovered and see how he reacts."

"I'll come with you."

"No Chloe, I think you should keep clear. He may well want to cut a deal on letting you keep Venus Downs and I don't want you present if he does. I'd want to think about any proposal he comes up with as Ike would most certainly have a motive in mind and it would be entirely to his advantage, you can count on that. In the meantime, I'm going to make a phone call. Something has just occurred to me that Geddes has been gone from here for sometime, so where is he now? Probably still with the bank, but where is the crucial question?"

"Use the phone in Dad's office. You can't be overheard in there by a certain pair of listening ears."

Andrew returned grinning from ear to ear.

"Well, what did you find?"

"Arthur Geddes is the State manager of the bank. He certainly has risen in the world, but they wouldn't put me through to him unless I had an appointment."

15

*I*ke looked up in surprise as Andrew walked straight through into his office, ignoring his secretary.

"Andrew, what a pleasure. I was wondering when you would front." The sarcasm was evident in his tone.

"Why were you wondering that?"

"That's obvious isn't it? You've been interfering in my business arrangements, affecting my income and you've murdered the manager of Venus Downs, a manager who had my interests at heart."

"Don't give me that Ike. I didn't murder Collins. It was reported as a self-inflicted gunshot wound by your pal Smith, otherwise he would have pressed charges."

"So tell me what you've come to see me about."

"I believe you are behind the bank's decision to call the the loans. I want you to back off and let Chloe have Venus."

"And why would I do that? I've told you already I intend to have that property and I'm certainly not going to intercede with the bank, even if I could. No, Boyce is out and I'm in."

"So that's your last word?"

"It is."

"I've been going through Henry Boyce's diaries. They are quite meticulous in detail and describe how you set up the whole cattle theft operation and why."

Ike shrugged. "It was Henry's idea. He was going bust and I decided to help him. So he stole thousands of head, but I was only agent and didn't know what he was up to. At least that will be my defence. And yes, Hargraves was his accomplice."

"Henry indicated there was another person involved."

"Well if Henry's diaries are that detailed he would have named him, I would imagine. Are you telling me he didn't?"

Andrew was about to name Geddes, but something told him to ignore the question. "Ike, you're named along with Bill Hargraves and Henry Boyce. Of course I knew all this when I wrote Hargraves' Will. He named you, but you had a reasonable defence. However, now I've got the full details along with numbers, dates and value of the stolen property. Money trails are easy to follow when they involve bank accounts. You're going to have a real problem in getting out from under that by claiming you were only an agent."

"Hanna, you're flying a kite. You are a very smart lawyer, but I've no doubt you've already worked out it's your client Chloe Boyce who's going to be the real loser. Do your worst. I've got the money to fight, but your client will be wiped out when the Ascot Downs people seek damages. Either she goes now and I buy her properties at my price, or I pick up the pieces when the properties are auctioned off. Either way I can't lose."

"Your accomplice Smith will be in the firing line if I go public with this. He's not going to come to your defence."

Ike laughed. "He knew what he was getting into, so it's his problem."

"What hold do you have over the bank Ike?"

"Hold? I've no hold over the bank. They don't work that way. They've called the mortgages and I'm going to buy them. It's as simple as that."

"I read in the diaries you were influential in Henry buying Remus Plains, along with Baracool and Ironstone in the

Pilbara. I can understand Remus because it adjoins Venus Downs, but why the other two?"

"Henry had more cash flow than he knew what to do with. It went to his head and he asked me for advice. I gave it to him, but it was up to him whether he accepted it or not. I'm not responsible for his actions, nor do I accept any liability."

"But I note from the diaries there appears to be a suggestion you purchased those properties in partnership. Is that correct?"

Andrew could see the question caught Ike by surprise as Ike studied him coldly as if trying to scan his mind as to what he knew.

"That's correct, but we dissolved it against my better judgement. I don't like partnerships or guarantees, too much bad blood if things go wrong. Henry made the mistake of dying otherwise everything would have been okay. However, as they say it's an ill wind that blows no good and in this instance it's blowing the right way for me."

"And Chloe is out on the road, so to speak?"

"Compassion is not something banks consider and it's not in my nature either. I'm strictly a business man and besides from what I understand Chloe Boyce is a wealthy woman in her own right. The loss of the cattle stations is not going to hit her personal fortune. She inherited what she didn't know she owned, so that's no loss in my opinion. The attachment to the place is only emotional. I cannot understand why she would never let on where that red diamond came from. She could have retired in luxury instead of walking around in cow-shit batting away flies."

"Hasn't it occurred to you she may have more scruples than you?"

"If you've finished Hanna, get the hell out of here. You've come in here to blackmail me and it won't work." Shulman rose and leaned forward, his face flushed in anger. "You're nothing but a hack law clerk with the arse out of your trousers and yet you have the hide to come in here and insult me. You're fucked Hanna and so is Boyce."

Andrew's open palm connected with Ike's jaw, sending him sprawling back over his chair and cannoning into the wall.

Andrew sat in his vehicle contemplating what he had just done. He felt good, but other than that he knew Ike had won the day. It had been a foolish move to confront the man. The violence was uncalled for and not in his nature, but the taunt had gone off like an explosion in his brain with the reaction beyond his control.

He did not notice Smith emerge from the police station, get into his Toyota and drive slowly past him. He was striving to recall what it was Ike had said that triggered something in his brain? Something nagged at him, but he could not bring it into focus as he started the engine and slowly drove out of town. Ike had dropped a vital clue, if only he could remember what it was.

It was on rounding a sweeping bend several hours later when he saw the Toyota parked in the middle of the road facing towards him. Smith was standing beside it trailing a shotgun in his right hand. Andrew looked around frantically, but he had no time nor space to swing around and head away from the danger, nor could he attempt to pass either side of the vehicle as the verge dropped away sharply into a deep drainage channel on the inside, while the other side marked the edge of a ravine several hundred metres deep. It was the perfect trap. He had a feeling his day was going to get worse as he pulled up a car length in front and waited. Smith realised the danger as he raised the gun and walked towards him. He was taking no chances Andrew would suddenly accelerate and run him down and Andrew was well aware the damage a twelve-gauge would inflict if he attempted to do so. Smith was smiling as he drew level and rested the barrel on the window sill. Death was only inches from the side of his head as he tried to remain calm, but he knew the inevitable was about to happen.

"What do you want sergeant?"

Smith laughed. "You've become a real liability Hanna. I thought we had an understanding, but now it would appear you're going to cause real trouble for me and Ike and we can't have that. You do understand don't you?"

"My meeting with Ike was to see if he would reconsider taking Venus Downs. Things got a little heated, but I've no intention of exposing what you're up to."

"Ike thinks otherwise and I have to go along with that. You've come to the end of the road fella. Now step out of the vehicle." Smith moved back a couple of paces and indicated for Andrew to move to the side of the road which dropped down into the ravine shielded from view where the vehicle and body would never be seen. He could have shot him in the cab, but that would result him getting splattered with blood and brain matter before steering the vehicle to the edge and pushing it over. Shoot the man first and then push the clean vehicle over. The pigs and wild dogs would clean up the human evidence and the vehicle would remain a hundred metres down hidden by thick scrub.

"Not a bright move Smith. Chloe has all the evidence she needs to put both you and Ike away. Henry Boyce left a trail a mile wide leading to you both."

"I'll deal with you first Hanna and then take care of her. I'm not really worried about what evidence you may possess because it will never see the light of day. Now stand with your back to the slope. I want to give you this right in the guts."

Andrew watched as Smith slowly raised the gun and he waited for the blast that would send him backwards over the edge. He would feel nothing. The shock would mask all pain, as he resigned himself to it.

Smith heard it first and turned towards the source while Andrew sucked in his breath as the vehicle swung into view. The scene was a set stage which an observer would quickly grasp. A man with his back to a ravine confronted by a man with a gun aimed at his stomach. Smith remained calm as the vehicle approached and slowed down to a walk as it eased around Smith's vehicle and drew level with them. At first Andrew did not recognise him, but when the face broke into a row of glistening white teeth surrounded by a smiling black face, he heaved a sigh of relief.

"Hi there sergeant. Hi there Mr Andrew. What you two doin? Nuthin worth shootin out here sergeant." It was not an innocent question or comment. Joey Moonlight had realised immediately what was about to happen.

Smith leaned the gun back on his shoulder and froze the enquiry with a look of menace. "Where are you headed Moonlight?"

"Goin into town for supplies sergeant." The smile was infectious, but the attitude subservient. He knew better than to comment on what he had just witnessed or make any smart remark. The jackaroo beside him sat silently with his eyes fixed straight ahead. He knew trouble when he saw it. Too often he had been arrested drunk and suffered at the hands of Smith.

"Well get on your way then."

Joey nodded, but the smile had disappeared as he passed Andrew. They watched as the vehicle slowly drove off and stopped on top of the rise leading into the bend Andrew had just rounded. They saw Joey get out and stand with his hand on the door looking back, well out of range of a shotgun.

"I think you're snookered sergeant." Andrew was trying to maintain a confident tone as he walked over and climbed back into the cab of his vehicle. "That's unless you're going catch up and shoot them as well." He expected at any moment to feel the blast of the pellets tearing at his skull.

He edged around Smith and gathered speed. When he was out of danger he glanced up at his rear vision mirror to see Joey Moonlight's vehicle disappearing in a cloud of dust.

Andrew then recalled the comment Ike had made. It was a long shot, but it could be the key to the bank's actions.

Chloe was waiting as he pulled up. "Hi darling, how did it go?"

Andrew shrugged and kissed her. "Ike wouldn't budge and he just brushed my threats off. He's determined to take over and kick you out."

"I thought that would happen, but it was worth a try. Did you pass Joey on the road? I sent him in for supplies."

"Yes I did, but I didn't stop for a chat."

Chloe laughed. "All you would have seen was an approaching cloud of dust, and then a passing cloud. Joey only knows one speed and that's flat out. You would have seen those teeth though?"

"I saw his teeth alright and they were the most welcome teeth I've ever seen."

She looked at him oddly. "What do you mean by that?"

"Oh nothing. He really does have a magnificent set of pearly white's doesn't he? He should audition for a Colgate ad."

They were sitting at dinner and she could see he had something on his mind. "You look troubled. Something's bothering you isn't it?"

"It's nothing." He tried to pass it off with a drawn smile, but he could see he was not being believed. "Yes, there is. I've got to go to Perth to try and talk to Geddes now I know who he is and how he fits into the picture, or at least I think I do. They refused to put me through to him on the phone, but that doesn't mean I can't see him."

"I'm coming with you."

He could see the look of determination etched on her face and nodded. "What time do flights leave, do you know?"

"Only in the morning. Let me check now." She went into the kitchen. Five minutes later he heard her put down the phone. "Too late for tomorrow as I've got to pack, but we'll drive in tomorrow afternoon, stay the night at Marge Tilley's and catch the flight in the morning. I don't know who's older, Marge or the pub. Probably not as salubrious as the hotels I've been used to, but it will be fun as long as I'm with you."

"The beds make an awful racket. Marge will soon broadcast what we've been up to."

"To hell with her. Why don't we make the whole building shake and give her something to really talk about?"

Andrew gave a half-hearted laugh, but his mind was otherwise engrossed. He was playing with fire if his assumptions were wrong. Even if he was right and his bluff was called, he ran an extreme risk. Blackmail was a crime, no matter how you tried to describe, present it, or mask it. At best he would lose his licence to practice law and at worst he would do a stretch and no doubt reacquaint with some of the felons he had put behind bars. It would not be a pleasant reunion. He did not sleep well as the strategy and dangers churned over in his mind. It had also taken some time before he was convinced Chloe was asleep before he quietly crept back to Henry's office to where Joey was waiting on the veranda, his teeth gleaming in the filtered moonlight.

Chloe was usually cheerful at breakfast, but had become unusually quiet and he could sense she was troubled by the time they were due to leave around midday. The cheerful farewells to Dotti and Hazel were perfunctory with none of the usual warm feelings being demonstrated as they drove away.

"Come on Chloe. Spit it out and tell me what's on your mind."

"Can I trust you Andrew?'

"What kind of a question is that?"

"It's simple enough. Why didn't you tell me what really happened yesterday. Smith was going to murder you wasn't he?"

Andrew sighed and nodded. He should have known that Joey or the jackaroo would have not been able to keep their mouths closed.

"Joey told you what he saw?"

"Yes he did, but not before Dotti had told me. He told Dotti in confidence, but you know how long she kept that promise. You didn't really think you could keep that quiet, did you? I'm very angry you tried to hide it from me. Joey and Tinker saved your life. They witnessed exactly what was about to happen."

"It was nothing. Smith and I were just having a chat on the roadside."

"Don't be so damned flippant Andrew." She raised her voice a pitch in anger. "You should thank Joey and not lie to me. I don't like it."

"I'm sorry, but I didn't want to alarm you and I suppose you are quite right, Joey did save my life. I must thank him."

"What are you going to do about it?"

"Nothing. There's no point. Who do I lay a complaint with? Smith?"

"But the man tried to murder you. Don't you understand?"

"Chloe, calm down. Smith won't try that again and as soon as we get back we'll pack up and be gone for good. I'll admit I thought I was about to die. It's not a pleasant experience, but it's amazing how you can reconcile to something over which you have no control. I realised I would be dead a millisecond after he pulled the trigger."

She swung at him with her clenched fist, hitting him in the chest and shouting as the tears welled in her eyes. "Stop it Andrew, stop it. I love you. Don't talk like that."

He stopped and hurriedly gathered her in his arms as the tears flowed uncontrollably, the spasms shaking her whole body. He stroked her hair and whispered softly. "I'm sorry darling. I was trying to protect you, not lie to you. Please understand."

Gradually the spasms subsided and she sobbed quietly while trying to dry her eyes.

"Perhaps it's a blessing we're leaving for good. This place has only meant death to me. First Gramps, then Carl and Walter and Henry and that priest and finally Collins. I would have gone out of my mind if I'd lost you."

"I hadn't thought of it like that. I will be more considerate in future. I promise." They drove in silence until with uncanny timing she straightened up and looked over at him.

"It happened near here didn't it? Joey told me and this is the only place I can think of with a steep chasm on one side."

Andrew slowed and pointed as they drove over the spot. She just nodded, but said nothing as he began to accelerate again.

Marge Tilley greeted them with her raucous banter."Chloe, where have you been? Why haven't you been to see me?" She shouted in a loud patronising tone claiming a friendship Chloe was not aware of, as she could only remember ever meeting her once on a cattle drive with Henry. "And Andrew." She acknowledged him with a knowing grin. "Now what are you two love birds up to?"

"We're off to Perth in the morning."

"And what are you going to Perth for? I've heard you're selling up Chloe. Is that true?"

"We're going to see a man about a dog Marge." Andrew cut in sarcastically, the obvious message being she should mind her own business.

"Long way to go to get a dog." Marge ignored the sarcasm. "I've got a bitch out the back with a litter a couple of weeks old. You could have had one of those free. They're not pedigree as the dog that jumped her left without identification or forwarding address. Mind you that happens with most bitches on heat around here. They get jumped and the guy leaves town in a hurry." She turned and took a key off the wall, handing it to Andrew

Chloe fully understood the insinuation, but offered no visible reaction although she was seething at the effrontery. Andrew broke into a broad grin at the thought of any hapless Lothario attempting such a carnal transgression with Marge, let alone getting out of town in one piece if he did. Marge read the telepathy in an instant. It was obvious what Andrew was grinning about.

"Top of the stairs, first on the right. You've got the bridal suite to yourselves. Dinner's at six and breakfast from seven." The humour had suddenly drained from her face as she disappeared into the bar.

"Charming old bag, isn't she?" Andrew was still grinning as he picked up their bags and started up the stairs.

"Charming." Chloe hissed through her clenched teeth. "She's a nasty piece of goods I think."

"Well, the whole town will know we're sleeping together tonight. Radio Wyndham will be broadcasting it to the whole bar before we get to the top of these stairs."

He tried the key, but it just twisted in the lock. He twisted the handle and the door opened with a tortured groan. He looked at the ancient key in his hand before tossing it on the dresser. It was a symbolic gesture rather than some guarantee of security.

"The bed's okay." Chloe sat on the side and bounced up and down as she looked around the room at the faded prints on the walls and mirrored dresser with its single chair. "Not exactly the Savoy though."

"You've been spoilt Chloe Boyce. It's either here or the Argent, locally known as the snake-pit, and I don't think you'd like it."

"Hmm, no this will do nicely. A big bed and you is all I need," she taunted as she lay back and grinned at him.

The whole bar turned within seconds of one another as they walked through to the dining room. "I get the impression they're expecting us." Chloe sat down but was not intimidated by the onlookers. She was a hardened veteran of scrutiny and comment. As each pair of eyes met her expressionless gaze, they would turn back to the bar, their drink and their murmurings. "Have they all been to a funeral, or are they always this happy?"

Andrew laughed. "You'll have to forgive them. They've got the news straight off the press from Marge and they're over-awed by the celebrity status you've brought upon this establishment. They've all heard about the famous Chloe and now they want to see her."

"I didn't know cadavers moved," she quipped. "This place gives me the creeps."

A waitress appeared at the table and stood there silently scratching her head with a pencil, while in the other hand she clutched a dog-eared pad. Andrew looked around for a menu.

"No menus mate," she said catching his expression.

"Well then, what's good tonight?"

"I'm always good, but I'm not on the menu tonight." She tried to maintain a deadpan expression, but her eyes danced with mirth. "You can either have steak, salad and chips or battered or crumbed barramundi and chips and there's bread and butter pudding if you want sweets."

"Crumbed barra it is then."

"Make that two."

The waitress nodded at Chloe as she laboriously wrote the order down.

"Are you really Chloe the famous model?"

"I was a model, but not anymore."

"I think I may be related to you. My father Jimmy Shilling was related to a Quartpot and your name is Chloe Quartpot, isn't it? So we could be cousins," she beamed.

"Really? That's very interesting," Chloe replied graciously. "And what is your name?"

"Cynthia Shilling." She wiped her plump hand on her dress and held it out.

"I'm pleased to meet you Cynthia," Chloe replied as she shook the extended hand, expecting it to be the end of the conversation, but Cynthia remained fixed just staring down at her with an excited look.

"I would like to be a model. How do you learn it?"

"It's a lot of hard work Cynthia, but I'm sure you could do it if you set your mind to succeed."

Cynthia was about to ask another question when she was cut off by a shout from the kitchen. She spun around nervously. "I gotta go. Now what was it you ordered? Yeah, yeah, two fish and chips," she said studying her pad.

They watched as she waddled off as quick as her fat legs would allow. "She's been eating too much battered fish and chips by the look of her."

"She has Andrew, but I never try to discourage people. We both know she'll never get out of this place. She was born here and will die here, but I won't snuff out her dreams by telling her the truth."

"Do you think you're related?"

"The whole world is related in some way, either by birth or association. People love to be associated with celebrities, to be seen with them, to touch them, to be around them. I've seen every level of social caste all clamouring for recognition in some way. It's a natural tendancy; nothing abnormal about that. It's quite easy to slot that girl in. The glimmer of ambition will fade the moment I'm gone and she's back with her peers, but she'll have something to talk about."

"You're quite the philosopher. I would never have guessed it."

"There's a lot you don't know about me Andrew Hanna, but I'll educate you as we go along."

He nodded. "This is a dry argument. I'll get a bottle of wine." The bar went quiet as he picked up the bottle and two glasses just as Cynthia arrived with the meals.

"I picked out the freshest fish for you. It came in today," she whispered. "The dragon would go ballistic if she knew. Some of it's been in the freezer for weeks, so dried out you'd think you were chewing cardboard."

"That's very nice of you Cynthia." Chloe gave her a disarming smile.

"So you think I would make it as a model?"

"You can do anything if you try Cynthia, but you must try. Always keep that in mind."

"I will, I will. I can't wait to tell some of my friends I've met you and we're related," she said as she bounced away.

"She's claimed you and by the taste of this fish it's been well worth it."

Chloe was about to reply when she looked up with a frozen expression. "Look what just walked in."

Smith was standing in the entrance to the bar casting his eye over the drinkers.

"No trouble in here tonight Marge?"

"No Wally, these boys all love their mothers and go to church," she replied with a peal of laughter.

Smith slowly turned and looked into the dining room. "That's good to hear. There's a lot of vermin around now that's got to be cleaned out." He stood watching Chloe and Andrew for a few seconds before turning and walking out.

"He was giving us the message he knows we're in town and where to find us."

"He makes my skin crawl."

Andrew was awake and out of bed the moment the brass ashtray hit the wooden floor. He cursed as his foot contacted the side of the dresser in the dark. Chloe had wondered what he was doing when he put the solitary chair with its back inches from the door. She watched intrigued as he then balanced the old ashtray on top of the back.

"The improvised Hanna burglar alarm. Anyone opening that door will tip the ashtray off and it will make quite a racket when it hits the floor."

He pushed aside the chair and flung open the door. The hallway was empty, but he could hear the faint sound of someone on the stairway. He ran and hopped in pain to the top and looked down, but it was empty. He was not imagining things. Someone had tried to enter their room. He concluded it was just an opportunistic thief after money and whatever valuables they could lay their hands on. If it was someone with a more sinister intent in mind, the the attempt had failed.

Chloe was sitting up in bed with a frightened look on her face. "Did you see anyone?"

"No, but I'm sure I heard someone." He climbed back into bed while rubbing his sore foot. "It was probably some kid on the make, or someone Smith paid to give us a scare."

"Either way it worked."

Chloe turned off the bedside light. She slept fitfully, constantly nudging Andrew to make sure he was still there. They were wide awake just as the light began to show through the roll-up blinds.

"That's a night I would care to forget." Andrew put his feet out on the floor and stood up. "I think I'll shower and shave. Are you coming?"

They padded down the hallway together towards the separate bathrooms. "Two can fit under the one shower." He made to follow her in, but she turned and pushed him in the chest.

"No, I want to be out of this place as quickly as possible and if I let you in, playtime will get out of hand. Besides, someone may walk in on us. Also you haven't shaved and I don't want you giving me a whisker rash in the wrong place."

Andrew pulled a face of mock disappointment. Minutes later he was humming to himself in the mirror when the alert light flashed in his brain. He dropped the shaver into the basin, wrapped a towel around himself and ran silently as he could down the hallway. The door to their room was wide open. The youth had his back to him as he tipped the contents of Andrew's bag onto the bed. He had been told what to look for as he picked up Henry's black diary, and flicked it open to make sure it was what he had been instructed to look for. He quickly scanned the remainder of the scattered files and paperwork and the contents of Chloe's bags which he had already been through. His eyes focussed on Andrew's wallet on the bedside table. He flipped it open and removed the cash, stuffing it into his back pocket in one swift movement. Andrew's watch went the same way after a casual inspection. He turned to leave, but showed no shock or surprise to see Andrew standing in the doorway blocking his exit. This kid was an expert thief, well experienced in all forms of larceny and not phased in the slightest at being caught in the act. Andrew judged he could be no more than fifteen. He was surprised to see him break into a broad grin of challenge, before quickly adopting the look of a scared defenceless youth. He advanced holding out the diary for Andrew to take. "Here, you can have it back."

Andrew almost fell for the innocent defenceless ploy until he noticed the kid begin to turn with his right foot lifting off the ground. The warning flashed as he threw himself forward thrusting his right arm into the turning body to disrupt the pivot of the karate movement while his left he flung upwards to push against the inside of the turning and descending leg aimed at his head. The kid went backwards unable to control or cushion his fall. His head hit the wooden floor with a sickening thud and he lay motionless. Andrew turned him over and quickly retrieved his cash and watch. He then searched his other pockets and was not surprised to recover Chloe's watch, a necklace she always wore and another wad of cash. He looked around the room and saw her empty pocket book lying beside the bed.

Chloe was suddenly standing in the doorway with her hand over her mouth. "What happened?"

"Our intruder from last night returned to complete the job and I caught him in the act. He would have got away with it if you hadn't pushed me out of your bathroom."

She looked down at the prone bare-footed form with tattered shorts and filthy torn tee- shirt. "Poor kid, I would have given him some money if he'd asked."

"Chloe, this poor kid as you describe him, is a professional thief. He had been sent to get Henry's diary, but of course he couldn't resist taking our watches and cash. Another minute and he would have got what he was sent for."

"How did he know you had the diary?"

"I think I mentioned it to Ike when I approached him the other day. Smith obviously knows we're leaving for Perth today and he took a calculated guess I would have some sort of incriminating evidence with me. I've no doubt he put the kid up to it as he knew exactly what he was looking for."

"What are you going to do about him?"

"He'll come around in a minute I hope. If he doesn't, I'll have to call an ambulance and that's really going to put a spanner in the works. We won't be flying out today."

"He could have suffered brain damage then?"

Andrew gave a grudging laugh. "Undoubtedly his brain is already damaged from petrol or paint sniffing or other substance abuse. I just want him up and out of here."

After a few minutes the kid started to moan and stir until finally he sat up shaking and holding his head. He sat there for a few minutes, before staggering to his feet and walking groggily out the door.

"I'm tempted to toe him in the backside for good measure, but it wouldn't do any good. Smith will probably do it for me when he comes back empty handed, but still demanding money for a failed job. The little bugger nearly had me with that big innocent grin of his. Now I can go and have a shower. Prop that chair under the handle when I leave, but I'm sure he won't be back."

"Did the kid get it?"

"No Ike. Hanna caught him in the act and knocked him out and that has really caused me some heartache. The kid's old lady has been down here this morning screaming her tits off that her innocent child has been assaulted by Hanna. She won't stop screaming until I charge Hanna or get him to cough up some compensation. Bloody kid's a criminal, but he's one of the protected species we can't do much about."

"Did the kid actually recognise the diary? How did he know what he was looking for?"

"I showed him mine and explained it would have pages with dates and handwritten notes. He said Hanna had a similar black book with dates and it was full of handwriting, but he didn't have time to read it. I doubt whether he could anyway."

"What about Hanna? I hope you're not going to arrest him? Pay the kid's mother off and I'll reimburse you. That should take care of her."

"Hanna and Chloe Boyce flew out for Perth this morning and according to staff at the airport check-in they're not holding return tickets so it looks as though they're gone for good. They travelled light though. They only had one bag each."

"No, I don't believe they're not coming back. Hanna had only one diary with him. He told me Boyce had recorded everything from the year we started. He may be carrying the most incriminating, but the remaining diaries must be still out at the homestead."

"I can take care of that. I'll get old Hoben to sign a search warrant and I'll carry out a search in the morning. I'll get those diaries if they're still there. Tell me Ike, how did you know Hanna would have a diary with him. I told you he was catching the flight out, but I don't get the connection?"

"I believe he's going to try and see Geddes."

"But he hasn't done any good with you and me, so why would he front up to Geddes. He'll just tell him to get lost won't he? Forget it Ike, the guy's just spinning his wheels."

"I hope you're right Wally, but make sure when you carry out the search for those diaries you make it thorough. Make sure you get hold of every piece of paper Henry ever wrote on. In the meantime I'll put through a call to Arthur Gedddes. Hanna is very smart and he just might put the frighteners into Arthur. It's a pity about Hanna, he believes integrity overrides money. I'd really like that guy on my side if only he'd play ball."

"I came close to blowing him away the other day. All our problems would have been solved."

"Why didn't you then?"

"A couple of Venus jackaroos rolled up just as I was about to pull the trigger and then the cheeky bastards stopped a couple of hundred metres past and just watched me. Standing there with a shotgun pointed at someone's guts would ring alarm bells with anyone, no matter how dumb they are."

"Well if he comes back Wally, I think you should make another attempt. Mr Hanna is a real problem."

They picked their bags off the conveyor and made for the taxi rank. "I know a very nice hotel in Fremantle. Good restaurants, cafes and a stone's throw from the beach."

"No, we're staying with my aunt Liz. She's expecting us."

"You're aunt Liz?" Andrew exclaimed. "I'm not that broke. Anyway I want us to have time alone and I can't imagine anything worse than aunt Liz watching our every move."

"She's not a prude Andrew. You'll like her I'm sure and her cooking is great."

"Why didn't you tell me earlier?"

"I didn't want an argument. Better to spring it on you as a fait accompli. Besides, I don't want to mope around a hotel all day by myself. I couldn't stand being recognised and patronised by some magazine journalist. Those days are behind me."

Andrew laughed as he swung the bags into the boot of the taxi. The driver stood there with his hand on the upturned lid, not offering any assistance.

"Where to mate?" The driver got in and was looking at them in his rear view mirror.

"The lady will tell you where to go. I've only just met her."

Chloe dug him in the ribs, glaring at him in mock outrage as she gave directions.

They made small talk for the rest of the ride as they were aware the driver was listening to every word.

"Just here please driver." Chloe pointed the multi-storied unit block.

The driver opened the boot, but still did not offer any assistance as Andrew retrieved the bags and paid him.

"You've got a real stunner there mate." The remark was barely audible. "I wouldn't mind an hour with her."

"You don't make enough money." Andrew brushed him aside and joined Chloe on the pavement.

"What were you saying to him?"

"I said I couldn't give him your phone number, because you were far too expensive and I wanted you all to myself."

Chloe grabbed his arm tightly. "Behave yourself Andrew and don't make any jokes like that in front of aunt Liz."

"I thought you said she wasn't a prude?"

Chloe ignored him as she pushed the button and looked into the camera. There was a muffled greeting and the entrance door unlocked.

Elizabeth Murdoch was waiting for them when the lift opened on her floor. She threw her arms around Chloe and hugged her tightly. Andrew stood silently watching and listening to the usual squeals of delight and kisses mandatory with any loving relationship.

"And who's this dishy looking young man you've brought with you?"

"I'm just the porter ma'am," Andrew said holding up the bags. "Although I've been known to warm her bed on occasions.

Elizabeth looked stunned for a few seconds, before breaking into a shriek of laughter.

"This is Andrew aunt Liz, but he's not as funny as he thinks he is. He's trying to shock you."

He nodded sternly. "Yes aunt Liz, I've been appropriately admonished."

"Well, let's get one thing straight. I'm Liz to you both, not aunt Liz. Understood?"

They both nodded as they followed her in. Andrew took an instant liking. She was not like any aunt Liz he expected.

"The porter can put the bags in your room Chloe. You know where it is. You can make as much noise as you like in there. I've got a light lunch prepared when you're ready."

"I agree, she is a bit of a sweety." Andrew put the bags down and looked around. "Is she really your aunt?"

"She's Dad's sister, so she really is my aunt. Why don't you go and talk to her while I change and freshen up?"

Liz was busying herself in the kitchen as he went out into the lounge and marvelled at the view.

"So, Andrew what do you do if I may ask?"

"You can certainly ask Liz. I'm a destitute unemployed lawyer now."

"Where did you two meet?"

"In Wyndham. I bought a law practice and Chloe was a client of mine."

"So why are you now unemployed? Wasn't there enough work?"

"It's a complicated story Liz. It all has to do with Chloe, but she was not the cause. I was advising her and I got caught up in a conflict of interest, is probably the best way of describing it. Perhaps she can explain it better."

Liz nodded as she gave him a searching look. "When she phoned she didn't say much except to say she was coming to Perth with you on business. She's not in any trouble is she? It's nothing to do with that dreadful husband of hers is it? Oh, that reminds me, I think I saw his photo in the paper." She got up to move towards a cabinet. "I've got it here somewhere."

"She's already seen that Liz. I'm trying to locate him to push through her divorce."

"Any success? He should be easier enough to find now he's in the country as a refugee."

"No, it's not that easy because I think he would have tossed his passport overboard the moment he was sure their boat had been spotted by the navy. He's most probably using an alias and will apply for refugee status which may take some time while Immigration checks him out. He may even get around that because there are so many boat people arriving from Indonesia the authorities simply can't cope and will open the floodgates in the name of humanity. We know he arrived on Christmas Island, but they could have sent him to Nauru or Manus Islands, or he could be right here in Perth. Until I know exactly where he is, there's not much I can do about it."

"I cannot understand why she married him, but love is a strange animal. From what she's told me, he simply lived off her. I feel he will most certainly contest the divorce, because as you know Chloe is a very wealthy woman."

"I've no doubt that's exactly what he'll do, but he has to show himself to do that. I've put the necessary steps in place in the U.K., but must say I've simply been too busy to pursue it."

"So, what brings you two to Perth?"

"I think it best if Chloe's explains that to you."

Liz gave raised her eyebrows and nodded slowly.

"Explain what to you?" Chloe walked back into the lounge. "What have you two been talking about?"

"I asked Andrew what you've come to Perth for. I assume it's a social visit and a bit of shopping. You must miss the bright lights and the atmosphere of a city."

"No Liz, I don't miss it at all and we're not here on a social visit as you suggest." She sat down and looked directly at her aunt. "I'm about to lose Venus Downs and all the properties Henry left me."

Liz held her hand to her mouth in horror. "Surely not. How did that happen? You're not going bankrupt are you? If I can help in anyway..."

"No, I'm not going bankrupt, but I will lose my properties in the Kimberleys and Pilbara and there's nothing I can do about it. I've still got my house in London and savings so I'm well off in that regard, but thank you for your offer."

"Are you planning to move to Perth then? I would love to have you near me."

"I would like that to, but first things first. Andrew wants to talk to the bank that called the mortgages on the properties."

"Mortgages? That's unlike Henry. I know he nearly went under years back but when he recovered he insisted he would never be caught in that position again. He would never over extend himself."

"That's the part I can't figure out Liz," Andrew said breaking in. "The properties pay their way. They're not highly profitable, but nevertheless they do manage to meet the interest payments every month, but the bank has called the loans."

"But surely they can't do that?"

"Banks are a law unto themselves Liz. It's pointless to fight them as they have more money than any of us."

"But surely you can go to another bank?"

"Yes, Chloe could, but that would take time for them to peruse the books and decide the terms, if in fact they were inclined to replace the mortgages, but time is not on her side. I would say sometime in the next couple of weeks she will be dispossessed."

"Am I correct in thinking there's more to this than just the bank calling the loans? It just doesn't ring true to me."

Chloe looked at Andrew and nodded for him to explain. "You just mentioned Henry nearly went bankrupt. That was a year or so before Chloe left Venus Downs to come down here to train as a model before she went to England. You're not going to like what I'm about to tell you Liz, but Henry got mixed up in a major cattle theft operation. He was complicit in the theft of cattle from an adjoining station."

"Oh my God, I can't believe it." She gave them a horrified look of doubt. "Henry would never do a thing like that." She looked at Chloe for denial, but the slight nod confirmed her worst fears.

"If you say he was complicit, it must mean there are others involved. I take it you've stopped it?"

"Chloe can't stop it Liz. She has absolutely no control over what's going on. She's only found out in the past few weeks she's an unwitting party to the on-going crime."

"Why haven't you reported this to the police? Chloe you must stop it now. I'm horrified to believe you would continue to be involved."

"Liz, the police are involved."

The statement hit Liz like a thunderclap as she absorbed what Andrew had just said.

He nodded at her shocked look. "Yes Liz, the police are involved along with others."

"Andrew has already had his life threatened. He's in danger if he goes back."

"Why not report it here then? They would have to investigate it wouldn't they? What are you talking about in monetary terms? Have they stolen a few hundred head or is it much more serious?"

"It runs into millions of dollars Liz. It isn't just a petty offence that will incur a fine."

Liz straightened up with an indignant look. "Well, it's got to stop immediately and if you don't do something, I will. I happen to know the assistant police commissioner. His wife is a member of my bridge club. I could phone him now."

Andrew held up his hand. "No Liz, I would caution you to give this some thought. Of course Chloe could make a complaint here, but that would involve her in a full investigation which, although she's innocent, she would be dragged through the mud. Henry's name would likewise suffer. In some ways it's a blessing Chloe is about to lose everything, because the owners of Ascot Downs, the station from which the cattle have been stolen over the years, would sue her for theft and damages. Just because Henry is dead doesn't absolve the liability. His estate which has passed to Chloe would be directly in the firing line."

"How did you find out about this Andrew?"

"A member of the syndicate involved came to me to assist him with his Will. He was terminally ill and he disclosed everything."

"And you did nothing about it? I know enough about the law Andrew to know this is not a case of client privilege where anything said to you remains confidential. This is a crime and you were duty bound to immediately report it, weren't you?"

Andrew looked at the floor lost in thought before he raised his head and looked directly at his accuser. "Yes, I'm guilty as you say Liz. I'll be finished as a lawyer if I come under investigation, but I had a motive. I...."

"The motive is obvious to me Andrew. You're in love aren't you and your sole motive was to protect Chloe?"

"Guilty again Liz."

"And I love him," Chloe said softly. "Without him I would have been dead by now. That's how serious this whole thing is."

Liz held up her hand. "Chloe please stop there. But tell me, what have you come to Perth for?"

"Liz, whatever I say stays in this room. Let me explain it to you. The person who told me about this the day he died was Bill Hargraves, the manager of Ascot Downs which is owned by an English company which hasn't been paying attention to its holdings down here. The others involved were Henry and a person by the name of Ike Shulman, the richest man in Wyndham and an unnamed mystery fourth person."

"That's the police chief you're referring to?"

"No the police chief is a Sergeant Smith. He's not one of the main syndicate, but someone who obviously tumbled onto what was going on and had to be bought off."

"He would have murdered Andrew if Joey Moonlight my head stockman, hadn't arrived on the scene seconds before Smith was going to shoot him."

"You two do live dangerously don't you? I really can't believe what I'm hearing, but I accept it's all true. So who is this fourth person? I may as well know in case anything happens to you both?"

"I believe I know who it is Liz, but I can't be sure and until I can prove it, he shall remain nameless."

"And what if you do prove it? What's the point if Chloe is about to be thrown out? She can't lay a complaint because she'll also be charged. Why bother identifying the fourth person. Just walk away from the whole mess would be my advice."

"You'll have to leave that with me Liz, but suffice to say I believe he holds the key to why the bank is moving against Chloe. This is not a case of the bank simply calling the loans because it has the power to do so. That's not how banks work. I think the fourth person was the bank manager at Wyndham when Henry became involved, and if I'm correct he's here in Perth in a very senior position. However, if I'm wrong I've simply no idea of the identity of the other person involved."

"But that's not going to help Chloe is it? Either way she loses."

"At first glance she does, but I've got a very strong suspicion who's behind the bank's actions and who's pulling the strings and why. And the why is the real question I want answered."

"It sounds to me as though you two are playing with fire. You say you would be dead without Andrew, so someone must have threatened you and you Andrew, avoided death by seconds. Get the hell out of it now. I don't want to attend two funerals. You've got your whole lives to look forward to without getting further involved with something you clearly have no control over."

"I agree with you Liz. The situation looks hopeless at the moment, but there's a slim chance I may be able to unravel it."

"But you said yourself, even if you do get the bank to call off the dogs and Chloe by some miracle retains the properties, she still loses if the owners of Ascot Downs ever find out. It's pointless Andrew. Give it away and stop this silly quest."

"You're right of course, but I only want a few days and I can't stop now."

Liz let out a deep sigh and shook her head in disbelief. "I'm not trying to stop you Andrew, but you've got my opinion. In the meantime you're most welcome to stay as long as you like. I crave company and I can see you love Chloe, so I love you both."

Chloe got up and kissed her aunt on the cheek. "Thank you Liz. Venus Downs in my home and despite the fact all looks lost, I want Andrew to at least try."

Liz patted her arm. "I'm with you Chloe. Don't ever forget that. Now why don't we go out to a lovely restaurant I know and then take in a movie?"

"That would be fun. I haven't seen a film in years," Chloe replied looking at Andrew.

He grinned and nodded. "Neither have I, so I'll be in that. Dotti's cooking gets a bit repetitive and I could do with a little diversion."

Andrew was not aware of the movie or its content. His thoughts were elsewhere.

Liz and Chloe were laughing about something he could not recall as Liz opened the door and ushered them in.

"Oh, someone has been trying to get me." She noticed the message light flashing on her kitchen phone. "Four messages in fact." She pushcd the button and listened at the frantic garbled messages.

"I don't understand a word. No one I know." She made to delete them.

"Just a moment Liz, I think that's Dotti voice." Chloe listened intently as Liz played them again. "Yes, I'm sure it is, but I can't understand what she's saying. I gave her the phone number here so I'd better call to find out what's worrying her."

"I can guess why she's calling in a panic." Andrew had slumped into a lounge chair with a despairing look. "Smith has raided the homestead."

"Why would he do that? What could he be looking for?"

"Henry's diaries and papers. However, he won't find anything of interest as I got Joey to hide everything in anticipation of Smith's move. I still haven't gone through all his papers properly and there may be something significant I'm yet to discover."

Chloe talked to Dotti for about twenty minutes, the first ten just trying to calm her down, before she put the phone down.

"Smith just stormed into the place with two constables, waving a search warrant in her face and demanding to know where Henry kept his papers. Dotti showed him into Henry's office, but the place was empty of records. Even the safe was empty. He got very angry when she couldn't tell him where they had gone. He went through every room and even demanded to speak to Joey Moonlight who told him you had removed everything, but didn't know where to."

"Good for Joey. I knew I could count on him." Andrew laughed at the thought of Joey adopting a cowed look before the menacing policeman's threats, while underneath gloating at his frustration. "Smith must really be getting worried that I'll lower the boom on him."

"I would have done so already," Liz chipped in.

"I can't do that Liz. As I've already explained, Chloe is too exposed."

"Yes, yes, it's just that I'm so confused and worried for you both. What to you intend to do tomorrow?"

"I've got to try and get a meeting with someone at the bank, someone who will listen, because their attitude doesn't make any sense at the moment."

Andrew stopped outside the St George's Terrace entrance and looked up at the imposing glass structure of the bank inhabited by faceless people who hid behind its edifice and administered its rules and directions with compassionless impunity.

The bank could look to view the world outside and demand and make its own terms, because it was that inanimate structure called the 'Bank' and not the people within who were ultimately responsible. All he could see was the wall of opaque obstruction he was attempting to penetrate. He was aware security guards and cameras were watching as he walked up to the desk. The receptionist was all smiles.

"How can I be of assistance sir?"

"I would like to see Mr Arthur Geddes if I may. I don't have an appointment."

"And your name is sir?"

"Andrew Hanna. I'm a solicitor acting for a client of the bank."

"And the client's name please?"

"Chloe Boyce of Venus Downs pastoral company in the Kimberleys."

He watched her as she picked up a phone, punched in an extension number and relayed his credentials and client name to the person on the other end. She put down the phone and wrote his name on a tag and asked him to fill in the visitor book.

"If you take the lift to the fourteenth floor someone will meet you there Mr Hanna."

He was met by a nameless receptionist who directed him to a small meeting room consisting of a table and four chairs. "Mr Spurling will be with you shortly. Would you like a tea or coffee or cold drink?"

He declined and she nodded and disappeared, closing the door behind her. It was not a room signifying hospitality or comfort, but a room signifying the cold hard facts of banking and business. He mused he was probably being observed by some hidden camera as he looked around drumming his fingers on the table for ten minutes growing impatient with the staged delay. The door finally opened and a tall balding individual with rimless glasses entered and placed a folder on the table.

"Good morning Mr Hanna. I apologise for the delay, but your visit was unexpected and I had to bring myself up to date with the file on the Boyce matter. Do you have authorisation and some form of identification?"

Andrew handed him a signed letter authorising him to act on Chloe's behalf and his driver's licence. They were studied and handed back without comment.

"And your name is?"

"Peter Spurling. The Boyce matter is within my portfolio. Now what can I do for you?" The question had no warmth or meaning. It was perfunctory and demanding.

"I would like to know why the bank is calling the overdraft and loan facility when the mortgages are not in default."

"I agree, they are not in default, but without that facility the mortgages become exposed and the bank simply does not want to accept that risk. The mortgages appear to be in a healthy position at the moment, but as you know conditions in the cattle industry are subject to any number of negatives and the bank has made the decision to de-risk in that area."

"But why the sudden haste? Why not let her sell one or two of the properties and completely extinguish the mortgages on the whole package? Why the bank has taken this attitude is beyond my comprehension. I believe it is an unconscionable action that requires explanation."

"It is out of my hands Mr Hanna. The bank has made the decision and it cannot be changed." Spurling's attitude was clinical and expressionless.

"Mr Spurling, the bank is people. It's not some Darlek or automaton that can think for itself, so don't hand me that bank-speak. It's total spin and you know it. If it's not you, then someone in this bank, a real person with the vital signs of life, has the authority to review this file"

Spurling's expression flinched momentarily at the insult, but he showed no other outward emotion as he picked up the file and began to rise.

"I believe I have explained the bank's position Mr Hanna. I can do no more."

Andrew could see he had lost, but a sudden thought occurred to him. "Other than the bank, are there any guarantors supporting those mortgages?"

"That would be a confidence between the bank and the guarantor and I wouldn't be at liberty to discuss it with you. However, if a guarantor does exist then your client would not necessarily know about it. That confidence would be between the guarantor and the bank."

"I take it from that equivocal answer Mr Spurling, a guarantor has precipitated this action by the bank?"

"I have a busy day Mr Hanna. You'll have to excuse me. Would you wait here for a minute until I can have you escorted to the elevator."

The surgical strike had been delivered by the bank and Spurling was the messenger who disappeared as quickly as he had arrived. Andrew wasn't left waiting as the receptionist opened the door and with a plastic smile, beckoned him to follow her. Spurling was in a hurry to get rid of him.

"By any chance would Arthur Geddes be on this floor?"

"Mr Geddes is not in this department. He is the general manager" She ignored his further questions as she rode down in the lift with him. Spurling was indeed making sure he was seen off the premises.

Andrew strode across the foyer to the reception desk to hand back his pass. "Could I make an appointment to see Mr Geddes please?"

The welded-on smile did not diminish as she called the extension and made the request.

"I'm afraid Mr Geddes is not available Mr Hanna. He has a busy schedule and cannot fit you in anytime this month."

Andrew smiled and turned to walk away. A month would suit Geddes. Chloe would be out of business and Geddes could quietly forget the whole matter. He was passing a wall of elevators, with muted bells ringing and doors opening and closing. A door was closing when a girl ran up with a coffee in one hand and urgency on her face. She stabbed the button and the doors hesitated before momentarily sliding open again. There was no mistaking Ike Shulman. He was shuffling backwards in the crowded lift and had not noticed Andrew. However, he had no doubt Shulman would soon know he'd been trying to see Geddes.

Andrew sat in the coffee bar beside the exit ramp from the bank and waited. He had a clear view and was warned by a pedestrian alarm to any vehicle leaving the building. If Ike was lunching with Geddes he doubted whether Geddes would invite him into the executive dining room where every guest was vetted and recorded. And it would be beneath his status to simply walk out the front entrance with a client and look for a restaurant. No, he would travel down in the executive lift, climb in his car and drive off to some quiet location with his guest. At least that is what Andrew assumed and anticipated he would do. He waited for half an hour just watching delivery trucks and obscure cars come and go and then the nose of a Mercedes coupé appeared. He had a clear view of the driver, with Ike beside him in an animated conversation. He could have quickly moved around the rail and walked in front of the vehicle, but thought better of it. He did not want Ike around when he finally confronted the man.

Chloe was waiting anxiously for him when the lift door opened. She could see the depressed look on his face.

"It didn't go well did it?"

"No, I saw a Peter Spurling who's in charge of your portfolio. He wouldn't budge or listen to me. He confirmed the bank will not change its position. However, I did see something of real interest and that was Ike Shulman arriving at the bank. He didn't see me, but I waited and sure enough I saw him leave in a Mercedes I can only assume was driven by Geddes."

Liz was putting a salad and cold cuts on the table when they came into the lounge. "Sit down and eat you two. You don't have to tell me the bank wouldn't listen."

"Liz, do you have a phone book?"

"In the cabinet under the phone. Who is it you're looking for?"

"A man by the name of Arthur Geddes, the general manager of the bank. He refused to see me. I wonder if he's listed." He ran his finger down the column. There were two Geddes listed, a Ronald J, and a Malcolm R, but no A. Geddes.

"Where do these two live?"

Liz reached for her reading glasses and looked at the addresses. "I doubt whether either of them is the person you're after. Very much the wrong side of the tracks if you're looking for a wealthy banker. He probably has an unlisted number."

She straightened and put an upright finger to her lips as she searched her memory. "I recall a name like that. Anyway I think it was Geddes. I was introduced to her when her bridge club visited ours and that would have been more than a year ago. She's was a tall dour woman, hardly spoke, but knew how to give her partner hell when she made the wrong call. You could crack a brick on her face and she wouldn't flinch. She had that appearance. Any man married to her would toe the line. I vaguely recall now that someone said she was married to a banker."

"Could you find out about her Liz? I've got to meet Geddes and confront him in person."

"Hmmm. Rachel Frick may know, she's the president of our club. In fact I think it was Rachel who introduced me to her." She picked up her phone and dialled. "Hello Rachel, it's Liz Murdoch speaking."

The usual pleasantries followed until Liz pulled a face and held the phone at arm's length while tapping her forefinger against her thumb to signify an endless stream of chatter from the other end.

"What I'm phoning about Rachel, is do you remember introducing me to someone by the name of Geddes who was married to a banker? She was visiting from another club."

Her eyes lit up and she nodded to them while listening. "Maud Geddes, known as Maudlin Maud you say? Yes, I agree with you. She did look as though she was just waiting for the mortician to come and collect her, but she could play bridge, I'll give her that. Rachel I...." Liz held the phone out again as she was cut off by the unceasing chatter. Finally, she cut in. "Rachel I've got an appointment in fifteen minutes, so I'll be brief. Would you know her address or phone number. No, I don't want to talk to her, but I know someone who wants to speak to her husband. He's a personal friend he hasn't seen for years and he wants to just drop around and surprise him."

Liz put her hand over the speaker. "She's got both, but will have to go through her contact book. I wonder what they refer to me as. Talk about a bunch of gossips. I don't play much any more for that very reason." She quickly put the phone back to her ear. "Oh, yes Rachel I'm still here. Just give that to me slowly would you?" She scrawled down the address and phone number and then repeated them. "Yes, I've got that Rachel and thank you so much. I must go now. Bye."

Liz tore off the notepaper and handed it to Andrew. "That's the person you're after. Maudlin Maud let the whole bridge club know husband Arthur is indeed a very influential banker. She and Arthur have only been married a few years. They met at a bank function when Maud appeared with her father, the bank chairman. According to Rachel she was well past her used-by-date. She thinks Arthur couldn't believe his luck and neither could Maud. You can draw your own conclusions as to why Arthur has risen to be general manager."

"I'll know when I see him. I got a clear look at him in the car this morning with Shulman."

"Are you just going to knock on his door and front him?"

"Unless you can come up with a better approach I can't see any other way than being up front and direct Chloe. He refuses to see me at the bank, so yes, I'm just going to walk up to him when he gets home."

"Take my car Andrew. It wouldn't pay to be seen loitering around in that upmarket neighbourhood on foot. The police would pick you up within five minutes of a complaint being made about a possible rapist or burglar at large."

"Thanks Liz, I'll accept your offer."

"I'm coming with you Andrew. I want to see what Geddes looks like."

"Okay, but you must promise to stay in the car. I don't want to drag you into this in case I've got the wrong person. On the other hand, if he's the person I'm looking for, then I believe it would be in your interests to remain out of sight. This man will undoubtedly have power and influence and he may immediately call my bluff and call the police. Blackmail is a nasty charge to defend and he'll be well aware of that. I wouldn't want to see us both banged up and applying for bail in the morning."

Liz looked horrified. "You're not going to blackmail him are you Andrew?"

"I can't think of any other way of doing it Liz. I will call it a demand for an explanation, but if it hits the fan a prosecuting barrister will level blackmail at me and at the mere mention of that word, any judge's frown will turn decidedly dark."

17

The imposing house was set back on the lower side of the road with sweeping vistas of the Swan River.

Andrew gave a low whistle. "This pile would have cost a buck or two and I'll bet Ascot and Venus Downs contributed a significant portion of that. And the her's Mercedes in the driveway is a nice touch. Arthur and Maud are doing very nicely, but I intend to pull it all down around their ears if Arthur doesn't play ball."

"Do you think we'll have to wait long?"

"Chloe I'll bet he punches the Bundy at five on the dot. He'll be home by five thirty and Maud will have his dinner on the table by six sharp."

"Bundy? What the hell's that?"

"I can see you've never worked in a factory. A Bundy is a clock which punches the time and date a worker checks in or out."

She laughed. "You've got to be kidding aren't you? Surely, Geddes would't have to do that?"

"Yes I am." He leaned over to give her a quick kiss. "Oh, oh, a Mercedes has just swung into sight so let's see if it's our man."

Geddes looked directly at Andrew as he drove slowly past and then into his driveway.

"That's him and I recognise the plate on his Merc. Now Chloe, don't get out of the car."

She was about to say something, but he was already out and striding up the driveway as Geddes, realising that someone was about to accost him, was also in a hurry to get out of the car. However, as he was dragging his brief case across the steering wheel it opened and the contents spilled out onto his lap and onto the driveway. Andrew picked up those that were fluttering down the driveway towards him.

"No need to rush Arthur. I'm not a bailiff here to serve a summons." He held out the documents which Geddes took and shoved in with the others.

"Who are you? How dare you accost me at my own home? You are trespassing and I order you to leave now or I will call the police."

"You might not know me by sight Arthur, but the look on your face tells me you know exactly who I am. My name is Andrew Hanna and I'm Chloe Boyce's legal representative. I called on you today, but you refused to see me."

"I, I am an extremely busy man Hanna. I can't see every blow-in who demands a meeting without an appointment. Now remove yourself immediately from my property."

"I find it strange you had time for a nice lunch with Ike Shulman today, but had no time to see me." Andrew was holding the door of the Merc open and boxing Geddes in. The banker made to move past, but Andrew shoved him up against the car. "Listen Arthur you had better find time to talk to me otherwise I'm going to drop an anonymous letter to the bank about your clandestine activities over the years with Shulman. I don't think the directors will like what they read."

"I don't know what you're talking about, now get out of my way."

Andrew could see he was going to lose the threat if he allowed Geddes to think rationally. At present he could see the banker was trying to stifle the panic, so he stepped back.

"Arthur you were and no doubt still are, the silent partner in a very significant cattle theft operation. Your cut was ten percent which by my calculations must run into very serious money."

"That's a preposterous allegation. You're trying to black-mail me," Geddes exploded.

"Arthur you can cut the bullshit and bluster. I've positive proof you were the fourth member of the partnership in crime along with Ike Shulman, Bill Hargraves, and Henry Boyce with a third each and you holding the balance. You see, Henry Boyce kept very detailed diary notes of the numbers of cattle stolen and sold through Ike Shulman along with a calculation of the distribution of the ill-gotten gains. I know your name was to be kept secret from Hargraves, but Boyce recorded it as such with your initials AG. You've got some explaining to do as your superiors will quickly follow a money trail back to you, no matter where you've hidden it and I've no doubt you're still receiving your cut. Shulman is panicking and that's why you got together with him today, wasn't it? You can probably feel the heat Arthur, but that's nothing compared to the blow-torch I'm about to apply to your arse."

"Arthur, what are you doing out there? Who are you talking to?" Maudlin had heard the car drive in and wondered what was keeping him. She was standing in the doorway with a look of concern and annoyance.

"You don't know what you're talking about Hanna. I will sue you for defamation and lay a complaint with the Law Society. You'll lose your practising certificate over this."

"I can live with that, but in the meantime I can assure you'll be out of a job, you'll be doing time and Maud may not wait for you. I don't think she'll be able to bear the disgrace of her high-profile banker husband suddenly crashing her social standing."

Out of the corner of his eye Andrew saw a person walking across the road and pausing at the bottom of Geddes driveway.

"This person appears to be hassling you Arthur? Can I be of assistance?"

Geddes waved his hand. "No, no Tom. No problem at all." The neighbour shrugged and turned back.

Maud became more demanding. "What are you doing Arthur? Why don't you answer me?"

"I'll be there in a moment dear."

"Do you want the whole street and your wife to hear this, or can we get together and discuss this in a sensible manner."

"What do you want Hanna?" He hissed in Andrew's face, shaking in rage.

"I want to discuss the Boyce matter with you Arthur, nothing more. So why don't we get together tomorrow?"

"I'm busy tomorrow. I can't possibly see you."

"Well, you've just cancelled your appointments for an hour or two because if you don't agree now, I'm going to drop a memo to the bank. Capice?"

"Arthur what are you doing? Who is that man?"

"Give me your hotel and I'll phone you in the morning." There was a note of desperation in his voice. He could see his wife approaching.

"No Arthur. Give me your mobile number and I'll phone you. I don't want to open my door to any surprises during the night."

Geddes handed him a business card, slammed the car door and stepped around him.

"I'll phone you at nine sharp in the morning to set up a meeting Arthur and you'd better take the call, otherwise you know the consequences."

Andrew could feel the glare of Maud's wrath on his back as he casually walked down the driveway.

"It looked as though Geddes didn't appreciate the intrusion? I thought you were in trouble when that neighbour wandered across the road. And when big Maud appeared I imagined there would be a real scene."

Andrew laughed as he started the car and turned across the centre of the road. "I thought Arthur was going to call my bluff for a moment, but when that neighbour appeared he began to deflate somewhat. A leading banker must keep up appearances and it wouldn't look good to be seen getting into a heated argument with a stranger. The tongues would wag and Maud would have trouble defending her Arty."

"What are you going to do now?"

"I told him I'd phone him at nine in the morning for a meeting and that's where I could get myself into deep trouble, or make some progress."

"How would you get into trouble?"

"If Arthur suggests a meeting in his office, it means he will have taken legal advice, the meeting will be recorded and I'll be facing a charge of blackmail and extortion. If on the other hand he suggests a quiet meeting in a discrete location, it will mean I've got him on the run and I can negotiate."

Chloe squeezed his arm. "I'm worried darling you are going too far out on a limb for me. I don't want to see you go to jail. I've lost everything, so why don't we just call it a day and get on with our lives?"

"Because I believe there's a conspiracy going on with Shulman the conspirator and Geddes a now very frightened co-conspirator, by assisting Shulman to get hold of your properties. I will know conclusively if Geddes agrees to meet me tomorrow somewhere away from his office. I'm convinced it is him Henry referred to as AG in his diaries. He's been party to the theft for years, but now if I'm correct, he wants out. The only problem is that Ike won't let him out. Why would he, when all he has to do is phone up Geddes if he wants to finance a deal. He's got him hooked and he has no intention of letting him off the hook. What's more, I now believe Ike is the guarantor for Henry's mortgages and it's him who has put pressure on the bank to call them."

"But why doesn't Ike just remove himself as guarantor? The bank would be forced to act then, wouldn't it?"

"He can't, as the bank wouldn't let him unless he could find a replacement guarantor, and there's little chance of that. There's something I can't put my finger on at the moment. So many things just don't add up. I can only surmise Ike is forcing Geddes and therefore the bank, to sell the properties to him at a knockdown price. He gets the properties at half their real value, or less and the guarantees are gone. Geddes can explain his actions to those higher up by saying he did not believe you as a woman, whose career up to now has been far removed from cattle, would be able to successfully manage such a huge holding. The result is the bank calls the mortgages and sells you out in one lot, a far better outcome than selling individually, dealing with a succession of buyers and their lawyers and financiers and waiting months for it all to be completed. The bank has no interest in protecting your position. It just wants its money, a quick resolution and can walk away with its integrity unblemished. Also I believe Geddes wants to distance himself from the crime by handing his ten percent to Ike and washing his hands of the whole affair."

"But Andrew, I've still lost everything either way. I can't beat either of them. Even if Geddes is going along with the conspiracy as you put it, Ike is going to get what he wants. I can't possibly stop them now."

"Don't give up hope just yet. Let's see what Geddes does in the morning. I've got to phone an old friend of mine and call in a few favours so I can be ready for Geddes if he doesn't agree to meet me."

"What kind of favours?"

"Oh, I just want to know what real estate Geddes owns in this town and whose name it's registered in."

Chloe gave him an odd look, but decided not to pursue the enquiry.

Geddes answered his direct line immediately. It was as though he had been waiting with his hand poised.

"Andrew Hanna speaking Arthur. Where can we meet?"

Andrew heaved a sigh of relief at both the voice speaking in hushed tones and the instructions to meet him at a café two streets north of the bank for lunch. It looked as though the blackmail risk was off the table, but he was wary. The risk he was being set up was very real. He caught a taxi into town and located the café within a whole group of lunchtime eateries spread around a concourse. No upmarket restaurant for Geddes where he could easily be spotted by his contemporaries. His presence in a non-descript café would go unnoticed amongst the milling and chattering throng of lunchtime officeworkers. Andrew picked an adjoining café with a table partially obscured by a pillar, but with a clear view of the meeting place. He ordered a coffee and picked up a newspaper someone had left on the other chair. The whole concourse began to fill with young people crowding sandwich bars, takeaway eateries and coffee bars. Andrew felt the faint chime of an alarm bell as he dropped the paper and paid more attention to the patrons starting to fill the designated venue. He started focussing more intently until his gaze fell upon a solitary figure seated with his back to him, facing out onto the street and gazing idly at the passing crowds. Any other tables were filled by gossiping housewives, groups of girls or guys and mixed groups all in animated conversation. He looked at his watch and then glanced up to see Geddes arriving right on time. He made to get up, but froze when the solitary figure at the table got up and nodded to Geddes before walking off. Geddes claimed the table and sat down. If he had not been watching Andrew would never have picked up the signal. He followed the departing figure and watched him sit down at a table at the back of the café. He was looking directly at Geddes back. Andrew felt a sickening feeling as his heart started to race. He did not have the look of a cop, but decided he could not take the risk. It was obvious a trap was being set and he would have walked right into it if he had ignored the premonition. There was no use running away from it. Another trap would be set if he did not tackle this one head on. He got up from the table and walked out of the café knowing that Geddes had not yet seen him and he was safe in the knowledge the accomplice did not know who he was supposed to be looking for. He walked down the road about fifty metres and opened the door of the solitary cab sitting on the stand. "Just hold it a moment driver, I want to call someone."

"Arthur, you'll see a cab pull up right in front of you in about thirty seconds. I want you to join me in it."

The cab driver looked up in bewilderment as Andrew pointed towards the café.

"But I thought we were meeting here? This is very inconvenient." Geddes was still talking into his phone when Andrew pulled up, opened the door and shouted. The taxi was far enough forward that Andrew was obscured from the accomplice. Andrew smiled as he saw Geddes look around in consternation and then walk quickly towards the him.

"Come on sport, this is a bus stop and I've got one up my ginger now." The driver yelled at Geddes as he got in. "That's a two hundred buck fine if I get lumbered." He pulled out into the traffic. "Where to?"

"Subiaco, anywhere in the café strip please."

Geddes sat stunned as Andrew leaned across and quickly patted his chest and sides. "Just taking precautions Arthur. I'm not making a pass at you."

Neither of them exchanged a word until they were seated under the footpath awning of a quiet café.

"Much better here don't you think Arthur? We can hear ourselves talk."

Geddes looked at his watch. "I don't like appointments changed without notice Hanna. I don't have a lot of time as I'm due back in an hour." He adopted the tone of indignant authority, but Andrew could see it had a very thin veneer.

"I changed it Arthur because you decided it wasn't just going to be you and me. I saw your accomplice acknowledge you and surrender his table."

"He was a perfect stranger. I just took his table."

"Oh, cut out the bullshit Arthur. He signalled to you and then moved to where he had a direct view of us both. Was he a cop?"

Geddes did not reply.

"Look Arthur, I'm going to drop you right into the shit unless you tell me what's going on. If he wasn't a cop, who was he?"

"I, I really don't know who he was. I had nothing to do with him."

"Ike really has got your dick in one hand and is squeezing your nuts with the other, hasn't he?"

"Hanna, I find your remarks crude and extremely offensive." The banker flustered as the colour in his face rose.

"Why? Doesn't Maud ever stroke your dick, or do you only do that yourself?"

Geddes began to rise as his face went crimson with rage. Andrew reached over and pushed him back into his chair. He decided to go in for the kill. He was either making the biggest mistake of his life, or he was about to hit a home run.

"Calm down Arthur and don't come the holier-than-thou tone with me. I've no doubt you go to church, piss in the bishop's pocket to give him a warm feeling at the size of your tithe every year, are seen with the right people in the correct settings and functions, and generally come across as a pillar of society, but I'm about to tear all that down around your grubby ears. The veil of respectability will be pulled away and you'll be exposed as nothing but a lying, cheating, thieving shit. Maud won't squeeze your gonads, she'll cut them off along with your dick when this breaks."

Geddes did not react so Andrew played his trump card. "And my title searches show your house, and another in Cottesloe, along with a vineyard in the Margaret River, are all registered in her name or in the name of a company of which she is the sole shareholder, director or trustee. Arthur, you're going to be living under a culvert along with the other homeless derelicts when you get out of the pen."

"Enough, enough." The banker threw his hands wide. A tear started to roll down his cheek as his face screwed up in the rage of defeat.

"I can have you charged with blackmail."

"You certainly can Arthur. Hopefully we can be assigned adjoining cells so we can reminisce. You about Maud and all you've lost and me about my law career being over. Mind you I can appeal and probably get my licence to practice back within a couple of years, but in your case, you're stuffed for all time."

Geddes leaned down and buried his head in his hands. "Tell me what you want?"

"First of all, who was the person back at the café?"

"I don't know. Ike described him to me and arranged the meeting place. I've never laid eyes on him before today."

Andrew felt the surge of relief. If Ike had arranged it, it meant the person was not a cop, but it still smelt of real danger. "Okay, I'll accept that explanation for now, but you had better warn Shulman if anything happens to me or Chloe Boyce the balloon is going to go up just the same. Maud will be in and you'll be out on the street."

"For God's sake Hanna, tell me what you want. I can't stand this."

"I want the bank to back off on pulling the mortgages, it's as simple as that."

"I can't and besides, Ike has given written notice he wants to withdraw the guarantees."

Andrew nodded slowly. "That confirms what I've suspected. Ike is behind all this. He knows no one will replace him as guarantor because of the money involved, so he just pulls the guarantees and gets the properties for a fraction of their worth. But tell me, I'm mystified why Ike went guarantor in the first place?"

"I've often wondered that myself and Ike would never explain it to me. I could understand Remus Plains because it borders Venus Downs, but why they bought Baracool and Ironstone in the Pilbara was beyond me."

"Did they buy them in partnership?"

"Yes they did and that's why Ike's guarantees were required. At some point in time though Ike wanted to sell his share to fund a new project. Henry would not agree to splitting the partnership, but agreed to buy Ike out as long as he maintained the guarantees. That was good enough for the bank. I then arranged a rather large loan for Ike on the strength of his other assets. The arrangement was running along smoothly until Henry died."

"What was that loan for?"

"He wants to build a modern high-tech abattoir to export the finished product rather than live cattle to Indonesia, Korea, Malaysia and anywhere else in the rapidly expanding and increasingly wealthy Asian market."

"How much did he borrow?"

"Twenty million, but can be extended to forty if he can secure Asian partners with marketing and outlets to ensure long term contracts for supply."

Andrew gave a low whistle. "He sure is sticking his neck out. From what I've read dealing with the likes of Indonesia is risky business."

"That was the view of the bank when I put the proposal forward. It took me some time to convince them, but Ike finally sealed it by introducing a couple of strong Indonesian players who wanted to split the business between them. Ascot, Venus and Remus are central to his supply chain and that's why he wants them."

"And Ike is still paying you isn't he? You're still getting a cut from the cattle being stolen from Ascot Downs."

"He won't let me out of it. I was just a rural manager when I first met Ike and persuaded him to give me his account. I thought I'd really staged a coup in getting his business. I didn't realise it was the other way around, I wasn't stalking him, he was stalking me. He said the theft would stop once Henry Boyce was out of trouble. Ike wanted to buy him out, but Henry was not prepared to sell. However, I soon learned that once you've touched the spider's web you're trapped."

"And the money trail can be traced right back to you if I divulge Henry's diary entries."

"Hanna, you keep driving that nail in." He was shaking his head and moaning in despair. "But you're wrong about one thing. I'm a banker and know how to bury money. You can forget that as a threat although those diaries might throw up some awkward questions, but I'll handle that problem when it arises."

Andrew shook his head. "No, it's you that's wrong so don't try that on me. You may be able to hide the money trail, but you certainly can't avoid the smell of corruption. You're position in society and at the bank is finished the moment Henry's diaries see the light of day."

The banker went silent while looking blankly at Andrew. "Yes, I suppose you're right. I just pray Ike is successful in buying Ascot Downs after he gets hold of the Boyce properties. If he achieves that, there'll be no longer any point in duffing cattle from Ascot. He will have achieved his goal of a huge vertically integrated operation. It will give him the numbers to supply live cattle to Asia as well as the highly lucrative packaged processed meat through his new abattoir to the same region."

"You say Ascot is being sold?" A sudden thought occurred to Andrew as he tried not to show any real interest.

"It's about to be put on the market. Our rural division has been commissioned to handle the sale."

"Does Ike know about this?"

"No, not at this stage, but I was planning to tell him tonight when I'm meeting him for dinner. I'm caught between two evils. If it's not him, it's you trying to blackmail me. I just don't know which way to turn and as you can imagine I will not get any support at home."

Andrew could see the banker was descending into the depths of depression.

"Can you stall the sale of Ascot Downs?"

"Oh, that's not going to happen overnight. We'll have to advertise it and then there'll be the usual inspections and negotiations. It won't be a quick process, but I know the Ascot owners would like a quick sale. And I believe Ike would likely snap it up when it comes on the market."

"So it could take a month or more?"

"At least, but that's not going to help you."

"Can I ask you how long you've got before you retire?"

"I've got eighteen months to go, but I'm already being treated for depression. I just don't know if I can handle the pressure."

"Tell me, in your position it would be relatively easy for you to cancel Ike's guarantees? It would be at your discretion in view of the fact the properties are paying their way and have been debt free for years."

"The bank would not agree to it. When he pays out Boyce he could request the guarantees be extinguished, but that isn't going to happen if he buys Ascot. He's already into the bank for twenty million for the abattoir and those guarantees will have to remain until his totally liability has been satisfied."

"Pull yourself out of that dark abyss you're falling into Arthur. This is what's going to happen. Chloe is going to buy Ascot Downs but, there are a few steps prior to be slotted into place. However, with your help I'm convinced this can be achieved."

Geddes gave a small derisive laugh. "I don't see how that can be achieved Hanna. The Boyce properties are to be sold and you know who the buyer is. I cannot stop that process."

"But you could if your bank was informed Chloe Boyce intended to file a court injunction to stop the sale on the grounds it is an abuse of process. You know very well the properties are worth more individually than being offered to one man as a whole at a knockdown price. My understanding is banks don't like controversy and this could be a nasty one that could blow up in its face and in your face as well Arthur. I don't believe she would have any problem getting an injunction. In fact, as a solicitor I could prepare one tonight and lodge it with the court in the morning and that would mean a delay until a date was set for a hearing. I've no doubt I could get that hearing date extended, so who knows when it would go to trial, but it would be at least six months. The bank cannot ask for it to be expedited as there is no loss being suffered nor likely to be. The properties are paying the principal and interest and have never been in default. This could drag out for a year. If I were you, I would remind your superiors that in matters of equity the complainant has to come to court with clean hands which Chloe Boyce could clearly establish. Even a half-baked barrister could show the bank has very grubby hands in this matter. The bank has no valid reason to call the mortgages. It can be clearly demonstrated the bank is not acting in good faith and is under undue pressure from a client. You will be subpoenaed to give evidence and your involvement is going to come out. You're going to be torn to pieces Arthur and no matter what happens, management will be looking for a head to roll and that will most certainly be yours. The directors will want the mess cleaned up and the garbage tossed out. Have you ever smelt prawn heads when they've been left out overnight? The room is uninhabitable and that's what you'll smell like to the directors and needless to say Maud will also want to distance herself from the odium."

Geddes wrung his arched hands as he fought with his demons. "Tell me what you have in mind."

"The first thing I want you to do is not to tell Ike that Ascot is up for sale when you meet him this evening. Don't cancel the meeting as I believe you should go through with it. We'll meet here tomorrow for lunch and you'll tell me what transpired and I'll tell you how everything is going to fall into place. If you don't turn up then I'll carry out my threat."

"Wh... what, if I can't make it?" He stammered. "Can you give me your phone number."

"You'll make it Arthur. If you don't I'll know you got depressed and jumped off the pier in Fremantle. However, I don't think you have the balls to do that. I'll see you tomorrow."

Andrew did not look back as he got up and hailed a cab. Geddes remained seated staring into space.

18

It was as though he had not moved since the previous day. He was staring out into the street vacantly watching cars go by. Andrew had been watching him for a good ten minutes from the bench of a sheltered bus stop someway down and across the street. He could not spot anyone who might be Geddes' accomplice. He was nervous as he got up, crossed the road with a group waiting at the lights and walked towards his target.

"I thought you weren't coming."

"I got a little held up Arthur." Andrew sat down opposite and picked up the menu. "What do you feel like?'

"Just a toasted sandwich and coffee will be fine."

Andrew nodded to the waitress as she took the menus. "Make that by two please." He studied Geddes, but remained silent. The man was under strain, the dark lines under his eyes signifying lack of sleep while he tried to control the small involuntary spasms of his hands that overtook the control he was trying to exert on his addled brain.

Andrew was equally as tense as he waited at any moment for an arresting hand to be placed on his shoulder. Geddes certainly had enough evidence to level a charge of attempted blackmail.

"Mr Hanna I can assure you no one is watching us."

Andrew ignored the remark. "Did you meet Ike?"

"Yes, I did, but I didn't tell him I'd met you. He knows you're in Perth of course and he did ask me if you'd come to meet me at the bank. He specifically referred to a meeting at the bank, so I could see no reason to put him straight. If he'd asked whether I'd met you otherwise, I would have told him the truth, but he didn't so I did not feel obliged to inform him."

Andrew smiled at the man's justification. "Did you plant my suggestion the bank maybe querying the transaction."

"I did and I told him the bank was concerned Chloe Boyce would make a formal complaint and there was the likelihood she would proceed with an injunction to stop the sale of the properties if the bank proceeded to sell to him as the pre-ferred purchaser. I told him the bank would most likely offer the properties at auction to remove any taint of impropriety."

"How did he take that?"

"As you can imagine he got very upset. We only met for about an hour and the conversation revolved around the Boyce subject."

"Excellent. Well, what I want you to do now Arthur is to plant a seed in his brain he should perhaps make a sensible offer to purchase the properties."

Geddes shook his head. "No, he's adamant he will get own-ership on his terms and is demanding to take it higher if I will not proceed with the sale."

"The way I see it Aurthur is that with the commitment to the abattoir construction, which I believe is a brilliant idea, he must be really going out on a limb financially and is des-perate to lock in supply of cattle by gaining control of Ascot, Venus and Remus."

"That is the main reason the bank is supporting his abat-toir financing. They are well aware of his intentions and that's why they're supporting the cheap acquisition of the properties."

"So the bank is up to its neck in this conspiracy?" Andrew was astounded.

"I wouldn't call it a conspiracy Mr Hanna. It's just good business. Shulman has been a very good customer and the bank wants to support him. He's going to turn an industry shipping out live cattle to one of vertical integration of live cattle, or packaged meat to the consumer's plate via the arrangement with his Indonesian partners. The bank wants progress and it sees this as a positive for the region and the state of Western Australia."

"Yes, I can see its justification, a very lucrative arrangement if Ike can pull it off."

"The abattoir will go ahead with or without the Boyce properties Mr Hanna."

"I don't believe that Arthur and neither do you. Banks don't like incidents that impact on the original intent and if Ike fails to deliver, because Chloe Boyce mounts a delaying tactic, the finance might just get pulled without explanation. Ike would really be up the creek then."

"We did in fact study and factor in the possibility of Boyce mounting some sort of delaying action, but it was considered it would not be sufficient to overrule the bank's support. The bank believes Boyce is bluffing. Ike has also guaranteed he can come up with an additional ten million once he gets hold of Ascot."

"So what you're saying is there is no way the sale will not proceed? The bank is going to ram it through." Andrew stifled the inner glow of satisfaction. Shulman was getting desperate with his assumptions and planning. It was clear he had to acquire Ascot Downs at all costs. "And Shulman has shown you proof of that finance, has he?"

"Yes, and he has the support of the bank, so there's not much that can be done. You've got to believe me Mr Hanna, if I thought there was a way I could assist you, I would."

Andrew could see he was genuine as the cloud of despair descended on his face and his hands started to shake. "This whole thing is going to blow up in my face, isn't it?"

"Tell me Arthur, what if Chloe Boyce decided not to contest the sale? What if she came to arrangement with Ike that would conserve his cash? After all he must be scraping every penny he's got together to make sure the abattoir deal proceeds smoothly?"

"That's why he's desperate to get the properties cheaply and that's why the bank is supporting him. It really is a package deal where everything has got to slot smoothly into place. Where are you leading with this?"

"You help Chloe and I promise I won't undermine you Arthur, but if you cross me you may as well jump out of your office window. I want you to hint to Ike that Chloe may be ready to buckle and he should approach her personally and not with threats."

"Is that all? I can tell you now Mr Hanna nothing is going to save her. You are wasting your time."

"Arthur will you just do as I ask? I will not ask you to do another thing if you will just do that. I've got something in mind, but I don't want to go into it at this stage."

Geddes nodded trying to work out what Andrew was up to. As far as he was concerned Chloe Boyce was in a hopeless position. On the other hand, so was he if Hanna carried out his threat. He would be fired on the spot and marched out of the building by security.

"Of course I will. Let me get this straight. You just want me to hint now maybe the right time to approach Boyce? The problem with that proposition, is how am I aware of that?"

"Arthur. How long have you been a banker? I'll bet you've witnessed many an occasion when someone putting on a brave face has suddenly crumbled looking for a way out of the dilemma. After all, it all comes down to money. Chloe Boyce won't get what she wants, but has probably realised it's better to sell now and walk away with something along with her pride, than be completely wiped out. Common sense would suggest she will agree to a deal. It may take a bit of horse-trading, but that's the very nature of negotiation. I'd be surprised if Ike didn't revel in it. He's not going to look into the chicken's entrails and conduct a forensic investigation of how you know she may be open to an approach. It's a suggestion on your part. Approach her with some compassion and understanding rather than threats. I've got the distinct impression it may work. It's going to save the bank and Ike the angst of having her challenge them in court. The bank is taking a hell of a risk if they believe she's bluffing. She may just call it and there'll be a lot of directors with egg on their faces if she does. Ike will get what he wants and the bank will be saved from any embarrassment if Chloe decides to challenge. If that should happen you would be finished and both Shulman's and the bank's complicity would be exposed. I've no doubt both you and Shulman would be doing a stretch in rock college together."

"I haven't a clue what you're attempting Mr Hanna. It won't work, but I'll go along with it if it gives me some breathing space."

"I'm not saying it will work either Arthur, but you've no choice. Chloe may turn my advice down flat, but it's well worth a try. If it does work the way I envisage, Ike will never know you were involved, I can promise you that."

"But how do I know I can trust you?"

"You don't Arthur, but I'm not after your scalp. I have an axe to grind with someone else, and you might drop it to Ike we're heading home on tomorrow's flight."

"We're going back tomorrow?" Chloe looked shocked. "What are you up to Andrew?"

"There's absolutely no point in staying here Chloe. I've had two meetings with Geddes and I accept his assurance it's all over as far as the bank's concerned. However, it's far from over in my book."

"If that's the case why are you smiling? You look delighted, not depressed."

"My advice to you is to strike a deal with Ike now and sell out."

Chloe looked aghast with shock. "What are you talking about Andrew. What's going on? One moment you're the fighter inciting me to injunct the bank and the next you want me to roll over and accept what he offers?"

"What's your alternative?"

"It looks as though I don't have one, but that doesn't explain why you've got a grin a mile wide."

"That's why I'm going to play a dangerous game with Ike Shulman. The man is the sharpest of the sharp. It's in his very nature and genetic makeup, but greed often clouds the perspective and in this case I think it will work. However, I can't guarantee it. All I want you to do is trust me I've got your interests uppermost. Ike is going to roll up at the homestead unannounced a few days after we get back. I want you to leave me to conduct any negotiation and don't be surprised at what I say or do. Promise me you will leave it entirely to me. I don't want to go into it now because I'm still thinking it through, but you must trust me."

"Of course I do, but will the bank agree?"

"The bank will be only too happy to go along with the terms. You've sold out and they're in without any threats of legal action on your part and you will not have to move off Venus Downs."

"What do you mean, we won't have to leave? If I sell out, Ike will want me out of his sight."

"He may want you out of his sight, but he'll have no choice but to agree to your terms, which i will negotiate for no fee. The satisfaction of beating Shulman will be enough compensation."

"You're not going to tell me what you've got planned?"

"No, I'm not Chloe. If I tell you now it would only be a bitter disappointment if I fail and I cannot have you showing any enthusiasm. You are losing your properties to an opportunistic thief supported by a corrupt bank, and bank official. You're depressed and I don't want you appear to be enthusiastically supporting what I may say. I'm acting strictly as your legal adviser, not your lover. It's strictly business and anything I may negotiate I will of course refer back to you for consideration. You may even appear antagonistic to some things I may suggest and I want you to play it that way. I want Shulman to believe he's got the complete upper hand, which he undoubtedly has at the moment, but I've no doubt he won't believe he's pulled off the deal that leaves him in complete control on terms he would have thought not possible."

"What do you think Liz?"

"It's not for me to say Chloe, because I don't know what Andrew has in mind. However, if you're asking me whether I trust him, I've absolutely no doubt on that point. You can trust him with your life."

Andrew blushed. "Thank you for that vote of confidence Liz."

"You don't have to thank me Andrew. The moment I laid eyes on you I thought here's the right man for Chloe Boyce. I can't wait for the day you divorce that wastrel you're married to and you two say, I do. Look, I'll clean up, so why don't you two go for a walk. It's a lovely evening for a walk along the river."

Just as Chloe was about to open the door, the intercom from the foyer buzzed and she could see a face she did not recognise looking back at her through the camera.

"Can I help you? Who are you looking for?"

"My name is Inspector Morrison from the Federal Police." He held up his warrant badge. "I want to speak to a Chloe Boyce if she's available."

"I'm Chloe Boyce. Can I ask you what this is about?"

"I think it would be best if we discuss this in private. Can I come up please?"

Liz nodded at Chloe's enquiring look as she pushed the door release button. Minutes later two men knocked and Liz let them in.

"I'm Elizabeth Murdoch. Chloe has been staying with me along with Mr Andrew Hanna."

The policeman smiled and nodded. "I'm Inspector Frank Morrison and this is Senior Constable Peter Sutherland."

Liz indicated the lounge suite. "Please take a seat. Would you like a tea or coffee?"

"No thank you." He turned to Chloe. "Ms Boyce, I just want to confirm you were married or are still married to a person by the name of Marcel Faroud?"

"Yes, I'm still married to him, but I've no idea where he is and I haven't seen him for some time."

"When was the last time you saw him?"

"In London more than a year ago. I left him in fear of my life and came back here to my home in the Kimberleys."

"And you haven't seen him since? Has he contacted you in any way?"

"I have seen him, but only in a newspaper cutting of him landing on Christmas Island with a group of refugee boat people. I don't want to ever hear from him again."

"Is this what you saw?" The policeman pulled a colour photo from a large envelope and handed it to her.

"Yes, that's him." Chloe studied the photo. The monochrome newspaper cutting had disguised the discolouration to his face and she had not noticed the bleeding laceration to his forearm now brought out in colour.

"You're quite sure of that?"

Chloe nodded as she looked at the photo one last time before handing it back. "Yes I am. That is my husband Marcel Faroud. May I ask why you're asking me these questions?"

"Your husband goes by the name of Amir Tabakali. He was granted a temporary protection visa when he arrived. He's been travelling in and out of Australia on fake passports since then and we have just identified him as the head of an illegal people smuggling ring involving boat people arriving from Indonesia. He's also very heavily involved in drugs."

"How did you identify him? How did you find out his real name?"

"We very much doubt Marcel Faroud is his real name. We know he's of Lebanese extraction, he holds a cancelled U.K. passport in that name, but we have since found out it was issued to an Oxford educated Lebanese who died in a skirmish with the Israeli army six months before Faroud moved to the U.K. He was a member of the Hezbollah. The Faroud who died was a medical practitioner. Was your husband a doctor?"

Chloe laughed and shook her head in disbelief. "No, Marcel had a very poor understanding of medicine. He would rush off to the doctor demanding antibiotics at the slightest sign of a cold or pain. He was obsessed with his own well being. He did not mind inflicting pain on anyone who crossed his path, but he could not bear it himself."

"I'm Andrew Hanna, Ms Boyce's solicitor Inspector. I've been trying for some time now to locate him so I can serve divorce papers. Is he still in Australia?"

"We don't know, but we would certainly like to track him down. We also believe he's in danger himself. He's been extorting large sums from desperate Iraqi, Pakistani, Iranian and Afghani refugees by guaranteeing them safe passage to Australia. As you know those boats are largely unseaworthy and thousands of people have died in the attempt. However, there appears to be a small group of Afghanis whose complete families drowned when a boat sank. Understandably, they would like to catch up with Faroud or Tabakali, or whatever he calls himself."

"It sounds as though it wouldn't be any great loss Inspector."

"I agree it would not, but before they catch up with him we would like to see him put behind bars. Whatever you may suggest Mr Hanna, we cannot condone murder."

Morrison turned to Chloe. "Are you sure you haven't seen or been in touch with your husband? I must warn you that lying to me or sheltering your husband is a serious offence."

"I've told you the truth Inspector. I have not seen my husband since I left London. I would be petrified if he suddenly appeared or even tried to contact me in any way." Her face was angry. "Are you accusing me of lying?"

"Ms Boyce, we know your husband was in Wyndham less than a month ago." He let the statement sink in as he witnessed the shocked look.

"How do you know it was him?"

"He was recognised by one of the boat people who he landed on Christmas Island. The man lost his wife and daughter when the boat broke up in heavy seas. Faroud was not on the boat, but had arranged the passage saying they would be met by an Australian Navy patrol vessel which would rescue them. The refugee was working as a kitchen hand in a hotel when he saw your husband sitting in a car outside. He ran inside to get a carving knife. He admitted he was going to slit your husband's throat, but when he got back outside the car had driven off. We checked with the local police and a Sergeant Smith confirmed some hysterical person who could hardly speak a word of English had attempted to make a complaint about someone who had killed his wife and daughter. He noted the complaint and recorded someone with a swarthy appearance had enquired the previous day about the location of Venus Downs. However, he didn't make the connection between the complaint and enquiry at first. That was until he was looking at some recent Federal Police bulletins of wanted persons that he recognised Faroud. We also interviewed the refugee who identified Faroud as the person he was going to kill. If your husband does make contact Ms Boyce would you please contact me immediately." Morrison stood and handed her his card.

Chloe was trembling as she took the card, but made no reply as Liz showed them out.

"How did they trace me to here?"

"Quite simple. Smith obviously threatened Dotti and she gave him Liz's phone number. He passed it onto Morrison. No problem for the police to match a phone number to a name and premises."

"I, I can't go back there Andrew. What are we going to do?"

He put his arm around her shoulders and kissed on the forehead. "You can and must. It's no use running from

Marcel. He knows where you are, but that doesn't mean he means to harm you. He wants money. He's wanted and he's on the run and I've no doubt the Feds will catch up with him eventually. He'll serve time for people smuggling, but from what Morrison has just said he needs to be one step in front of some very angry people who've lost their families and relatives. I've no doubt the kitchen hand would have knifed him if he'd got the chance. Put him out of your mind for now. We're heading home in the morning and I don't intend to leave you."

"Andrew, I don't know what I'd do without you," she said squeezing his hand. "I would simply go to pieces if he ever confronts me again. I get cold shivers every time I think about him. Do you think that inspector believed me?"

"I was watching him closely. At first I believe he suspected you were lying, but by the time he left I'm convinced he thought otherwise?"

They picked up their bags from the trolley and walked out to the car park. The blast of humidity and heat were stifling as they opened the doors of the vehicle. They stood outside as Andrew leaned in, started the motor and turned on the air-conditioning full volume. He had not noticed the flat tire until he glanced down as he began to get in. It had been deliberately cut. He stepped around the vehicle parked nose to nose with his and studied the offside tire. It too had been deliberately cut. Chloe followed his look.

"Someone's left their calling card." He retrieved the bags and slammed the door shut. "And no guesses for who is responsible."

"Who do you think did it?"

"I don't know who did it Chloe, but I know why they did it. It will require two new tires and whoever ordered the vandalism will get the tip-off the moment I order them to be fitted at the airport. No need for someone to be out here every day to see if we're on the incoming flight."

The taxi driver was asleep with the motor running to keep the inside of the vehicle cool. Andrew tapped on the window and indicated the bags and boot as the man shook himself awake.

"Where to sport?"

"Jimmy's Tires and then you can drop us off at Marge Tilley's."

The taxi drove into the yard. It was littered with discarded tires and rims. The scream of airguns removing wheel studs on heavy trucks and machinery was overriding. Andrew knew the man by sight as he walked towards them.

"You want two new tires fitted at the airport, right?"

Andrew handed him the keys. It was pointless asking him how he knew. "Can you do it today and can you drop it back to Marge's hotel?"

"Not a hope in hell today mate." He was cleaning his hands with a piece or rag when he glanced over at the cab to see Chloe smiling at him. He gave a little wave of sudden recognition. "I'll get it done by late this afternoon." He turned and walked away.

"That guy has got real personality," Andrew remarked as got back into the cab. "He wasn't going to do it until he recognised you."

Chloe laughed. "I don't really know him. I met him a couple of times at rodeos and races Henry took me to. Can you imagine working in grease and filth all day in this heat? It's not a lawyer's office."

"That was a cheap shot Chloe Boyce, but I'll forgive you as I can see you have influence in this town."

The cab pulled up in front of the hotel. "Now for the dulcet tones of Radio Marge, she would have broadcast we're back in town by now I would imagine."

Marge greeted them with the usual cackle of laughter and with the false bonhomie of a hovering vulture. "Hello Chloe, I hear your husband has been in town looking for you."

"So I heard Marge.We won't be staying the night. As soon as we get a couple of new tires we'll be off. We'll just sit in your lounge out of the heat if that's okay."

"I'm a publican Chloe and by law I can't refuse you. You're welcome. Who do you think slashed your tires?"

"I can see there's no need for a newspaper in this town Marge." Andrew smiled as he guided Chloe past.

Marge gave him a withering look that passed in a split second. She knew full well what her nickname was, but did not appreciate it being attached to sarcasm. "You two make yourselves comfortable. What would you like to drink?"

"A pint for me and a lemon, lime and squash for Chloe thanks."

"That's the second time you've had a shot at her." Chloe chuckled under her breath as Marge busied herself behind the bar. "She won't like you if you keep doing it."

"Nosey bloody old bag. It must have been Smith who told her about Marcel and I bet she knows the person responsible for slashing your tires. Nothing is private in this town."

"Now listen, unless I miss my guess Ike Shulman will soon walk in here and express surprise to see us. He'll want us to stay overnight so he can discuss business with you in the morning. I want you to make out you're very tired and want to get home and will be leaving as soon as the vehicle is fixed. Let me handle him and don't contradict me, and above all don't let him talk you into staying. I want you to meet him on your ground and not his."

"I wish you'd tell me what you're doing. Is there a real point to all this?"

"Just trust me Chloe. Just trust me."

It was not Ike who poked his nose into the bar two hours later, but an overall-clad kid in his teens. "Your Toyota's outside all fixed and ready to go."

"Can we give you a lift back to the yard?"

"No thanks chief, the boss followed me here in the repair truck."

Andrew was about to pull out from the curb when he caught sight of Ike hurrying across the street. "I thought he would have made a move earlier than this."

Chloe looked across wondering who he was referring to when Ike tapped on her window. She rolled it down. "Hello you two, I was hoping to catch you earlier, but I got held up. I would like to talk to you urgently Chloe."

"We're just leaving," Andrew broke in. "Chloe's tired and she wants to get back and see how much of mess Smith left the place in. Can you give me an idea of what do you want to talk about? I am Chloe's legal counsel after all."

"The bank has moved and I'm about to complete a contract to buy all your holdings as you are well aware. I would like to talk about that as I want vacant possession immediately on completion. You may be claiming personal property and livestock such as horses. I also want to talk to you about staff and retainers and what entitlements are owed."

"Don't rush Ike, as Chloe won't be moving out in the foreseeable future. I will be lodging an injunction against you and the bank. By the time it gets to court another year will have ticked by if I have anything to do with it."

"On what grounds may I ask? You're bluffing Hanna."

Andrew shook his head. "No I'm not Ike and you should know enough about the law to realise I can delay your plans.

And I think the bank will run for cover the moment the injunction is slapped on them." Andrew made to move off. "You're in for a fight my good man. On the other hand if you want to talk sense then come out tomorrow and we'll discuss it. Chloe has had enough, but I'm going to make damn sure she doesn't get fleeced by the likes of you."

"Well, come in and let's talk about it now. I want to know what you have in mind."

"A fair price Ike, but it will keep until tomorrow. It will give you time to think about it overnight."

Ike was still standing in the same spot as Andrew watched him recede in his rear vision mirror. "Well, that should start the ball rolling."

"You're joking aren't you? He's won, and what's this about selling out? We won't be seeing him tomorrow."

"That's where you're wrong Ms Boyce. The suggestion of an injunction has got him worried, just as it shook Geddes when I mentioned it to him."

"Can you really stop the sale?"

"Probably not, but I can hold it up for a considerable time and Ike runs the real risk the court will determine the properties must be put up for auction or offered in separate lots. However, we're not going to let it get to that stage as you're going to sell everything to Ike tomorrow. And what's more he's going to agree to your offer and make a very substantial deposit as well. The bank will agree because I've already told Geddes I intend to injunct the present arrangement so the whole sordid affair can get a proper airing before the court. No bank wants an adverse finding or dirty linen shown in the public domain."

"Andrew I've been thinking about it and I believe it's time to let go. I don't want to get into any more arguments or court fights. He won't offer me anything near what the properties are worth. I may end up with something and that combined with what I get for my London house and my savings is more than we need."

"Chloe don't give up on me now. I've only just started having fun and I don't want it to stop until I've buried that greaseball Ike Shulman. I know you'll think I'm out of my tree, but not only will you sell to Ike, but if my plan works, you will get them back within twelve months at no cost to you."

"I agree, you really are out of your tree."

"We'll see, we'll see, but are you prepared to lay a bet that Ike will be out bright an early tomorrow?"

"I would be foolish to bet against you Andrew Hanna. I don't believe he will come, but you're not telling me what you have up your sleeve so I'll fold my hand."

"Wise girl. Just remember, you must let me do all the talking and negotiating. He's going to try and sideline me and address you as he perceives you are the weak link. I intend to step on him very quickly and the situation may get very tense. There are a few things that puzzle me about his motives for wanting everything. I can understand Venus and Remus. They make sense, but two properties in the Pilbara don't. I can't fathom why Henry bought them. Have you ever visited them?"

"No, I didn't know he owned them. They appear to be paying their way though."

"That's true, but why buy something that doesn't exactly fit with your business plan? From what I can gather reading his diaries, and I must say I only gave them a cursory look, I can only figure he must have had some ulterior motive not apparent to me. I'll have to dredge through them a lot more closely. I hope Joey hid them well and the termites or rats haven't got at them. Another thing that interests me is as to why Ike would have gone into partnership with Henry on those two. Ike just doesn't operate like that. He wants everything within easy reach like his other holdings to the south and west. All are within a day or two of Wyndham. It just doesn't make economic sense for him to operate outside his comfort zone."

"You never stop thinking, do you Andrew?"

"When it involves people like Ike Shulman, you either keep thinking two steps ahead of his next move, or you're in check then check-mate before you realise it."

ndrew glanced at his watch as Ike's vehicle rolled up. "I knew he'd be early, but not this early. He mustn't have slept at all last night. Here comes one very anxious man, so remember let me do all the talking." Ike tried to adopt the composure of complete control; the chess master only a move from trapping the king; his opponent already in check with no escape possible. He sipped the cold drink, but did not touch the sandwiches Dotti had prepared.

"So where to we go from here Chloe?"

"A fair price is what she is after Ike. If we can arrive at that the properties are all yours."

"Andrew, the properties are as good as mine now. Why should I pay what they're worth when I can get them for what I want to pay?"

"And what are you prepared to pay?"

"I'll get them for thirty million."

"That's preposterous," Andrew exploded. "You wouldn't get them for twice that figure, let alone complete with the tens of thousands of cattle included. The whole package would be a bargain at fifty million."

"I'm a business man Andrew, not a charity. It's too bad Chloe has run into trouble, but I've of no mind to relieve her position. I believe thirty million would keep Chloe and yourself out of the poorhouse."

"It's not going to happen Ike. I'll be flying back to Perth tomorrow to lodge an injunction against the bank and I don't think you will have any say in the matter when the bank realises the dirty linen might get an airing. Even if Chloe loses, you're still not going to get hold of the whole parcel. The bank will be forced to put them up for auction and that means offering them as a whole and then individually if the whole doesn't attract a high enough bid. You might wind up with one or possibly two, but not the whole four. You're attempting to steal them Ike, but you won't succeed. And another reason for that is your connection to Geddes and Smith. You may claim you have no connection to the cattle duffing from Ascot Downs, but I can connect you to it through Geddes. It's all contained in Henry's diaries and despite what Geddes may have told you, I can prove he's the person annotated as AG in those diaries. You sent Smith out here to try and find them, but I can assure you they're well hidden. However, they will be used as evidence at any trial which will most surely follow the injunction. I want to make it perfectly clear Ike, you won't be kicking Chloe off her land in the next twelve months, because that's how long a good legal team will be able to string this out for. What chance then of you being able to finance your abattoir?"

He saw Ike flinch as the smile momentarily disappeared. "You appear to be very sure of yourself Hanna. What makes you so certain a court will grant you an injunction in the first place? You're assuming a lot."

"Ike, I can easily make an ex-parte application where I don't give any notice to the bank of what is about to happen, or I can make a full blown application by giving them notice of what I'm about to do. I think I know a little more about the law and banks than you, but I believe the moment I do, the bank will buckle when I implicate both you and

Geddes. It wouldn't be Chloe trying to put the pressure on, it would be the bank and that would be game, set and match I would think."

"You're forgetting something aren't you?"

"And what's that?"

"I realise you will cause me a great deal of discomfort, embarrassment and money defending myself. Geddes will lose his job and along with Smith do time together, but the other person affected is Chloe here. She may escape being named in what's been going on, as she had no knowledge of it, but she's going to be sued for her eye teeth when all is revealed to the Ascot Downs people in court. The damages and interest on those damages will be colossal. Wouldn't it be better to accept what I'm offering?"

"Mr Shulman, Andrew has warned me of that likelihood, but I can tell you now I intend to take you down with me if you run me off my property. It's true, I did not play any part in what I've inherited, but that doesn't mean I'm going to be disinherited of what my father clearly meant me to have. I will find a way to recompense the Ascot Downs owners."

Ike clapped his hands softly in a mocking gesture. "I applaud your forthright attitude Ms Boyce. As for your honesty I will leave open to question and posterity. People have all the best intentions and expressions of remorse when a crime is discovered, but when it remains hidden, the crime can be justified with the passing of time. With the exception of murder, there is a statute of limitations to most crimes."

"Ike, there's a question I would like answered? You bought the Pilbara properties in partnership with Henry and then sold him your share. What is the interest in those properties today? They're too far away and simply don't fit in with the core business you're planning?"

"That's my business Hanna, but I want them included. What is the core business you're referring to?"

"Ike, you're into the bank for twenty million in regard to the abattoir you're building and you've got to find a partner with equally deep pockets. You're so confident that contracts have been let and construction is underway. Why not let Chloe have Baracool and Ironstone Park?"

"I'm not prepared to do that."

"Look Ike, the two properties integral to your plans are Venus Downs and Remus Plains and without them your whole pack of cards comes crumbling down. It's obvious whoever is now managing Ascot Downs is complicit in the theft, therefore guaranteeing supply of cattle. That's why at some point in the future you have to buy Ascot Downs. You've based your whole model on that plan and that's what you've sold the bank and your intending Indonesian partners on. You really are in a dangerous position Ike. You are certainly aware of it and I know it for sure. I'm certain Arthur Geddes is a very stressed and worried man. I know exactly what you've pledged to the bank by way of collateral and I know exactly what you're in the hole for. One wrong step and you're going to be in a very big bind."

Ike remained silent. Inwardly he was cursing. He believed Andrew was bluffing, but could not be sure Geddes had not divulged his financial arrangements with the bank. Geddes denied seeing Hanna, but a desperate man will say anything. "Perhaps a compromise is in order then?"

"And what would that be Ike?"

"Join me. I will call off the bank and we leave it as the status quo. In return Chloe gives me a five year option to buy the properties at anytime based on an independent valuation. We stand to make a great deal of money out of what

I've got planned. The Asian market is going to be huge and I doubt whether even the abattoir I've got planned, will be able to keep up with demand. I will have to adjust my expectations somewhat, but I can live with that."

"And you will delete Baracool and Ironstone from that agreement?"

"No, they are to be included."

"And what about Ascot Downs?"

"I've already spoken to Ray Massie, the new manager who's taken over from Bill Hargraves. He was already in on the game, so there's no problem there. He just gets a bigger share now."

"I won't allow you to run the cattle through Venus Downs. I'm not going to be party to a criminal action."

"Ms Boyce, you're already party to a criminal action, as you put it. You've now been made aware of what your father has been doing over the years, so unless you report it now you are a co-conspirator, and equal partner in crime. You cannot just let it go on by turning a blind eye and the longer you let it go on, the deeper the hole you're going to dig for yourself. I would point out you would not have been in this position of owning these properties if I had not proposed the original arrangement with Henry. He would have gone broke. The drought was severe and prolonged and the bank was about to pull the rug. I saved him, so you've a lot to thank me for. It's your call, but I believe my suggestion is the only way forward. You join me and forget about your moralistic virtues."

Chloe turned to Andrew for support. "Is he correct?"

"Yes Chloe. You are aware a crime has been committed and unless you report it immediately you will be front and centre if it is ever revealed at a later date you allowed it to continue."

There was a long silence as Chloe looked out at the barren red earth surrounds of the homestead before turning back to face Shulman with an etched determined look.

"In that case Mr Shulman, I'm going to reject your offer and sign an affidavit as to what I know. If it costs me everything, then so be it, but I cannot agree and go along with what you are proposing. My father obviously did what he did out of desperation and he hoped I would accept the bequest with gratitude. I had two adopted brothers who I believe must have known about the duffing and would have no doubt complied with your present suggestion, but they are both dead. That leaves me and I am not going to condone it any longer. The game is over Mr Shulman. I'm well aware it will most likely cost me everything, but that's a position I must accept. As for yourself, I've got absolutely no compassion as to the consequences. That's your problem."

Ike looked stunned. It was not the reaction he expected. "Ms Boyce, listen to reason. You'll be wiped out."

"And you'll be wiped out and most likely behind bars," she snapped back at him.

"For the sake of everything she owns Hanna, can't you talk some sense into her?"

"It's not my call Ike. I'm only her legal counsel, but if she were to ask me for my advice I would be duty bound to repeat what she has just told you."

"I, I just don't understand it. How could you just turn your back on everything your father worked for and have him branded a thief?"

Andrew was revelling in Ike's dilemma as the full import of what Chloe had just said, sank in. He could not have choreographed it better.

"If he were still alive I would probably not have known what was going on. I'm sure he wouldn't have told me, but the simple truth Mr Shulman is that he was a thief and if he's branded as such I'll just have to live with it. You obviously have a different set of morals and standards to me, but I'm prepared to live with the consequences of mine."

"Do you think you can arrange for Smith to shoot us both before she files the affidavit?" Andrew had Ike fixed with an icy look. "Smith almost got me the other day and would have unless Joey Moonlight hadn't come along. You must have known about that. The problem is now Smith will have to shoot Moonlight as well, as there'll be a lot of questions asked."

"Don't be so bloody ridiculous Hanna. Smith's a cop, not a murderer."

"He's as big a crim as you Ike. It's common knowledge he took Mark Tippet for a ride from which he never returned. He tried to kill me and if he'd achieved that, I've no doubt Chloe would have been next on the list."

"I'm not interested in killing anyone." Ike almost screamed in his vehement rebuttal.

"You're only interested in money Ike, but if anyone stands in your way you'll turn a blind eye if they should suddenly disappear or meet a violent end."

Ike stood up and turned to leave. "I just can't understand you Chloe. It would appear to be some act of revenge on your part. Can we compromise on what I've offered and what you believe the properties are worth? Can we meet halfway?"

The attitude of complete control was dissolving before Andrew's eyes. Gone was the cockiness of surety to be replaced with a pleading voice.

"I agree with you Ike. There should be a compromise and this is how it's going to happen."

Ike looked to Chloe to see if there was a hint of duplicity, a hint that Chloe's statement was part of a pre-arranged plan, but he could see she was shocked by Andrew's sudden intervention.

"What do you have in mind? I take it you've already discussed this with your client?"

"No, I haven't Ike, but I've been giving it some thought and it's the only course by which you get what you want and stay out of jail and Chloe gets out from under this mess with some dignity."

"I'm listening."

"You sign an option agreement for the purchase price of thirty million for all Chloe's properties." Ike was about to protest when Andrew held up his hand. "You pay fifteen million on the barrel head within a week with the balance, including interest, anytime within the next three years. You know you'll have to come up with at least thirty million to buy out Chloe in the next week or so, if you persist with your present intentions. Chloe remains on the property at her pleasure, if she chooses to do so, but you assume all liabilities including those to the bank on her receipt of the fifteen million. That should give the bank some comfort in the knowledge you're not stretching yourself too far."

Shulman did not react, but it confirmed Andrew must have met Geddes, and coerced him into divulging his financial position.

"By agreeing to my proposal you can apply the extra fifteen million you would have had to pay to buy out Chloe towards the twenty you've committed to the abattoir financing. Not only have you saved fifteen, but you've gained extra breathing space in getting the abattoir up and running and your cash flow into a healthy positive position within three years. The only real cost is the interest you'll pay on the fifteen million outstanding to Chloe, and even that may not be significant if you extinguish the debt earlier. I would say that's good business. Isn't the motto of a successful businessman to always use someone else's money if you can? It's your business what you do regarding Ascot Downs. Chloe will no longer have any interest or liability if things should go wrong in that direction and you will have to sign an indemnity in that regard. The ball is in your court now Ike and you'd be foolish not to accept."

Andrew held his breath and ignored the dark telepathy he could feel coming from Chloe. He just prayed she would stay silent. The plan was proceeding exactly to plan, but he was worried she may object or express some doubt about a particular point. She remained silent and just sat watching Ike as he pondered the proposition.

"So no injunction, no affidavits filed away in some drawer, no complaints about Smith or Geddes and nothing about what's been happening here on Venus in regard to Ascot? It's all buried is it?"

"It certainly would be if you agree to the terms."

"I would like to hear that confirmation from Chloe please?"

"Whatever Andrew has outlined I will agree to Mr Shulman. On receipt of the fifteen million the place is all yours, but I won't vacate until I receive the balance."

"What if I pay it immediately?"

"Then I will leave immediately."

She played it exactly how he wanted her to play it. The last question was just a test. Andrew knew full well Ike would not pay the full purchase price immediately as it was not in his interests to do so. The proposal was giving him enormous breathing space.

Ike held out his hand to her. "We have a deal then Ms Boyce. I will draw up a contract of sale and phone when I've got the documentation and initial payment arranged."

"We'll see you in your office within the week Ike. My client will require a bank cheque on signing."

"Andrew." The pressure valve had released. Ike was trying to hide his triumph, the light dancing off his coal black eyes. "You should stay and work for me? You certainly know how to negotiate."

"Thanks Ike, but as in the old western movies, this town ain't big enough for both of us. You're simply too big for me."

They stood and watched as Ike almost ran to his Toyota cruiser and drove off. "I don't know what you did just then Andrew, but I've a feeling this is not the end of it. You've got something up your sleeve. Are you going to tell me what it is?"

He pulled her towards him and kissed her. "I can't at this stage. The first stage has fallen exactly into place. It's the next part that presents the real risk, but one thing's for sure is that you're not going to lose. You're guaranteed another fifteen million."

"And I might get all the properties back. Isn't that what you said?"

"Don't hold me to that, but I believe that is what will happen."

"So Ike pays me fifteen and it's just a matter of waiting from then?"

"Chloe, I've no doubt Ike will try to slip some nasty clauses into the contract, but I'll soon knock those out. He has no choice, but to agree to your terms and conditions. What I want you to do is pack your bag as we're going on a little trip. You can tell Dotti and Joey we'll be away for a few weeks. And as for where we're going we'll first fly to Perth so you can do a little shopping."

"I don't need any fancy clothes, I've got all I need right here."

"Your current wardrobe would look out of place in London."

"London? Why London. Mind you it might be a good idea because I can put my house on the market and tidy up some loose ends."

"That's settled then."

"No it's not. Why are we going to London?"

"We're going to talk to someone about a business proposition."

"What business proposition? What are you talking about?"

"If Ike signs and pays up I'll tell you part of it, but only part of it."

"You're impossible Andrew Hanna. Impossible."

Andrew read the contract slowly looking for any escape clauses Ike may have had inserted.

"It's all straight forward Andrew, in plain English and easily understood. I pay Chloe fifteen today and the balance at anytime within the next three years."

Andrew picked up a pen off Ike's desk. "Just a simple addition. If you don't come up with the balance within the time period, the contract is void and the properties revert to Chloe. In addition you lose your deposit. You also assume all past and future liabilities from the moment you sign."

"That's a harsh condition. I can't go along with that. I at least want my deposit back."

"Look at it this way Ike. You're getting a great deal and you know it. I don't know what it is about the two in the Pilbara you're intent on keeping, but I'm sure you're not disclosing something."

"I, I will have to get my lawyer to make the amendments and consider those terms before I accept."

"You should have had him here now Ike. I'm a lawyer and I'll write the amendments in clear terms. There's no need for it to be retyped."

Ike began to protest.

"Take it or leave it. I have my instructions from my client. We're on today's plane to Perth, so if you don't sign, the deal is off."

Ike turned to Chloe for a sign of weakness, but she looked at him in stony silence. He took the pen from Andrew and signed the inclusions before handing it over to Chloe for countersigning.

"You've stolen some wonderful properties Ike."

"Andrew, Andrew it's only business. There's nothing personal." Ike handed over the bank cheque with a beaming smile. Andrew glanced at it before handing it to Chloe.

"I hear what you say about it being just business, but that's not how we view it. Just remember one thing Ike, and I would impress it upon you, always keep that final settlement date in mind because there will be no extensions. Either you pay or Chloe gets her properties back."

"I'm very comfortable with that. I can assure you, I'll be settling well within the option period."

Ike stood and put out his hand, but Andrew ignored it.

"There's nothing more for us here. The properties are now your responsibility along with all the livestock, goods and chattels. I'll leave the key of the Toyota at the desk at the airport for someone to pick up."

"I'll drive you out."

"Probably a good idea Ike, otherwise Smith might get someone to slash the tires again."

Ike tried to start a conversation, but gave it up when he saw he was not going to get a response. He pulled up in front of the terminus and watched Andrew as he unloaded their two bags and a couple of cardboard boxes.

"Is that all you're taking?"

"It is for now. What remains is potentially all yours."

"What's in the boxes?"

"Oh, those contain Henry's diaries and papers you and Smith were trying to get your hands on. I've not read them in full, but I'm sure I'll find something more of interest. Call them my insurance policy. Goodbye for now Ike."

"You're coming back then? I thought you were leaving for good?" Ike was trying to make light of the comment.

"Ike, if you ever see me again in this neck of the woods you'll know you're in trouble. However, I can assure you it will be strictly business and I trust you'll view it that way." Andrew turned and followed Chloe inside.

20

It was cold overcast day when the flight touched down at Heathrow.

"What are you thinking?"

"I was just reminiscing on the number of times I've been in and out of this airport. In those days it was first class and first class treatment, five minutes in Customs and then whisked through to my waiting car. I remember the first time I landed here was on an economy ticket. Customs took close to an hour while they studied my entry and work visa and then the tube into London was almost another hour. It makes me shudder when I think about it now."

"I've only been here a couple of times. Once as a broke uni student backpacking around Europe for three months and then for two years getting some work experience with a law firm here. They offered to sponsor me if I wanted to stay on, but two years was enough in this climate, although I do love the London life."

He recognised the carpet as they queued at Customs. "They must have got a bulk lot on this carpet. I could never work out whether it was red or mauve or a combination of both, but they haven't changed it since I was here last."

Chloe just smiled as they shuffled forward. "All I want is a nice shower and hotel bed. I've no interest in carpets."

Half an hour later they were on the Heathrow Express to Paddington Station, and then by taxi to the Westbury Hotel in Mayfair. It was early evening when Andrew awoke and looked at his watch.

"Come on Cinderella." He nudged the sleeping form beside him. "Enough sleep, otherwise you'll be awake all night."

Chloe guided them to a quiet restaurant in Mayfair. Andrew ordered a bottle of wine while studying the menu.

"You could buy a first class ticket back to Australia with the prices they charge here."

"Andrew this is London, or had you forgotten? You're no longer backpacking and you're no longer a broke law clerk. Everything's on me, so order what you like. I know this place and I can assure you the food is good."

"Good evening Ms Chloe." The impeccably dressed maitre de unfolded a napkin and draped it on her lap. "It is so good to see you. Are you staying long?"

"Oh, hello Claude," Chloe smiled as she looked up. "A few days. Just a holiday."

Claude nodded to Andrew. "I'm here at your service. Enjoy your meals."

"I can see you haven't been forgotten. I was wondering when he was going to ask you about Marcel."

"That doesn't happen in London. It's assumed that everyone is cheating on everyone else, so you don't make those sort of gauche enquiries. Ask one too many questions and you're liable to lose the patron for all time, and that of all their friends and acquaintances. Discretion is everything although everyone knows about everyone's indiscretions, dalliances, affairs or assumed wealth, or if they don't know they guess. Claude learned all he wanted to. It would be all over London by now Marcel and I had split up. It's old news, so he just wanted to get a good look at you. He could tell in an instant your nationality; an Australian. You will be on the gossip wire by this time tomorrow."

"A celebrity at last. How far off am I from getting on the A list?"

"You're not even on the first rung yet," Chloe laughed. "It would take a year or more before you're even noticed let alone being included on any list. You're a hayseed from the backwoods so don't try and rise above your station just yet."

The waiter opened the pinot noir, poured a little into Andrew's glass and stood back. Andrew tasted it and nodded acceptance. The entrecote of beef followed and he had to agree with Chloe's recommendation. It was excellent.

"What are you going to do tomorrow?" Andrew was swilling the last of the wine in his balloon glass.

"I'll call the estate agent in the morning. I want to find if there's been any interest in my house."

"And you?"

"I'm going to look up an old acquaintance, Martin Amesbury, a partner of my previous employer here. He knows everything about what's going on and has excellent contacts. Probably the best net-worker I've ever come across. If he didn't know someone, you could bet by five o'clock he'd spoken to them and introduced himself. I just don't know how he does it. I don't know how many exclusive game shoots and parties he got me into and introductions to very interesting people. He's not an aristocrat, but he comes from a wealthy background and just knows how to play the game. Mind you, he does all the right things, plays polo, royal tennis, grouse and pheasant shoots in Scotland, skiing in Gstaad. You name it Martin does it."

"Just a social call is it, or is it something to do with this mysterious business we're here about?"

"Social of course, but I will be dredging for any worthwhile information that will be of assistance to our cause."

"And what is our cause?"

"Burying Ike Shulman if I can." Andrew drained his glass with a wry smile. "That was a nice wine and a great meal. Now how about I pay the bill, we go somewhere for a quiet drink and then hop into bed and sleep off the last of the travel lag?"

"Why don't we skip the drink and hop into bed. I'm still suffering the effects of that flight."

Andrew looked at his watch and then the light from the street lamps penetrating the cracks in the curtain. He got up and pulled the curtain aside to look out at the heavy overcast and sodden street below where the traffic and buses were already nose to tail edging into the city. Pedestrians all had that fixed and determined look as they dodged each other and the danger of open umbrellas. It was such a day when he flew out of London on his return home those years before. He was pleased to go then, but now he could feel the overall cloak of the depressing weather being overcome and thrown off by the vibrancy and excitement of this huge city. Chloe was still asleep as he showered and dressed. She finally rolled over and smiled at him.

"Are you going to stay there all day?"

"I'm going to stay here for another hour. It's nice and warm. Then I'm going to see the real estate agent, and from there I'll probably walk around Harrods and have lunch somewhere."

"Okay, I'm going down for breakfast and then I'll phone Martin Amesbury and see if I can see him today. Maybe he'll have time for lunch, but I should be back here by five. You can take me to another of your favourite restaurants."

She held up her arms to pull him towards her as he bent down and kissed her. "On second thoughts, it's dark outside. I should really hop back into bed."

She laughed as she pushed him in away. "Save your strength darling. You're here on business don't forget and I am a demanding client who only pays for results, so get on with it."

Andrew finished his breakfast of bacon and eggs, pushing the ubiquitous baked beans and black pudding aside. He could never get used to, or understand the English love of the two ingredients. He finished his coffee and went looking for a phone in the lobby, but decided against making the call. It was cold, but the rain had ceased as he walked up Piccadilly, crossing over at the Ritz and then down Regent into the Strand, and the ever crowded Fleet Street, before wending his way to Cheapside and its maze of tiny streets and lanes. Fitzgibbon & Lascelles was the name he was looking for on the multiple brass plaques inside the doorway.

"Can I help you sir?"

He turned to see the portly concierge approaching.

"Yes, I was looking for Fitzgibbon & Lascelles, but they must have moved."

"No sir, they're now under A for Amesbury & Lascelles."

"Oh, I see Martin has made real progress since I was last here." Andrew noted the floor and turned for the lift.

"I know you, don't I sir? It's the voice and I've only just placed it. You are Andrew Hanna aren't you?"

"Yes, and if I remember your name is Porrit isn't it? My apologies for not having recognised you. I never did know your Christian name."

"Just Porrit sir, that's the name everyone knows me by. Even my dear wife addresses me as Porrit in rising or descending octaves of the scale depending on mood or level of demand, but never of endearment." He maintained a perfectly straight face as he pressed the button on the lift and walked away to direct someone else.

Andrew did not recognise the receptionist as he pushed open the door. She looked down at her appointment pad.

"You have an appointment sir?"

"No I don't, but I was wondering whether I could see Mr Amesbury please?"

"That won't be possible sir. Mr Amesbury is extremely busy."

He gave her his most disarming smile, but the response was not reciprocal. It was what he expected as protocols had to be strictly adhered to. No use wasting billing time on someone walking in the door with a matter unrelated to the firm's particular practice area. Those six minute billing segments were the revenue stream to be maintained at all costs. And the cost to the hapless solicitor who did not maintain at least eighty segments a day was a quick exit. It did not matter whether the work was a genuine billing, or a hapless client who was unlucky enough to get billed to make up the eight hour quota at the end of the day. What client would give any thought to another six minutes being added to their account? Pick ten clients and add six minutes each and there was another hour billed at a senior partner's hourly charge. No use complaining the work could have been handled by a junior on a lower hourly rate. The excuse was it was mandatory for a partner to overview the file. After all, the aim was to protect and ensure the client's interests, wasn't it? Andrew had been acquainted with the practice the moment he walked in the door. The learning curve was immediate and it all boiled down to billing, billing, billing. Pro bono was a term anathema to commercial law practice in the City, the money centre of the world.

"I used to work in this office when it was Fitzgibbon & Lascelles. Mr Amesbury knows me well. Would you tell him I'm just in London for a day or so and would like to see him for a few minutes if possible?"

She looked hesitant as she picked up the phone and spoke to someone Andrew knew would be Martin's secretary.

"Would you take a seat please Mr Hanna? His secretary will see if he's available."

Andrew looked around at the drab office he knew so well. He was sure it was the same plastic ficus in one corner wedged between the battered leather lounge suite and chairs. The dust on the leaves suggested it was. There were no pictures or anything adorning the panelled walls and the same coffee table contained a copy of The Times and Country Life. The only expense appeared to be that of a recent deep green carpet.

He recalled the first day when Henry Fitzgibbon had welcomed him to the firm. Andrew was about to be interviewed for a job and had been looking around the waiting room with some trepidation when Fitzgibbon appeared with pipe in one hand and manila folder in the other. He did not have time to wipe the distaste of the surrounds from his face before Fitzgibbon read his thoughts in a flash.

"You're not here to study or make comment on the woodwork Hanna. I've read your file. I don't think much of your qualifications, or where you got them from, but you can start at eight in the morning." The old man tossed the file onto the receptionist's desk. "Get him signed up Margaret." He was about to disappear when he swung around. "And I'll give you a week to get yourself a decent suit. You look like an east end barrow boy."

Andrew did not have time to express his thanks. His entry into the world of high pressure commercial law was about to commence.

"Andrew." Martin Amesbury beamed as he burst in. "Come in, come in. Tell me you've come for a job. I can fit you in as a senior immediately and make you a partner within twelve months. I'm desperate."

"You haven't changed Martin. You're still full of it."

"That's a very offensive remark Hanna. I shall commence proceedings for defamation unless I get a written apology. But tell me, what brings you to London?"

"Is the metre on, or off?"

Martin slapped him on the back. "The metre is always on. You know that, but I've got plenty of files I can bill your time to."

"The ghost of Dick Turpin still lives on, despite being hanged at Tyburn. The practice of highway robbery is still considered a legitimate crime in the City."

"Now Andrew, don't point the finger." Martin laughed as he signified a chair opposite his desk. "You were very adept at pointing the blunderbuss at client's yourself, if I recall."

"I learned it from you and that tyrant Fitzgibbon."

"Old Fitzgibbon thought the world of you."

"He retired did he?"

"No, he died last year at eightyfive. I bought in and am taking over soon as George Lascelles wants to retire." He looked at his watch. "Let's go to lunch. I've got feeling this is not entirely a social call."

Andrew went along with Martin's order of Dover sole and a bottle of Marsanne.

"So what have you been doing?"

"I bought a small country practice, but it hasn't been very successful in that I became involved with a criminal syndicate."

Martin raised an eyebrow. "You did what? You're not on the run are you?"

"Of course not. Just relax and I'll explain everything."

Martin finished his fish by the time Andrew explained the events of the past few months.

"You really have dug yourself in deep haven't you?" Martin commented as he sucked his teeth. "Why didn't you just walk away? Never get involved with your client's personal problems. You should know that? Who is this female client you keep referring to?"

"Her name is Chloe Boyce."

"Oh, oh, what gives me the impression this is more than a professional relationship? Don't tell me she's here in London with you?"

"Yes she is, and yes it is more than a professional relationship. I intend to eventually marry her."

Martin broke into a broad grin as he thrust out his hand. "Congratulations, but I still think you're a bloody chump. The only Chloe I knew of was a simply gorgeous drop-dead model I would have given anything to ravish, but unfortunately she's just disappeared off the scene."

"That's her."

Martin sat bolt upright in shock and spilt his wine. "My God man, what a lucky fellow you are. I can understand why you've thrown caution to the wind. I met her a number of times at functions, but never long enough to chat her up. That sleaze of a husband, or one of his minders always made it very clear she was not for talking to. By the sound of it she's one very wealthy woman whose been cheated out of her inheritance and you're so smitten you've taken on the role of Sir Galahad riding to rescue the young maiden. You mentioned the Ascot Pastoral Company as being the victim of this crime. Is that why you are here?"

Andrew caught the knowing smile. "I can see the name rings a bell with you. You haven't got a conflict of interest have you?"

"Ascot Pastoral is part of the Arnold Rotherheim group so I'm clear of any conflict, although I do know some worthwhile contacts. I know the group had substantial land holdings in Argentina and Australia. Argentina has been going belly-up for years and they've flogged most of those holdings and since old Arnold went to meet the Messiah last year, I know the new blood is directing all efforts to its real estate developments here and in the States. Am I correct in thinking Chloe would like to buy Ascot Downs?"

"She knows I'm here on business, but she doesn't know what that business is, but yes, I want her to buy Ascot Downs."

"Andrew, I'm trying to figure out what you're up to. Why the hell doesn't she just live on the fifteen million she's got to date and wait for the payout from this Shulman fellow? I must say that guy must have big ambitions getting in so deep. Still if he's that successful I suppose he's got it all figured out. He and Chloe's old man have been robbing Ascot blind for years and now you want to turn around and buy the place. I smell revenge, but as to how you're going to achieve it, I don't understand. However, I've every confidence you know what you're doing."

His eyes suddenly lit up and he started to laugh. "I can now see why Henry Fitzgibbon thought you were so good. You mightn't know it, but you were only supposed to be here for two months until a smart young lass got back from maternity leave. However, he paid her out and got her a position with another firm when she screamed discrimination. You would have been a partner now if you'd stayed on. You are very clever Andrew and I wish you every success with this one. Will she still love you if you stuff it up?"

"Will you help me?"

"Certainly, what would you like me to do? And by the way I demand a dinner with yourself and the gorgeous Chloe."

"That's a deal. I want you to tap the contacts you have and try and get some feeling as to what Rotherheim's attitude is? I know they want to sell the place, but how keen are they and would they negotiate on price and terms?"

"My observation is if they've been hammered in Argentina and apparently haven't paid any attention to the Australian holdings. They might be very amenable to any sensible suggestion. What I do know is that Albert Rotherheim, Arnold's son, is now in control and his predilection is property, office buildings and shopping centres. Arnold Rotherheim was big in the days of feeding Europe, but those days are long gone. I wouldn't expect Albert to declare a fire-sale, but I believe you've arrived just at the right time."

"I don't just want to go and knock on his door. I would really appreciate if you could make some phone calls, get all the intelligence you can and see if you can't get me a face-to-face meeting with the man. By the way this is not pro bono. This is business."

Andrew held out his hand as he stood up. "The lunch is on you, but the metre will run from now. Where can I get you?"

"The Westbury in Mayfair."

"And go and buy a sim card for your mobile and phone my secretary with the number. I don't want to be hanging on while the hotel tries to locate you. I'll get back to you tomorrow. In the meantime, try and explain to Chloe how handsome I am and that she's going out with the wrong guy."

Andrew watched him leave as he signalled for the bill. If anyone could deliver it was Martin Amesbury. He chose a different route as he slowly walked back to his hotel through a myriad of unplanned streets intersecting and crossing one another with black cabs making seemingly impossible turns in order to catch a fare. He hung over a rail in Covent Garden along with other tourists and listened to amateur opera singers testing the acoustics in the shopping pit below. It was as he remembered. London, a timeless static city caught in a time warp, inwardly calm, but outwardly vibrant and alive. He bought a card for his phone and walked slowly through Leicester Square and back go the hotel.

Chloe was sitting by the window looking out over the street when he entered.

"How was your day?"

"Marcel has lodged a caveat over my house. I can't sell it until the caveat is lifted."

Andrew leaned down and kissed her before slumping in the seat opposite. "I don't think that will be too much of a problem really. I'll get Martin Amesbury to handle it. So you're going to leave it empty in the meantime?"

"No, I've rented it out for two years to a Russian businessman. He will pay a year in advance and meet all outgoings."

"Sounds a good deal to me. Probably a member of the Russian mafia if the truth be known."

"Well, that's my news. What about yours? Were you successful?"

"I'll know tomorrow. Martin is going to talk to a few people and see if I can't get an introduction to the man who controls Ascot Downs."

"Ascot Downs? You've come over here to see someone about Ascot Downs? What are you really up to Andrew?"

"Ascot Downs is for sale and I want you to buy it if the price is right. It's as simple as that."

Chloe broke into a bemused look. "What would I want Ascot for? I've already sold everything to Ike. Ascot is not my home and I've no intention of living there or owning it. The place has no memories for me and I've never been there. Is this some sort of fanciful jaunt you're on, or are you serious?"

Andrew held up his hands. "Okay, I will tell you. I should have told you before this, but now I've a feeling everything is going to fall into place. Prior to my meeting with Martin I was not so hopeful, but now I am." Chloe listened as he outlaid his plan and answered objections and questions. She remained quiet for a few minutes looking out the window and churning it over in her mind when he had finished.

"Andrew you have a very devious mind. I would hate to be in Ike Shulman's shoes if you drop this one on him. The god's smiled down at me when you walked into my life."

"So you'll go along with it?"

"Of course I will. Now you've got me really excited. However, I suppose it all depends on what sort of agreement you structure with Rotherheim, if any?"

"Well, all I know is Ascot Downs is for sale and Geddes' bank has been instructed to handle it. I'm putting my trust in Geddes he'll delay the appraisal and won't tell Ike. If he does, then this trip will have been a waste of time. However, he did get the message very clear what I would do if Ike beat you to the property. I suppose we're trusting each other, but he's aware he has to put greater trust in me rather than the reverse. He has much more to lose and that's why I believe he will keep his end of the agreement. He can easily claim ignorance when Ike does find out. He may not be believed, but there's not much Ike can do about it. In fact Ike will by then have much more pressing problems on his mind without taking Geddes to task."

"So Martin's going to phone tomorrow? He sounds a very interesting character. I'll look forward to meeting him."

"You already have, but his advances were repulsed by Marcel or one of his hired thugs. He wants to ravish you, as he put it."

Chloe looked shocked. "Is he that bad? You're not talking about some old leach are you? I experienced plenty of them in my time modelling. They all thought wealth and influence would mask their wrinkling skin, drooping bellies and dyed hair. I'll thank Marcel for one thing. He really did protect me, but then again to him I was just a trophy he could parade and live off."

"Martin is my age, and mirrors my good looks and charm, but being English I don't know whether he changes his shirt or showers every day, so I believe I'm ahead and won't lose you to him."

He ducked as Chloe tossed a cushion at him.

"Where are you taking me to eat? Why don't we find somewhere more remote where you're not going to be recognised?"

"Not much chance of that and I hate dining in bijou out of the way little restaurants with rats and cockroaches investing rubbish bins at the back door. I've already booked Scots for tonight. Very expensive and the place to be seen. You'll love it."

"Can't we put that off until after I meet Rotherheim? We'll have something to celebrate then?"

"By the sound of it, if Rotherheim agrees we'll only be able to afford McDonalds. I've never shared a Big Mac, but there's always a first time. No, I think we should do Scots tonight while there's money in the bank. Anyway if I cancel tonight, we won't be able to get in again. You don't cancel Scots at the last moment and expect them to forget."

"Scots it is then."

The restaurant was full when they walked in. Andrew was ignored as the maitre de recognised Chloe instantly and beckoned her to follow. They were shown to a table right against the window in full view of the whole restaurant. This maitre de was not going to let a prize exhibit be secluded in an obscure position. He wanted the attraction and advertising for which he was not paying.

Chloe looked around. "Do you have a table a little more private?"

The maitre de swept his extended hand around the restaurant. "Not at he moment madam. As you can see we are booked out."

Chloe nodded as he pulled out her chair with a huge smile before turning to Andrew. "A waiter will be with you shortly sir for your drinks order."

"I get the feeling he knew who to expect? What name did you make the booking in?"

Chloe looked thoughtful for a moment and then gave a soft laugh. "I got the concierge at the hotel to make the booking. I was surprised we actually got a table. I just assumed the glitterati must have downgraded it. The place is generally booked out weeks and sometimes months in advance, so although he would have made the booking under Boyce he obviously disclosed my identity."

"That's what I couldn't fathom for a moment. He didn't even refer to his booking list, but showed us directly to this table. I'm really impressed, you do have some pull. Not that I really appreciate the attention."

"You should revel in it darling. This is your moment in the limelight. Haven't you noticed the room has gone somewhat quiet and descended into whispers and surreptitious glances in this direction? The gossip will be running hot. I bet Martin would be playing to the gallery if he was in your position right now. I just may trade you in and stay in London."

"You can't do that. I come with a non-returnable, non-refundable lifetime guarantee. It's just not possible to arrange a trade."

"Are extras optional or do they come with the appliance?"

"Any extras you want are included in the price?"

"Then I think I may have one to add."

The comment passed right over his head until he noticed the odd way she was looking at him. He broke into a broad grin. "When's this extra due to be delivered?"

"In around seven months, give or take a few weeks."

"Are you sure?"

"As sure as my obstetrician can be."

The whole restaurant paused as he let out a cry of joy and leaned over to kiss her. "Now I know why you booked this place. And you have the hide to call me devious? This calls for champagne." He looked around to catch the waiter's eye.

"Andrew, calm down. You wanted a quiet place and now you're broadcasting to the whole of Mayfair."

He grabbed her hands and squeezed them. "I don't give a damn what this toffee lot think. I'm over the moon. A bottle of Krug please."

The bottle arrived, was opened with practised flare and effect and poured delicately into each flute.

"Should you be drinking this in your condition?" Andrew adopted a mock look of concern.

"Oh shut up Andrew. You've been reading too many women's magazines. We're here to celebrate, so let's do it."

They raised and touched their glasses. "Now our cover is blown darling. They'll guess we're either getting married or having a baby. Affairs are clandestine and never to be celebrated in public, and never in London."

"I think the bubbly is going to your head already," he laughed as he topped up their glasses much to the displeasure of the hovering waiter.

21

"Andrew, I've set up a meeting with Albert Rotherheim for eleven tomorrow. Be in my office at ten. No need to phone me back as I'm unavailable for the rest of today."

Andrew had left the phone in the room when he and Chloe had gone down for breakfast. He smiled at thought of his friend being able to organise a meeting so fast, but that was Martin's style. He on the other hand, would have taken days to get to talk to someone within Rotherheim's, let alone get anywhere near the principal. Cold calling was unacceptable and not the London style. Contacts were the vital key to introduction.

"Cab sir?" The doorman enquired as Andrew emerged from the hotel.

"No thank you. It's a lovely morning and I'll walk."

The doorman nodded as Andrew began to retrace his steps of two days before. It was churning over in his mind of how to structure the deal with Rotherheim and what the man may demand. He hoped for a perfect match, a willing seller and a willing buyer. He knew he would be up against an opponent long-schooled in how not to show any emotion. He wondered if he could likewise maintain the same clinical, emotionless approach to business.

"Good morning sir."

"Good morning Porrit."

He looked at his watch as the lift door opened on Martin's floor. It was right on ten. Martin was standing there ready to step in. A look of surprise crossed his face. "Where's Chloe?"

"Is Rotherheim expecting her. Did you tell him she was my client?"

"No, I just said I would like to introduce a client who is interested in buying Ascot Downs."

"I don't think parading her before Rotherheim at this point is going to make the slightest difference, do you?"

"Perhaps not." Martin nodded his agreement. "Let's go. We'll have coffee somewhere on the way."

Martin strode off down the street with Andrew endeavouring to keep up on the small crowded footpath with obstructing scaffolding, signifying the endless recycling of London, blocking an easy passage.

They found a small crowded coffee bar.

"What have you said to Rotherheim?"

"Nothing directly. I called in a favour from one of his financial advisors, told him what you wanted to talk about and suggested a meeting with the man himself. He confirmed Rotherheim wants out of the cattle industry. Too remote, too hard to control and too little return for the investment."

"As simple as that?"

"Not really Andrew. This fellow has done me a real favour which I will no doubt have to repay at some stage. However, the long and short of it is, I've been warned Rotherheim will listen and then politely show you the door if he doesn't approve of you, and by that I mean first impressions are very important to him. If he does approve, he will open a cigarette case and offer you one. If you decline he will then ask if it's okay if he does. I don't have to tell you the answer to that one. It is well known the man is impeccably polite and charming and he expects the same in return. If you make the grade you will stitch up a deal today, subject to me handling the legals. Is that agreed?"

"Certainly Martin."

"Now tell me what you propose so I'm not in the wilderness."

"A buyout with a twelve month settlement. Ten million on signing, the balance of fifteen million to carry interest at Libor."

"Very clean, but have you thought of any variations?"

"Martin, the key to this deal is I don't believe Rotherheim has the faintest idea of how many head of cattle Ascot is carrying, or at least I hope he doesn't."

"I would imagine he would have those numbers at his fingertips."

"Not if he's unaware he's losing thousands of head a year through theft. The absentee landlord is being right royally ripped off. If Rotherheim accepts my terms, Chloe will easily pay off any balance by mustering and selling off the Ascot herd. She can't lose."

"You're not going to mention that, are you?"

"Hell no."

"Do you have a plan B?"

"Yes, but it will take a bit of explaining."

"Well don't. I would advise you to make it a straight buyout, lock stock and barrel. If he asks you about cattle numbers, just tell him you've no idea, which you haven't. Don't get sidetracked. You've got plenty to play with even if you have to agree to a higher overall price."

They were kept waiting for about five minutes before being shown into the cavernous office with a clear view of St Pauls. Albert Rotherheim put down the phone, got up from his desk and walked around to greet them. Martin introduced himself and then Andrew. The handshake was warm and friendly.

"Gentlemen, please sit over here. It's more comfortable." He indicated a coffee table surrounded by leather lounge chairs. "Can I offer you a coffee or tea?"

Martin took the cue. "No thank you Mr Rotherheim. We don't want to take too much of your time."

Rotherheim picked up a small wooden box and offered them a cigarette. Once again they declined. "Do you mind if I do?"

"Not at all, please go ahead." Andrew caught Martin's fleeting nod of approval as Rotherheim leaned over to pick up the lighter.

"Now gentlemen, I believe you're here to discuss the purchase of one the properties in our portfolio. Ascot Downs I believe?" He indicated Andrew with his cigarette. "And you are acting for the purchaser Mr Hanna?"

"That's correct Mr Rotherheim."

"Well, I'm listening. What are you offering?"

"My client would like an extended settlement. Ten million dollars on signing and fifteen million within twelve months."

The room went silent as Rotherheim contemplated the offer and occasionally drew on his cigarette. Andrew was restraining himself from saying another word and Martin remained motionless. They both knew when to shut up. Rotherheim finished half of his cigarette and stubbed it out before looking at them.

"Fifteen million now and twenty in twelve months with the usual interest clause. You're client is not committed enough at ten Mr Hanna. Fifteen is a lot more to lose if they don't finalise and I want your answer now."

Martin was about to say something when Rotherheim held up his hand and looked directly at Andrew.

"If you say you have to discuss it with your client, you're wasting my time and yours. My offer is final."

Andrew held out his hand. "Mr Rotherheim, your proposition is acceptable."

"Good, that's settled. I'll have my attorneys prepare the contract and sent over to Mr Amesbury in the morning." He walked back to his desk and flicked over a page of his diary. "Why don't we make it here at three Thursday for signing and exchange? And Mr Hanna would you be so kind as to bring your client with you. I have met her previously, but I'm sure she probably doesn't remember me. I remember her as a young lady of absolute charm and delight."

Andrew could not hide the look of shock as he turned to Martin. Rotherheim saw the fleeting accusatory furrowing of the brow.

"Mr Amesbury has been most discrete in regard to the identity of your client Mr Hanna. I have my sources, but in this case I was sitting in a certain restaurant a few evenings ago when I recognised your client and who was sitting with her. Until Thursday at three then gentlemen."

Neither said a word as they caught the lift down. Martin started to laugh and shake his head as they hit the pavement.

"That would have to be the fastest deal I've ever witnessed. You are one lucky stiff Hanna."

"You got me in the door Martin. I've really got to thank you for that."

"Yes, but you do have a certain panache about you, despite your ugly head. Tell me, what does Chloe see in you? Obviously Rotherheim saw something not apparent to me."

"She's in love with me Martin and that's all that counts. As for Rotherheim, he wanted out and was happy with the terms."

Martin took out a card and scrawled on the back. "These are my bank details. Get Chloe to telegraph the funds, plus fifty grand for my services to my trust account. Rotherheim will want to see the funds before he signs."

"Sounds good to me."

Martin was studying him for an adverse reaction to the fee. A fee on straight hourly billing was an ambit figure only, and not to be taken seriously, the final fee being the weight of the file, and the wealth of the client with the ultimate figure being calculated on the result and worth to the client.

"Delighted to be of assistance Andrew. Now why don't we meet at midday Thursday for lunch so we can go over the contract and I can discuss it with your gorgeous client. I can see Rotherheim was impressed."

"You forget Martin, I used to be employed by Fitzgibbon & Lascelles. I can read a bloody contract. I wrote enough of them in my time here."

"Yes, but now you're dealing with the senior partner of Amesbury & Lascelles and I have to be very careful of my obligations. Professional indemnity insurance is a killer in this business."

"Who's paying for lunch then?"

"You ungrateful cheapskate Hanna." Martin adopted a look of mock horror.

"It goes without saying the client pays. Mind you if I want to impress a client I pay then add it to the final bill. Didn't you learn anything while at F&L?" With a wave of his hand he was gone.

Andrew was lost in his thoughts as he slowly took more than an hour to walk back to the hotel. He was unaware of the traffic or the sights and sounds or the milieu of human life set on pursuing their own individual tasks as they flowed around him in both directions. He could not believe his success. He was a lucky man in both the personal and business sense.

Chloe did not see him as she got out of the taxi, paid the driver and was about to walk into the hotel when he hugged her and spun her around off her feet.

"Are you mad Andrew? Stop...", but he smothered her mouth before she could protest further.

"I love you Ms Boyce. I'm the happiest man in London and you've just bought Ascot Downs. Let's get a drink and I'll tell you all about it."

The doorman tipped his cap as he opened the foyer door. "I can see we have two very happy people staying here. Enjoy your day."

Andrew slipped five pounds into his hand. "It's been a great day, and tomorrow is going to be the same."

He grinned and pocketed the money. "Thank you sir."

The doorman had hailed a cab the moment he saw them get out of the lift and begin to walk towards the entrance. He held the foyer door open and then quickly moved in front of them to open the cab door.

"I figured you would not be walking today sir."

Andrew muttered his thanks as he climbed in behind Chloe and sat down giving Martin's address to the cabbie. Martin was waiting at the kerb and quickly got in and pulled down a seat. "Savoy Hotel please." With a glance in his mirror the cabbie swung the vehicle across the road and into the crawling traffic.

"Are you going to introduce me you country oaf?"

"Martin Amesbury Chloe and Chloe, Martin Amesbury."

Chloe leaned across and shook his outstretched hand. "I've heard all about you Martin. Andrew has told me he didn't really need your assistance, but only agreed for old times sake. Is that true?"

Martin shook his finger at her. "You don't want to believe half of what he tells you. He's just trying to get out of buying lunch. However, it's really on me today Chloe. I've met you before, but you would not remember. I suppose half of London can lay claim to that fame though."

The talk was all banter as the cab approached the clogged Savoy driveway. "Drop us off here please cabbie."

The short driveway was congested with Rolls Royces, Bentleys and a Ferrari driven by a frustrated looking middle European trying to extricate himself from the jam.

Martin led them into the dining room where, upon seeing him, the maitre de indicated for them to follow. He had raised his eyebrows when he saw Chloe, but was too trained to acknowledge her with any familiarity. He quickly seated them and arranged their napkins before standing back.

"Would madam like a drink to start with?"

"A bottle of Moet please," Martin chipped in. "Now Chloe you must tell me why you're buying a cattle property?"

"I was brought up on a cattle station not far from Ascot Downs. I am tired of modelling and travelling the world and now I want to go back to the land."

"Going from such a glamorous life back to branding cattle. The attraction must be very strong?"

"It is very strong Martin. You must come and visit sometime. In the meantime, here's to your health and thanks for the assistance you've given us. Without you Andrew said he would never have got to meet Rotherheim."

They raised and touched glasses. "And to you both. I wish you every happiness for the future."

"Thank you Martin. Has Andrew spoken to you about a problem I have with my husband and a caveat he's put on my house?"

"He mentioned it and it will be no problem. I will make application to have it lifted. I can't see him defending if he's hiding in Australia somewhere. Anything else you would like me to look into?"

"No, I think that's about it."

"Now let's order as I don't want to be late for Rotherheim."

"I get the feeling we should have waited until after the contracts had been exchanged, before we celebrated."

"Andrew, it's in the bag. Once Albert Rotherheim shakes on an agreement, that's all there is to it. Like his father, the man is rock solid. If you're staying around for a few days we'll have dinner at my place. My wife Astrid would love to meet you Chloe."

"Thanks Martin, but I think we'll head back tomorrow evening. The pressure is really on."

"I can understand, but the invitation stands anytime you're back in London. You know, I've got the distinct impression there's something more to all this. Why would you make such a huge investment and take the risk in a business where even the likes of the Rotherheim's could not make it work?"

"The Rotherheim's are absentee landlords," Chloe replied smoothly. "You cannot run a business from twenty thousand kilometres away. We'll be hands on. Some years may turn out to be bad, others may be a real bonanza, but I'm not doing it for the money. It's a way of life and I intend to bring my children up in the atmosphere I love."

"I see, I see. Well, I'll just have to accept that explanation. I've no doubt Chloe with your determination, I will read about you as turning into a cattle baron."

The roast beef trolley rolled up and served them the portion size requested, and preferred level of cooking, along with Yorkshire pudding.

The cab pulled up in front of Rotherheim's a quarter of an hour early, but they were shown into Albert Rotherheim's office immediately the lift opened on his floor. He greeted the two lawyers before turning to Chloe with a beaming smile.

"Pardon my ignorance madam, but I've only ever known you as Chloe. May I call you Chloe?"

"Chloe will be just fine." She returned his warm smile and shook his hand. "My mother's name was Quartpot, but I took my father's name when he died. He was Henry Boyce."

"Henry Boyce? How do I know that name?"

"Ascot borders onto Venus Downs which was his property."

"Oh yes, I remember meeting him when I visited Ascot years ago. And you inherited it?"

"Yes I did."

"And you have a particular affinity with the land of your ancestors?"

Chloe was about to say something when he went on.

"I think that's a wonderful sentiment. I to want to return to my ancestral home one day." Rotherheim broke off his train of thought and turned to Andrew. "I take it everything is in order with the contract?"

"There's just one clause I would like to add."

"And what is that Mr Hanna?"

"It doesn't in anyway alter the terms of the contract. It's merely a protection for Chloe that has no affect on you whatsoever."

Rotherheim gave him an irritated look. "Very well Mr Hanna, pen it in now and let me read what you propose.

I warn you however, that if I don't agree this meeting is at an end."

Andrew completed the wording and handed it to Rotherheim who studied it for a few seconds and then initialled it.

"I can't see any problem with that, now let's get on with the signing."

Andrew quickly worded another contract and they exchanged signed copies.

"And fifteen million as agreed Mr Rotherheim." Martin handed over the bank cheque.

Rotherheim glanced at it and held out his hand to Chloe. "It's been a pleasure Ms Boyce. You know I'm pleased in a way you left London. My wife attended every one of your shows and cost me a fortune. Mind you, her buying pattern hasn't changed," he chuckled to himself. "You now own Ascot Downs and I'm very pleased to be out of the industry. I wish you every success. However, there is something that puzzles me and that is why did you buy Ascot when you've just sold Venus Downs and three other holdings? I would have thought they complimented one another?"

Rotherheim noted the surprise and hesitation on her face and held up his hand. "I don't need to know Ms Boyce. You obviously have your reasons which are none of my business."

"How would he have known that?" Chloe asked as they got into the lift.

"Simple. One of his minions would have phoned Geddes and told him Ascot had been sold. That would have drawn the obvious question of who to and your name would have surfaced."

Martin was shaking his head. "I cannot fathom you Chloe as to why you would sell your two central properties and then buy an adjacent property. I can understand why Rotherheim was scratching his head."

Andrew slapped him on the shoulder. "I'll let you know when it all falls into place as I'm sure it will."

They were standing on the footpath when Martin flagged a cab. "What are you doing now?"

"We're going back to the hotel to check out and then we'll catch a flight home this evening."

"Take this cab then and the best of luck. I've got work to do."

Chloe kissed Martin on the cheek. "Thank you so much and you won't forget that caveat on my house?"

"I won't." He shook Andrew's hand and clapped him around the shoulders. "You two look after yourselves. I may get out there oneday."

"Arthur Geddes speaking Ike. I've got some news for you about Ascot Downs."

Ike broke into a broad grin. The last piece of his grand plan was about to fall into place. "Tell me it's on the market."

"It's been sold."

"What the hell?" Shulman exploded. "You were supposed to keep me informed. Who bought it?"

"Chloe Boyce."

"How did this happen Geddes? You told me you thought it was going to come onto the market and you would be handling the sale. What are you up to? Listen, if you've been dealing behind my back with Boyce your future won't be worth a nickel. Do you hear me?" Geddes held the phone away from his ear as the blast of anger reverberated.

"I had nothing to do with it Ike. Boyce went to London with Andrew Hanna to speak to the Rotherheim group directly. The agreement was signed within twenty four hours. I received an email saying the property had been sold and was therefore off the market. I phoned and managed to get through to Albert Rotherheim, who confirmed the sale and the identity of the buyer. He would not disclose the price or terms. He justified the sale by saying the buyer had cash in her hand and he wanted to sell. There was no favouritism involved and if the bank had come forward with a prior client, a reasonable offer would have most probably been accepted. Perhaps you should have got on a plane immediately I told you the property was likely to come onto the market."

"I don't need your bloody gratuitous advice Geddes. It's too late. I would have topped any offer Chloe Boyce was able to make"

"Ike, as you realise this does somewhat leave you exposed as to the bank's continued involvement in the financing of the abattoir, don't you?"

"Fucking bank. A bit of a setback and the bank wants to pullout and run for the hills. You're committed to support me."

"The bank's support was conditional as you well know. It was dependent on you adding Ascot to Venus Downs and Remus Plains and obtaining further backing from an Indonesian partner. You were relying very heavily on getting your hands on Ascot because of the forty thousand head it is carrying and it was on those numbers the bank agreed to get involved. That collateral has now disappeared completely unless you can do a deal with Boyce. I'm just putting you on notice it will be out of my hands when I report this to the directors."

"Well, don't report it until I've figured a way to make up the numbers."

"Easier said than done Ike, but where are you going to conjure up forty thousand head from? I would say it's impossible unless you do a deal with Boyce."

"Ah, would you stop crowding me. I've got to think without you hammering away. How long have I got before you have to report it?"

"I'm in possession of the email and there will be a record of my call to Rotherheim. However, I asked Rotherheim to officially confirm it in a letter. You've got a week at the most."

Ike cursed as he slammed down the phone. He poured himself a Scotch and began pacing around his office. He opened a filing cabinet and began to read the contract of sale for the Boyce acquisitions. Any loophole had been closed off by Hanna's seemingly innocuous final amendments. He should have paid more attention and thought through their purpose, but he was in a hurry and he wanted to conclude the deal with Boyce as quickly as possible. He felt sick in the stomach when he realised the fifteen million deposit had been used against him. How much did Boyce pay for Ascot? It would have been more, but how much more and on what terms? She probably got it for nothing as the forty thousand head would surely account for the rest of the commitment to Rotherheim. He flung the glass at the wall in fury. How could he have been outsmarted? The colour drained from his face as he sank back into his chair. Hanna's plan was exploding into his brain, but was he that clever? The warning Hanna had given him rang in his head. "Ike, if you ever see me again in this neck of the woods you'll know you're in trouble." The threat was now very clear and very real.

He picked up the phone. "Smith we've got to talk. My office at ten this evening."

The policeman began to object, he had an appointment, but Ike cut him off.

"Well, tell Tilley you've got a bloody headache. You can shag her anytime."

It was ten after when he heard a vehicle pull up in the laneway behind his office. The door opened and closed followed by the heavy breathing of the overweight cop.

"What's so important Ike?" He said as he dropped his bulk onto the lounge suite.

"Chloe Boyce has bought Ascot Downs."

Smith slowly nodded his head as his mind absorbed the implications. "I thought you were going to buy it? Has Geddes double crossed you?"

"It wouldn't appear so, but I do have my doubts. Boyce and Hanna flew directly to London and bought if off the owner yesterday. I've been completely blindsided."

"You mean some half-breed chocolate-coloured gin beat the mighty Ike Shulman at his own game?" Smith slapped his knee and let out a belly laugh. "I don't believe it."

Ike gave him a withering look. "It wasn't her that came up with the idea. I'm sure it was Hanna."

"And to think he worked for you at one time. You obviously didn't pay him enough."

"You can cut out the sarcasm Smith. I've got a real problem and I want you to help me solve it."

"I will if I can Ike, but if she's bought Ascot, isn't that the end of the game?"

"Wise up Wally. Do you really think Hanna's going to forget you tried to blow him away? No man would forget that."

"There's nothing to connect me directly to the duffing from Ascot Downs so I don't see how I can assist. The game's over. We've both made money. You've made millions no doubt and I've been happy with what you've slung me, but I'm quite happy to pull the curtain down on the whole game. As for Hanna, he can make all the accusations he likes, but he's not going to get to first base. So what if Moonlight came along and saw me talking to him with a shotgun in my hand? It doesn't mean a damned thing and would never rate an investigation."

"You don't understand, the bastard could finish me off completely."

"Ike, I don't see how that affects me. We both knew the risks, but you got outplayed. It's as simple as that."

Ike lowered his voice. The threat was evident. "You don't think I'm going down alone do you? The shit will hit the proverbial if Hanna does what I think he's got in mind and some of that is going to stick on you."

"Don't threaten me Ike. I'm the last person you should rub up the wrong way. You're not suggesting Hanna and Boyce meet with an accident are you?"

"Tippet met with an accident. Why can't those two meet a similar fate?"

"Ike, I had Hanna in my sights once, but he's going to be really on his guard if he comes back, and as for killing Chloe Boyce, that's not my style. I'm afraid you're on your own from now on. I was going to tell you earlier, but I've only got a week or two to go in the job before I hang out the shingle 'gone fishing.' Marge and I are tying the knot and we're moving south to buy a small pub by the seaside. I tossed in my resignation three months ago. The force will close ranks around me if there's an investigation, but I can assure you my involvement will be swept under the carpet. If I get charged the Police Union will fund my defence and they don't muck around with run of the mill barristers, they always hire the top boys. I'm not in the least bit concerned Ike. It was fun while it lasted, but the show is over and I'll give you one last warning, take care before you point the finger at me, because you're really going to bring yourself undone if you do." Smith heaved himself off the couch and walked out.

Ike sat back in his chair rolling a pen between his fingers. Smith was right, his threat was hollow and the policeman knew it.

On one front it looked hopeless, but on another there was a stronger instinct of survival.

22

Andrew raised his glass of champagne the hostess had just poured them. "Here's to you Chloe Boyce. You're back in the business of cattle and you've bought yourself one hell of an enterprise."

"The question is, can I pay for it?"

"Don't even give that a thought. You'll have paid Rotherheim in full within six months and have regained your properties from Shulman in about the same time. I plan to make you into a real cattle baron."

"I don't want to be a cattle baron as you put it Andrew. I just want Venus Downs back, and you by my side."

"I promise you that will happen. You'll have the perfect drought proof run by combining Ascot, Venus and Remus into a year round production platform. The two in the Pilbara might not fit in and you can sell them to raise more capital. However, before you do that I would like to try and find out more as to why Henry bought them in the first place."

"Andrew, I don't know anything about running a business of the size you're talking about. I just want to build a real homestead on Venus Downs and settle down with you and have children."

He leaned over and kissed her. "You look after the house and the children and I'll run your empire for you. You're smart Chloe. You're worried now about the enormity of what

I'm proposing, but in a short time you'll be very comfortable. We'll hire some good managers for each of the spreads so it won't be as though you'll be hands on."

"Where are we going to live in the meantime?"

"Ascot Downs of course. I've heard there is a substantial homestead built for old Arnold Rotherheim's occasional use. It's maintained, but no one lives in it. There are also a couple of manager's houses. I want to go there and sort out the new manager as I'm sure he'll be on Ike's payroll. The duffing has now ended and he's out of a job."

"Are you going to see Ike?"

"Of course I am. I want to tell him his racket has ceased. I'll appoint a new sales agent and immediately begin to sell cattle to get the cash-flow going. He'll want cattle for that new abattoir he's building and I suspect he may now be in a bit of bother with the bank. I've no doubt he factored in buying Ascot to supply the numbers."

"Why would that make any difference? Now he can buy them from me, so why would the bank be affected?"

"Chloe darling, I suspect Ascot is carrying tens of thousands of head not on the books. Hargraves recorded a static number every year with minor variations. It was the natural increase that compounded significantly, which he never recorded because he was selling through Ike. Now you own those unbranded cattle and I intend to conduct an aerial survey to get an accurate head count. If I'm correct, and I'm comfortable I am, it is those numbers which will provide the balance to pay Rotherheim."

"And if you are wrong?" Chloe sat back and let out a sigh of exasperation. "I hope you know what you're doing Andrew. You've just spent all the money Ike paid, plus you've committed me to another twenty million. I'm way out of my depth."

Andrew laughed and squeezed her hand. "It's cost you nothing to date. The fifteen million is covered. In effect you haven't paid a cent to get hold of Ascot Downs. It's the smartest move you've ever made."

Chloe glared at him. "What are you talking about and what's so funny? Tell me now; I'm getting annoyed at your smug attitude." She punched his arm in mock annoyance.

"It's quite simple, I am the executor of Bill Hargraves estate; I wrote up his Will. He had an estate worth in excess of twenty million, accumulated from some very smart investing in stocks and real estate generated from his share of the illicit cattle duffing over the years. He got the guilts when he found out he was dying and left his entire estate to the owner of Ascot Downs in restitution for his crime. You now own Ascot Downs, so you are the beneficiary."

"B...but, I don't understand, Doesn't that money really belong to Rotherheim?"

"That clause I inserted in the Rotherheim purchase agreement stated you were entitled to any of the benefits attached to the purchase. It was an innocuous clause that Rotherheim agreed to because he could see no disadvantage – he wanted out. I didn't explain it to you at the time because I was determined to get hold of Ascot Downs and smash Shulman. Hargraves had no relatives and no claimants have come forward, so I as his executor have the sole power to determine who should benefit. And it's quite clear from the terms of the Will who that is. You will easily discharge the liability to Rotherheim with six months and you will send Ike Shulman to the wall."

"Aren't you forgetting something? I will have to refund Ike his fifteen million."

'That's why you employ me as your legal counsel my dear, If he doesn't complete the purchase, the contract is void and his deposit forfeited. He was so sure of himself, he ignored the clause I had inserted. Ike Shulman is finished or he certainly will be when I walk back through his door."

Chloe smiled and slowly shook her head while vacantly looking out at the overcast sky. "That wasn't the smartest move I've ever made: you Andrew Hanna, are the smartest move I've ever made."

He patted her on the stomach. "You just look after that one and I'll handle everything else."

After a night in Perth with Liz they were on the flight to Wyndham the next day.

"I'm very nervous Andrew. I fully expect Smith to be waiting."

"I don't think he will be. I'm sure Ike will have found out by now what's happened and Smith will realise his cash-cow has stopped milking."

They stood and waited for their bags and the boxes he had retrieved from Liz to be unloaded. A few people nodded recognition at Chloe, but there was no sign of Smith.

"What's your plan now?"

"We'll buy a Toyota cruiser and head on out I think. There's no point in sticking around."

"You're not going to call on Ike then?"

"No, it's probably around town by now you've been spotted at the airport. Ike can stew for a few days until I've sorted out what's going on at Ascot and I want to take a bit of time really getting into Henry's paperwork. Ike will know where to find us."

"Are we going straight home?"

"No, let's go and look at Ascot. I want to see what the homestead's like."

It took an hour to conclude the vehicle purchase and another three before they pulled up in front of the imposing homestead built of local stone with wide surrounding enclosed verandas. It was situated a few hundred metres above a string of permanent billabongs and running streams, with broad vistas in all directions and surrounded by towering ageless eucalypt trees.

Andrew gave a low whistle. "Wow, this is a little different to Venus. What a magnificent place. Old Arnold certainly knew how to rough it in style. And look at those air-conditioning units and solar panels on the roof. It must have cost a fortune to build. You'll be happy here."

Chloe nodded as she saw the look on Andrew's face. He was beaming with delight and wonderment. She would be happy here, but Venus Downs ran deep in her veins.

"Come on let's have a look inside."

Andrew thrust open one of the big double doors and led her in. They stood gazing around the cavernous interior furnished with green leather lounge chairs and suites, a huge wooden coffee table strewn with neatly arranged magazines, cabinets full of hardback books, mounted buffalo heads with massive horn spreads, a writing desk and separate roll-top desk with captain's chair, magnificent wooden lamp bases shaped from the burl of swamp mahogany and fine Persian rugs spread on the polished hardwood floor. Either side of the entrance were large tables that had no purpose other than ornamentation. The ceiling of the room was cathedral like with cedar panelling and hardwood supporting beams. They wandered slowly through the remainder, with five bedrooms complete with en-suites, billiard room, library, a cinema with soft leather lounge chairs, two separate reading rooms, and a gun room with shotguns and assorted rifles securely locked and chained behind glass fronted cabinets. All rooms faced outwards through screened French doors leading to the enclosed veranda.

Andrew studied the guns. "There must be a couple of hundred thousand bucks worth of shotguns in here. I can see a couple of Purdeys, Holland Holland and look at those engraved Beretta's, and he's left it all here. Unbelievable!

"This place is vast." Chloe was taking in the furnishings and layout, unaware that someone was standing behind them.

"There is a separate guest wing as well along with five self contained cottages. Mr Rotherheim senior loved coming here and entertaining his guests."

Chloe turned to see an immaculately dressed woman in her fifties observing them with a warm smile. "Ms Boyce and Mr Hanna I presume? Welcome to Ascot Downs. Mr Albert Rotherheim phoned to tell me the news and to expect you. I'm sorry I didn't hear you arrive, I was taking a nap. My name is Alice Booth, I am or was the housekeeper, although I must admit I don't do any housekeeping myself."

"Why did you use the past tense Alice?"

"I don't know whether I'll have a job now you've bought the place."

"I would certainly like you to stay on Alice, and please call us Chloe and Andrew."

"I love it here Chloe and will certainly accept your offer. Please come and let me introduce you to Rosebud the chef, Violet her assistant and Lillian the maid."

"Chef and assistant, not cook and assistant?"

"No Chloe, although they are locals Mr Rotherheim sent them to cooking schools in London, Paris and Italy for training. Ask them for anything and they'll astound you. Lillian is also a charmer."

"I can see it's a very happy household Alice. Please lead on."

The kitchen was vast with every appliance. A huge Aga stove dominated one side under an all encompassing range hood, while on the other was a double oven and hotplates also under an extractor range hood. A vast central bench ran the full length with pots, pans, saucepans, ladles and an assortment of utensils hanging from an overhead rail. A huge door concealed the walk in fridge and adjoining pantry. Hardwood panelling covered a never ending array of highly polished cupboard doors and drawers. The whole place was immaculate.

"I've never seen anything like this." Chloe was in awe.

"Mr Rotherheim loved entertaining guests who he flew in from all parts of the world. He only wanted the best for them."

Three woman in their thirties quietly entered. Alice introduced them each in turn.

Chloe shook their hands. "I'm Chloe and this is Andrew and that's how you'll address us. We don't want any formality."

"That's what Mr Arnold used to say." Violet piped up in a cheerful voice. "He thought it was very funny when he saw the shocked look on his guest's faces when we called him Mr Arnold. However, after a few days they became very informal themselves. Mr Albert only ever came here once. He was the opposite. We had to call him Mr Rotherheim, but he didn't like the place at all. Flies and dust and cattle were not his thing."

"I'm pleased they weren't. I think this place is a real compliment to Arnold's taste.

Are you sisters?" The olive skin, large brown eyes and gleaming white teeth suggested the white connection to her obvious indigenous ancestry.

"No Chloe, but we are all related," Lillian the older of the trio replied.

Chloe nodded. "I thought you must be. I want to assure you I want you to stay on here, if you would."

The smiles increased in a cloudburst of joy as they thanked her and then quietly disappeared at a glance from Alice.

"Alice, I take it that accounts for the house staff. Where do the manager and other staff live?"

"The manager is Ray Massie. Bill Hargraves was the previous manager, but he died in a car accident. Massie has his own home about a kilometre from here and there are any number of houses and outbuildings for other staff. However, Massie runs everything, but not the homestead and that's the way I like it."

Andrew noted she had dropped the Christian name. "I take it you don't like Ray Massie?"

"He's been here for a number of years. He did try and order me around and attempted to move in here when Mr Hargraves died, but I soon disavowed him of that notion. I phoned Mr Albert and he put him in his place."

"What do you know about him?"

"Nothing. Apparently Bill Hargraves took him on at the recommendation of that shifty eyed Ike Shulman. That's one man I detest.

"Has Shulman ever been out here since?"

"He certainly has. He's been a constant visitor since Bill died. I see him drive past and on down to Massie's house."

"When was the last time he was here?"

"Yesterday. He was in a real hurry when he came in and was full speed when he left. He would always wave if I was on the veranda, but he sure didn't yesterday."

"How long did he stay?"

"He arrived early and left late afternoon and then Massie left early this morning. You must have passed him on the road?"

"No, we were the only vehicle, so he must be still in town."

"He never stays, so he'll be back sometime tonight."

"Thanks Alice. We'll look him up in the morning."

"What would you people like to eat tonight? Just name it?"

"Alice, we'll have what you and the girls are having and why don't we eat in the dining room? I want to get to know you all better."

The crows, cockatoos and corellas were in competition in a cacophony of discordant harmony when Andrew pushed open the door and sat down in one of the squatters chairs. He had slept fitfully, waking constantly at the strange surroundings and sounds of the house. They were lost in the king sized bed with its ornately carved river-gum headboard depicting the native bird life and flora of the Kimberleys.

The door opened and Chloe emerged with a coffee and sat down in another chair beside him.

"I thought I was being very quiet. I thought you were still asleep," Andrew commented."

"I just couldn't sleep. I kept thinking about this place and what I've bought. What's your first move this morning?"

"After breakfast I'll go and see Massie. I heard a vehicle come in late last night so I guess it was him."

"Alice is going to serve breakfast out here. Apparently Arnold Rotherheim just loved to get up at dawn and sit out here and watch the sun come up."

Alice held the door open as Violet and Rosebud appeared with trays containing pastries, toast, tea and coffee. With the exchange of cheerful greetings of good morning, they disappeared as silently as they had come.

"I think you've made a fantastic buy Ms Boyce." Andrew buttered a slice of toast. "I could easily give away the law and become a country squire."

"Your law days are over Andrew. You got me into this and you've got to help me run it. You're also responsible for another growing event and I don't want you in some stuffy office and leaving me alone here. You're not thinking of leaving me are you?"

"No I'm not. How could I leave you and this place?"

"Would you move back to Venus?"

"You can at anytime, you have a right to live in the homestead until he pays up and takes over, but to you really want that? We'll go and see Dotti and Hazel and make sure they're comfortable. They wouldn't fit in here and I'm sure they wouldn't want to move."

"If that's what you want, I'll be quite happy to make this our home. It really is beautiful."

They finished breakfast and sat in silence listening to the bird life and looking down at the glistening waterholes strung out like a linked band of non-conforming boudinage formations.

A Toyota cruiser appeared and pulled up. A rugged individual in a sleeveless shirt stepped out. The humourless unshaven face was topped with a dark stubble, the battered jeans and shapeless R.M.Williams boots completing the picture of a person used to working with cattle.

"Hi, I'm Ray Massie." He pushed the flyscreen door open and looked at Chloe with a strained smile. "You must be Chloe Boyce the new owner of Ascot Downs."

Chloe shook the outstretched hand. "Yes, I am and this is Andrew Hanna."

Massie nodded with a deadpan expression and shook Andrew's hand.

Chloe indicated a chair for him to sit down.

"Nice vehicle you've got there Ray. Is it new?" It was a seemingly innocuous question.

"Yep Andrew, I picked it up yesterday. Special order. I've been waiting months for it."

"What did that set you back? It looks like it knocked a hole in a hundred grand?"

Massie suddenly realised where the questions were leading. "There's not much to spend money on out here. I save. I don't spend like a lot of other people."

"Tell me Ray, when you took over did you continue the same arrangement Bill had with Henry Boyce and Ike Shulman?"

"What arrangement is that?"

"The duffing of unbranded cattle off Ascot and moving them through Venus for branding and sale through Shulman."

Massie shook his head as fidgeted uncomfortably. "I don't know anything about that."

"Why is it that I don't believe you?"

Massie flashed a look of annoyance before averting his eyes to look at the floor. He could not conceal his quilt.

"Okay, well let me ask you how many cattle have been mustered from here onto Venus in the past three weeks since Ike Shulman bought the property from Chloe?"

"None."

"You're happy then if I check with your head jackaroo later this morning?"

"No, I'm not. I'm the manager here and I don't believe you have the right to undermine my authority."

"When it comes to theft Ray, I've every right to check. Look, you must know what's been going on over the years and I've no doubt you've been mustering cattle off this property of late. The vehicle was a payoff from Ike, wasn't it?"

Massie remained silent as he contemplated his position.

"Ray, you may think you can shelter behind Ike, but I intend to lay a charge of duffing. Even Smith can't ignore that."

"Smith has resigned."

"Has he now? We'll whoever takes over will probably conduct a swifter investigation than Smith would have. You may have some very awkward questions to answer. Have you ever been convicted of anything?"

The question touched a nerve as Massie flinched. "Let's just say I've had my ups and downs, but that was years ago before I married. That's all behind me now. I'm no angel, but I'm a good cattleman and a good manager."

"So how many cattle have you moved onto Venus Downs in the past three weeks? Answer me that?"

"About five thousand. Look Andrew I was under threat first from Hargraves and then from Shulman when he found out Ascot had been sold. I saw him yesterday and he was furious he'd missed out."

"So you've been party to the duffing, haven't you?"

"Yes, ever since I've been here I have. I suppose this means I'm fired?"

"Not necessarily. I may call on you as a witness at some time, but for now I can't see the point in booting you off the property and having you charged along with Ike Shulman."

Massie gave him a startled look. "You mean you're not firing me?"

"No," Andrew replied shaking his head. "It's better the devil you know than the devil you don't. You've been working on this property for years and you know everything about it and that knowledge is an extremely valuable asset I don't want to see drive out the front gate in that new vehicle of yours."

The big man screwed us his face and tried to hide the tears rolling down his cheeks. He wiped them away with the back of his hand. "I really appreciate that Mr Hanna." He snuffled as the acknowledgement of guilt followed by relief lifted from his shoulders. "My wife Tina and kids think this place is heaven. It's been killing her that we'd have to move. She's known what's been going on and has been fearing the worst. She's even started packing up the house ready to leave. I would never get another job managing a property if I'm fired with duffing hanging over my head."

"It's not Mr Hanna, it's Andrew and you can go back and tell Tina to start unpacking."

Massie started to rise and then sat down and started to open his mouth, but Andrew cut him off.

"Ray, the first thing I want you to do is give me an accurate head count of how many cattle this place is carrying?"

"I can give you a very accurate count the bank carried out a month or so back. It was done at the request of the bank because Ike Shulman was going to buy the place. It's just over forty five thousand head. I don't think the five thousand we moved the other day would have much bearing on that figure as there would be easily that many head we missed. The place is just that vast, it's impossible to get down to the last thousand."

"Just as I thought." Andrew smiled as he looked at Chloe.

"You knew what the place was carrying?" Massie asked with a look of surprise.

"I can see what you're thinking Ray. You're thinking, how does a lawyer know anything about cattle or what a property the size of Ascot should be carrying with its limitless water and good grasses, aren't you?"

Massie nodded. "It had crossed my mind. Does this mean you have some other instructions for me?"

"Yes, you're to retrieve as many cleanskins as you can from Venus Downs. Just go over with as many boys as required and drive them back. I'll phone Joey Moonlight and tell him to expect you. And don't worry about Ike. Then I want you to tighten this whole operation up so it becomes a working proposition and not a target for theft and easy crime. I want a complete management plan drawn up. I want to know how many breeding cows we have, how many weaners, salers, steers, calfs and anything else that moves that can be turned into an economical proposition. I want to know about herd improvement and what's being done about it. I've no doubt Arnold Rotherheim introduced new bloodlines. I want to know what they are and a report from you as to the effectiveness and any opinions you may have. Just like this homestead, I want Ascot Downs to become a showcase. Do you think you can handle that assignment?"

Massie reached out with his wiry fist. "Yes, I can Andrew and thank you for giving me back my life. I won't let you down, or you Chloe. You know, when I was driving back last night I stopped at the scene of Bill's accident and although I'm a Christian and supposed to forgive, I cursed him for getting me into this. I've been distraught with worry at the pain my wife has endured and the thought of the effect on my kids. I was weak in not resigning when Hargraves first pulled me into this. Tina wanted me to resign and we had endless arguments until she finally gave in. She hasn't said a word since you bought the place, but she's been packing. We just don't talk to one another any more and the kids know something is wrong. I can see it in their expressions and the way they look at me."

"Go home and talk to her then Ray. Tell her everything is okay and tell her you've just received a ten percent pay rise. We know you won't be complicit in duffing another cow off this property. Let's have a fresh start."

Massie nodded and without another word opened the screen door and walked out. They watched him start up and slowly drive away.

"That was a lovely thing you did just then darling. I thought you were going to fire him."

"Oh, I was, but then I began to study the man and I realised the hard outer exterior was a camouflage, easily penetrated. Why destroy the man and bust up his family when his guilt and remorse could be turned to advantage. I would safely bet Massie is now part of the Ascot furniture and he'll be here for life. This is his home and I'm sure things are going to improve in the Massie household."

"I'll go down this afternoon and introduce myself to Tina. Andrew, you have a wonderful way of managing and under-standing people and getting what you want, don't you?"

"I know that. It's worked on you hasn't it?"

"Oh, I don't know why I bother. You're a conceited..." She didn't finish as she burst into laughter and then adopted a serious look. "I love you dearly. Don't you ever dare leave me."

"Leave all this, you've got to be joking," he replied sweeping his hands around the horizon.

"I would never be able to handle anything if something was to happen to you. I thank God every day you walked into my life."

"I feel the same way. You're in no fear of losing me," he replied squeezing her hand.

"Now you've got Ray sorted out, where do we go from here?"

"I'm going to hire a permanent bookkeeper. The days of the manager scribbling out a few notes for London on stock numbers and handing over everything in a shoebox to the accountant at the end of the year are over. This place is got to operate like a well oiled machine."

"What do you intend to do about Ike?"

"That's a tough one, but it's got to be done. In the words of the ancient Chinese wise-one Confucius, if you seek revenge, dig two graves. I keep asking myself if it's revenge in seeking to destroy him or is it business."

"He would surely maintain it was business. After all, he impressed that on us."

"Yes he did, but it may be a matter of timing. I need to think about it further. You know, something has always nagged me about why he wanted Baracool and Ironstone Park. I think I'll spend some time over the next couple of days really going through Henry's diaries and papers. There's got to be a clue in there somewhere. I also want to go through the diaries to tally up how many cattle have been stolen over the years."

"Does that matter now? It's in the past isn't it?"

"Perhaps you're right, but let me go through everything first."

It was two days later when he finally tallied Henry's diary notes. He calculated more than one hundred thousand head had been duffed over the years, a staggering figure in dollar terms, but a figure he had suspected all along. He turned to a folder full of press cuttings containing beef prices, weather statistics and general agricultural articles and was about to cast it aside when a small headline in an article mentioning the name Ironstone Park caught his attention. Further down it noted both Ironstone Park and the adjoining property Baracool had been bought by Boyce and Shulman. Then there was a paragraph of speculation that perhaps the pair had brought them not only for cattle production, but for the underlying iron ore deposits. Andrew clapped his hand to his forehead. He had been looking for a clue and there it was staring him in the face, Ironstone Park; iron ore the commodity China and Asia were now demanding to feed their blast furnaces. He had noted the box tied with string and marked "Mining" many times, but had overlooked it as being unimportant. He tore the string away and spread the contents on the table. More press cuttings about gold, copper and diamond discoveries in the Kimberley and then he turned over a folder containing gridded maps of the Pilbara. He unfolded it and picked up a mineral application form applying for the iron ore rights to a huge block covering large areas of both Ironstone and Baracool. He counted the blocks noted on the legend. They added up to more than five hundred square kilometres. Then he found the certificate of grant of the titles dated two years after the original application in the names of Boyce and Shulman. Andrew felt sick in the stomach. Ike had outplayed him. Shulman had sold his rights to Ironstone and Baracool to Henry, and now Chloe had sold them back to him, but had he also transferred the mineral rights? He searched through the rest of the papers, but there was no evidence to suggest he had. Ike was too astute not to now know the value of the two properties and the real wealth they contained. Five years had passed since the initial applications were made. The Chinese were now bursting into the iron ore market buying every ton they could lay their hands on. Ike could see no value when Henry bought his share, but now he realised what he had missed out on and wanted them back and had got them.

Andrew tossed the documents back on the table and sat back lost in thought. His gaze focused on the row of phone books neatly stacked above his head. He picked out a Perth phone book opened it to Government Departments and dialled a number.

"Yes, I want to check on a mining title. Could you transfer me to the right department please?"

Moments later a voice answered. "Titles. How can I help you?" Was the polite enquiry.

"I would like to check on the status of two exploration titles in the Pilbara region."

"Can you give me the numbers of the those titles please?"

Andrew read the two numbers out and waited.

"According to our records the titles were applied for in the names of Boyce and Shulman and are still held in those names. No, wait a minute I'm just scrolling down and I note Shulman transferred his share to Boyce a year after they were granted so Boyce owns the titles. All rentals and charges are up to date so the titles are in good standing."

"Can you tell me when were the last lot of rental charges paid?"

"Just a moment. Ah, here we are. They were paid about three weeks ago, and it looks as though Boyce has made application to transfer the titles back to Shulman. I'd hate to think of the tax implications of that transfer would be. It would run into millions based on the present value of those permits."

"When did Boyce lodge the transfer?"

"On the same date the latest lot of charges were paid by the looks of what I can see here."

Andrew felt his heart leap. "How long does it take before the transfer is processed."

"Oh, that could happen anytime within say the next three months."

"And you say it was Boyce who made the application?"

"I can only read to you what I see on the screen sir. The transfer is made out in the name of Henry Boyce of Venus Downs station, which is the name of one of the original applicants and the current transferee."

"Thank you. That's all I need to know for now." Andrew put on the phone and crashed his fist onto the desk with a shout of joy.

Chloe appeared with a concerned look on her face. "What's happened? What are you so excited about?"

"I've just found out why Ike was so desperate to get hold of Baracool and Ironstone. They contain vast iron ore deposits."

"So why the excitement? Ike owns them and there's nothing we can do about it."

"You don't see. The minerals titles are separate to the land titles. The State owns everything under the ground. Henry did own the mineral titles to the iron ore, but he transferred them to Ike three weeks ago."

"He couldn't have."

"Precisely, so Ike Shulman has forged Henry's signature and lodged the transfers. He is banking on the fact you don't know about the iron ore. While he owns title to the land, you in fact, still own the mineral titles."

"What are the titles worth?"

"I don't know, but we've got to move fast and lodge a caveat. I think it's about time I had a word with Mr Shulman. This is no longer business, this is more theft on a grand scale he's attempting."

23

"Andrew, I wondered how long it would take you to call in. And how is Chloe?"

The attempt at bonhomie was greeted with a look of contempt as Andrew sat down. "Do you recall my warning the next time we met, you would be in trouble?"

"I seem to recall that threat, but I can't possibly think what I'm in trouble over."

Andrew pulled the writ out of his jacket pocket and threw it in front of Ike. "Ascot Downs is suing you for the theft of one hundred thousand head of cattle stolen and marketed by you over the past eight years. That figure includes the five thousand you've duffed since Chloe bought Ascot Downs."

Shulman attempted a full belly laugh, but it came out almost as a stifled groan as he slowly read the claims. "You're nuts Hanna. I haven't stolen a single head. You can't prove a thing. In any event if there was any theft, Henry Boyce was the guilty party. I note you've joined Venus Downs to the writ so you're going to sue your girlfriend too are you?"

"Ike, I have Bill Hargraves' affidavit which puts you squarely in the frame along with Henry Boyce, and Arthur Geddes. Wally Smith even gets a dishonourable mention. I have Henry's diaries which give dates, numbers duffed and the split up of proceeds. You were the principal of the scheme and were quite aware you were handling tainted property. Geddes had ten percent and Smith was only minor player getting a sling from you. Hargraves and Boyce are both dead so that leaves just yourself and Geddes, with you as the standout ringleader. As for Chloe's involvement I would suggest you read the indemnity clause I wrote into the sale contract. I was surprised you actually accepted that clause, but you were in such a hurry to take control you obviously didn't realise the full import. The contract states you assumed complete liability for all claims made against the estate of Henry Boyce and therefore Venus Downs. You've got a real problem Ike."

"I don't accept that Hanna. I'll tie you up in court for years."

"You're bluffing Ike. I'm about to slap a caveat on the properties Chloe sold you under duress. You're into the bank for untold millions to build your abattoir and have no doubt put up a mountain of collateral for that loan. You were banking on getting hold of Ascot Downs. Ray Massie has already told me of the audit carried out by the bank, but all that supposed collateral Rotherheim wasn't aware of, has now slipped through your fingers, along with the proceeds of Hargraves' estate which I've no doubt you pledged to the bank. That's why I was determined to beat you to the punch and remove Hargraves' legacy from your grasp. Banks don't like litigation of any kind Ike. Your backside is going to be toast and the moment the Indonesian partners hear about legal problems, they'll likewise terminate any interest they may have indicated. I think that's game, set and match."

"Okay, it may get a little difficult with the bank, but I'll still own the properties."

"Ike, you don't own them, you only have an option to buy them. You still owe Chloe fifteen million and you signed an indemnity for Henry's share of any liabilities. You've been party to the theft of more than one hundred thousand head which at say a knock-down price of threefifty per head leaves you with a liability of thirtyfive million bucks. At a more likely figure of five hundred you're staring down the barrel of fifty mill."

"This is extortion Hanna. You can't make threats like that. It's blackmail. I'll sue you." Andrew could clearly see the bead of sweat running down the side of Ike's face as he lashed out in frustration.

"No Ike, it's only business. I learned that from you. It's straight business and nothing personal. Isn't that the way you operate?"

"You'll send me to the wall Hanna, but I'll rebuild." He muttered in fury through clenched teeth.

"Ike you won't be rebuilding in either cattle or iron ore. You're finished. Even Smith hasn't got a big enough shotgun to get you out of this predicament." Andrew let the statement sink in as he watched the colour drain out of Ike's face.

"Iron ore? What do you mean by that?"

"I'm talking about the signatures you've forged transferring the iron ore rights on Baracool and Ironstone Park. Now that's an easy one to prove, isn't it? I think you'll be serving time if Chloe presses charges on that one."

Shulman buried his face in his hands and slowly shook his head as he contemplated his predicament. "What am I left with, what am I left with? I've already invested twenty million into the abattoir. How about compensating me for that? You've certainly got the collateral now to take over. It's a great project and I don't think you'll have any problem in getting the bank to support you. The sale of those iron ore rights are worth a fortune."

"I know it's a great project Ike, but I don't think I could get Chloe to go along with it. She knows nothing about running an abattoir."

"Well, what more do you want me to offer?"

"First of all you'll transfer Venus, Remus, Baracool and Ironstone back for a one dollar consideration. You can forget about your fifteen million deposit. It's gone. In return Chloe will not sue you for the theft from Ascot, nor will she lay charges just so you're clear in that regard. Rotherheim had no problems with my drafting of the clause in the contract requiring Chloe to assume and pursue all debtors along with the standard clause of accepting all creditors. Your investment to date in the abattoir is valueless, but Chloe will buy you out for a dollar."

"But that's a major asset, and yet you are only going to pay a dollar?"

"It's only business Ike," Andrew replied with a smile. "It's entirely up to you. You can fight and lose the lot and face a little time in jail, or you can agree and escape the humiliation of court and some time breaking rocks."

"I've got to think about this. You're going to wipe me out. What are you going to do about Geddes and Smith?"

"Nothing. They're only bit players and I hear Smith is about to retire and marry Marge Tilley. And don't go tattle-taling to the bank about Geddes otherwise Chloe might change the terms of the settlement and sue you for every penny you have. I need Geddes so I won't be saying anything, and Ike I don't believe you'll be wiped out. I could turn you upside down now and a million bucks would fall out of your pockets."

"You're a smart man Andrew and you've really fallen on your feet. Did you set out to get into Chloe Boyce's bed?"

"Don't piss me off Ike by making silly cracks. I strongly advise you to leave her out of this."

"Did you know her husband was in town again a few days ago? He went out to Venus looking for her and got really upset when she wasn't there. Dotti, the old cook phoned Smith in a hell of a state claiming he had threatened her and only left when Moonlight heard the commotion and went to investigate. Has she divorced him? I wouldn't be surprised if he doesn't put his hand out once he finds out how wealthy she is. What's his name anyway?"

"Marcel Faroud. Do you know if he's still around?"

"I haven't seen him, but I know there's an Afghani cook over at the Argent who is very keen to talk to him."

"What's that about?" He raised an eyebrow in an expression of ignorance.

"From what I can gather Faroud showed up in town once before and was spotted by this Afghani who wanted to carve him up. It was something to do with people smuggling and the loss of his family. Faroud is dead meat if he catches up with him, as he most surely will. They're a close knit mob and the Afghani will soon find out where Faroud is working or hiding out."

Andrew was worried, but tried to hide it. Chloe was in danger and this was Ike's perverted way of telling him and watching for any reaction.

"Thanks for that Ike. Now I'll be back this time tomorrow with transfer and release agreements, so you've got twenty four hours to decide whether you're going to fight or accept the terms I've offered which are non-negotiable of course."

Ike sat staring into space as Andrew walked out.

Smith looked up in surprise. Ike Shulman had never been to his office before. It was he who was always summoned to Shulman's presence. Ike closed the door behind him and sat down.

"What the hell do you want?"

"I want your co-operation Wally."

"I've already told you Ike I've resigned from the force and that's the end of it. The game is over and I don't want to know about it or your problems."

"I've just had Hanna in my office."

"So?"

"He's coming after you Wally," he lied. "Chloe Boyce bought Ascot Downs and as the new owner she's going to sue everyone involved in the theft of cattle and that includes me and you and Geddes."

"That's bullshit. She can't sue for cattle she didn't own at the time."

"That's where you're wrong Wally. Hanna negotiated the sale directly with Albert Rotherheim who owned Ascot. He wrote a clause into the contract which allows Boyce to claim any property or monies found to be owing to Ascot. He's a clever bastard is Andrew Hanna."

"I've already told you Ike, that Hanna or Boyce can make all the allegations they like, but the Police Union will fund my defence. It won't cost me a nickel"

"You may be correct if he lays a criminal action, but if he launches a civil case it's an entirely different matter and the Police Union will wipe you like a dirty rag."

Smith gave a sickly smile. "So what's the difference?"

"As I've said, one is a criminal action where you're defence is that you did not act corruptly as a police officer. The other is you received the proceeds of stolen property and Boyce wants recompense. Believe me, there is a subtle difference and if you don't believe me you need to get legal advice immediately. Boyce will launch an action against me and join you and Geddes to it. She will nail me as the evidence is compelling and of course I will implicate you and Geddes because I will be under oath. Once I'm convicted she will then come after you and Geddes for restitution. The court will order damages with interest on what you have received to date and of course there will be the crippling court costs if you decide to defend the action. You're broke now, but you just don't realise it. I think Marge's love for you will quickly disappear the moment she hears of this. She will immediately think you'll want to borrow money to defend the action and knowing Marge as I do, she's still got the first buck she ever made and doesn't intend to share it. She's as tight as a cat's pussy. The costs will break you, so you'd better think again about hanging out that gone fishing sign as you'll be under a tree down by the riverbank with some of the town's less fortunate citizens sleeping in the dirt and drinking watered down wine. Mind you it will do wonders for your waist line. You'll be a classic ad for a slimming clinic before you know it."

Ike could see the attack had hit home as Smith began to grasp the enormity of what he had just told him.

"I wouldn't be sitting here telling you this if I was bluffing. In effect Boyce and Hanna want to clean me out. I'll lose everything."

"You're the guy with the brains Shulman. Mr Big who owned the whole town and now you're telling me you've got the arse out of your trousers. I'm a simple copper. What do you expect me to do?"

"Use your brains for once Wally. The problem must disappear or we disappear. It's as simple as that. You've already bumped off Tippet so it's not as though it would be the first time."

"I just can't go out there with a gun and blow them both away."

"No, you do it one at a time starting with Hanna. Once he's out of the way I'm sure I can deal with Boyce."

"Okay, so it's your turn. I took care of Tippet so you can take care of Hanna. That's fair isn't it?"

Ike ignored the question. "You've met Boyce's husband Marcel Faroud haven't you?"

"Yes, I intercepted him on the road back from Venus Downs when he caused that commotion."

"What's Faroud like?"

"Smooth as silk on the surface, but as mad as a cut snake underneath. He started to argue with me about trying to locate his wife. He was ranting on about how his wife had left him and how he had every right to make threats as her property was his. Said he was going to kill Walter Boyce for taking her away from him. He obviously doesn't know Walter is dead, but he does know she's living with someone. I wouldn't give much for Hanna's chances if he finds out it's him. That hothead wouldn't think twice about sticking a knife into him." Smith trailed off when he saw Ike nodding slowly and smiling at him.

"You know where Faroud is now?"

"I warned him off. I told him if he came back and made trouble I would arrest him. He's staying with someone in Kununurra. I have his phone number. It was ironic when the next morning I opened the mail to find a bulletin from the Federal Police. Faroud is wanted for people smuggling."

"What did you do about it?"

"Nothing. The Feds can go screw. I've got enough on my plate without assisting that bunch of self-centred arseholes."

"Why don't you arrange a meeting?"

"Why would I want to meet him? I would have to arrest him and I don't want to know about the paperwork involved. I'm done with policing. I'm just waiting for my resignation to be processed and then I'm out of here?"

"You approach him saying Hanna would like to meet him to discuss Chloe Boyce as he intends to marry her when her divorce comes through. That will really get Faroud stirred up. He'll bust his gut to cut the balls off the man who's stolen his wife."

"So I shoot both of them? You're out of your bloody mind Ike. I'm holding the gun that shot two people. How do I explain that?"

"Just hear me out Wally." Ike replied throwing up his hands. "Faroud is going to kill Hanna and won't require any urging to do so by the sound of what you've told me."

"That would be a fair assumption."

"You can easily explain to Faroud you don't hold a high opinion of Hanna and would turn a blind eye if anything should happen to him. You could even make it worthwhile for him to do it by offering him ten grand. After all he's wanted, so he's got every incentive to accept and then bolt once he's carved up Hanna. It's obvious he's so blinded by revenge. I could spare ten thousand for that."

"So that gets rid of Hanna, but that still leaves Faroud. What guarantee do I have he won't plea bargain when the Feds catch up with him, as they most surely will. They'll promise him the world for information about who else is involved in people smuggling. He's sure to let it drop in return for leniency, he knows who was behind a couple of murders. Those boys would love the kudos of pinning an accessory to murder rap on a senior sergeant in the State police. They would revel in the publicity. Here was a sergeant who was aiding and abetting a wanted criminal is the way the press would print it. Pure sensationalism."

"Is that Afghani still working at the Argent Hotel?"

"As far as I know he is. That's another of those mad raghead bastards who think nothing of picking up a knife and slicing someone up."

"Well, why don't you let him hone his slicing skills on Faroud. He had a chance once and missed, so why not give him another chance? Faroud knifes Hanna. The Afghani knifes Faroud and then you shoot the Afghani in self defence on the pretext he came at you with a knife. A perfect scenario I would say Wally. I will then take care of Boyce, so all our problems disappear."

"You're a devious bastard Shulman. I want to think about it. It just might work."

"I'm desperate Wally and so are you. It will work and you've got to make it work."

"But how do I get Hanna and Faroud together? Hanna will smell a rat if I phone him and say Faroud wants to meet him. I wouldn't mind betting Hanna already knows Faroud is wanted and I'd be shot down in flames if he contacts the Feds. The old cook at Venus Downs must have told him by now what happened."

"I'll take care of that. Hanna is due in my office tomorrow. I'll mention it to him. I'll say that Faroud just wants to discuss some sort of settlement which he thinks would be agreeable to put to Boyce. He's been warned off by you, so he just doesn't want to front up and cause trouble. Hanna will fall for it."

"And the Afghani?"

"You go and see him and invite him to meet Faroud. You won't have to repeat the invitation. He'll have that knife stuck in Faroud's guts before he can open his mouth."

"Where does this all take place? Hanna will be suspicious and is not going to walk into a trap by trying to lure him to some out of the way place."

"It will happen in Hanna's old office in my building. He'll be comfortable with that and it will also be easy for you to explain. I will lock the back stair fire escape so there's only one other way up and that's by the internal stairway. You heard the disturbance and shot the Afghani when he came at you with the knife. You set the meeting up so that the Afghani is in the room next door. He will know when Faroud sticks the knife into Hanna and can catch him as he leaves. Faroud will be completely unprepared for the Afghani and even if Faroud should get in first and kill him, you can then say Faroud came at you with the knife."

"And if Hanna survives?"

"He won't. He'll be completely off-guard and won't survive."

"Christ, this is far-fetched. Isn't there another way?"

"Wally if you can think of one, I'm all ears. You can't entice three guys out into the bush. I don't think any of them would be that stupid. It's got to be right out in the open."

"When do you want this to happen?"

"Tomorrow night. Phone Faroud now and arrange for him to get here. I'll phone Hanna and put off the meeting until tomorrow evening and it will only take you a phone call to round up the Afghani."

Smith hesitated and then picked up the phone. Ike listened on an extension as the arrangement was confirmed.

"He didn't seem suspicious at all."

"No, I couldn't have handled it better. I loved the bit about Hanna acting as Boyce's solicitor and Boyce wanting to come to some amicable settlement to finalise the divorce, so he can marry her. I can just see the dollar signs flashing in his eyes. If as you say Faroud is not his real name, he'll realise he won't have a marital claim against Boyce' assets."

"Now I'll phone Hanna."

"Not from this phone Ike. I don't have any excuse to call him and all my calls are traceable. Do it from your office."

Andrew put the phone down slowly and then shrugged.

"Who was that Andrew?"

"It was Ike. I'm supposed to see him tomorrow morning, but he's going to be out of town until late afternoon. He wanted to know if I could make it in the evening."

"Is that all he wanted?"

"Yes, he just wanted to know if he could change the time."

"You seemed to be doing an awful lot of listening for him to be just changing the time."

"Oh, he was just saying he would like discuss Baracool and Ironstone Park."

Andrew was confused and it was the only convenient lie that sprang to mind. It looked as though Faroud had come to his senses and wanted to discuss a divorce settlement, but he wanted a discrete meeting with Andrew first, as Chloe's attorney, and did not want Chloe to know about it. He thought they may be able to work something out on amenable terms. He was wanted by Immigration and the Federal Police and wanted to get out of the country quickly. It made sense to Andrew but from what he had heard about Faroud, was he really that rational? There was only one way to find out and that was to meet the man and get an idea of what he was proposing.

"Do you want me to come with you?"

"No, I don't think so. I'll just get Ike to sign the papers and drive straight back."

Chloe noticed the concerned look on Andrew's face, but said nothing. She was sure there was more to the phone call than he had told her.

It was just on dusk when Andrew pulled up in front of Ike's office.

Ike was sitting at his desk engrossed in a document. He looked up with a smile and indicated Andrew to take a seat.

"Let's have them Andrew. I want to sign off and get that part of my life over. It's time for a new start."

Andrew took the transfers and wavers of claims out of his folder and handed them across the desk without comment. Something was not right. Ike was being too casual. He expected a pleading of leniency, of understanding or an attempt at negotiation, but Ike read them carefully, signed them and slid them back across.

"That's it then Andrew. If only a beautiful woman hadn't come between us we'd have made a great team. You'd have made a fortune."

"Where's Faroud. I thought you said he would be here?"

"He's down the street your old office. I don't want any meetings or divorce negotiations in my office. It's none of my business."

Ike stood up and offered his hand. "Just to show you I don't have any hard feelings toward you. It was business and you out manoeuvred me. I wish you the best of luck, although I think you've had more than your fair share already."

Andrew shook the small almost lifeless hand out of courtesy. He could have crushed it with one powerful reflex. Underneath, it took him all his time to restrain the contempt he felt for the man.

He walked out and down the street. He hesitated as he began to climb the stairs contemplating how he would handle Faroud and what mood he would find him in. He was fully expecting aggression, but Ike had informed him when he phoned that he had calmed down. Without thinking he pushed open the door. It was a split second later when he saw the blade coming towards him he realised he had been led into a trap. He pushed at the knife with the folder, but it slid past and he felt it enter his chest before he went over backwards and crashed to the floor. The unyielding hardwood did not absorb the sickening crunch of his skull as all sense of being disappeared.

Faroud stood over the dying man. He grunted with satisfaction and reached down to deliver the coup de grace.

The look of pleasure disappeared a split second later as he sensed danger and began to turn and feint to one side out of the range of the carving knife. The Afghani, like his countrymen, was an expert with the assassin's blade. *"Al Akhbar"* was the last sound Faroud heard as the blade slid effortlessly into his throat and was ripped outward to sever the carotid artery and windpipe. He collapsed to the floor grasping at his throat, trying to stem the flow of blood clogging his breathing. The Afghani watched with a maniacal grimace of pleasure as Faroud's eyes rolled back and his lifeless hands lost their grip. With two quick flicks of the knife he picked out each of Faroud's eyes and flung them aside.

"Jesus man, did you really have to do that?" Smith stepped into the room and dry retched at the two empty sockets staring back at him. He stepped around the lifeless form and looked at Andrew. He felt his neck for any sign of a pulse. There was none. The Afghani muttered something unintelligible and indicated Andrew's eyes with his knife.

Smith pushed him away. "No, you bloody heathen."

Ike stepped past him trying to avoid looking at Andrew's lifeless form and averting his gaze from Faroud's mutilated corpse. Smith picked up the folder and began to flick through it, before Ike reached over and took it out of his hand. Smith turned and began to descend the stairs. The Afghani followed and was halfway down when Smith turned and levelled the shotgun. The recognition of what was about to happen and the scream of betrayal was drowned by the discharge that took away half his head. The contents of his skull sprayed over Ike who was close behind and he fell forward with the dead Afghani's blood obscuring his vision. Smith raised the gun slowly and took deliberate aim before releasing the contents of the choke barrel. The confined discharge had the desired effect.

"And that takes care of you as well, you little shit." He ejected the cases and slowly reloaded. Satisfied there was no sign of life he leaned the gun back over his shoulder as he began to turn. He caught the sudden movement, but was too late as the iron fist smashed into his jaw and he crumbled to the floor senseless.

24

Andrew slowly came out of the drifting cloud. He could not see through it, but could sense movement and sound. He realised the movement was someone holding his hand. The sound was a voice saying something he could not understand, but kept re-occurring in a soothing monotone. The hand touched his face and slowly stroked it. He screwed up his eyes to gain focus, but all he could see was hazy outlines of fixed profiles. A head descended and kissed him on the forehead.

"You're going to be okay darling. Just rest." He recognised the voice as he tried to resist being overtaken again by the induced dream. It was a futile fight as the blackness overtook and enveloped him. Every time the cloud began to disperse, the hand was still holding his and the soothing voice returned.

"It's Chloe darling. Do you hear me?" He felt the hand tighten on his as he tried to respond. "Hey, I felt that. Now, don't try to talk because you can't."

Chloe looked at the tubes inserted through his nose and the covering mask. A feeding tube was inserted in his windpipe and various other wires and tubes appeared from under the bedclothes and were hooked up to monitors and constantly blinking machines. His head was swathed in a bandage covering the brain surgery. There was bandaging covering the wound in his chest. He was unrecognisable and she cried out when she first saw his inert form lying naked as two nurses hovered over him.

"My God, is he dead?" She burst into tears as she saw the sheet being flicked over his head before being folded back to leave only the top of his chest and head exposed.

"No he's not." The nurse turned and smiled. "Nurse Hussein and I are just making him comfortable. Please sit down. We'll only be a couple of minutes and then we'll leave you alone."

As they walked out the older male nurse gave her a nod and warm compassionate smile through a rugged swarthy face that had witnessed suffering and trauma.

Chloe was dabbing her eyes when she became aware of someone standing beside her.

"You must be Chloe? I'm doctor Carl Gibson, the registrar here." He extended his hand with a bright smile. "I was at university with Andrew and I'll make sure he's looked after."

"How is he really doctor?"

"He's in an induced coma at the moment. He's very lucky to be alive. He was either hit from behind or more likely fell backwards and cracked his skull which caused pressure and bleeding to the brain. I operated by removing part of the skull to relieve the pressure. He's stable but the condition is still rated as critical. I saw him when he first came in. The knife wound to his chest was bad enough as it resulted in a collapsed lung and major blood loss, but when I noticed the head trauma I thought he could not possibly survive. He was terminal in my opinion and could do nothing but take him off life support. To be honest I just didn't have the skill or training to attempt surgery. But then someone with more experience came to my aid."

"Another doctor?"

"It was divine providence and if and when Andrew pulls through this, I'll introduce him to the man who saved his life."

"How long will he be in a coma?"

"That's a hard question to answer. It might be a week, two weeks or months. Injuries to the brain are not something that have a defined healing period. He may recover in a week or so and be his normal self very quickly. The worst case scenario is there is a hematoma that cannot be contained which would be fatal, or damage that leaves him partly paralysed or with minor to serious motor skill function deficiencies. The brain is a very delicate organ requiring specialist knowledge and care. We will keep him induced to take the pressure off the blood vessels, but I'm afraid I cannot give you a prognosis of when and in what condition he will be in when he finally awakes. In the meantime you can be assured he's in very capable hands with Hussein."

"Is he that capable? He looks very tired and detached."

"He may look tired, but he's as tough as an ironbark tree. We go bike riding and jogging together sometimes and it's me who has to take a breather, never him. If you wanted someone to carry you up and down Mt Everest, it would be him you would choose. I can assure you that look of disinterest is an illusion, he's pure titanium with a massive heart. I'll get them to make up a bed for you in here, because I can see you're not going to leave his side."

"Thank you and you are correct, I won't be leaving. He just means too much to me."

For the next week Chloe sat and held Andrew's hand, talking to him, reading and watching television. She would leave and walk around the gardens when Hussein would change the dressings, attend to his needs and bed-wash him. He was like an insect flitting in and out of the light of an incandescent bulb. It was in the third week when Hussein kept looking in every hour, standing over and looking at the inert face and then across at the monitors.

"Next week, he should come awake. Signs good."

Chloe looked up in surprise. She could barely understand his heavily accented English, but she could read the look of pleasure in his eyes. They were the first words he had ever directed at her. Generally it was one of the other nurses who always greeted her and told her of Andrew's progress. Hussein was always the silent background presence, but she noticed the other nurses did not query his muttered inaudible instructions or peremptory hand movements if he wanted some adjustment or placement of the tubing and wires of the monitors. She noticed even Gibson appeared deferential when he came in twice-daily to inspect the progress chart.

As if on cue Hussein appeared mid-morning and picked up Andrew's hand and leaned down to look into his eyes. They were open with the pupils fully dilated trying to focus through the haze. Hussein smiled at Chloe on the other side of the bed and held up his thumb. "You speak to him. It will help." He left as quickly as he had appeared.

Chloe was talking to Andrew and stroking his arm when Gibson walked in ten minutes later.

"Hussein tells me our patient is coming out of the coma. I thought he was being a bit premature in reducing the drugs, but I can see his advice was correct. Andrew is on the way to recovery, although he's got some way to go yet."

"Tell me doctor Gibson, who is the doctor, you or Hussein?"

Gibson screwed up his face and looked around to see if anyone else was present. "It was Hussein who saved Andrew's life, not me. When he was admitted I just threw up my hands in resignation when I saw the extent of his injuries. The knife wound I could handle, but the brain and the obvious trauma suffered, was way outside my field of expertise. Hussein was with me in theatre and just took over. Hussein is in fact a highly skilled and I would say, brilliant neuro-surgeon, a refugee whose credentials are not recognised in Australia. He was wielding a scalpel in the battlefields of Iraq after he qualified from Tehran University. He's witnessed every kind of trauma known to man. I can't claim any kudos whatsoever. It was me who was the junior surgeon."

"Why doesn't he get qualified here?"

"He claims it's too late for him now. He did try, but failed both the written exams. I think there was a lot of prejudice involved. He couldn't prove he had qualified in Iran because he had no papers when he arrived here as a refugee. Iran refused to confirm his credentials other than to say he was a criminal and should be deported back to Iran. I have a suspicion he might have been fighting on the wrong side and the Americans tipped off our security. The prejudice would have ensured the shutters would have been pulled down on any hope of him being licensed to practice here. Uncle Sam has an unforgiving memory. There's got to be something in his background that hasn't come out, because I've seen some hopeless foreign doctors with qualifications from dubious universities gain accreditation here. Some of them have gone through this very hospital. It just doesn't make sense. However, he's happy here and I'm more than pleased to have him. I hope he never leaves. Please tell Andrew that saying thanks to me is directed at the wrong person. And please keep what I've told you in the strictest confidence. I would be before the Medical Board if it ever came out I'd let a nurse perform an operation."

"That confidence is safe with me doctor."

It was a week later when Andrew was able to sit up and eat without taking sustenance through a tube. The knife wound had healed, but his brain was still being monitored. A further week of utter boredom and frustration and he was sitting in a wheelchair ready to go home. Carl Gibson was standing alongside Hussein, along with two other nurses and Ray Massie.

"I'm walking out of here." Andrew slowly got up out of the chair. "I'm not going to be wheeled out in that bloody chair."

"I'll give you a hand," Massie stepped forward. "After all I carried you in here."

Andrew hesitated and then accepted the offered arm as he got up and steadied himself.

"Thank you all, and particular thanks to you Carl." Andrew offered his outstretched hand.

Gibson shook it and laughed as he slapped him on the back. "It wasn't only me Andrew. We're a team in here."

They were at the door when Chloe threw her arms around Hussein and burst into tears. "Thank you so much. Thank you. If I can ever repay you in some way, please let me know."

Andrew was mystified by the sudden burst of emotion, but said nothing. Surely it was Gibson who deserved the praise.

Hussein patted her on the back and then gave her a final squeeze as the embarrassment overcame him and he stepped back out of the limelight.

Ray helped him into the back seat of the Cruiser and made him comfortable before getting into the driver's seat alongside Chloe.

"Ray, what was that remark you made about carrying me into the hospital?"

"Let me tell him Ray."

Chloe turned in her seat. "I sent Ray after you when you said you were going into town to see Ike. I sensed something was wrong and I'm glad I did. He saw Smith shoot the Afghani and then Ike and would have turned the gun on him if he hadn't knocked him out. He even broke Smith's jaw. He then went upstairs and found you with the knife sticking out of your chest, carried you out and drove you to the hospital. He saw the blood coming out of your head and figured every second counted. He wasn't going to wait for an ambulance and Carl has since agreed with that decision, although he wouldn't have agreed with it at the time. Your blood pressure was critically low through the loss of blood. Even a delay or another five minutes could have been fatal."

Andrew was silent for a few seconds. "Thank you Ray. I owe you one."

"You owe me nothing Andrew. You gave me a life remember?"

"What happened to Smith? Was he charged at all?"

Ray shook his head and gave a mirthless laugh. "No, he's gone. He's out of the police force. Marge Tilley gave him the flick and I guess he realised he had few friends in town so he just disappeared one day. The police interviewed me because I'd been seen by a number of people carrying you out. Smith claimed he shot the Afghani in self-defence and didn't see Ike standing behind him. He knew nothing about Faroud being there, but was able to give an explanation of why the Afghani slit his throat. I saw him deliberately take aim at Ike, but how could I prove it. A detective did approach me and suggest very strongly I accept Smith's explanation as he was sure to be acquitted if charges were laid. I took his advice. I don't feel sorry for Ike. He had it coming."

A sudden thought occurred to Andrew. "The transfer papers. What happened to them?"

"I don't know why, but I picked them up without thinking and shoved them into my jacket pocket before I found you. Don't ask me what possessed me to pick them up, I just did."

"That's a load off my mind." Andrew let out a sigh of relief. He was lost in thought as the countryside rolled by.

"I've decided to make Ascot Downs our home Andrew. I agree, it will be a wonderful place to bring up kids."

"Oh, oh, please forgive me, I'd forgotten all about that. My brain is just not functioning in the right sequence. How is the bump coming along?"

Chloe laughed. "The bump is just doing fine and as for your brain, Carl did explain you're not out of the woods yet. You may feel confused or disorientated for some time and you'll need further scans."

"Now that you mention confusion, I'm confused about the emotion and tears you showed with Hussein? Why didn't you hug them all? They all deserved it."

"I know that, but Hussein was something special."

"But what was so special about him?"

"Someday I will tell you Andrew, but not today, I have an obligation to fulfill."